CRICKET HUNTERS

CRICKET HUNTERS

by Jeremy Hepler

www.silvershamrockpublishing.com

For my wife Tricia and all the other lovely Garcia-Ayala women.

HOW TO CRAFT A CRICKET STICK

Instructions given by Yesenia Garcia-Ayala, Bruja, Curandera

The crafter should sever the limb from a living tree with their bare hands, alone. No tools. No onlookers. No help from anyone else. Preferably, the crafter will have grown with the tree, watered its roots, climbed its branches, danced in its shade, sung with the birds it housed. The deeper the crafter's connection to the tree, the more powerful the weapon.

Upright, the limb should stand shoulder-high to the crafter and be slightly tapered, the fattest end measuring about half the size of the crafter's wrist. Using a single stone or series of stones found as near to the tree as possible, the crafter must sharpen the skinny end of the branch to a fine point.

Once the point is honed enough to pierce flesh, it should be used to shed the crafter's blood. A slice or jab to the palm, usually. The wound must be deep enough to draw at least four drops of blood. One for the earth the tree seeded from, one for the air it swayed and spread its seed in, one for the water that nourished it, and one for the fire that will strengthen it. These four drops must soak into the sharpened tip, and then the tip must be hardened by a flame sparked by the crafter, preferably using only nature's tools—loose twigs, dry sticks, and tinder gathered from underneath the tree. If a friction fire is unattainable, a wooden match that has undergone a purity ritual will suffice.

After the tip cools, the crafter must mark the stick with a number, letter, or symbol sacred to them, a unique design or stamp that represents their spirit's greatest strength. The mark should be carved into the stick with the same stone, or one of the many stones, used to sharpen it.

Finally, with one hand on the giving tree and the other holding the stick above their head, the crafter must say the bonding spell out loud three times.

Prepared properly, the stick will be bound to the crafter, a servant to their will, forever.

SEPTEMBER 2013

Chapter 1 – Cel

Cel closed her eyes when Parker's cell phone vibrated just before seven A.M. She'd been lying in bed an arm's distance away from him for nearly an hour, watching him snore, remembering when they used to sleep with their legs woven seamlessly together, their heads on the same pillow. They'd been together fourteen years, married six, and she'd never felt this disconnected from him. Sure, they'd suffered their fair share of rough patches over the years, survived a couple of temporary splits even, but this time the gap between them felt wider, deeper. Almost impassable.

She pretended to sleep as Parker grabbed his phone off the nightstand, eased out of bed, and snuck into the bathroom. When the door clicked shut, she smothered her face with his pillow and pushed hot, heavy breaths into the cotton. She had no doubts about whom the caller was: Lauren Page. Miss fucking Page. The new seventh grade English teacher at Oak Mott Middle School. Parker's fresh-out-of-college mentee. The skinny brunette who called and texted with no regard to time. Cel had met the woman face-to-face twice, both times when she'd gone to the school unannounced to visit Parker during lunch, and she'd found Miss Mentee's bubbly greeting and perfect smile as much a façade as her cherry red lipstick and fake nails.

Cel tossed the pillow aside when she heard the toilet flush and made her way to the closet. She had her jogging shorts and tank top on, her hair pulled back in a ponytail, and her blue running shoes in her hands when Parker came out of the bathroom. He stopped at the foot of the bed and adjusted his boxers.

"You leaving?" he asked.

Without looking his way, Cel knelt, slid on a shoe, and cinched the laces tight enough to make a hiss. She didn't have any proof he'd slept with Lauren, only a hunch, a fear. An intuition so strong she couldn't hold it inside any longer. "Are you fucking her?"

"What?"

"That was Lauren, right?"

Parker tossed his phone onto the unmade bed and smirked. "Are you serious?"

Cel scooped up the other shoe and stood, eyeing him with unbreakable focus.

Parker hesitated, ran his hand through his hair for a few seconds before answering. "Am I...No. I'm not *fucking* her. We're just friends. Co-workers. You know that."

Cel squeezed the blue sneaker with both hands as her pulse quickened. She wanted to believe him, wanted to give him the benefit of the doubt, but she knew him too well. He'd hesitated too long. "Don't lie to me, Parker."

"I'm not."

Cel glanced at his phone on the bed, took a deep breath. "It's pretty obvious something more than lesson planning is going on between you two."

Parker dipped his chin and pinched the bridge of his nose. "Jesus Christ, Cel." He looked up. "You're freaking out over nothing again."

"Am I? *Am I?* Then tell me why you talk and text with her all the fucking time? Why do you leave the room every time she calls? Why do you hang out with her for hours after work?"

"It's my job to talk to her. To listen to her. To help her. I'm her mentor, remember?" Parker enunciated the word mentor slow and loud, as though Cel wouldn't understand the meaning otherwise. "I leave the room for privacy when I talk to a lot of people. The same way you do when you talk to Natalie or your *abuela*. Get over it"

Cel fought against the urge to throw the shoe at him. "Why have you suddenly decided to start going to the gym again after years of not giving a shit? The same gym she goes to."

"It's the only gym in our neighborhood. And I haven't...wait..." An inquisitive look passed over Parker's face like a shadow. "How did you know she goes there, anyway?"

"I didn't until now."

Parker pushed out a loud breath. "Listen, I started going there before she even moved here. I've only seen her there once, for God's sake." He grabbed the flabby flesh drooping over his boxer waistband and jiggled it. "This is why I go. Not because of *her*."

Cel's gaze slid to Parker's wallet on the nightstand. A key to Lauren's apartment was wedged between his driver's license and debit card. She'd supposedly given it to him so he could feed her fish when she went to Austin over Labor Day weekend. "Why do you still have the key to her apartment?"

Parker's brow knitted. "Have you been going through my wallet?" When Cel didn't immediately answer, he stepped toward her. "Is that what this is about? Her stupid fucking key?" He tapped his chest. "I tried to give it back, but she asked me to hold onto it in case of an emergency because she doesn't know many people in town yet. I keep it in my wallet so I won't lose it." He marched to his nightstand, fished the key out of his wallet, marched over to Cel and held it out. His face and neck had reddened to match the color of his boxers. "Here. If you're that fucking paranoid, then take it."

Cel searched Parker's face but didn't move. She could tell by the look in his eyes and the sour adrenaline stench of his breath that his frustration would soon boil over into anger if she continued peppering him with questions. Her emotions were on the brink as well, and she didn't want another physical-altercation-notch on their belt. She swallowed hard and flashed a submissive yet condescending smile. "Taking that will serve no purpose on my end."

A thick curtain of silence dropped between them. They held eye contact for a long moment, until Parker's phone sliced through the tense silence. The vibration was just a slight rattle, barely audible in the mess of sheets, but it impacted Cel with the force of a fire alarm. She shook her head, turned, and stormed out of the room with an awkward gait due to only wearing one shoe.

As she approached the kitchen at the end of the hall, Parker mumbled something and slammed the bedroom door shut. The force rattled the pictures hanging on the wall beside her. She whispered her go-to calming spell, her security blanket, put on her second shoe, grabbed her cell phone and earbuds off the kitchen table, and closed the front door hard enough for Parker to know she'd left.

Chapter 2 - Cel

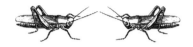

When Cel rounded the corner onto Matador Lane, Parker's Camry was no longer in the driveway behind her Envoy. She slowed to walk and laced her hands behind her head. The five-mile jog through Woodway Park and a good dose of The Eagles had calmed her nerves some, loosened her rigid muscles, and she hoped a hot shower would finish the job.

In the foyer, she instinctively whispered a dissolving spell as she removed her earbuds. She'd learned the spell, like all spells, from her *abuela*. After every fight or disagreement they'd had when Cel was a child, Yesenia would walk around the house with a fistful of burning sage, whispering the spell, forcing Cel to follow and whisper it as well, in order to dispel any lingering *energia maligna*. Cel knew the spell couldn't work without Parker participating, or without the sage for that matter, but she couldn't help herself. The spell came without thought. Like many of them did.

She threw on jeans and a T-shirt after showering, and then made her way to the kitchen, where she filled Mila's food and water bowls and downed a shot of wheatgrass before locking up the house and heading over to her *abuela's*. Yesenia had retired from Allied Foods two months earlier, and they'd met for brunch three days a week since.

Yesenia lived in a small, three-bedroom house in the Gateway neighborhood on the east side of Oak Mott—the same painted-brick house Cel had grown up in. A hurricane fence blanketed with ivy bordered the front yard, and two giant slippery elms stood guard on either side of the walkway leading to the front door.

On the porch, Cel readjusted the potted herbs, peppers, jasmine, aloe, and plumeria, allowing the dappled sunshine to kiss new leaves. She'd helped care for her *abuela's* plants as a child, one of the few chores she didn't mind back then. She'd hated mowing the lawn, having to use the clothesline in the backyard to dry the laundry, and washing the dishes by hand, but she loved tending to the plants, nurturing them. A group of similar plants were in terra cotta pots on her own back porch, most grafted from these.

She called out for her *abuela* as she stepped inside the house. The smell of jalapenos and the hiss of sizzling grease filled the air. She called out again as she made her way into the kitchen and found Yesenia in front of the stove stirring a pan of *migas*. Yesenia stuck out her cheek without looking at Cel, and Cel kissed it. "Good morning, *mija*."

Cel sat at the table in the center of the kitchen behind Yesenia and sighed as though a weight had been lifted off her chest. Nothing in the kitchen had changed in thirty years. The same grease-stained, flower-patterned linoleum covered the floor. The same yellow paint flaked away from the cupboards. The same pouch of blessed, dried bay leaves—*maleta de curacion*—dangled from a hook above the sink. The same long silver braid fell down her *abuela's* back. And this morning, the same spicy version of *migas* was cooking in the same cast iron pot on the same gas-burner stove as it had most mornings when Cel was a kid. In her teens, she'd constantly complained about the never-ending sameness, calling Yesenia dull and predictable, but now, especially given the recent instability in her own home and marriage, she found comfort in it. Stability felt good.

Yesenia loaded two plates with steaming *migas*, placed one in front of Cel, and sat down across from her. Her forehead was slick with sweat, the chest of her knee-length purple dress speckled with grease. She picked up one of the two glasses of black tea she'd brewed earlier and smiled. "*Fuerza y salud.*"

"Strength and health," Cel repeated, and sipped her tea.

Inspecting Cel's face with her eyes, Yesenia scooped a forkful of eggs into her mouth and spoke as she chewed. "What's wrong?"

Cel picked at her eggs, took a small bite. Like the house, her *abuela* never changed. Direct and to the point as always.

"I can tell something's off with you, *mija*." Yesenia shoved another forkful into her mouth, then drew an invisible circle in the air around Cel's face with the fork. "*Tirada.*"

Cel chewed slowly, swallowed. "Parker and I had a fight this morning."

Yesenia continued eating. "About?"

Cel took a warm tortilla out of the *comal* in the center of the table, tore off a small chunk and shoved it in her mouth. "I asked him if he was sleeping with Lauren."

Yesenia nodded. "What did he say?"

"He got pissed and denied it. Said I was paranoid and freaking out over nothing."

Lightly shaking her head, Yesenia smirked with half of her mouth. "Of course, he did. He's a man."

Cel shoved another small chunk of tortilla in her mouth and shook her head. "If he hasn't slept with her already, I'm afraid he might soon if something doesn't change."

Yesenia took a drink of tea as Cel poked at her eggs. "Did you try the rekindling spell we talked about last month?"

"Uh-huh. A few weeks ago. But it obviously didn't help much."

The grooves bracketing Yesenia's mouth deepened as a knowing smile touched her lips. She pointed at Cel with her fork. "I told you that spell was a cooperation spell and would only work if in his heart he wanted the same as you." She took another big bite and eyed Cel as she chewed and swallowed. "It would've been better to use a stronger spell on him that might be able to bend his will enough to—"

Cel waved her hand, cutting off Yesenia. "I don't want to bend his will. I just want that Lauren bitch to leave him alone. She swooped in when we were already in a rocky place because of the miscarriage and started throwing herself at him like a temptress. I think it's a game to her. A few weeks ago, she even gave him a key to her apartment."

Yesenia's stopped chewing mid-bite, her eyes widening.

"*Right*," Cel continued. "He said she gave it to him so he could feed her fish when she went out of town to visit her parents, but I don't know. I just..." She trailed off, scanned the yellow and white mushroom-shaped jars lining the counter, then locked eyes with Yesenia. "He still has it. He said she told him to keep it in case of an emergency since she doesn't know many people in town."

Shaking her head in disbelief, Yesenia pushed the last of her *migas* into a small pile. "*Dar de comer al pez. Chingao.*" She shoveled the bite in her mouth and set her fork on the plate. "Are you going to confront her?"

Cel shrugged. "I don't know what to do."

Yesenia wiped the corners of her mouth with a napkin, dropped it on her plate, and clasped her hands together on her lap. "Have you tried any spells on her?"

Looking down at her plate, Cel lied by shaking her head. She'd been raised to believe that if spells and rituals were used in the right way, cast or performed by a dedicated, well-versed *bruja* with an enlightened spirit, they could influence anything from hair thickness to emotions. Yesenia had pounded into her head that failure to achieve results was never the craft's lack of power. It was the *bruja's*. Although, at thirty years old, Cel didn't crave her *abuela's* approval as strongly as when she was a child, she still felt ashamed admitting that the rekindling spell she'd tried on Parker had failed, and she didn't want to add to that humility by admitting failure with the one she'd tried on Lauren, too.

Yesenia stood and picked up her plate. "I know a few that might help keep her away. If you want, I'll write them down for you."

Cel smiled a pleased smile not at the offer, but at the thought of how her *abuela* wrote everything down with pencil and paper like it was 1920. Another example of how time stood still at 314 Cobalt Street. Despite repeated attempts by Cel, at least on the cell phone end, Yesenia had refused to acclimate to the Internet age. She still occasionally sent Cel letters in the mail. "Okay."

Yesenia gestured at Cel's plate. "*Acabaste?*"

Cel nodded, and Yesenia took the plate and dumped the eggs in a scrap bowl beside the sink. As Yesenia washed the dishes, Cel brought the *comal* and glasses over to the counter. She tossed the leftover tortillas into the scrap bowl, wiped down the table, then dried the dishes and put them away as Yesenia cleaned the stovetop. They'd repeated this sequence of events so many times that they moved around the small kitchen like two mute dancers gliding through an obstacle course. Each knew exactly when to twist sideways to make room for the other, when to pause before opening a cupboard, when to pass the other a towel or rag or spray bottle.

Yesenia passed Cel the scrap bowl to end the dance. "Take that to the *ninas*, and I'll go write down those spells."

Cel stepped out onto the back porch, and all four hens noticed the bowl and sprinted for her. They knew the multi-colored bowl better than they knew their own talons. "Hey, ladies." They followed her into the center of the yard, and she scattered the scraps beneath the pear tree. As they pecked, she scanned the tree line beyond the hurricane fence that cordoned off the large backyard. The wooded area was known to locals as Hunter's Haven because of the large number of white tail deer and rabbits that lived there. It stretched for miles beyond the eastern edge of Oak Mott. Sparse patches of leaves had already begun to change into fall shades of maroon and gold, speckling the dark green canopy like distant stars.

Much of Cel's childhood had been spent in the heart of Hunter's Haven. She'd first kissed Parker in those woods, on Table Rock by Mesquite Creek, and she'd lost her virginity to him on a bed of leaves under a nearby gnarled elm months later. The thought brought on a swell of emotion. She bit at her lip to fight back the deluge rushing up her throat, but her eyes welled with tears anyway. What was she going to do? How was she going to fix this? They'd fought through so much. She didn't want to give up. She didn't want to lose him.

She took in a deep breath, whispered a calming spell, and headed inside where she washed and dried the scrap bowl, then sat on the living room couch petting Mina while she waited for Yesenia. Mina was the oldest of Yesenia's three cats, Yesenia's familiar, and also the mother of Cel's cat. Mina purred with pleasure as Cel scratched the nub where her front right leg used to be, a leg that had been tied to a string and worn around Yesenia's neck, hidden beneath her clothes, for fifteen years now.

When Yesenia walked into the room a few minutes later, she handed Cel a sheet of paper with writing on the front and the back. "Here you go, *mija*. There's one on each side."

Cel glanced at the spells. One was the same blocking spell she'd already tried on Lauren, but again she kept that to herself. She flashed a grateful smile as she stood and hugged Yesenia. "Thanks, *Buela*. I better get going. I have to go to the store. Mila needs food, and I need laundry detergent."

Yesenia nodded, placed her hands behind her back, and cocked her head so Cel could kiss her cheek. "You know where I am if you need me."

Chapter 3 - Cel

Cel purchased the items she needed and drove to Oak Mott Middle School. She parked her Envoy curbside across the street from the teacher's parking lot, where she had a good view of the window looking into Parker's room.

The second time she'd visited him unannounced earlier in the month, she'd brought three ivies, claiming she thought he needed "something green to liven up his room." She'd raised the blinds about two feet, placed them on the window sill, and told him he had to leave them there so they'd get plenty of sun. She'd figured the gap would provide enough space for her to see into his room at lunch time, and it had.

She didn't enjoy spying on him, but for her own peace of mind, she needed to see if he was lying about the nature of his lunches with Lauren. Were they really work-lunches, or were they locking the door and screwing each other's brains out on his desk? As a faithful wife, she felt she deserved to know the truth. She'd only watched them three times so far, and each time Lauren had sat on a stool across the desk from him and done most of the talking. Parker had laughed a lot, more in those thirty-minute snippets than she'd seen him laugh in years. And sometimes Lauren had placed one hand over her mouth and the other on Parker's wrist when she giggled, but as far as Cel could tell, that was the extent of their physical contact. Although there were a couple of times they went to the far side of the room out of view for longer than she liked.

Shortly before the lunch bell rang, Cel fished the binoculars out from under the seat that she'd bought at Gander Mountain the day before she'd taken the ivies to the school. She aimed them at the window and focused the lenses. Today, she wanted to see if Parker would act jovial and pleasant, like nothing had happened at home this morning, or if he would act cold and upset, perhaps even give Lauren her apartment key back.

A few minutes after the kids cleared out of Parker's room, Lauren walked in wearing an inviting smile and carrying a sack lunch. With slumped shoulders, as if the upper part of his spine had turned to jelly, Parker rose from his seat and put his hands in his pockets. They talked only for a moment before he pulled his cell phone out of his pocket and either read a text or checked the caller ID. Then he pointed at the phone, said something, and Lauren nodded and left the room, closing the door behind her.

Parker spent the next fifteen minutes pacing around in front of his desk talking on the phone. Cel assumed he was talking either to a student's parent, which happened frequently, or to his oldest sister Jennifer—the only other person Cel imagined he would answer a call from during school hours. Jennifer had moved back to Oak Mott to help care for their ailing mom, and she often called and asked Parker to pick up medications or groceries after work and drop them off on his way home.

When Parker shoved his phone back in his pocket and exited the room a few minutes before lunch ended, Cel put away the binoculars and headed home, not happy, but content with the small victory. ("Small victories pave the road to reconnection," was the motto of marriage counselor Dr. Les Dean's book, *The Road to Reconnection*, a book both she and Parker had read after their first temporary split.) Although he hadn't given Lauren the apartment key back, Cel was glad he'd looked downtrodden and hadn't perked up when she'd walked into the room. She was also glad he'd sent Lauren away while he talked on the phone.

Chapter 4 - Cel

In the kitchen, Cel washed down a multi-vitamin and two *maca* pills with a swig of partridge tea, then made her way to the living room for her daily meditation. She'd been taking the pills, drinking partridge tea, meditating, and running ever since her second miscarriage two years earlier. After tests proved she had no obvious anatomical or genetic problems to blame for the first two miscarriages, and Parker's sperm tested ready and willing, Dr. Benson had given her a suggested exercise regimen and a list of natural remedies that might help prevent future miscarriages. "A tweak here or there can sometimes make a world of difference," he'd said.

She dove headfirst into Dr. Benson's suggestions not only for herself, but also for Parker. He'd always said he wanted a big family, two girls and two boys, ideally, and his family constantly badgered them about grandchildren. Even in the months right after each of the first two miscarriages, every time they talked to his mom, Beverly, she would ask when they were going to start trying again, reminding Parker that he was the only male left on their side of the family to pass on the Lundy name. Beverly would also often pat Cel's belly and make comments like: "Those eggs won't last forever, you know."

So Cel ran daily. Switched to eating only organic fruits and vegetables. Cut soda, soy, and wine out of her diet. Took multi-vitamins and herbal supplements twice a day. Performed fertility massages on her abdomen every evening. Grew partridge plants on her back porch to make the tea many Native American women used for fertility. And she continued performing the fertility rituals her *abuela* had given her. She lost ten pounds in the first month, and mentally and physically felt sharper, toned, ready. A viable vessel. Parker praised her efforts and seemed to love her trimmed body as well. He couldn't keep his hands off her.

Then came the third pregnancy, and the third miscarriage.

Afterward, she battled through a tough depression but fell back into her fertility routine within a few months. Parker seemed discouraged but never said as much. When it came to discussing the miscarriages, he promised her it wasn't her fault, that everything would be okay. They would try again when she was ready.

Then came the fourth miscarriage in July, which was followed by a darker bout of depression. Dr. Benson urged Cel to go on antidepressants, but she refused. For the next six weeks, she kept the house dark, slept nearly eighteen hours a day, ate way more than she needed when awake, often cried herself into a daze with blankets pulled over her head, and couldn't bear to be in the same room with Parker. It hurt too much to see the sadness in his eyes, to hear the pity in his voice. It was also embarrassing, shameful. She'd failed him again. She was not a mother. She killed every piece of him he gave her.

By the time she emerged from her depression and restarted her routine, Parker had already gone back to work and met Lauren Page, halting any relationship-recovery efforts she attempted. No matter how many leading questions she asked, he never seemed interested in talking for more than a couple of minutes. No matter how flirtatious she tried to be, even if she walked around the house naked practically begging him to fuck her, he never seemed interested in touching her.

Cel finished meditating an hour before Parker usually arrived home. She ate a couple of carrots, folded and put away the clean towels, and went outside to water her plants. When she came back in, she turned on the radio and started preparing turkey tacos for dinner. She wanted to be busy when Parker walked through the door. Activity made awkward greetings easier for her. She would simply cook and follow his lead. If he wanted to talk about this morning or continue arguing, she'd oblige with honesty. If he wanted to make minimal eye contact and skirt the problem for a while, she'd play along.

Classic rock songs played as the smell of seasoned meat saturated the kitchen. Four-thirty came and went without Parker arriving. Cel left the meat on the warm burner, made a salad with fresh tomatoes from her garden and a fresh pitcher of tea. Thirty minutes passed. Parker had only stayed later than five o'clock a handful of times, all of which were this school year. With Lauren. Cel waited another thirty minutes before texting him.

Are you coming home? I cooked tacos.

Twenty minutes later, she put the meat and salad in the fridge and called Parker. The phone rang six times and went to voicemail. She didn't bother leaving a message because he never checked his voicemail. She typed a second text, asking if he was at the school with

Lauren, but thought better of it and sent a text to her friend Natalie instead.

Do you have time to chat?

Natalie was Cel's best friend, one of the few people she was honest with about Parker. They had all three been friends since their Gateway Elementary School days. Natalie texted back immediately saying she had two more houses to show this evening and would call afterward. Cel sent back a smiley face emoji and patiently waited.

When Parker still hadn't come home or texted by seven, Cel headed to his mom's house. If he didn't want to come home, fine, but she deserved to know where he'd gone and who he was with. Sometimes he could be such an asshole.

Best case scenario: he'd gone to his mom's house after work. He frequently went there and vented to his oldest sister Jennifer after he and Cel fought.

Worst case scenario, one Cel didn't want to fully consider until faced with the reality of it: he was somewhere secret with Lauren.

She slowed to a stop on Union Street and parked angled where she had a direct line of sight at the Lundy house on Evergreen. It was the third house on the right, the one rimmed with rose bushes. The blinds in the front windows of the two-story brick home were open. Jennifer's Audi sat in the circular driveway behind Beverly's Durango, but Parker's Camry wasn't there.

Cel exhaled a loud breath. Where was he? She briefly considered knocking on the front door and asking Jennifer if she'd heard from Parker, but the idea left her as quick as it had come. She knew better than to go inside the Lundy house and ask if they'd heard from Parker. His mom Beverly and favorite sister Jennifer would freak out. Parker was the baby of the family, the happy accident, more than ten years younger than both of his sisters, and although he'd turned thirty-one in May, they still treated him with kid gloves. If they hadn't heard from Parker, they would unleash a barrage of questions on Cel and insist they all go search for him. She couldn't handle hours of Jennifer's and Beverly's underhanded judgement and criticism right now.

Cel pulled away from the curb and headed for the Grandview Apartments, Lauren's home, just in case. She'd followed Lauren to the complex a few weeks earlier, after her suspicions had gotten the better of her and she wanted to know where Miss Mentee lived. She went the long way, passing Oak Mott Middle School in hopes of finding Parker diligently working alone in his room, maybe grading papers, avoiding a fight at home, but he wasn't there. The lot was empty, the school abandoned for the evening.

Half of the sun had slipped below the horizon, coloring the sky dark orange, by the time she reached Grandview Apartments. She looped through the circular complex twice, searching for Parker's Camry, to make sure he hadn't sneakily parked on the opposite side of complex from Lauren's apartment. He'd been sneaky a lot since meeting her. His Camry was nowhere in the complex, but that didn't mean he hadn't parked a block away and walked to Lauren's. Lauren's yellow rag top Jeep *was* in its designated spot, so Cel parked in an empty slot facing Lauren's one-bedroom apartment—building 14, apartment 212, upstairs on the right.

Cel watched the sliding glass doors on Lauren's balcony for a few minutes before Lauren appeared. The blinds were pulled back, the living room well-lit. She watched Lauren move from the kitchen to the living room a couple of times before sitting down on the couch with a bowl of food and turning on the TV. Satisfied Parker was not in the apartment, Cel left the complex just as the building's security lights popped on.

Chapter 5 - Parker

Parker cancelled his afternoon tutorials and left the school right after the final bell rang. He didn't want to stay and talk to Lauren. He didn't want to lie and tell her everything was fine, to hide the fact that Cel had confronted him about their relationship, but he didn't want to tell her the truth either. He didn't want to talk at all. He wanted a break. A quiet break. Some time alone before heading home and facing Cel again. He took FM 24 around the southern edge of Oak Mott, and about a quarter of a mile outside of town turned onto an overgrown dirt road that penetrated the southern reaches of Hunter's Haven. Shrouded by tree shade, he drove at a snail's pace with the windows down for a while, inhaling the scent of mud and creek and weed pollen, before stopping in the center of the road and killing the engine.

Although he hadn't been out to Hunter's Haven since the school year started, since he'd met Lauren, he'd used the old road, the only one that lead into the woods, as an escape route for years. And based on the constant fresh supply of cigarette butts along the side of the road, many people in Oak Mott did. Most came to hide a vice like drinking or smoking from their spouse or parents, or to rendezvous with a secret lover, or talk to God, or contemplate divorce or suicide, but he came to simply be alone. Escape. Decompress. With a population hovering around fifteen thousand, Oak Mott wasn't a tiny town, but it was small enough that hideaways were few and far between.

Parker unbuttoned the cuffs of his shirt, rolled the sleeves up to his elbows, then opened his briefcase and pulled out a worn paperback copy of Jack Ketchum's *Red*. He'd had his nose shoved in books since his sister Jennifer had taught him to read when he was five years old, making him read aloud from her Sweet Valley High collection every night before bed. Back then, Jennifer was an overweight loner with a horrible case of pubescent acne. Books were her best friends, her magic portal, her escape from the comments and ridicule her cruel peers often bombarded her with. And although Parker hadn't had the same social problems in school, he'd followed in her footsteps when it came to reading, especially as an adult. To him, reading was therapy. When he read, he didn't fret or worry, overthink or rethink, assume or regret. When he opened a book, all of his daily problems vanished for a while. He relaxed. He healed. He forgot himself. Over the years he'd spent hundreds of hours reading out here under the canopy of Hunter's Haven, jumping from world to world, journeying with friends and fighting foes. He muted his cell phone, opened the book, and began reading.

For the next hour he didn't look up. He didn't think about Lauren finding his room empty and his door locked after school. He didn't think about how to greet Cel when he arrived home. Or if he'd even go home for that matter. He didn't worry about the parents who would be pissed that he'd canceled after school tutorials at the last minute. He pored over the words, through the sentences. He followed Avery Ludlow on his quest for justice after three heartless teens had shot his best friend, his dog, Red, for no reason other than malice. Parker had read the book three or four times, but Ketchum was one of his favorite wordsmiths, a master at pulling him in, and each time felt like the first.

He was twenty pages away from Avery's revenge when the roar of an engine pulled him out of the story. He closed the book and watched through the rearview mirror as a gray F-150 came into view. The truck slowed to a stop about fifty yards behind his Camry, and after a brief pause, made a three-point turn and drove off.

Parker smiled to himself. *Looks like I stole someone else's idea,* he thought.

He continued reading for twenty more minutes, finishing *Red* and starting the other short novella in the book, *The Passenger*, before checking his phone. It was almost five-thirty. Cel and Lauren had both texted, both asking where he was. As he set the phone on top of his briefcase in the passenger's seat, movement in the trees to his left caught his attention. He looked that way and saw a girl with thick brunette hair standing beside an elm tree thirty yards away. She wore a light-colored summer dress and had her hand on the tree trunk as though holding it upright. She had pale skin, slender legs, and was staring at him.

Parker watched her for a moment as an impossible possibility moved slowly through his mind, like a sodden leaf finally too heavy to float on a lake's surface sinking to the bottom. When the thought settled, his pulse quickened. It couldn't be her.

He opened the door and stepped out of the car to take a better look. The dancing shadows, overgrown shrubbery, and untrimmed trees made it hard to see well, but the girl's long brunette hair was parted down the center just like Abby's. And the style of the dress looked similar to the last one he'd seen her in. He felt like he'd stepped into the past, into a dream. It couldn't be her.

The girl darted behind a tree when he took a step toward her. She emerged a moment later between two others, farther away. She moved lithely and quick, like a ghost. She smiled a familiar smile and gestured for Parker to follow her. Gooseflesh sprung to life on his arms, but he didn't move. She gestured again, slowly, and then moved deeper into the woods. Parker hesitated, but eventually his feet tore loose of the dirt and he ran after her.

He kept his eyes forward, searching, as he kicked through the shrubbery and shoved through the branches grasping at his skin. By the time he caught sight of her again, he'd tripped twice, ripping a hole in his slacks, and had scrapes on his forearms from using them as shields as he barreled through the woods.

He followed her, crossing two game trails, catching momentary glimpses of her behind this tree, around that tree as she zigzagged with ease through the thicket. It wasn't until he heard the water flowing that he realized how deep into the woods he'd gone. When she reached the large, two-foot-high, flat rock nestled up alongside Mesquite Creek, she stopped and looked back at him. She eyed him for a second or two, then leapt off the rock, splashed through the water, and disappeared in the woods on the opposite side of the creek.

Short of breath, a sharp stitch needling his side, Parker hopped onto the rock and put his hands on his hips. Mesquite Creek split Hunter's Haven into two nearly-equal halves. He couldn't go on any farther. He sat down on the same rock he'd sat on a hundred times as a kid—"Table Rock," the Cricket Hunters had called it—looped his arms around his knees, and watched the woods on the opposite side of the creek, his mind struggling to rationalize the situation.

What the hell was going on? He didn't believe in ghosts. Auras and spiritual energy, okay, but not human-shaped apparitions haunting forests. There had to be a logical explanation. She was real, right? If she wasn't, was he hallucinating? Was his mind slipping? He'd definitely been stressed lately, not sleeping well. And his family did have a history of mental illness. Depression. Bi-polar disorder. Alzheimer's. Name the problem and one of his relatives had it. Or...couldn't hallucinations be signs of a stroke? A brain bleed? His blood pressure had been through the roof the last few months. So high his doctor had upped his medication twice. And, of course, there was family history there, too. His dad had had two strokes before his fatal heart attack five years earlier. Or, what about a brain tumor? He'd read that those could cause hallucinations, too. And he'd been having frequent headaches lately. Cancer could rear its ugly head anywhere, anytime, right? Jesus-fucking-Christ.

Beginning to panic, he closed his eyes and shook his head as if the movement would jar the anxiety and worry loose, allowing the unwanted parasites to fly out of his ears. He took a series of deep breaths, focusing on the movement of the air in and out of his lungs and nothing else.

When he opened his eyes, he stood and looked back the way he'd come. He'd spent enough sunsets in Hunter's Haven to know it would be pitch black soon. Without the flashlight app on his cell phone, he wouldn't be able to see two feet in front of him. He needed to get back to his car. He hopped off the rock, glanced back over his shoulder, and searched the tree line on the opposite side of the creek one last time. "I'm losing my mind. I couldn't have—"

His consciousness cut off mid-thought when something slammed into the back of his head.

Chapter 6 - Cel

After leaving Grandview Apartments, Cel drove by Whiskey River and The Pub, two local bars Parker occasionally met his sister at for drinks, but she didn't see his Camry or Jennifer's Audi in either parking lot. She drove by the public library he frequented. Nothing. The gym. Nope. Out of ideas, she decided to drive to his parent's house again. Jennifer's Audi and Beverly's Durango were still there, but not Parker's Camry. She watched the house for almost an hour before heading home, texting and calling him multiple times in vain while she waited.

As she turned onto Matador Lane, she stiffened her back and tilted toward the windshield, her eyes wide with foolish hope. But when the headlight beams lit up her house, she found the modest brick home at the back of a deep lot dark and empty, the porch light off, blinds closed, none of the windows lit from the inside, Parker's car nowhere to be seen. "He's not here," she whispered, slumping back against the seat as she pulled into the driveway.

In the foyer, she slipped off her shoes and called out Parker's name anyway. Mila immediately emerged from the darkness and rubbed against her shins, meowing. Cel stroked Mila's back. "Hi, girl. Did you miss me? Has Daddy been here?"

Cel made her way to the kitchen and flicked on the light. All the clean dishes and cookware were neatly stacked in the doorless cupboards. The countertops were empty, the chairs neatly pushed under the table, place mats perfectly aligned. Just as she'd left the place. She looked in the fridge and found the food she'd cooked untouched.

With Mila on her heels, she walked to the bedroom. She turned on the overhead light and saw that the bed was still made. No clothes were on the floor. Most days when Parker came home, he tossed his dirty clothes on the floor at the foot of the bed and changed into sweats. If she didn't pick them up, he'd add to the pile the next day.

She went to the bathroom and sat down on the toilet to pee. She'd been holding it for over an hour. As she checked her phone to make sure she hadn't missed a text or call from Parker, she heard a soft crash somewhere on the other side of the house. Her heart hiccupped, and her urine flow stopped. She shot up straight as though stroked down the spine with a sharp instrument. Had she locked the front door behind her when she'd gotten home? There had been two break-ins in the neighborhood last month. The perps broke into the houses in the evening when the residents weren't home, stealing TVs, laptops, weapons, and jewelry. As far as Cel knew, they hadn't been caught.

"Parker?" she called out. "Is that you?"

She pulled up her shorts and sent her ears out as far as she could, hoping to hear Parker's voice. The house answered with cold silence.

"Parker, is that you?" she tried again as she made her way through the bedroom to the light switch by the door. She flicked it on, peeked out into the hall, and looked both directions while reflexively reciting the protection spell her *abuela* had whispered to her every morning before she'd boarded the school bus as a child. She didn't realize she was saying it until she finished the last verse and the house grew eerily silent again.

Feeling like she wasn't alone, like she was being watched, she suddenly craved a physical form of protection, a weapon. She hurried to the kitchen, turned on the light, grabbed a steak knife from a drawer, and checked the French doors leading out onto the patio and the window above the sink. They were both locked and secure.

She held the knife head-high as she moved into the living room and turned on the lamp on the end table beside the couch. Nothing appeared broken or amiss in the room. The two windows were closed and locked, their outer screens undamaged.

"Parker," she hollered again as she headed to the front door to check if she'd locked it behind her when she'd entered. She hadn't. Damn it. She fastened the deadbolt, flicked on the porch light, and then made her way back down the hall. After checking the bathroom, she went into the spare bedroom that doubled as their office space and turned on the light. She took a couple of steps into the room, and that's when she noticed the paperback books in the center of the closet floor to her right. They always left the closet door open because house settling had made it impossible to fully close. The walk-in closet shelves housed CDs, photo albums, Parker's collection of paperback novels, and Cel's overflow of clothes.

She cautiously made her way into the closet. Seven or eight of Parker's books, some Stephen King and Agatha Christie, and

Bradbury's *The Illustrated Man*, had fallen onto the floor. *The Illustrated Man* was upright, spread-eagled like a tepee. On the upper shelf, many of his other books were askew, another hanging over the edge about to fall, and Cel's stacks of folded sweaters next to them were knocked over. It appeared as though a strong wind gust had whipped across that side of the closet and that side only.

She spun around and faced the bedroom door before squatting to gather the books. When she reached for *The Illustrated Man*, she noticed a picture sticking out from in between the pages. She slid it out as she rose.

For a brief moment Cel thought the girl with thick brunette hair parted down the middle and dark eyes was Lauren Page. The similarities were uncanny. The face shape. The body shape. The smile. But her breath caught in her throat when she realized the face didn't belong to Lauren. It belonged to Abby Powell. One of her best friends when she was in elementary and middle school. One of the Cricket Hunters. The one whose disappearance had all of Oak Mott on edge fifteen years ago to the month. And she was sitting on Table Rock in Hunter's Haven, wearing the yellow and blue summer dress she was last seen in.

Stunned and confused, Cel stood in the center of the closet, staring at the image as the past roared toward her like a runaway locomotive.

SEPTEMBER 1998

Chapter 7 - Cel

Four weeks before Abby disappeared, just before sunset, the Cricket Hunters met in the field that separated Yesenia's house from Hunter's Haven to compare cricket sticks. Yesenia had given Cel the instructions on how to craft them a week earlier. She'd copied the spell from one of the grimoires she kept locked in a wooden chest in her closet, books once owned by her mom, and *her* mom before that. The weapon wasn't specifically designed for crickets, but that's what Yesenia wanted the kids to kill. She'd promised to pay each of them ten dollars a week if they kept the crickets around her house at bay until winter arrived.

"Did you guys have to use the matches to start the fire like me?" Cel asked, her eyes sliding across her friend's faces.

Parker, Natalie, Abby, and Omar nodded in unison. They'd spent every afternoon out in Hunter's Haven since receiving the instructions, spinning twigs and rubbing their palms raw, trying to learn how to spark a friction fire. The abundant elm trees and dry air were ideal for the process according to the library books they'd checked out, but mastering the art still proved difficult. Yesenia had given them purified wooden match sticks as an alternative, just in case.

"And you did everything else like we practiced, too, right? Especially the part about the blood? That was the most—"

"Relax," Parker interjected. "We did everything just like we were supposed to. Look." He extended his hand, palm up. A fresh gash ran from his lower thumb to his wrist, still bloody.

Omar, Natalie, and Abby followed suit, placing their hands palm-up alongside Parker's. All had similar wounds, the one on Omar's bony hand the shallowest, but adequate.

A blend of relief and gratitude mushroomed in Cel's chest as her eyes slid from hand to hand, cut to cut. Although none of the other hunters had said so to her face, she knew they each carried a growing degree of skepticism about her family's beliefs. At one time, back when Santa Claus and the Tooth Fairy were as real to them as their parents, there was zero skepticism. They would participate in rituals like the evil-eye-egg-roll and body sweeping with excitement sparkling in their eyes, just like her. They would sit rapt on the back porch with Yesenia for hours, listening to her tales of magic and mischief, curses and revenge, *knowing* it was real. But over the past few years, Cel had noticed them shooting each other hesitant looks more and more when she asked them to participate in a ritual, or help her cast a spell, or hang out with Yesenia on the back porch. She figured her *abuela* had noticed too, which was why she'd offered to pay them to craft the sticks and help hunt the *espiritus venganza* rather than just asking. They might not have agreed to follow the specific instructions as diligently, or hunt as eagerly and frequently, if there had been no monetary gain. Cel would never know. And right now, she didn't care. All that mattered was that they had followed the instructions and were ready to hunt. She slid back the sleeve of her worn, over-sized blue and black flannel, and stuck out her hand to join the Bloody Hand Club. Her cut was deepest, flayed open.

Parker shot her an ornery look. He was a head taller than her, his hand nearly twice the size. "Mine's bigger."

She playfully elbowed him. "*Whatever.*" Then she tilted the handle of her stick forward, revealing the symbol she'd chosen as her mark—the same symbol that adorned the necklace she wore around her neck. A necklace that had belonged to her mother. "I carved the infinity symbol on mine."

"I knew you would," Natalie blurted out, nervously adjusting her Houston Astros cap when everyone looked at her. She'd been forced to chop her bouncy curls down to nubs at the beginning of summer after her little brother spat a wad of gum into her hair while she napped. She'd worn her dad's Astros cap every day since. Strands were finally beginning to poke out of the edges and tickle the tops of her ears.

Cel smiled at Natalie. "What did you pick?"

"Well, since I'm always having dreams where I'm flying through the sky like a bird, I picked this." Natalie laid her stick across Cel's, a small four-feathered wing carved into the handle.

Parker immediately placed his stick on top of Natalie's and twisted it until an X inside a circle became visible, his recent obsession with Deadshot in the Batman comics on display. "I put a sniper's crosshairs on mine."

Abby and Omar added their sticks to the crisscrossed stack. Omar met eyes with Abby, and they simultaneously said, "You go first," which caused Abby to giggle and her chest to jiggle, catching everyone's eye. Over the past six months, her breasts had blossomed into C cups, but her shirts had remained the same size. In early June, when Cel had jokingly remarked about Abby's new assets, Abby had guffawed and covered her chest and told Cel to "shut up," that she couldn't help it. On the surface, Cel apologized for teasing and embarrassing Abby, but deep down she knew—*everyone knew*—Abby welcomed the attention. Abby and attention went hand-in-hand. She thrived on it.

Omar snapped his gaze back to Abby's face and flashed a guilt-ridden smile. "Go ahead."

"Mine's a star," Abby said. Her eyes bounced around the group, gauging their reactions. Two of the points were round rather than sharp, and one was a dwarf compared to the others. "Not great, I know, but it's the best I could do with the shitty rocks around my tree." She looked at Omar, eager for him to take over.

"I picked the Pi symbol," he said, surprising no one. Everything was numbers and angles and percentages with him. Every day, rain or shine, hot or cold, he carried a Texas Instruments graphing calculator in the front of pocket of his cuff-rolled, hand-me-down jeans. It was a hand-me-down, too, given to him by his oldest sister Sophia after she graduated from high school, but he treated it as if it were sacred.

"All right," Parker said. "Now that we have everything settled, can we get to cricket hunting? They're singing like crazy."

A quiet giggle seeped out of Abby's mouth.

Parker glanced at her. "What?"

"It just sounds funny, saying it that way...cricket hunting." She giggled again and lightly shook her head. "I mean, *really*, who hunts for stupid crickets?"

Parker put his hand on his waist and puffed out his chest like Superman. "We do," he said in a comically deep voice. "Because, by the power of our blood, we are now..." He raised his cricket stick high in the air and looked upward as if there were something fantastical in the sky. "Ordained Cricket Hunters." He opened his mouth and let loose a victorious scream reminiscent of the pig-slaughtering boys dancing around the camp-fire on *Lord of the Flies*.

Seconds later, the other four jabbed their sticks at the sky and joined in.

All five had been friends for as long as they could remember. They'd played t-ball together, eaten cheap popsicles on Table Rock in Hunter's Haven together, ridden their bikes to the municipal pool every summer together, trick-or-treated the streets of their middle-class neighborhood together, worked on their homework together, lied to their parents together, fought off bullies together, stolen together, danced together, but they'd never discussed or used a collective name. Others had. Natalie's dad had occasionally referred to them as the Gateway Gang. Omar's mom, the Rotten Bunch. But they'd never embraced a name themselves. That night, punctuated with guttural howls and blood purified sticks, they embraced one without discussion.

The Cricket Hunters.

As their yells faded and they lowered their sticks, Cel noticed movement behind Abby, near the Hunter's Haven tree line about thirty yards away. She pointed. "Looks like we have a visitor."

Everyone's heads swiveled. Abby put her hand on her cocked hip and whispered, "Jesus."

"Not Jesus," Cel responded, "Jeff."

Abby's only sibling, her younger brother Jeff, waved enthusiastically and trotted toward the group. He was eleven years old but could easily pass for nine. Doctors said his constant battles with pneumonia as a toddler had resulted in his smaller than average frame. He wore a dirty T-shirt and carried a long stick in his right hand. A stick sharpened to a point. A cricket stick. Having no friends of his own in the neighborhood, and, with a natural desire to grow up faster than needed, he constantly chased after Abby and her friends. Sometimes they allowed him to hang out, sometimes not. Abby voted no every time.

He stopped a few feet from the group, beaming ear-to-ear, proud. "I just finished mine." He dipped his head and held the stick out in front of him horizontally, like a blacksmith offering a finished sword to a knight. "I followed all the rules."

Abby glowered at him. "I told you that you couldn't come tonight."

Jeff's smile dissolved.

"Go home. Before I make you sorry you came."

Jeff looked away as his eyes watered up, and he clenched his teeth to fight back tears. "I just wanted to help kill crickets."

"Go," Abby yelled, pointing in the direction of their house. "Now."

Not wanting to hear another Powell-sibling screaming fight, Cel nudged Abby's arm down. "It's okay." She walked over to Jeff and took his stick. "You followed the instructions, huh?" She met eyes with him. "All of them?"

He'd been shadowing and questioning and spying on the hunters all week as they'd prepared to craft their sticks. They'd caught him peeking out from behind tree trunks many times while they practiced starting fires. They'd heard him whispering under Cel's back porch the night she'd taught everyone the bonding spell, repeating it with them over and over. They'd allowed him to look on one afternoon as they sat on Table Rock flipping through a book called *Native Trees of Central Texas*, studying the differences of the various trees in Hunter's Haven, discussing which would be best to craft a stick out of. Abby had put up with him hanging around and bombarding them with questions for the most part, but she did occasionally go off on him, telling him more than once that he should "give it up," that he was "too much of a pussy to ever cut himself anyway."

He nodded. "I did it. All by myself. I used rocks under the tree I got the stick from, and I started the fire with one of the matches I stole from Abby." As Cel examined the stick, tracing the lightning bolt he'd carved into the handle with her finger, he excitedly thrust out his palm, fingers spread wide. He angled his head toward Abby. "I even cut myself. Deep." He pushed the words at his sister, as though trying to knock her back with them. His cut was still bleeding.

Omar stepped next to Cel and looked at the carving. "Cool lightning bolt." He mussed Jeff's thick hair. As the youngest of seven siblings and often on the butt end of his older brothers' pranks and disdain, Omar had a soft spot for Jeff.

Abby rolled her eyes. "He's not coming with me. I'll tell you that."

"He can search the vacant lot on the north side of the house with Omar," Parker said. "Cel, you come with me to the south lot. Abby and Natalie, you guys check the front and back yards. We'll meet back to scan this field when we're done." He pulled a flashlight out of his pocket, held it up, and jiggled it. "Everybody got theirs?"

They all nodded, and Jeff added, "Yep."

"Good. Let's go make some money."

Chapter 8 - Yesenia

Yesenia sat at the kitchen table sipping chamomile tea, waiting for the kids to return. Five ten dollar bills and a plate of *pan de polvo* were on the table in front of her. The scent of cinnamon and caramelized sugar sweetened the air. The Country Roland Band's 20 Greatest Hits album spun on the record player in the living room, the Tejano music drowning out the crickets singing in the distance. Her younger sister, Dolores, was sleeping soundly in the bedroom at the end of the hall.

She and Dolores had been raised in a tiny rural community outside of McAllen, Texas. Their mom, Berta, was born in Mexico and had bounced back and forth across the Rio Grande with her own mom as a child, following men and friends and work opportunities, but she eventually settled in Texas after becoming pregnant with Yesenia at seventeen. Dolores came two years later, and shortly after, Berta relocated the girls north to Oak Mott for reasons she never revealed, where she took a job at Allied Foods and bought a couple of acres of land outside of town using cash she shouldn't have had.

She enrolled them in public school so they could learn English, but they spent most of their childhood on the homestead, speaking Spanish, tending to gardens and goats, learning and mimicking their mother's ways.

They were both teens and working at Allied Foods, Yesenia a mom to two-year-old Rebecca, when Berta died of a heart attack. Soon after that, the sisters sold the homestead, and Yesenia used her portion of the money to secure a small house on the edge of town, a solid home in a solid middle-class neighborhood, closer to the schools and Allied Foods. Dolores spent her money on frivolous things, booze and smokes and trips to Mexico mostly. She lived with Yesenia and Rebecca for a year before moving into her own apartment on the north side.

That apartment had served as Dolores' home until three months ago when a prolonged sickness had forced her to quit her job at Allied Foods, leaving her unable to pay her rent. Over the last half year, she'd lost thirty pounds, suffered regular bouts of weakness, nausea, and headaches, and recently had begun having seizures and periods of disorientation. But despite all that, she refused to visit a doctor. Like Yesenia, she didn't believe a bacteria or virus was to blame for her sickness. She didn't believe pills or injections or ointments that catered only to the body would help. No, she believed Maria Lopez was to blame for her sickness and that only her mother's healing methods could cure her. Methods passed down for hundreds of years. Methods that treated both body and spirit as one. Methods she and Yesenia had successfully used their entire lives.

Her downward spiral had begun shortly after Maria, a squat, middle-aged *bruja* with a thick accent and penchant for gaudy jewelry, caught Dolores in bed with her husband, Arturo. Maria and Dolores had been friends for more than two decades, sharing clothes and spells, recipes and remedies, everything except men. They'd often traveled to Mexico together to perform rituals for pay, and had spent many Friday and Saturday nights drinking cheap wine and reading tarot cards for strangers. But as Dolores scooped up her clothes and ran out of Maria's house that afternoon, Maria hurled curses at her, vowed to make her life *"un infierno viviente"* for her betrayal. Soon after came the headaches, then the nausea, then the weakness and disorientation, and three weeks ago, the maddening cricket songs. Songs of the *"espiritus venganza."* Music meant to fracture her sanity and cripple her spirit. The final nail in the coffin.

With Yesenia's help, Dolores had cast countless protection spells and counter curses, performed multiple blocking rituals, and drunk numerous healing, strengthening, and cleansing potions. She'd even made a few animal sacrifices. But with the exception of a good day here and there, she continued to decline. Feeling helpless to stop her sister's downward spiral, Yesenia had decided to have the kids hunt the crickets in hopes that limiting their noise would at least provide Dolores a little respite. And it had. Dolores had been less anxious and wild at night since the hunting began, sleeping more, writhing and moaning less. She seemed more lucid, more there. More Dolores.

When the Country Roland album ended, Yesenia turned on the radio and checked on her sister. Dolores was still asleep, balled-up like a caterpillar in a cocoon under a colorful quilt their mother had sewn. Yesenia turned off the bedside lamp, and as she made her way back to the kitchen heard the kids laughing in the backyard, approaching the house. She grabbed the money and *pan de polvo* off the table and headed outside before they stormed in and woke Dolores.

The kids hushed when they saw her and stopped in the farthest reaches of the porch light, where the grass met the raised oak porch. She sat in front of them on the top step and held out the plate. As they eagerly grabbed the sweet pastries, thanked her, and began shoveling them into their mouths, she said, "You kids have done good. I don't hear any crickets nearby."

Parker swallowed the partially-chewed glob of dough in his mouth, then gestured at the woods beyond the backyard with his cricket stick. "The only ones left around here are out in Hunter's Haven."

Yesenia smiled and nodded. She understood why Cel, Abby, Natalie, and, if her instincts were right, Omar, all had crushes on him, whether they admitted it to one another or not. He was handsome and polite and funny, and he possessed a sense of charisma and confidence uncommon in most his age. But she also saw something their young eyes couldn't. Hidden in the depths of his inviting, All-American smile and soft eyes was a streak of selfishness and disregard. A look she'd seen in too many men over the years. Men who thought the world was their oyster. She set the empty plate on her lap and handed each of the kids a ten dollar bill, which they accepted with pleased smiles and nods of gratitude. She waited a moment for the kids to examine and pocket the cash, then said, "I'll give you each five more a week on top of that if you'll go ahead and hunt the edge of the woods from now on, too."

"Sweet." Parker high-fived Omar. "That'll give us more to spend at the fair next weekend." His eyes swept across the girls'. "You guys are game, right?"

They all nodded enthusiastically.

"*Bueno*." Yesenia stood and brushed the crumbs off the plate. "Now, you kids better go home so you don't get in trouble. It's getting late."

Cel stepped onto the porch next to Yesenia, and they watched the other hunters cross the backyard. Parker glanced back at Cel and flashed a trace of a smile before he closed the metal gate, crossed the field, and disappeared in the darkness with the others. A few seconds later, a howl of elation followed by a faint chorus of laughter drifted through the night air.

When Yesenia turned to head inside, Cel continued to stare in the direction her friends had gone. She was biting her bottom lip, fighting back a giddy smile, but her eyes were unable to contain her excitement. Yesenia shook her head, fighting back a smile of her own. She could practically feel the air around Cel tingling with electricity. Young love. Stupid love. She touched Cel's shoulder. "Come on, *mija*. You need to wash up."

Yesenia checked on Dolores, washed the plate, heated another cup of chamomile tea, and was sitting at the kitchen table when Cel walked into the room in her purple fuzzy robe thirty minutes later. She sat across from Yesenia, patting her wet shoulder-length black hair with a towel. The radio played softly in the background to help drown out any crickets that crept up close to the house.

"How's *Tia* Dillo?" Cel asked. "Is she asleep?"

Yesenia nodded, sipping her tea. "She's okay. Been asleep for a while now." She loved that Cel called Dolores *Tia* Dillo just like Rebecca, Cel's mom, had. She also loved how Cel could pass as Rebecca's clone. It was almost as if Rebecca had been resurrected. They had the same fierce cheekbones, the same comely smile, the same piercing eyes, eyes so dark it was hard to locate a pupil. They even shared a bean-shaped skin blemish below their left eye, and both had a slightly twisted right incisor—the same anomaly obvious in Yesenia's and Dolores's smiles, and *their* mom's, as well. Yesenia had never met Cel's father, but she assumed his family's pedigree must've been weak because Cel didn't appear to carry any traits other than her mother's.

Cel set the damp towel on the table. "You think she's getting better?"

Yesenia took a sip. "I think you guys help her feel better." She gazed out the window above the sink for a long moment before looking back at Cel.

"You think she'll die?"

"We'll all die, *mija*."

Cel pushed out an irritated breath. "I know we'll all die *one day*. But…" Her eyes dropped to the towel on the table. She rubbed her hand over it as if it were fragile. "You think she'll die soon?"

Yesenia shrugged. "*No se.*"

Cel looked up. "There's nothing else we can do? No stronger healing spells or potions?"

"We're doing all we can to help her."

"What about doing something to stop Maria then? Can't we curse her back or something? If she gets sick enough, or weak enough, won't she stop hurting *Tia* Dillo?"

Yesenia set down her tea. "It's not that simple." *Or safe*, she thought but kept to herself. When it came to the craft, vengeance could carry harsh consequences.

Cel looked away from Yesenia, her eyes fraught with pained frustration. "It sucks watching her hurt." She shook her head. "I just wish I could do more."

"I know, *mija*." Yesenia reached across the table and touched Cel's hand. She didn't want Cel involved in the feud any more than necessary. "More involved" meant more danger. She had no doubts Maria would attack Cel if needed. "But, by killing those crickets, you are helping her more than you know." She squeezed Cel's hand, and Cel made eye contact with her. "This dark stint will pass, I promise."

Cel nodded.

Yesenia scooped up her tea and held it close to her chest with both hands, allowing the steam to warm the underside of her chin as she thought of a way to steer the conversation away from her sister's troubles and Cel's emotions away from worry. "So, when did you and Parker become more than friends?"

The frustration in Cel's eyes instantly changed to happy shock at hearing the question. A change only possible for the young. She bit at her lip to fight back an explosive grin. "What?"

Yesenia chuckled. "I see the way you've been looking at him this summer when he's not looking at you." She took a slow, calm sip. "I saw the way he looked at you when he was leaving tonight."

"We're just friends."

Yesenia cocked one eyebrow and flapped a hand at Cel. "*Por favor*. Have you kissed him?"

Blushing, Cel buried her face in her hands as though she knew Yesenia could see the answer in her eyes, in her smile, which she did. Any right-minded woman would've.

"Is he a good kisser?"

Cel looked up sheepishly and nodded, biting her lip again. Just like her mother always had.

Yesenia could tell Cel was struggling to keep from gushing about the kiss, or kisses, and part of her would've loved to listen to her granddaughter relive the pleasures of her ignorant, youthful lust, but her motherly instinct overrode that desire. She knew all too well as a woman who'd become a single mom at sixteen that if fostered, the toxic mixture of teenage hormones and infatuation easily led to kisses, and kisses easily led to touching, and touching easily led to babies. Although she felt blessed that she'd had a second chance at parenting with Cel, she had no desire to raise another child ever again, kin or not. Two was enough. "Just make sure that's as far as it goes. *Muchachos* only have one thing on their mind, and you're too young to let him—"

Cel jumped up, her chair screeching across the linoleum as it slid back. Her eyes and smile slathered with embarrassment. "*Buela*! I haven't even thought..." She picked the towel up off the table and headed down the hallway toward her room. "I'm going to bed now."

"Goodnight, *mija*," Yesenia called after her in a singsong voice despite being a little concerned about the squeaky tone of Cel's attempt at a denial. Cel may not have slept with Parker, but the idea wasn't foreign to her.

Chapter 9 - Cel

Cel rode her bike to Abby's house a little after seven in the evening. The Cricket Hunters had separated an hour earlier after hunting the area around the house, each heading home to touch base with their parents, wash up, and eat. Although they'd accepted Yesenia's offer the night before to start clearing the edge of Hunter's Haven, they wanted to wait until Sunday to start. They wanted the last Saturday night of the summer break to be like all the others. Saturday nights were movie nights at the Powell residence. All summer, Abby's mom had worked the closing shift at Brookshire Grocery on Saturdays, and the Cricket Hunters had taken advantage of the empty house.

Cel opened the front door and walked into the living room. The TV was off, the dingy couch unoccupied. The scent of cigarettes and Abby's perfume clung to the air. As Cel made her way through the living room, she heard whispering in the kitchen. She stopped just before the entrance and turned her head sideways, listening, but couldn't make out what was being said or who was talking. She peeked into the kitchen. Parker and Abby were standing in front of the sink, their backs to her, Abby's shoulder touching Parker's chest as she dried a glass. The paperback copy of Ray Bradbury's *The Illustrated Man* Parker had been carrying around all summer was shoved into the back pocket of his cargo shorts. They both looked back at Cel when she stepped into the room.

Parker held eye contact with Cel for a moment before moving away from Abby and greeting her. His hesitation made Cel's heart hitch. He looked nervous, unsure of what to say, uncomfortable. He'd never looked at her that way before. He and Abby must've been gossiping, talking about her, she just knew it.

Abby flashed Cel a quick smile of acknowledgement, then started pulling glasses from the cupboard and lining them on the counter next to a three-liter bottle of Dr. Pepper and the five Coors Light beers Parker had lifted from his dad's garage stash. The speed of her movements along with the way she kept glancing back at Cel spoke to her nervousness—*guilt*—as well.

"Will you grab the popcorn bag and put it in the microwave?" Abby asked Parker in a normal volume. No more whispering.

Parker winked at Cel and mouthed, "I'll tell you later," as he made his way to the pantry.

Cel released a clutched breath, as though a tight corset had been snipped off her chest, freeing her lungs. "How long have you been here?" she asked him.

"I don't know. A couple of minutes."

More relief. With a spring in her step, she headed toward the cupboards. "You want me to get the bowls out?"

"Sure," Abby answered as she filled five glasses with soda.

They carried the glasses and beers and bowls of popcorn into the living room and set them on the coffee table, then Abby suggested they go out onto the back porch while they waited for Omar and Natalie to arrive with the movie. They always alternated who picked the movie, and this Saturday was Omar's day. He and Natalie lived next door to one another on Malibu Way, the farthest street on the northern edge of the Gateway neighborhood, and knowing his tendency for indecisiveness, Natalie had offered to ride her bike along with him to Hastings to help him choose a movie.

On the porch, they lined up three lawn chairs and sat down. Parker pulled out his Bradbury book and began flipping through pages as Abby dug a pink lighter out of her pocket, retrieved one of her mom's partially-smoked menthols from an ashtray under her chair, and lit up. She took a couple of small puffs, offered the cigarette to Cel who shook her head, then offered it to Parker who took a long puff and handed it back. After she finished the cigarette with a series of delicate puffs and dropped the butt in the ashtray, Parker closed his book and turned his head sideways, aiming his left ear—the ear he claimed was his better cricket ear—at the backyard fence. "Man," he said. "We should've brought our sticks. Sounds like there is a good twenty or thirty horny crickets out in your alley."

"Right." Abby agreed, giggling. "I never noticed them before we started hunting, but now that's all I can hear when I'm trying to go to sleep at night." She shot Cel a wry grin and flipped her off. "Thanks a lot."

Cel reciprocated the expression, rose, and gave a sarcastic curtsy. "My pleasure."

They were both chuckling when the sliding glass door opened and Natalie and Omar walked outside. "We're here," Natalie announced, a broad smile decorating her plump face. Abby and Cel had been helping her brainstorm new hair styles for school all week, spending hours in front of a mirror with roll-brushes and cans of hairspray, and although she'd already decided on a slightly parted, unkempt hair-do, she still wore her dad's Astros cap every time she left the house.

Parker nudged Omar's arm. "What movie did you get? Nothing cheesy, I hope."

Omar held up a DVD and smiled as though he were holding up a well-deserved award. "*Real Genius.*"

Parker took the DVD, read the blurbs, and examined Val Kilmer in his I Love Toxic Waste T-shirt on the cover. "Looks old."

"It's hilarious," Natalie said, snatching it out of his hand. "You'll like it. Let's go."

Cel led the way inside and saw Jeff's head poking around the hallway corner. She waved, and when he immediately jerked his head back, she called out, "Hi, Jeff."

He poked his head back out, his dark eyes full of glee. "Hi."

Abby skirted Cel, marching at Jeff with one hand on her hip and her other arm pumping like a piston. He walked backwards, retreating into his room. "I thought I told you not to spy on us anymore!"

"It's my house, too," Jeff yelled. "I can do whatever I want!" Then he slammed his bedroom door in her face.

She pressed her hands against the door and kicked the bottom so hard the wood gave a little. "You better not come back out!"

As she marched back toward the living room, the door creaked open, and she spun around. Jeff's small hand poked out, his middle finger shot up, then the door slammed shut again.

Abby plopped down in her usual spot on the end of the couch and crossed her arms over her chest. "I swear. He's such a fucking pest." She glanced at Cel who was sitting on the opposite end of the couch— her usual spot. "You're so lucky to be an only child."

Cel ignored the remark, slipped off her *chanclas*, and pulled her legs up onto the couch into what her kindergarten teacher had called crisscross applesauce position. If engaged, Abby had the tendency to rail for hours about her brother.

Parker put in the DVD, found the remote, and sat between Cel and Abby on the couch. Omar grabbed the two beanbags from the corner of the room and tossed one to Natalie. They sat on either side of the coffee table like always, beanbags snug against the couch armrests. Abby flicked off the lamp on the end table, and for the next hour and a half, sharing beer and popcorn and soda, they laughed and chatted and watched science geniuses exact comical revenge on a selfish professor.

When the movie ended, Abby turned the lamp back on, and Natalie noted the time. It was almost ten o'clock. Her parents, Omar's, and Parker's, expected them home by ten-thirty on Saturdays. Cel's *abuela*, the same. After helping Abby wash the dishes and hide the beer cans in the bottom of the kitchen trash, they all gathered on the driveway. A gentle breeze tickled the night air.

Abby stood next to Parker while the others mounted their bikes. She glanced up at the diamond-studded sky and then at him. "So, we'll meet tomorrow at Cel's after dinner to hunt, right?"

"Yep," Parker confirmed. "The last hunt of summer."

Natalie moaned. "Don't say that. I don't want school to start."

"With a haircut like that, I wouldn't either," Omar said.

Everyone but Natalie laughed. Her mouth fell open in a huge, *I-can't-believe-you-just-said-that* smile, though. "You're going to get it, little man." She outweighed Omar, and every other hunter, by at least thirty pounds.

Omar pedaled out of the driveway, the electric assist motor he'd attached to the pedals humming to life, and veered left. He was laughing so hard he nearly toppled over when he lost his balance at the end of the driveway. Natalie furiously pedaled after him, yelling for him to stop and take his punishment like a man. When they were about half a block away, Natalie yelled back over her shoulder, "See you guys tomorrow."

Cel hollered back, "Goodnight," and turned to Parker. "You want a ride?"

"Sure."

Jill, the younger of his two older sisters, had accidentally run over his bike and bent the frame in June. He'd been bumming rides with Cel ever since. Although her bike was the only one with wheel pegs, and they lived only one street apart, she liked to believe he rode with her because it gave him an excuse to be alone with her, to touch her. He hopped on her bike's back wheel pegs and placed his hands on her shoulders. As she steered out of the driveway and onto Chaparral Street, Abby hollered, "Bye," and they both waved back at her.

Cel zigzagged through the Gateway neighborhood, coasting from street to street, cutting across vacant lots and weaving down dark alleys when needed, eliciting dog barks and triggering automatic security lights on houses. Parker kept a firm grip on her shoulders and leaned into her, keeping his head just to the right of hers. She could feel the warmth of his breath on her neck, the heat from his hands on her shoulders through her blue flannel and T-shirt.

He whispered into her ear as they turned onto his street, "Let's walk the rest of the way." The words raised gooseflesh on her neck that quickly spread down her back and across her upper arms. He'd whispered stupid jokes and funny remarks into her ear countless times over the years with no such effect, but ever since their first kiss on Table Rock last May that had changed. Now, every time he whispered directly into her ear, her entire body responded with joy.

Cel slowed to a stop, Parker jumped off, and she started walking her bike toward his house. She'd only taken two steps when he put his hands on top of hers and their eyes met. "Let me do it," he said. "It's the least I can do since you did all the work to get us here."

She held eye contact with him for a couple of steps before slowly sliding her hands out from under his. "What were you and Abby whispering about in the kitchen earlier?"

"Oh yeah. That." Parker shook his head. "You have to promise not to say anything. I swore to her I wouldn't tell anyone."

"You know I won't say anything."

"I know. It's just one of those things you have to say." He smiled at her. "She was telling about how her dad just got out of jail and has been calling and harassing her mom again."

Everyone in Oak Mott knew that Abby's and Jeff's dad, Tom Powell, had gone to jail for armed robbery a couple of years earlier. He and a buddy had held up a convenience store in Caprock, Texas, a small town about sixty miles northwest of Oak Mott, and were caught two blocks away with a measly seventy-six bucks between them. His mugshot was on the local news and in the Oak Mott Daily. He and Abby's mom, Sheila, had been separated for years at the time, supposedly because he was an abusive crack addict who, according to the town rumor mill, had been caught "touching Abby in the bad way," but they'd never legally divorced.

"He keeps demanding to see Abby and Jeff." Parker glanced at Cel. "Abby's afraid he might show up and try to hurt her mom, or take her and Jeff or something. I don't know. She said she's been having nightmares about it and wanted to know if she could call me in the middle of the night if she got scared."

Cel fidgeted with her flannel shirt sleeves. Abby had never talked to any of them about her dad. The one time Omar had asked her about him right after the arrest, she started crying and said she didn't want to talk about it and ran off. Since then, they only talked about him when she wasn't around. "I wonder why she doesn't want you to tell the rest of us about it."

Parker shrugged. "I don't know."

They passed the house next to Parker's in silence, walked up his driveway, and stopped behind his dad's truck. He leaned the bike against the tailgate and looked at Cel. "Based on what my parents say about her dad, he'll probably be back in jail soon, so it won't matter anyway. My dad says he's been a no-good shithead who comes from a no-good family."

Cel nodded, but before she had the opportunity to respond, to ask Parker if he thought Abby could be lying, if Abby just wanted sympathy and attention, *his* sympathy and attention, he grabbed her hand, pulled her toward him, and kissed her. When he slipped his tongue in her mouth, she threw her arms around his neck, and pushed her chest and pelvis into him. He tasted of salt and sugar, popcorn, and beer. When he started sliding his hand toward her breast, she stopped him. "No." Their faces were two inches apart, sharing air. "We can't. Not tonight. Someone might see us out here."

"I'm sorry. I just can't—" he broke off when the porch light popped on and the front door swung open.

"Parker?" Lionel Lundy, Parker's dad, a self-proclaimed plumber extraordinaire with a gut like a beach ball and long spindly chicken legs, stepped onto the porch. "What are you doing?"

"Nothing, Dad. Just talking to Cel. She gave me a lift home."

"Well, you need to come inside. And don't lean that bike on my tailgate like that. It'll scratch up the paint."

Parker looked at Cel, crossed his eyes, jiggled his head, and mockingly worked his mouth silently open and closed as his dad headed back inside. Fighting back laughter, she pulled her bike away from the truck and mounted it. "I better go." As she turned and pedaled away, Parker ran up and smacked her butt, and she let out surprised squeal.

"Bye, bye, little piggy," he said, and broke into laughter.

Smiling so true the joy reached her eyes, Cel looked back over her shoulder and flipped off Parker. "You're the only pig around here."

He laughed again, shoved his hands in his pockets, and sauntered to the edge of the driveway as she sped down the center of the road, in and out of the glow of the streetlights, constantly glancing back at him.

Cel felt as though she were ten feet off the ground, gliding on a cloud. What a night. What a summer. What a kiss. She sailed through the alley at the end of the road, but when she turned onto Cobalt Street and her house came into view, the cloud whisking her home suddenly vanished. Her grip on the handle bars tightened, and she found it almost impossible to pedal, to breathe, as though her round wheels had turned square, the air to thick sludge. An ambulance with its lights on was parked in front of her house, strobing red across her house. Two paramedics in blue uniforms were loading a gurney into the back. The person on the gurney was covered up to their chin with a white sheet.

Cel recited a calming spell, the same spell her *abuela* had whispered over her when she was scared or angry or panicked for as long as she could remember, as she jumped the curb into her front yard. She hopped off her bike and dropped it on the ground. The back wheel was still spinning as she sprinted inside.

"*Buela?*"

"*Buela?*"

When Yesenia emerged from the kitchen and walked into the living room, Cel ran over to her and hugged her. "What's going on? Is it *Tia* Dillo?"

Yesenia nodded. She had tears in her eyes, which caused Cel's eyes to well up. Cel had never seen her *abuela* cry. "Is she going to be all right?"

"*No se,*" Yesenia said. "I came back from the store and found her lying on the bathroom floor and her head was bleeding and I couldn't wake her up and the spells wouldn't work and I didn't think she was breathing, so I called 911. I know she didn't want to go to a doctor and I don't like them much either but..."

Yesenia spoke so fast and with such a thick Spanish accent that her words ran together into one long continuous ebb and flow of sound. Cel didn't understand everything she said, but she understood enough. She hugged Yesenia again, longer and harder this time.

Chapter 10 - Cel

Three days after Dolores was admitted to Oak Mott Memorial Hospital, Cel decided to take action. She'd spent all day Sunday at the hospital with Yesenia, helping perform healing rituals over Dolores, and had ridden her bike to the hospital after school on Monday and Tuesday and sat with Yesenia for an hour or so before heading home to eat and cricket hunt with the others. Dolores was unconscious but stable, weak but alive. An MRI had found a golf ball-sized tumor in her frontal lobe. More tests were scheduled for later in the week.

Cel hated seeing *Tia* Dillo, a woman whose signature color palette knew no bounds, lying like a corpse in a white gown, under a white blanket, on a white bed, surrounded by white machines, in a white room. She hated the beeps from the machines and the invasive antiseptic smell. She hated how hollow and pale Dolores looked. How frail. How dead. She also hated seeing the desperate, lost look in her *abuela's* eyes as she sat guard over her sister. The look assured Cel that if Dolores died, a part of Yesenia would die, too.

Cel didn't doubt the doctors about the tumor, she doubted the cause. Like her *abuela*, she didn't blame chance or genetics, she blamed Maria Lopez. Maria had cursed Dolores, plain and simple. She had planted an evil energy, a devouring growth fueled by cursed crickets, inside of Dolores's head for revenge, for retribution, and despite her *abuela's* refusal to discuss the subject, Cel firmly believed that if she weakened Maria, the evil would lose its hold over Dolores. She also knew that if Dolores's and Yesenia's magic hadn't been able to remove the curse, hers alone stood no chance. She had to try something different. Something other than magic. She needed to cut off Maria's strongest power source.

Yesenia had asked them to please continue hunting even though Dolores was in the hospital, so after leaving the hospital Tuesday night, Cel, Parker, and Abby cleared the crickets from around the house and the edge of Hunter's Haven. They returned to Cel's back porch around nine, propped their sticks against the railing, and sat on the steps. Omar and Natalie had hunted with them the two previous nights but were absent because they had to attend a band fundraiser at school.

The three sat in silence for a while before Parker said, "Not too many out tonight."

"Nope," Abby agreed.

Cel didn't chime in. She was leaning forward with her elbows on her thighs, chin propped on her fists. Her eyes were aimed at the ground, lips pinched. Parker touched her arm. "You okay?"

Cel looked in his direction and slowly nodded. When he looked as though he were about to say something else, she blurted out, "I need your help tonight." She would've preferred to wait until she and Parker were alone to tell him her plan, to only work with him, that's how she'd envisioned it, anyway, but she hadn't had any alone time with him in the past few days, and she knew Abby wouldn't head home without his escort.

"Sure," he said. "With what?"

Cel sat up straight. "I think I know how to help *Tia* Dillo."

"How?" Parker's tone conveyed his confusion.

Cel's eyes slid back and forth from Parker to Abby. "I have to take Maria's familiar away from her."

"Her what?" Abby asked, befuddled.

"Familiar," Parker answered. "It's a magical pet, right?"

Cel simpered and nodded. He remembered. Years back, Cel couldn't remember exactly when, Yesenia had told him and the others about familiars while they nibbled on fresh tortillas during one of her magical back porch story sessions. "Hers is a cat named Frito."

"*Seriously?*" Abby shook her head. "You really think stealing a stupid cat will help your aunt's brain tumor?"

"Frito works hand-in-hand with Maria," Cel snapped back. "Their bond is so strong, she says he doubles the power of her spells. If she doesn't have him, her pull on *Tia* Dillo won't be as strong, and then my *abuela's* healing spells might work better."

Abby sighed and addressed Cel as if she were five years old. "Listen, I feel horrible about your aunt, I do, and I know you might believe that taking that cat will help, but—"

"It will." Cel cut in. "And I'm doing it." She looked to Parker, hoping her determination was evident in her eyes. "I have to. It's the only chance she's got."

Parker searched her face. "Where does Maria live?"

Cel smiled. She knew she could count on Parker. He *got* her. "On Clover Lane. I've gone over there with my *abuela* and *Tia* Dillo a bunch of times. We can get there in about ten minutes."

Abby shot Parker a look of disbelief. "Are you really going to do this? If you get caught, you could get arrested." She stood up, cocked her hip to the right, crossed her arms over her chest. "I'm not going to break into anybody's house."

"You don't have to," Cel said, keeping her eyes on Parker. "No one should be there. All I need is someone to be lookout."

"How do you know no one will be there?" Parker asked.

Cel glanced down at her feet and bit her lip, treading the fine line between nervousness and shame. "I've been spying on the house the past few nights, riding over there after you guys leave." She met eyes with Parker, and he smiled as though pleasantly surprised by her antics, which made her smile, too. "She kicked her husband out after she caught him cheating with Dolores, and she works until ten every weeknight at M and R Liquor."

"What about Jose? Doesn't he still live at home?" Abby asked. Maria's only child, her nineteen-year-old son Jose, was short and stocky and had a penchant for gaudy jewelry like his mom. Cel couldn't stand him. He constantly stroked his lucky stache and seemed to not own a single shirt. Every time she'd been at the Lopez house when he was home, he'd teased her about her flat chest and boy clothes, about how he knew she was a dyke, but he could change that if she'd let him.

"His car hasn't been there any night I've gone," Cel said. "I think he spends most nights lifting weights and smoking pot at his friend Felix's apartment. If he is home, though, I won't go in."

"How do you plan on getting in?" Parker asked.

"She leaves her bedroom window cracked open so Frito can come and go as he pleases while she's at work."

Parker stood and excitedly rubbed his hands together. "All right. I'm in." He looked at Abby. "Come on. You have to come."

Shaking her head, she twirled her hair with her finger. Cel could tell by the look in her eyes that she didn't want to go, but she also didn't want to reject Parker. They shared a secret now. A bond. She trusted him. He was her *special* friend. If he asked her to jump off the Empire State Building, she would contemplate it. But if Cel asked her the same question...

"We won't get in trouble," Parker assured. "If someone is there we'll just come back. Right, Cel?"

Cel nodded.

"The more people we have as lookouts, the safer it'll be." Parker nudged Abby's shoulder with his, then he put his hands on his hips and artificially thrust out his chest like he had the first night of cricket hunting. "Come on. We're the Cricket Hunters. One for all and all for one..." He shrugged and smiled. "Or some shit like that, right?"

Abby smiled back. "Okay." She held up a defiant finger. "But I'm not going in the house."

Cel led the way on her bike with Parker perched on the back wheel pegs, his hands on her shoulders. Abby followed on her silver, banana seat Schwinn. When they reached Clover Lane, Cel slowed to a stop in the shadow of the same rusty camper half a block from Maria's house that she'd hid her bike behind the past few nights. Parker hopped off, and she propped the bike against the camper. Abby pulled up next to them and rested her bike next to Cel's.

Cel walked to the front of the camper. "It's up there on the left." She pointed. "The white one with the blue trim."

"The one with the porch light on?" Abby asked. "Don't you think that means someone's home?"

"No," Cel answered. "That light stays on all day. Besides, look. Neither one of their cars are there."

"So how do you want to do this?" Parker asked. "We need to hurry."

Cel scanned the street for a moment, chewing on her bottom lip. She pointed at a tall cottonwood across the street from Maria's house, the same tree she'd hid behind when she'd watched the house the past few days. It stood on the corner of a large sloping front yard, the small house behind it dark and quiet. She'd busted out the streetlight that lit that yard and Maria's yard and the street between the two houses, with a rock days earlier. "Abby, you hide behind that tree over there and watch for cars." She met eyes with Parker. "While I go around back to the window, you wait on the side of the house where you can see her." She looked at Abby. "You have your lighter?" Abby nodded. "Good. If you see Maria's green Explorer or Jose's Mustang coming just hold it up and flick it so Parker will see and he can warn me."

Abby pulled out her pink lighter. Her hand was slightly trembling. Her eyes bounced from house to house, driveway to driveway, car to car, Cel to Parker. "How long is this going to take?"

"It should only take a couple of minutes," Cel answered.

As Abby scuttled across the road and positioned herself behind the tree, Cel and Parker quick-walked to Maria's house. They cut across the driveway and crouched under the eave between the A/C unit and a length of hurricane fence that separated the back corner of the house from a detached garage. Cel looked at the cottonwood across the street and could see a vague oval shape extending out from the side of the trunk like a tumor. Abby's head. "You see her?" she whispered.

Parker nodded and waved at Abby who waved back.

"All right. Wait here."

Cel hopped the fence, and as she crept along the back side of house, she quietly recited two spells. The first was the same protection spell Yesenia had cast over her every time she left for school since the age of five. The second, a disarming spell she'd memorized from one of her *abuela's* grimoires while Yesenia was at the hospital watching over *Tia* Dillo. She recited the protection spell more out of habit than necessity, as quick and thoughtless as a Catholic girl would a nighttime prayer, but she whispered the disarming spell slow and mindful. Yesenia had taught her that seasoned *brujas* trained their familiars to stay alert for malicious spirits and humans, and that familiars could telepathically communicate dangers to their masters if the bond between them was strong enough. Cel knew her casting ability was weak compared to the connection between Maria and Frito, but she hoped the disarming spell, if cast with enough conviction, would make Frito view her as a nonthreat long enough for her to catch him.

Cel passed under the kitchen window, a tiny bathroom one, then stopped under Maria's, which was open about ten inches as expected. She placed her back against the house and listened. She heard the steady whirring of the ceiling fan above Maria's bed but nothing else. No voices, no TV, no signs of life.

She held her breath as she rose and peeked into the bedroom through the parted curtains. She knew it was possible that Frito had left the house and was scouring the neighborhood for rats or mice. But she also knew that Frito was old, fifteen or so, fat and spoiled. Both times she'd looked in the window earlier this week, he'd been sleeping on Maria's bed. Tonight proved the same. A pulsing swirl of orange fluff dotted the center of her pillow, the head aimed at the headboard.

Cel released the air trapped in her lungs and examined the rest of the room. The queen-sized bed sat against the wall to her left. A talisman with an azabache pebble in the center like the one in her own room hung above the headboard. On one side of the bed, a humidifier sat on a small rocking chair that had sweaters draped over the back. On the other was a nightstand with a lamp. A purplish blue, silk scarf covered the lamp shade, dimming and tainting the faint glow. The wall opposite Cel had a closed closet door and an open doorway leading out into a dark hall.

Her eyes stayed trained on Frito as she eased the window open as far as her arms allowed. She placed her hands on the window sill, and with the help of her tennis shoes gripping the wood siding, hoisted herself up into the opening. Without taking her eyes off Frito, she lowered her right foot down onto the carpet as gently as possible, twisted, and did the same with her left. She stood there for a moment waiting to see if the cat would sense her. It didn't. Perhaps the disarming spell *was* helping. She tiptoed over to the doorway leading into the hallway and started slowly closing the door to prevent Frito from bolting out of the room. When the door was about a foot from shut, the hinges squeaked, and Frito's head snapped her way, his pupils dilated with intense focus, ears perked and rigid.

"It's okay," she whispered as much to calm herself as Frito. Her insides felt as though they had been tossed into a blender. Her breathing and heart rate escalated. Familiars were smart, fierce. She needed to hurry. She extended her hand as an olive branch, palm up, and took a couple of steps toward the bed.

Frito stood and turned her way.

She continued along the side of the bed, whispering soft assurances as she moved, and stopped in front of the rocking chair.

Frito's nostril's flared, sniffing at the air as though he'd been trained to recognize the enemy's scent. Her scent. He stared at her for a moment longer, then his back arched, his teeth bared, and he hissed.

Cel lunged at him and grabbed the back of his neck. He yowled as if his warm insides were being torn out, and he slashed at her forearm with his front claws. She reached across the bed with her other hand and pulled him to her chest. He dug harder into her arm, biting down with his needle teeth for added effect. His hind paws pushed against her torso, the sharp claws ripping through her shirt and fileting the top layer of her flesh with the ease of a razor. She gritted her teeth against the sharp stings and squeezed him tighter. So tight his ribcage crackled, and the air rushed out of his lungs.

When she turned to make her way back to the window, her foot knocked the foot of the rocking chair. The humidifier crashed to the floor with a plastic clatter, and seconds later, a voice called out, "What the fuck, Frito?"

Jose. It had to be Jose. When did he get home?

Keeping Frito pinned against her chest with one arm, she rushed to the window. He was still struggling but with less vigor. She threw one leg through the hole, ducked her head just low enough, and toppled out of the window onto the ground. She landed on her right shoulder and hip, sending a current of thick, painful vibration through her body, rattling her to the bone. But she didn't release Frito.

As the sensation faded, she opened her eyes and saw Parker running toward her. He dropped to a knee and placed his hand on her hip. "Are you okay?"

"We have to go," she said weakly, as though it hurt to talk. "Jose. Coming."

"What? But nobody's gotten home." He grabbed her arm and helped her stand.

"He's—"

The light in Maria's room flicked on.

"Shit," Parker said. "Come on."

They ran, a deep pain piercing Cel's hip each time her foot slapped the ground. Parker hopped the fence first and reached for Frito. "Give me the cat."

Cel obeyed, and, as she hopped the fence and landed on the other side, Jose yelled, "Hey! What the fuck are you doing?" It sounded as if he were close, outside, probably hanging out the window.

Parker called out to warn Abby as they sprinted across the driveway and down the sidewalk. "Run! Run! Run!"

When they reached the bikes, Parker shoved Frito at Cel and mounted her bike. "I'm driving."

Cel stood on the back wheel pegs. She pressed Frito to her chest with one arm, cinching her hand around his neck tight enough to feel bone, and wrapped the other arm around Parker's waist. She leaned on Parker, hard, mashing the cat against his back with all her weight. Frito weakly struggled but soon stopped fighting. Parker rolled the bike out from behind the camper and glanced up the street. Abby was running toward them, about fifteen yards away, pressing one arm across her chest to keep her breasts from bouncing. The few seconds it took her to reach them felt like an eternity. She jerked her bike away from the camper and hopped on. "What happened in there?"

Neither Parker nor Cel answered. Parker took off, and Cel craned her neck to watch behind them. Jose was standing in his front yard, shirtless and shoeless, with a baseball bat in his hand. The porchlight highlighted the anger etched on his pinched face.

"Go, go," Cel urged.

Parker pedaled across the road, cut through a yard, and was turning onto an adjacent street when Abby squealed just before the hiss of metal scraped loose gravel. Cel looked back and saw Abby scrambling to stand, her bike sideways, the handlebars and front wheel twisted at an odd angle. Jose stepped off the porch and started marching her direction.

"Abby's in trouble," Cel said into Parker's ear. He slowed to a quick stop and looked toward the house. Abby already had her bike upright and one leg over the frame. He watched until she'd pedaled a good ten yards, far enough to escape if Jose ran after her, and then took off.

"I *will* find out who you and your friends are, Tits!" Jose yelled, his deep voice rattling the still night air, chasing Abby as she turned off of Clover Lane and closed the gap between her and Parker. "Pussy motherfuckers!"

They made the return trip to Abby's house in half the time it had taken to get to Maria's. Parker pedaled furiously, occasionally glancing back to make sure Abby was nearby. Cel closed her eyes and laid her head on the back of Parker's neck. Despite the growing sting from the tiny slashes on her arms and abdomen, and the dull ache dominating her hip and shoulder, she felt mentally elated. She'd successfully broken into Maria's house and stolen Frito. She'd separated Maria from her strongest ally and power source. She'd done everything she could to help *Tia* Dillo. And now she was pressed up against Parker, allowing the sweat from his neck to wet her cheek, fleeing a crime scene like Bonnie and Clyde. Two rebel lovers riding the thrill of taking a stand. She wished the ride home could've lasted forever. She opened her eyes and raised her head when Parker slowed to a stop in Abby's driveway.

Abby ditched her bike in the grass on the side of the house and walked over to them. A sheen of sweat covered her face. Strands of her hair clung to her cheeks and forehead. Blood trickled from a scrape on her knee. She put her hand on her hip, shot daggers at Cel with her eyes. "I told you it was a stupid idea. Now what are we going to do? What if Jose calls the cops?"

"I told *you* that you didn't have to come," Cel snapped back.

"Hey," Parker interjected, carrying out the *eeyyy* like a mom trying to shush feuding toddlers. "Everything's going to be fine." Abby's eyes met his and softened a bit. "Jose didn't get a good look at us. Even if he does call the cops, he doesn't know who we are."

"He may not have seen you guys, but he saw me good enough to call me Tits." Abby's eyes filled with tears, and she looked up at the sky for a moment, pinching her lips together. "He'll figure it out. And when he does..." She trailed off and shook her head.

Parker touched Abby's arm. "Listen, I promise everything will be okay. If by some chance he figures it out and calls the cops and they come to us, we deny everything. We were at your house watching *The Goonies* with your little brother tonight. Jeff will vouch for us as long as we promise to hang out with him for a while this weekend or something, right?"

Abby took in a ragged breath and nodded.

Cel wanted to tell Abby she shouldn't worry about the cops, that Jose would never call the cops. That's not how the Lopez family worked. Not with something like this, anyway. When Maria found out her sidekick, her best friend, her confidant, Frito, was missing and had probably been stolen, she would want revenge, not justice. But Cel didn't say anything. Abby had made it very clear more than once that she didn't believe in the curses, anyway.

Abby glanced at the tufts of orange fur poking out from between Cel's chest and Parker's back. "What are you going to do with it?"

Again, Cel withheld the truth. She knew what she had to do with Frito. But the less Abby knew, the better. "I'll probably take him deep into Hunter's Haven and let him go."

"You better do it tonight. If anyone catches you with him, we're all screwed."

Cel nodded. "I will. I don't want to get caught any more than you do."

Following a short silence, Abby glanced at Parker, and he gave her a caring smile. "Is your leg okay?" he asked.

Abby looked at her leg as though she hadn't realized she'd been injured. She looked back up, her pleasure with Parker's concern evident in the expression on her face. "It's just a scrape. I'll be fine." She glanced at her house. Jeff was peeking out of the blinds in the living room. "I better go talk to him. I want to tell him what to say before my mom gets home."

"Don't tell him about the cat, though," Parker said. "The less he knows the better."

Cel smiled to herself. She'd thought the same thought, was going to give the same advice. They were on a wave.

After watching Abby enter the house, Parker told Cel to hold on and then pedaled away. He cruised at a slow pace as they navigated the alleys and short cuts through Gateway. Cel kept her eyes open this time and didn't ask him why he didn't stop when he pedaled passed his own house. A couple of times he turned his head sideways, cut his eyes at her and smiled, his mouth inches from hers. When they reached Cel's house, Yesenia's car, a beat-to-hell '82 Starlet, wasn't in the driveway, meaning, like Cel had hoped, she was still at the hospital.

Cel eased off the bike pegs and followed Parker around the side of the house into the backyard where he leaned the bike against the house next to the mess of cricket sticks. She still had a firm grip on Frito's neck and was pressing him against her chest. The cat's eyes were closed, legs and tail limp as noodles.

Parker eyed the cat. "Is he dead?"

"It doesn't feel like he's breathing."

Parker placed his hand on Frito's chest. "I don't feel a heartbeat." He took Cel's hand, gently pulled it away from Frito's throat, and twisted it back and forth, examining her wounds. Some of the scratches had bled enough to color her fingers and palm crimson. The skin around each cut was red and raised, irritated by dirty cat claws. Streaks of blood also colored the chest of the white Nirvana T-shirt she wore under her unbuttoned blue flannel. Frito's talons had ripped through the fabric and flesh. "You better clean these off good when you go in so they don't get infected."

"I will."

They held eye contact for a moment before she leaned in and kissed him, the cat once again separating their torsos. When their lips parted, she thanked him for helping her and bringing her home, and he replied by kissing her again. She moaned into his mouth when his hand slid down and gripped her hurt hip.

"Sorry," he said. "Sorry."

She smiled and looked down at Frito.

Parker followed her gaze. "You think it's going to work?"

"I hope so."

"You want me to go toss him into woods?"

Cel looked at the cricket sticks leaning against the house. She knew Frito was technically dead, but she feared that Maria might know some dark way to bring him back, to resurrect him with some mystical ritual if he hadn't been destroyed properly. The sticks were on the same plane with familiars, the plane of the *brujas* and *curanderas* and *videntes*. Yesenia always said to inflict damage on that plane, you had to use a weapon designed for it, an enchanted weapon. Hence the cricket sticks. Cel didn't want to take any chances. "I need to..." She met eyes with Parker, hoping to convey her intentions, hoping he could read her mind.

"You need to make sure he's dead?" Parker gestured at the sticks. "And you need to use the cricket stick to make sure, right?"

Chewing on her bottom lip, Cel nodded. "Just in case...you know...for *Tia* Dillo."

Parker grabbed the stick with the infinity symbol carved on it, and the one with the crosshairs. He handed Cel hers, took Frito out of her hands, dropped him on the ground, and rolled him onto his back using his foot. "Let's do it together. On three."

Cel clenched her jaw to fight back the happiness trying to coerce her lips into a smile. Together, she liked that word. When she'd imagined doing this the past few nights while lying in bed staring up at the water stain on her ceiling, she'd always imagined Parker there with her. They aimed the pointed ends of their sticks at Frito, Cel's a few inches above where she assumed, hoped, the heart lied, and Parker's, the center of the gut.

"Ready," Parker said.

Cel nodded.

"One...two...three."

Blood and a pasty, greenish yellow liquid gushed out of the gut as Parker drove his stick all the way through Frito and inches into the soil. Cel met resistance but pushed and twisted until her stick pierced the skin between ribs and punctured soft tissue. Frito responded to the stabs with the indifference of a ragdoll.

They carried Frito out to Hunter's Haven and buried him in a shallow grave that Parker dug with Yesenia's garden shovel. They covered the site with leaves and twigs and placed a giant stone on top for good measure.

SEPTEMBER 2013

Chapter 11 - Cel

Cel inspected each room in the house a second time with the knife still clutched in her hand, double checking all the windows and doors before brewing a cup of tea and heading to her bedroom. She sat at the foot of her bed with the warm mug in her hand, eyes glazed over, muscles tense and rigid, her mind bouncing from question to question, assumption to assumption, present to past.

Where was Parker? Was he pissed enough to sleep at a hotel for the night? Why had she never seen that picture of Abby before? Had he taken it? How had those books fallen? Had he contacted Lauren tonight? His mom or sister? Was he injured? In an accident? Should she call the emergency room? The police? Was he planning on leaving her? Divorcing her?

Her texts and calls to Parker went unanswered as her tea grew cold and the hours crept by. Eventually, the calls went straight to voicemail. Shortly after midnight, she drove by his parents' house again, then Lauren's apartment, and then the bars he occasionally frequented, but she didn't see his Camry at any of them. Her head felt like it was going to explode by the time she returned home. She needed to talk to someone. She needed to hear someone else's voice besides her own to help slow the avalanche of possibilities barreling through her head. She sat down at the kitchen table and texted Natalie.

I KNOW IT'S LATE. ARE YOU AWAKE?

She waited five minutes, reheated her tea in the microwave, and was typing a second text when Natalie responded.

SORRY I DIDN'T CALL. CRAIG HAD MADE DINNER WHEN I GOT HOME. AND AFTER THAT, WELL...☺

Natalie's boyfriend of ten months, Craig Jenkins, had moved in with her two weeks earlier. They both worked as realtors in Oak Mott, Natalie at Balke Realty, Craig at Triangle Realty.

NO PROBLEM.

SO WHAT'S UP? CAN'T SLEEP?

Mila sauntered into the kitchen and hopped into Cel's lap. The previous weekend Cel had told Natalie her suspicions about Lauren and Parker's relationship, about the abundant texts and calls, late work days and buddy-buddy lunches, the dreaded tell-tale apartment key.

I ASKED PARKER ABOUT LAUREN THIS MORNING. HE DIDN'T COME HOME TONIGHT.

OH NO. CALLING.

Cel started stroking Mila's back, took a sip of tea, and answered on the first ring.

"You want me to come over?" Natalie posed as a greeting. "I can be there in ten minutes."

"You don't have to. It's late. I know you have to work tomorrow."

"I actually don't have anything scheduled, and if anyone needs me, they'll just call my cell."

"What about Craig?"

"Are you kidding? He's been snoring like a pig for the last hour. I probably won't be able to get any good sleep anyway. I'll just leave him a note."

Cel nudged Mila off her lap and stood. "Thank you, Nat. I'll have tea ready when you get here." She retrieved another mug and two bags of chamomile tea, Natalie's favorite, from the cupboard, filled the kettle with water, and turned up the heat.

Not long after the kettle whistled and Cel had filled the mugs and covered them to steep, Natalie knocked on the door. Cel greeted her with a hug and led her to the kitchen where they sat at the table next to one another.

Natalie wore white pajama bottoms decorated in red lips that clung to her thin legs, a pink tank top that revealed her toned arms. She looked pale but healthy. Shortly after graduating from McLennan County Junior College with an associate's degree and earning her realtor license, she'd decided she was tired of being known as the pudgy girl with pretty eyes, the woman always in the friend zone, so she'd joined Weight Watchers and a gym, dropped forty pounds, and never looked back. She'd also recently chopped her hair down to a length reminiscent of the haircut her mom had given her fifteen years earlier after the gum incident with her brother, the one she'd despised and hidden under an Astros cap for the entire summer.

"Your hair looks great," Cel said. "Very professional and business-chic."

Natalie flashed a grateful smile, but her eyes conveyed her desire to skip the small talk. She placed her hand on Cel's knee. "Are you okay?"

Cel nodded though her eyes welled up. She took the cover off her mug and gently blew at the escaping steam for a moment before revealing the details of her day. For the next half hour, as Cel vocalized the fears and assumptions about Parker and Lauren that had been circling her head like a mad carousel all evening, Natalie sipped tea and listened, giving supportive nods and throwing out words like "bitch" and "asshole" when warranted. The only detail Cel withheld was finding the picture of Abby in Parker's book. She knew bringing up Abby would steer the conversation down a dark path she and Natalie rarely ventured down—that she didn't want to venture down. When she finished her verbal vomit, she felt a sense of relief, and fatigue. She inhaled deeply through her mouth and let it fall out her nose.

"Are you going to call the cops?" Natalie asked.

"I'm going to wait and see if he shows up for work in the morning. I don't think the cops will do anything about a missing adult until he's been gone for at least twenty-four hours, anyway."

As Cel carried the two empty mugs to the sink, Natalie said, "I need to go pee."

Cel washed and dried the mugs, and when Natalie hadn't returned to the kitchen a few minutes later, she made her way to her bedroom. The lamp on Parker's side of the bed was on, the bathroom door closed, a dim light knifing out from underneath. Cel turned her ear to the door and heard retching followed by a toilet flush. She lightly knocked before opening the door. "Nat?"

Natalie was kneeling over the toilet, a line of drool dangling from her bottom lip. Sweat slicked her face. The stench of bile encased her.

Cel squatted and caressed Natalie's back. "You okay?"

Natalie nodded. "Just feeling a little nauseated."

Cel jerked the hand towel off the rack beside the toilet and passed it to Natalie. "I thought you looked a little pale. Parker said there's a stomach bug going around the schools. I wonder if you caught it somehow."

Natalie blotted her face with the towel and then made her way to the sink. While she rinsed out her mouth and splashed cold water on her face, Cel flushed the toilet and lit the vanilla candle on the edge of the bathtub.

"You want a glass of ice water or tea or something?" Cel asked.

Natalie made eye contact with Cel in the mirror and nodded. "Water." With the bright light highlighting her now blotchy face, she appeared drained, hollowed, ten years older than when she'd arrived. As though a significant percentage of her essence had exited her body with the puke.

Cel gently ran her hand up and down Natalie's back a few times. "I'll be right back."

When she returned, Natalie was lying on her back on the bed with her hands over her face. Cel sat next to her. "Here you go."

Natalie sat up and took a tiny sip. She held eye contact with Cel for a few seconds before admitting, "I'm pregnant."

Cel's eyes bulged. "What? Really?" She hugged Natalie, careful not to squeeze or tug too hard. "That's great. Congratulations. When did you find out?"

Trepidation danced across Natalie's tired eyes. "A month ago."

"Oh." Cel paused, glanced at the floor, the gears in her mind churning, processing the answer, calculating how many times she'd spoken with Natalie in the past month.

"I didn't tell you sooner because I know you have had trouble with...and I didn't want to upset you...and I was scared the same thing would happen to me, too...but I swear the only people we've told are my mom and dad and Craig's parents."

"It's okay," Cel said, and loosened the damp hair clinging to Natalie's forehead. "You don't have to explain." She tried her best to not only smile, but beam. "I'm so happy for you guys. You're going to be a great mom."

Natalie smiled a wan but true smile, then lay back down and closed her eyes, holding the glass of water upright on her stomach. Cel watched the glass rise and fall in step with Natalie's breathing for a moment before her eyes slid to Natalie's stomach and her thoughts drifted to the bean-sized human floating around inside, to the mathematical odds of it surviving the first three months. Odds she knew all too well. The frightened, not-mother in her wanted to lay a hand over Natalie's womb and say a protection spell, a thriving spell, a strengthening spell, to tell Natalie everything Dr. Benson had told her, to take vitamins, exercise, eat right, but she pushed away the idea when she glanced at Natalie's closed eyes, her calm face. She didn't want to spread her infectious worry to her friend. According to Dr. Benson, anxiety was one of the top catalysts of miscarriage.

Natalie didn't open her eyes when Cel took the glass, set it on the nightstand, and turned off the lamp. Cel lay down beside Natalie, hip to hip, shoulder to shoulder, hand touching hand, just like how they'd slept in Natalie's twin bed during sleepovers back in elementary school when they were terrified they'd summoned Bloody Mary in the bathroom mirror. Within five minutes, both women were asleep.

Cel woke with a start when Natalie's cell phone chimed four hours later. As Natalie rose and checked her phone, Cel opened the bay window blinds. A thick, sunrise-tinged fog veiled the neighborhood, but it wasn't thick enough to hide the fact that Parker's car wasn't in the driveway.

"It's Craig," Natalie said. The color had come back to her cheeks, a restful solidity to her eyes. "Wanting to know if I want to meet him for breakfast."

"You should go," Cel said. "You need to get something in your belly for that baby."

"Are you sure? What are you going to do?"

"I'm going to call the school a little after eight and see if Parker showed up for work." Cel chewed on her bottom lip for a second. "If he did, fuck him, but at least he's all right. If not, I'll probably go to his mom's and see if they've heard from him."

"I'll wait and go with you. I know Beverly and Jennifer can be total bitches."

The corners of Cel's mouth rose, but her lips didn't part. "That's okay. You've done enough for me. You should go home and take a shower and eat with Craig before he goes to work. I'll let you know as soon as I find out something."

Natalie sniffed her armpits, cupped her hand over her mouth, exhaled, sniffed, grimaced. "I do need to clean up, don't I?" She put her hand on her stomach and glanced down as though it were talking to her. "And I am real fucking hungry."

They laughed, and Cel led Natalie to the front door where they hugged and promised to call or text one another with updates soon. Cel watched Natalie's Scion vanish into the fog before heading back inside. She was on her way to brew partridge tea and take her morning vitamins when she heard a series of light thumps coming from the kitchen. She froze and held her breath. Seconds later, another thump. Like a tiny, soft hand tapping on the tile or back door.

"Mila?" Cel called out. Mila usually slept on the foot of her bed, greeted her with meows and rubs first thing in the morning, eager for food. But she hadn't seen Mila at all today. She slowly continued toward the kitchen, her eyes and ears alert, her lips fluttering the protection spell. She stopped in the doorway, reached inside, and flicked on the light. "Mila?"

Another thump. From behind the island in the center of the room.

Cel stepped around the island and found Mila crouched low and staring down at her paws with dilated hunting eyes. A fat, one-legged cricket wriggled beneath the paws, struggling to escape. The tip of its jettisoned leg poked out from between Mila's lips like a freak whisker.

Cel's mouth fell open as her eyes slid across the floor, up onto the counter, and into the deep barn sink. Ten or twenty other crickets were hopping around inside, bouncing off the faucet, colliding, searching for somewhere to hide from the assassin cat.

Chapter 12 - Parker

Parker woke on his back, laying on a damp mattress, breathing in musky air that tasted reused. A dim, uncovered light bulb in the center of the ceiling buzzed like a swarm of bees. When he sat up, he cringed and closed his eyes. His head felt as though it weighed twenty pounds and had ballooned to twice its size. He fingered the back of his skull where the throbbing was most severe and found a doorknob-sized knot. No blood, wet or dry, though. He sat there for a moment, until the dizziness and pain of righting himself subsided enough for him to scan the room.

Cement surrounded him on all sides: four bare walls, the floor under the mattress, and the ceiling. A three-inch-wide pipe pierced the ceiling in the corner, for air he assumed. A wooden staircase on the left wall led up to a flat, coffin-sized, level-with-the-ceiling, cellar door. There was one small window with no latch high up on the wall behind him, but it had been bricked over on the outside. A plastic gallon jug filled with water sat on the floor on the left side of the mattress. A blue paint bucket with a scrap of cardboard lid on the opposite side. A toilet.

Where the hell was he? The place felt oddly both familiar and foreign, like the mash-up of real and fictional locations in nightmares. Had he been here before?

He stood, allowed a second wave of disorientation to recede, and headed for the staircase. A few feet from the bottom step, his right leg met resistance. He looked down and saw he was barefoot, a taut chain attached to a cuff around his ankle. He followed the chain back to a curved piece of rebar cemented into the floor under the foot of the mattress. The cement there was fresher than the rest of the pocked floor. *Poured just for me.* An eruption of terror and anger rushed through him. He grabbed the chain with both hands and jerked on it as hard as he could.

"What the fuck is going on?!"

As his panic-stricken voice echoed off the walls, he tugged and pulled and pried until he ran out of breath and his ankle was bleeding. He fell back down on the foot of the mattress and cupped his hands over his face, sweating, his heart jackhammering, his blood pressure undoubtedly sky rocketing. He could feel his raging pulse in his fingers and feet, the heat of his blood in his chest and cheeks. He needed to calm down. He straightened his back to lengthen his torso, placed his hands on his thighs, and took a series of slow, deep breaths. In the mouth and out the nose just like Dr. Gordon—an anger management therapist he'd visited once a week for three months after he'd punched Cel shortly after her third miscarriage—had taught him.

"Reactions are rarely productive," he whispered. Dr. Gordon's words. "You can't make good choices if you don't think them through first."

He repeated the mantra three more times, then picked up the jug of water, took a few gulps, and drizzled a little over his head. As he unbuttoned his shirt to allow air to touch his skin, he thought back on the series of events that had led him here. Fight with Cel. Work. Lunch with Lauren. Hunter's Haven. Reading. The gray F-150. Chasing Abby? Table Rock. The blow to the back of the—

The light above him cut off, swallowing the entire room in darkness. Absolute darkness. Parker gasped, and his chest tightened. His pulse escalated again, blood pressure soared. A surge of adrenaline energized his legs, and he jumped to his feet as rumbling and scratching sounds echoed down from the direction of the staircase and cellar door. Sounds reminiscent of heavy furniture sliding across a hard floor, of boxes being lifted and dropped.

He stayed perfectly still until the sound stopped and the cellar door eased open with a long painful screech, and he snapped his head toward the staircase. No light spilled through the opening, though the darkness up there was less encompassing, less black. He clenched his fists ready to throw blows when a slender silhouette appeared at the top of the wooden staircase. The indistinct figure held steady for a few seconds before slowly descending the stairs. It stopped on the third to last step, a black image on a black canvas, a specter within a shadow. Parker couldn't tell the age or gender or race of the person much less make out any specific facial features. It appeared to have either long hair or a hood on, though.

"Who are you?" Parker asked. In step with his balled fists, his voice trembled.

The person didn't respond.

"What do you want?"

Parker moved toward the stairs, until the chain stopped him about five feet from the person. The faint scent of cigarette smoke crept up his nose, the steady hiss of breathing into his ears. "Why did you do this?"

No response. No movement. Just the breathing.

Parker's voice grew stronger, louder. "Who are you? Huh? Who are you? What do you want?"

The person released a barely audible, airy chuckle, then turned and calmly headed back up the stairs.

"Hey! Hey! Come back here!" Parker stretched as far forward as he could, balancing on his left foot and holding his chained leg in the air parallel with the floor, watching the top of the staircase as the giant cellar door squeaked and lowered. "Hey! Wait!"

A moment later, the overhead light buzzed back on, and Parker squinted and aimed his eyes downward. As his eyes adjusted to the brightness, the sound of furniture sliding across the floor and heavy objects being dropped on the cellar door filled his ears again. He sat on the foot of the mattress and angrily eyed the cellar door for a long while after the noises ceased.

Eventually, he crossed his legs and sat up straight, put his hands on his thighs, and started Dr. Gordon's calm breathing method again. He needed to slow his heart down again. He needed to think rationally, without fear or anger. If the stranger had wanted him dead, he would be dead. They'd left him water. Left him a bucket to piss in. And they'd come down to what…check and see if he'd survived the head blow? Taunt him? Frighten him? Intimidate him? They hadn't said a word, this time anyway. But surely they wanted something from him. He had no doubts that sooner or later he'd find out what. For now, he was trapped, helpless, like when he'd gotten lost in Carlsbad Caverns as a Cub Scout and had to endure two days of pitch black horror before being rescued. He needed to remain calm and conserve his energy. Wait for an opportunity.

He continued taking measured breaths until he could no longer feel his heart pounding into the backside of his sternum and his hands stopped trembling. The back of his head still throbbing, he gently lay back and laced his hands behind his head. He gazed up at the ceiling as though he could see beyond the pale cement, wishing he hadn't gone to Hunter's Haven. Wishing he hadn't chased the girl. Wishing he had some Tylenol.

Wishing he had a book.

He closed his eyes and pictured himself standing in the closet in his computer room, sifting through the hundreds of paperbacks stacked on the shelves. He pictured himself finding *Ender's Game* by Orson Scott Card, a book he'd read countless times as a teen and written a book report over in college. He imagined opening it up, flipping to the first chapter, and sniffing the crevice. In his mind's eye, he could see the words on the first page as clear as day, and he began reading.

Chapter 13 - Cel

Cel assured and reassured herself the crickets must've come up through the rusty, cast iron drainage pipes. She'd found about ten more in the hall bathroom sink and tub, ten or so more in her own sink and tub. Yes, there must've been a temporary mainline backup in the area in the middle of the night, or a neighbor must've dumped insecticide or some other caustic chemical down a drain, forcing them her way. It was silly to think they'd come for her, that someone had sent them. She had no enemies like Maria. She didn't even know any witch other than her *abuela*. The crickets were, as always, a reminder of the past, a dark stint, a coincidence, a nuisance, nothing more.

She made short work of slaughtering the crickets, smashing them with a *chancla* and tossing them outside for the birds. By the time she texted Parker again, fed Mila, showered, and returned to the kitchen to warm her tea and take a shot of wheatgrass, the clock on the microwave read five minutes after eight. Five minutes after the first bell at Oak Mott Middle School had chimed.

Cel considered driving to the school to see if Parker had arrived but decided a call would answer the question quicker. She knew Patty Hendrix, the office secretary with fire-red hair and an equally fiery voice, and her husband Charles fairly well. They'd both grown up in Oak Mott, and Cel and Parker had sat next to them and their kids at the Baxter wedding two summers back. Cel took a deep, hopeful breath and found the school's number on her cell. Patty answered on the third ring.

"Oak Mott Middle School."

"Hi, Patty. It's Cel, Parker's wife."

"Oh, hi. Is Parker okay? Is he sick?"

Patty's questions seized Cel by the throat and told her all she needed to know. Parker hadn't shown up for work. Or called in. Cel struggled to put together a complete, coherent sentence and push it out of her mouth. The words and syllables floating around inside her head somehow seemed too thick and heavy to move. She had no idea if her husband was okay, or sick, or even alive.

"Cel? Hello? Are you there?"

Cel hung up. She stood motionless, staring out the window above the kitchen sink. When her phone rang and she saw the school's number, she silenced the call, hustled to her bedroom, slipped on shoes, pulled her hair up into a tight ponytail, grabbed her Envoy keys, and left. She had delayed going to the Lundy's house long enough. Parker may not want to talk to her, but if he'd contacted anyone about his whereabouts, he'd contacted Beverly or Jennifer. And they would have a harder time lying to her face than over the phone if he'd asked them to not divulge his location.

She drove by the middle school on her way to Clifton Heights, the upper class neighborhood on the northwestern side of town where Parker's mom and sister lived, and found what she'd expected. No red Camry in the parking lot. Lauren's yellow Jeep was there, though, which served as a modicum of relief. Little Miss Mentee probably had no idea why Parker hadn't shown up for work, either.

Cel parked curbside in front of the two-story brick home, checked her appearance in the rearview mirror, and headed for the front door.

The Lundys had purchased the thirty-five-hundred-square-foot monstrosity and moved from Gateway to Clifton not long after a law settlement handed Beverly a million dollars ten years earlier. Beverly's mini-van had been T-boned on the driver's side at the intersection of Main and 10th by an Oak Mott City Maintenance truck. The driver, a broom-handle-thin man named Benny Jameson, was seventy-six years old, almost legally blind, and drunk out of his gourd at ten that morning. He had somehow managed to buckle his seatbelt, though, and thanks to that and a functioning airbag, he suffered only minor injuries. Beverly, on the other hand, sustained a broken left hip and leg, damaged spine, ruptured small intestine, and a brain bleed. She spent three months in Oak Mott Memorial Hospital, one third of that time in a coma, and received the settlement two years later.

Cel walked between Jennifer's Audi and Beverly's Durango which sat nose to nose in the half-circle driveway. Had Parker been with her, they would've just walked inside and yelled, "Hello." But since she was alone, she rang the doorbell.

Jennifer opened the door a few seconds later. The younger, spitting image of her mom, Jennifer had a round face, calves and ankles as thick as young trees, and carried a tractor tire of blubber around her waist. Her thick bangs hung down to her eyebrows, and her gray sweat suit displayed more than one stain. As the eldest daughter, and because she'd never married or had children like her younger sister Jill, she'd volunteered to quit her job at an Austin Public Library and move back to Oak Mott after Beverly's accident. She'd lived in her parents' house ever since, her bedroom the largest spare upstairs. Other than reading paperback romance novels and watching Lifetime, her mom's care was her sole purpose. She looked annoyed to see Cel. "Hey, Cel. Come in."

Cel followed Jennifer past the staircase and into the living room. Beverly sat in a lift chair in the center of the room opposite a sixty-inch flat screen mounted to the wall, watching a *Golden Girls* rerun. Her pink cane was propped against the side of the chair. A hodge-podge of family pictures covered the wall above a leather couch on Beverly's left. To her right, on the other side of an end table housing a glass lamp and a cup of sweet tea with a straw, was a dingy recliner, the seat permanently hollowed into the shape of Jennifer's backside.

Beverly flashed a half-hearted smile but stayed silent as Cel greeted her, gave her a cordial hug, and sat down on the couch. The coffee table in front of Cel was littered with prescription bottles, magazines, and opened mail.

Jennifer plopped down in her recliner and started scrolling on her cell phone. "So, what's up?" She sounded unenthused, her face as inexpressive as a rubber mask.

"I just wanted to know if you've talked to Parker lately."

Beverly glanced at Cel, then moved her attention back to the TV. Jennifer didn't look up, continued scrolling. "About what?"

Cel repositioned herself on the couch, unconsciously shifting into a defensive position, as if minimizing her surface area in preparation for an attack. She leaned forward, closed her knees, and placed her hands in her lap, her elbows tight against her side. She knew that if they truly hadn't communicated with Parker, they would launch a verbal attack when she revealed how he hadn't returned home the previous night or shown up for work this morning. They would blame her. They always did. The Lundys, especially Beverly and Jennifer, had made their disapproval of Cel known from early on in the relationship. They had tried to convince Parker not to marry her, claiming she only wanted to marry him because "she came from a family of illegals and probably needed a green card." Which was as true as an *innocent* seven in the morning phone call or text from a beautiful mentee. Cel had been born in McAllen, Texas, on December

21, 1984, while her mom was there visiting friends, and Parker had shown them a birth certificate to prove it. They also claimed to "know" Cel's *abuela*, and all about her "dark beliefs," but in reality, they had talked to Yesenia less than a handful of times over the years. What they *knew* were rumors, the same rumors everyone in Oak Mott *knew*. On more than one occasion, Beverly had even made off-handed comments in front of Cel about Yesenia's "wacky voodoo and witchcraft" ways.

Cel fidgeted with her car keys as she told them how Parker hadn't come home the previous night or shown up at work this morning. When she finished, she finally had their full attention. Beverly's head snapped in her direction, her right eye rapt with fierce focus, the left, the one that had been damaged and temporarily dislodged in the accident, cloudy and askew. Jennifer looked up from her phone, her lips pinched into a thin line.

"Why would he...have you...what the hell..." Jennifer said, her tone escalating with each new attempt to voice a question.

"What did you do?" Beverly interjected. The blame.

"Nothing." Cel scooted to the edge of the cushion. "We had an argument yesterday morning, and I figured he was just pissed and stayed the night here to cool off."

"Well, he didn't." Jennifer found Parker's number on her cell and put the phone to her ear. "It goes straight to voice mail." She started typing a text.

"I know," Cel said. "I've been trying to get a hold of him all night."

"What did you start shit with him about this time?" Beverly asked.

Cel looked down at her keys. She didn't want to discuss Lauren Page with these two. Parker wasn't with Lauren. She knew that already. Besides, they would only twist the argument into a blame game, accuse her paranoia of driving him away. "I don't even remember. It was early. We were both tired." She looked up. "Something stupid."

Beverly grabbed her cane, maneuvered herself out of her chair, and headed into the kitchen. "Where's my phone?" she called out as her cane clacked on the tiles.

Jennifer was still staring at her phone, typing. "On the table."

Beverly lumbered back into the living room, plopped down, and began poking at her cell phone, as well.

"Do you guys know anywhere else he might've gone?" Cel asked. "A hotel or something?"

"No," Beverly shot back.

"He's not returning my texts," Jennifer said, shaking her head. She met eyes with Cel. The fury in her gaze scorched the path between them. "You should've called us last night. If anything bad has happened to him, if you've done something to him...hurt him again...I swear to God..." They held eye contact for a tense moment, then Jennifer started tapping on her phone again.

Cel squeezed her keys in her hand hard enough to sting. "I've only ever hit him as many times as he's hit me, but I've never *hurt* him."

Jennifer's eyes stayed down, her jaw clenched. "You've paid someone else to do it, though."

"Bullshit." Cel stood. "That's not how it went, and you fucking know it."

"Uncle Pete hasn't heard from him, either," Beverly said to Jennifer who was standing up and aggressively moving toward Cel. Beverly threw her arm up in front of Jennifer as though she could hold her three-hundred-pound daughter at bay. Jennifer stopped.

"I'm calling Chief Sterling," Beverly said. She cut her eyes at Cel. "Something's not right here."

Anger gripped every muscle in Cel's body from her face to her feet. "The only thing not right about this is Parker," she said. "*He* never came home. *He* didn't show up for work. *He* won't answer his phone. I don't know where he is. I didn't do anything wrong. Why would I come here if I had?"

Beverly and Jennifer eyed Cel, but neither spoke. Their stern, accusatory expressions answered Cel's question, though. They thought she wanted to appear like the innocent, gentle, loving wife—*the mother*—that she wasn't. They thought she wanted to cover up whatever horrible act she'd committed. They thought she thought she could outsmart them.

Beverly dialed the Oak Mott Police Department, and dispatch answered on the second ring. "This is Beverly Lundy. I want to talk to Chief Sterling. Now."

Cel stormed out of the house as Beverly greeted Chief Sterling in the background. She sped away but pulled to the side of the road half a block away as the realization that Parker hadn't contacted his sister or mom sank in. Her chest felt like it was caving in, crushing her heart, squeezing the air from her lungs. Her eyes tingled, threatening to spill tears. Where the hell was he? Maybe Jennifer was right. Maybe something had happened to him.

Something bad.

Chapter 14 - Yesenia

After tending to her plants and collecting the chicken eggs, Yesenia sat down on the living room couch with a cup of black tea to watch *Telemundo*. She had finished half of the cup, and her three-legged cat Mina, seventeen years old and plagued with severe arthritis, had just saddled up against her thigh when Cel walked through the front door. Cel's dark eyes were bloodshot, red-rimmed from crying.

Yesenia set her mug on the coffee table and turned off the TV. "What's wrong, *mija*?"

Without responding, Cel sat beside Yesenia and tipped sideways, resting her head on Yesenia's shoulder.

Yesenia patted Cel's thigh, kissed the top of her head, and whispered a soothing spell, the same one she'd whispered over an upset Cel a hundred times before. Some parents responded to their upset children with simple words of encouragement, others, prayers and blessings. Yesenia responded with the same spells her mother had responded to her and Dolores with, spells she still whispered to herself when needed. "It's Parker, isn't it?"

Cel raised her head and nodded. "He's gone."

"What do you mean? *Ido?*"

For the next twenty minutes Yesenia stroked Mina and listened as Cel recounted what had and hadn't occurred over the past twenty-four hours concerning Parker, ending with her visit to the Lundy household and Beverly's and Jennifer's reactions to the news Parker had possibly fled, Yesenia's mouth turned down at the sound of Beverly's name. She equated communicating with Beverly Lundy to cleaning out litter boxes. Necessary but ultimately worthless.

"I don't know what to do," Cel said, and wiped her eyes with the sleeve of her T-shirt. "I don't know where he could've gone."

"Well, you know how Chief Sterling and everyone else who works for this city reacts to Beverly. They have had their *cabeza en su culo* ever since that accident. *Ella dice saltar,* they jump. I'm sure they'll move finding him to the top of the list."

"What if something bad has happened to him?"

"Don't go there, *mija*. It won't do any good."

Yesenia spoke the platitude with a matter-of-factness, as though she had no experience dealing with the pain and uncertainty of having a missing loved one. But she did have experience. More than enough for one lifetime. She just couldn't share it with Cel.

The greatest lie she'd ever told, the one secret she intended to take to her grave, was that Cel's mom Rebecca had died in a bus accident in Mexico City shortly after dropping Cel off in Oak Mott. Yesenia had concocted the lie to shield Cel, only two at the time her mom abandoned her, from the truth. To shield her from the burden of knowing her mother had chosen the path of a prostitute and drug addict, a life of pipes and dicks, over that of a mother. To conceal the knowledge her father could've been one of a hundred men. Yesenia last heard from Rebecca a month after she'd left Oak Mott. Rebecca had called to say she was heading to Mexico with a guy (a pimp named Ivan, if Yesenia remembered correctly), and that she'd keep in touch. She didn't ask about Cel during the call, and Yesenia never heard from her only daughter ever again. Yesenia spent many nights over the following years worrying about Rebecca. Worrying if she was hungry, or hurt, or sick, or scared, or rotting naked face-down in a ditch somewhere. And in the end, all the worrying did no good. It brought no answers. No relief. Only misery. Yes, she had experience dealing with the pain and uncertainty of having a missing loved one, but she had locked that knowledge in a dungeon deep inside of her, where the pain couldn't reach Cel.

"Come on," Yesenia said, taking Cel by the hand and heading toward the kitchen. "I have some hot water on the stove. I'll make you a cup of *yerba buena*."

Cel sat quietly with her elbows propped on the table and a faraway look in her eyes while Yesenia gathered the herbs and prepared the tea. It was the same tea she'd brewed daily for Dolores in the months before Dolores's death, an ancient concoction designed to help soothe sick bodies and calm troubled minds. After Yesenia placed the warm mug on the table in front of Cel, she wrapped her hands around it, and a ghost of a smile touched her lips.

"Thank you, *Buelita*."

Yesenia slid a chair away from the table and had just sat down when someone knocked on the front door. She made her way through the living room with Cel following close behind. When she opened the solid door, a tall man in a dark suit was standing on the other side of the screen door mesh. He appeared middle-aged, fifty tops. Crow's feet marked the outside corners of his eyes, and wiry gray hair had infiltrated more than half of his scalp and goatee. His deep-set eyes projected a dullness, a surrendering, suggesting to Yesenia that he had experienced enough hardship to carry permanent scars on his heart.

"Can I help you?" Yesenia asked without opening the screen door.

He smiled, revealing a gap between his front teeth wide enough to roll a penny through. "Hi. I'm Detective Paul Hart from Oak Mott P.D." In step with his appearance, his voice sounded seasoned. "Chief Sterling talked to Beverly Lundy about her son Parker's whereabouts, and I was wondering if I could ask Celia a couple of questions about it." His eyes moved from Yesenia to Cel. "You're Celia Lundy, right?"

Cel nodded. "Cel."

Yesenia opened the screen door. "Come on in."

Cel sat on the end of the couch nearest the kitchen and held her mug on top of her thighs. Hart pulled his cell phone out of his jacket pocket and sat on the opposite end of the couch. After he politely refused Yesenia's offer to get him a cup of tea or glass of water, Yesenia twisted the rocking chair she'd inherited from her mom so that it faced the couch, adjusted the seat cushion, and sat down.

Hart tapped and scrolled on his phone for a moment, then met eyes with Cel. "I understand you told Beverly that you haven't talked to Parker since yesterday."

Cel nodded.

"Can you tell me when you last saw Parker?"

"Yesterday morning before he left for work."

"And how was he? In good spirits? Sad? Mad?"

Cel glanced at Yesenia, looked back at Hart. "He was upset."

"Why?"

"We'd had an argument."

"About what?"

Cel took a sip of tea. Yesenia could tell by the look in Cel's eyes that she was contemplating how to answer. Mulling over whether to lie about Lauren or not. "One of his co-workers. Lauren Page." Another sip and she set the mug on the coffee table. "And how I don't like how much time he's been spending with her."

Hart tapped on his phone, scrolled, tapped. "Beverly told us that you and Parker have had physical altercations in the past. Is that correct?"

Cel nodded.

"Did yesterday's argument get physical? On either his part or yours?"

"No. Just heated words."

"What about threats? Did he threaten you? Did you threaten him?"

"No," Cel responded harshly. "It was a short argument. I walked out on him and went for a jog, and when I came back, he'd already gone to work."

Hart's eyebrows rose in a sympathetic gesture, and he held his hand out as though he could calm the frustrated vibes wafting off of Cel. "I'm not accusing you of anything. I just need to know everything I can about Parker's recent mindset in order to better our odds at finding him." He tapped on his phone again. "Has he ever been treated for depression or tried to hurt himself or anything like that?"

"Never. He's not the type to do anything like that."

Yesenia's eyelids fluttered at the mention of suicide. She clasped her hands together on her lap. She looked down and to the side as an unwanted image of Cel lying face-down on the living room floor in front of the same couch she was now sitting on popped into her mind.

Parker wasn't the type. But Cel was.

The day after her fourth miscarriage last July, Cel had shown up at Yesenia's with a bag of clothes and toiletries in tow because she "couldn't stand to see the disappointment in Parker's eyes anymore." That night, after hours of talking and hugging and crying, Cel had taken a handful of sleeping pills and valium when Yesenia dozed off. By the grace of the Source, Yesenia had woken and discovered Cel unresponsive on the floor in front of the couch before it was too late. Two empty pill bottles were on the floor beside her. Yesenia yelled and shook and slapped Cel. She spat out frantic healing spells. She ran to the kitchen, ran back. She propped Cel upright, tilted her head back, and forced a concoction down her throat. Then she held Cel's head at an angle so the bile and water and pills wouldn't choke her. After struggling to hoist Cel onto the couch and cleaning up the mess, Yesenia put a pillow under her granddaughter's head, a quilt over her body, and slept sitting upright at her feet. When Cel woke the following afternoon, she gave Yesenia an embarrassed, eyes down apology, and they'd never spoken of it since.

Though the experience had terrified Yesenia, deep down, she hadn't been surprised. Cel had gone through a cutting phase in her teens, and had periodically experienced bouts of depression over the years where she would shut herself off from the world for extended periods of time. Yesenia had always tried to help Cel through these sad stints the best way she knew how, with love and potions, spells and rituals. But Rebecca had been in a spiritually bad way and self-destructive herself when carrying Cel. And although Yesenia had shielded Cel from that truth the best she could, she knew she would never be able to remove the dark imprint Rebecca had left on Cel's soul while Cel had grown in her womb and they'd shared tainted blood.

"Does he have any medical conditions like diabetes? Or is he on any medications?"

"He takes medicine for high blood pressure, but that's it. It runs in his family."

Hart positioned his phone where he could use both thumbs and smiled a half-smile. "Sorry," he said. "I'm still not very good at taking notes on cell phones like Sterling wants us to. He says it'll make it where we can share information quicker. I don't know. I'm a pen and paper man myself." He typed for a few more seconds then looked up. "Okay. What about alcohol or illicit drugs? Parker do anything like that?"

"He'll have an occasional beer at Whiskey River or something, and he smoked a little pot when he was younger, but nothing major."

"And how are you guys' finances? Any troubles?"

"No. I quit my job at the Activity Center after my...earlier this summer, but we're fine. We're not in debt or behind on our mortgage or anything like that."

"Good." Hart finished entering notes into his phone and slid it back into his pocket. Sizing up Cel with his dull, deep set eyes, he stroked his goatee twice. "Now, this may come off as harsh, but I have to ask it. Did you have anything to do with his disappearance?"

Cel held his gaze. "No. Of course not."

"I read in a report filed eight years ago that Josh Teague said you paid him to kick Parker's ass because Parker was cheating on you. Is that true?"

Cel's ears flushed. Her lips curled inward. "If you read the entire report then you know it's not."

Hart raised a defensive hand again. "Calm down. I'm not accusing you."

"Josh Teague was shit-faced drunk that night when Parker walked into The Pub. Had I been flirting with him? Yes. Did I drink a little too much and say some horrible things about Parker? Yes. But I didn't pay him or encourage him to do shit. After he was arrested, Josh tried to say any and everything he could to get out of that assault charge. Josh is a lying asshole."

"I hear you," Hart said. "I understand."

Cheeks puffed, Cel pushed out a loud, deep breath. As if attempting to expel a pocket of cursed air from her lungs. Tears formed in her eyes. "I don't know what happened to him. It scares me. I want to know where he is, too."

Hart reached across the cushion separating them and patted her knee. "More times than not people show up in a day or two at a hotel or in a nearby city because they just needed a breather. There's no evidence anything bad has happened to him, okay?"

Cel sniffled, nodded.

"Nowadays people can't go far without leaving a technological footprint. I'm sure we'll find him soon." Hart stood, pulled his phone out and scrolled. "He drives a 2008 red Toyota Camry, right?"

Cel nodded. "Uh-huh."

"Okay." He put his phone away and offered his hand to Yesenia. "Ma'am." She shook it, and he faced Cel. "I'm going to head over to the school to talk with his co-workers. They confirmed he showed up for work yesterday, so they might have some pertinent information. The quicker I get it the better." He tenderly touched Cel's shoulder, as though she were made of brittle glass. "Stay strong. I'll be in touch."

Yesenia followed Hart to the door and closed it behind him. When she returned to the couch, Cel placed her head on Yesenia's shoulder again, and Yesenia wrapped her arm around Cel. Yesenia's aged instincts told her this situation wouldn't end well. *Tiempos oscuros* were coming. A dark stint. She needed to stay vigilant for Cel's sake. She would prepare the spiritual rejuvenation ritual for this weekend. It had been nearly a year since she last performed one on herself.

Chapter 15 - Cel

Cel stayed on the couch only about five or ten minutes after Detective Hart left, long enough to finish her *yerba buena* tea and come up with a half-truth to tell Yesenia. After assuring Yesenia she felt better after talking with Hart, she claimed she thought a routine jog through Woodway Park would help quell her remaining anxiety, clear her mind. Which wasn't an outright lie. Jogs provided excellent stress relief for Cel on most days. But she had no intention of going to Woodway Park and jogging today.

She waved to Yesenia who watched her drive away from behind the screen door and then headed straight for the Grandview Apartment complex. She hadn't lied to Parker when he'd offered her Lauren's key from his wallet the previous morning. Taking the key wouldn't serve a purpose on her end. She already had one. She'd lifted the one from Parker's wallet two weeks earlier and had a copy made at Lowe's. Not for malicious purposes. Out of desperation, really. She had needed some of Lauren's hair in order to place a blocking spell on her, and also perform a small ritual to help keep Parker from entering Lauren's apartment, particularly lying in her bed. She'd hidden the key in the Envoy driver's manual in the glovebox.

Rather than parking in the complex lot, she parked on the side of Shipley Do-Nuts half a block away. She retrieved the key and the pair of gray cotton gloves she kept in a bag in the backseat along with a spare jacket and hat. She put them in her jean pockets and made her way toward Grandview.

Bright midday sunlight dominated a clear sky, but a chilly northern breeze lessened its effect on the temperature. Cel ducked her head into the wind, her hair flapping around her skull, and marched with a purpose down the alley behind Shipley's, following the wooden fence bordering the complex until she reached the backside of building 14. After peeking through the slats to make sure no one was out on a deck smoking or walking their dog in the sectioned-off dog area, she hopped the fence and hurried upstairs to apartment 212.

At the door, she slid on the gloves and whispered a protection spell. Lauren's Jeep had been at the middle school when Cel had driven by this morning, and now she was probably chatting with Detective Hart about Parker. Cel should have time to go in, remove the evidence under the bed, and get out without detection. Though unlikely, if the cops happened to search Lauren's apartment, Cel didn't want to be linked to it in any way. It would leave the wrong impression. She'd been honest with Hart about her and Parker's argument about Lauren because the longer Parker remained missing, the more Hart would dig and eventually learn the truth. If Cel had lied to him, any suspicion he might have about her involvement in Parker's disappearance would double. And if later he somehow found out she'd broken into Lauren's apartment and performed a ritual—a ritual he and the other officers would probably assume was threatening in nature, or possibly even satanic thanks to Beverly Lundy's lips being so close to Chief Sterling's ears—the suspicion would triple. Unfound suspicion. She'd watched enough ID Channel to know that any added suspicion would focus Hart's attention on her and slow his efforts to find Parker. She didn't want that to happen.

She slipped into the apartment and headed straight for Lauren's bedroom. The unmade queen-sized bed took up seventy percent of the one-window room. A smattering of papers and notebooks, pens and pencils covered half of the rumpled pink sheets and much of the floor. Cel lay down on her belly, reached under the head of the bed and grabbed the bound doll she'd placed behind Lauren's empty shoe boxes. Made from remnants of Cel's old white Metallica T-shirt and stuffed with Mila's fur and Lauren's hair, the four-inch doll had no features other than crude eyes and a mouth painted on with Cel's blood. Strands of Cel's hair were tied around its genitals, eyes, and mouth. With a swipe of her hand, she scattered the small circle of salt she'd placed around the doll, jumped up, and had taken two steps toward the door when writing on a piece of paper on the floor at the foot of the bed caught her eye. Parker's handwriting. She'd recognize his print anywhere. He wrote in all caps, block letters, sloppy sizes. Always had. She shoved the doll in her front pocket and picked up the half sheet of paper. The note was short.

MISS LAUREN LOU,

Lauren Lou? Really? A nickname?

I JUST WANTED TO SAY THANK YOU FOR LETTING ME MEET SAMMY LAST WEEK. YOU'RE VERY LUCKY.

A boyfriend?

HE'S MAGNIFICENT.

???

IT WOULD BE A DREAM COME TRUE TO HAVE A SON LIKE HIM SOMEDAY.

A kid? Lauren's a mom?

I'M GRATEFUL TO HAVE YOU IN MY LIFE. PARKER

Cel squatted and ruffled through the other papers, but only found spelling tests and vocabulary worksheets, a grocery list and countless blank pages. She dropped Parker's note. Her head was buzzing as though a beehive had been rattled inside her skull, its occupants furious for answers. So many questions were flying around in there she couldn't focus on any single one. She felt betrayed, jealous, inadequate. In a swirl of adrenaline and emotion, she marched out of the apartment, mindful to lock the door behind her. She slid off the gloves and put them and the key in her back pocket as she descended the stairs. She rounded the building at a brisk pace but was forced to abruptly stop when she almost slammed into Lauren who had her cell phone in one hand, keys and the sack lunch she normally would've consumed in Parker's classroom in the other.

They met eyes, their mutual dismay instantly generating an electricity all its own. In contrast to Lauren whose raised brows and gasp betrayed her shock, Cel's face remained stoic despite the chill running up her spine, causing her arm hairs to stand on end. How could she have been so careless? She'd never considered the possibility Lauren might come home for lunch.

"What are you doing here?" Lauren eventually asked.

"I wanted to know if Parker was here."

"Why do you think he'd be over here?"

Why do you think, you fucking whore? Cel wanted to scream. Instead, she fought back the urge and played as nice as her ramped up emotions allowed. "Well, he didn't come home after work yesterday and won't return my calls or texts." She put her hand on her hip. "And since I know you and he call and text every other second, and you gave him a key to your apartment, I didn't think it was too far-fetched that he'd be over here."

Lauren hesitated. Just like Parker had hesitated the previous morning. When she finally spoke, she did so with an air of nervousness. "It's not like that."

Realizing she had caught Lauren off-guard, Cel pushed harder. "What's it like, then? Because it seems to me you and him have developed a relationship way beyond mentor and mentee."

"We're friends. That's it."

Cel gave a sharp, humorless laugh. "Hmmm. That's funny. That's exactly what he said." She put her finger on the side of her lips in an exaggerated inquisitive gesture. "I bet next you'll say it's coincidence you two go to the same gym now, too. And that it's just work related when you eat lunch in his room every day. And, that the reason you gave him your apartment key was to simply...Feed. Your. Fish."

Lauren lightly shook her head. "He warned me that you would do this."

"Do what?"

"Freak out."

"You think it's freaking out for a faithful wife to want to know what her husband is doing behind her back?"

Sweat glistened on Lauren's upper lip and in the hollow of her neck. She appeared more scared than nervous now. "Listen, I know you've had a rough time since...this summer. But—"

"This summer? He talked to you about *my* miscarriage?" Cel tapped the center of her chest one solid time to emphasize the word "my."

"You know what? I don't need this right now," Lauren said. She tried to side-step Cel, but Cel mirrored her. "Move."

"No. Not until you tell me the truth. Do you know where he is?" A tense, brief pause. "Are you fucking him?"

"I already told the cops everything I know. Now get out of my way."

Lauren tried to move around Cel again, but Cel blocked her by sticking out her hands. "You owe me answers!"

"I don't owe you anything," Lauren said, her volume escalating to match Cel's. She held her phone up close to Cel's face and jiggled it as though Cel had never seen one and didn't know its purpose. "And if you don't move, I'm calling 911."

Cel grabbed Lauren's wrist, and after she shoved the phone away from her face, she realized they had a small audience. Not good. An elderly couple with their pants hiked too high and their shirts tucked too deep was standing on the sidewalk about five yards behind Lauren, holding hands and watching them. In the parking lot ten yards behind the couple, a woman wearing huge sunglasses and sitting in the driver's seat of a gray F-150 was also staring their direction. On the sidewalk ten yards from the truck, a kid about five years old on a Big Wheel stared their way.

"I think you know where he is," Cel declared, and then stormed toward the parking lot. She didn't want to draw any more attention to herself, and she didn't want anyone to see her scale the fence, either. Talk about suspicious.

The gray F-150 had backed out and driven off by the time she passed the old couple and reached the lot. A few seconds later, when she glanced back over her shoulder, the couple, Big-Wheel-boy, and Lauren were all gone. She cut across the lot, looped around building 12 and 11, made her way to a section of the fence behind the pool house that was shielded by bushes, hopped over, and sprinted to her car.

Chapter 16 - Cel

Cel sped home, choking the life out of the wheel. She could hear the tick of her pulse in her ears. Her stomach felt as if it had flipped upside down. She'd recited multiple calming and soothing spells with little results. She couldn't believe Parker had confided in Lauren about *her* miscarriage, *her* loss, *their* private pain. She accepted and welcomed him sharing personal details about their struggles with his mom and sister, or even Omar and Natalie. Everyone needed an emotional outlet, an ear separate from their spouse's, especially during dark stints. But she couldn't accept him sharing those struggles with the same woman who had spent the last two months seducing him, luring him away from his marriage. The same woman who had a child of her own—*magnificent Sammy*—to dangle in front of him as proof she had eager eggs and a working womb.

Cel parked askew in the driveway and hurried inside. On a normal day, she would've spent the afternoon taking care of household chores, meditating, and preparing dinner. But today wasn't a normal day. She spent the afternoon circling the house, moving from room to room, closet to closet, drawer to drawer, digging through notebooks and folders, searching under cushions and in between mattresses, looking for any letters or notes from Lauren Parker might have kept.

Like Yesenia, Parker had a penchant for writing longhand. He'd written Cel countless notes and letters when they were teens, usually taping them to the outside of her bedroom window at night while she slept, or hiding them in one of the pouches on her backpack or in her locker. Sometimes he somehow even snuck them into her pant pocket without her noticing. And after they moved in together in their early twenties, he continued surprising her, occasionally hiding one under her pillow, or putting one in a plant pot on the porch, or wrapping one around Cel's toothbrush or shampoo bottle, before he left for work. He said he liked to imagine the look on her face when she came across them; the way her eyes would hopefully inflate with fascination as the right side of her mouth crept happily up, revealing her awkward incisor, what he called the exclamation point of her smile. She had all the notes he'd ever written her in a shoebox in the back of her closet, the last one penned shortly after her second miscarriage, and she knew he had the few she'd written him in a worn cardboard box with his childhood baseball card collection in the attic. So, if Lauren had ever written him any personal letters or little cute notes, Cel figured he'd kept them. Probably in a drawer at the school because he was smart like that, but she wanted to check the house just in case.

She had pulled her hair up off her sweaty neck, stripped down to her bra and underwear, and was kneeling in the center of the computer room, sifting through a box stuffed with old tax forms and bills and manuals when the doorbell rang, startling her out of her obsession. She looked up and waited. A knock, three solid raps.

She rushed to the living room, slid the curtain back and peeked out the blinds. Two unmarked police cruisers and one official Oak Mott Police car were parked in front of her house, one blocking the driveway behind her Envoy. Her stomach torqued as she slid her eyes toward the front porch and saw four people. Chief Robert S. Sterling and Detective Paul Hart stood shoulder to shoulder, both eyeing the door like kids eagerly awaiting Jack to spring from his box. Hart was wearing the same dark suit he'd had on five hours earlier at Yesenia's and held a piece of paper in his hand. Sterling's ape-like arms hung down at his sides, his gut over his belt, mustache over his upper lip. His eyes were shielded by the tan-tinted bifocals most Oak Mott locals had never seen him without, day or night, church or work. He wore boots and jeans and a blue long sleeve button-up, a shiny golden star chief badge pinned to the left breast pocket. A short man with a scrawny neck, weak chin, and a wispy halo of hair flanked Hart, and a husky female with a freckled face and spiky hair flanked Sterling. The man donned dress pants and a Polo shirt, the husky woman, whose name tag read WILSON, a standard OMPD uniform.

"Coming," Cel hollered as she hustled to her closet. She threw on a T-shirt and jean shorts. "Be right there." When her hand touched the door knob, she paused and instinctively whispered a calming spell before opening the door. "Did you find him? Is he okay?"

Hart shook his head, his expression the definition of solemn.

Cel could feel the weight of all eight of their eyes pressing down on her.

"We didn't find *him*," Hart said. "But we did find his car."

Anxiety shifted Cel's heart into overdrive as she tried to digest Hart's response. "What? His... Are you sure it's his?"

Hart nodded.

She pressed her hand over her heart as if to stop it from bursting through her ribcage. "Where?"

"In Hunter's Haven, a couple of miles behind your grandma's house."

Beginning to feel light headed, she closed her eyes and placed her hand on the door jamb.

"Are you all right?" Sterling asked. "Do you need to sit down?" He sounded grandfatherly and soothing, the same as when he'd questioned Cel and the other hunters about Abby's disappearance shortly after becoming the chief fifteen years earlier.

She nodded and slowly opened her eyes. "But...then...he's got to be out there somewhere, right?"

"We've been searching all afternoon," Hart said. "But we haven't found any trace of him yet." He stroked his salt and pepper goatee, his deep-set, dull eyes glued to Cel.

"How can there not be a trace of him if his car is there?" Her eyes bounced from Hart to Sterling, Hart to Sterling. "No fingerprints or footprints or blood or anything?" Eyes bouncing back and forth again. "He couldn't have just vanished."

"It's not that simple, Cel," Sterling said. "These things take time. Our forensics team is still out there, working and searching. We even have our hound out there. If there is anything to find, we'll find it."

"Then why aren't *you* guys out there looking? Shouldn't *everyone* be out there? Isn't that your job?"

Hart glanced at the paper in his hand as though it had spoken to him, then met eyes with Cel. "We're here to search your house." He held up the paper for Cel to see. An official gold and black McLennan County seal marked the top, a fancy, undiscernible signature the bottom. "This is a notarized document signed by Beverly Lundy and Judge Exline, giving us permission to search this house. As you probably know, Beverly's name is the one on the deed to the property."

Cel knew, all right. All too well. Beverly had both discreetly and overtly reminded her that she'd bought the house as a gift for *Parker* many times. The anxiety brewing in Cel's chest bubbled as she eyed the paper. Although Beverly's longtime close friendship with Sterling, rumored to have been an affair that grew stale after Beverly's accident, had probably influenced the decision to conduct a search on the home, Cel suspected that wasn't the sole reason the police had agreed to do this so quickly. She feared the cops were lying about something, holding something back, information or evidence. She thumbed behind her. "Did you find something that makes you think something bad happened to him here?"

"No," Hart said. "But like I told you this morning, the sooner we explore all our options, especially now that we know he's not with his vehicle, the better."

Despite the gentle delivery, Cel had the impression his words carried an air of subtle accusation. "You mean the option that *I* did something to him and then dumped his car out there?"

Sterling touched her shoulder before Hart could respond. His hand felt as heavy as lead, and his sausage fingers seemed to trail half a foot down her back. "Relax. That's not what we're saying, Cel. There are a number of things we could find here that might help locate Parker." He removed his hand, adjusted his glasses. "Like a clue as to why he went out to Hunter's Haven in the first place, or where he could've gone from there. We just had to get Beverly's permission because she technically owns the house. It's a formality."

Cel bit her bottom lip and shot a quick glance back over her shoulder, thinking about how disheveled the house would appear when they entered, like a mini tornado had whipped through there. Every light on, closet open. Papers strewn everywhere in every room. Drawers and boxes open, contents stirred. She'd look moon-bat crazy. "Whatever," she whispered to herself as much as them. "Search all you want, but you're wasting your time. You won't find anything. I've already torn the place apart looking for something, anything, to help make sense of this, and there's nothing in there."

"Thank you," Hart said, and then glanced at Cel's bare feet. "You can't stay in the house while we search, and it could take a long while, so do you want to slip on some shoes?"

Cel nodded. "Do I have to stay here, or can I go to my *abuela's*?"

"We'd like you leave the Envoy here so we can clear it, too, but Officer Wilson can certainly give you a ride to your grandma's if you want," Sterling replied. "You need to leave any laptops, tablets, and other electronic devices in the house though, okay?"

Cel nodded.

"And if you could give us any of Parker's bank account or email passwords, things like that, it would speed up the process for us," the man sporting a wispy halo of light brown hair and weak chin said.

"Okay," Cel said. "Do I need to give you my cell phone, too?"

The man eyed Sterling, waiting for a decision from the man in charge. Sterling hung on the thought for a moment. "No. You can take it, so we can keep in touch."

You mean so you can monitor me, Cel thought but kept inside. "What about Mila, my cat?"

"That's up to you," Hart said. "We're going to be in and out of the house, so if you think she'll get scared or run away, you can lock her up in a carrier, or you can take her with you."

"I'll take her."

Cel felt numb, somewhat detached from her body, as Officer Wilson followed her into the house. In the kitchen, she collected her cell phone and jotted down all of Parker's passwords she knew on a notepad attached to the fridge, and in her bedroom, slid on her sneakers and scooped up Mila who was curled up on her bed.

When she exited the house cradling Mila in her arms, Hart, Sterling, and Wispy Halo Hair were huddled in front of one of the unmarked cruisers like a trio of warlocks hovering around a caldron. Hart had his cell phone to his ear, and the other two were talking in hushed tones. Melissa Herbert and her three young kids, the family who lived directly across the street, and a few other neighbors were standing on the sidewalk, watching the house, gossiping. An Audi the same color as Jennifer's was parked at the end of the block, facing the house. Two occupants were inside.

Wilson led Cel to the official Oak Mott cruiser and opened the front passenger door for her. As they pulled away from the curb and Cel watched Hart and Sterling enter the house, time slowed to a muted crawl. As though some deranged god with a vicious sense of humor had tapped the slow-motion button on a cosmic remote in order to relish one of the most harrowing moments in her life.

SEPTEMBER 1998

Chapter 17 - Cel

Cel was greeted by faint Tejano music when she unlocked the front door and stepped inside the house. At Yesenia's insistence, the radio in *Tia* Dillo's bedroom had stayed on ever since she was admitted to the hospital two weeks earlier. Yesenia had also bought a small portable radio for the hospital room. They were both tuned to the same station, *Tia* Dillo's favorite, and stayed on all night and day. Cel felt a sense of comfort knowing the hospital radio would be tuned to 95.7, *Today's Tejano Tunes*, every time she visited, and that the same station would greet her when she arrived home afterwards. It somehow connected the two places, provided a sense of hope. Made the situation in the hospital room seem less dire, the empty house more alive. But nonetheless, Cel didn't really enjoy listening to Tejano music. Not for personal pleasure, anyway. She preferred alternative rock, metal, industrial techno. Sounds with more bite. After kicking off her shoes and opening the blinds to awaken the house, she put a Massive Attack cassette in the boombox on her dresser and hit play. She didn't turn off Dillo's radio, she just cranked hers up louder.

She showered, dressed in cut-off jean shorts and her favorite Nine Inch Nails T-shirt, and then made her way to the kitchen for a quick bite to eat. When she opened the fridge, she found a plate of tamales and rice covered in Saran Wrap on the top rack. A sticky note was stuck to the clear plastic.

> HAVE FUN TONIGHT, MIJA! IT'S WHAT TIA
> DILLO WOULD WANT. I'LL BE HOME AROUND
> 11:00 AND WANT TO HEAR ALL ABOUT IT.

Two days earlier, when Cel had expressed guilt about going to the Central Texas State Fair with the other hunters on opening night because of *Tia* Dillo's condition, Yesenia had told her she had it backwards. "You need to go *for* Dillo. She loved the fairs and would want you to go. Besides, when she wakes up, if she finds out you didn't go, she'll smack you silly." This had elicited a chuckle from Cel (smack you silly), and lifted the burden of guilt off her heart (*when* she wakes up, not if).

Cel heated the tamales and rice in the microwave, ate, and then made her way out to Hunter's Haven to check on Frito's grave. She'd visited the site to make sure he hadn't clawed his way out of the ground every morning and evening since she and Parker had buried him. Tonight, like always, the large stone was still in place, the dirt untouched. When Cel returned home, she locked up the house, tied her flannel shirt around her waist, hopped on her bike, and headed to Parker's house.

The other hunters were already there. Plus Jeff. Abby's mom had told her earlier in the week that she had to take Jeff, or she couldn't go. Their bikes were positioned in a circle at the end of Parker's driveway. Parker stood in the center of the group, making goofy hand gestures at Jeff, whose giant-toothed smile took up half his face.

All eyes landed on Cel as she pierced the group, rolling to a stop between Omar and Natalie. Like her, all of the hunters except Parker, who still had on the black shirt and cargo shorts he'd worn to school, had cleaned up and changed. Natalie sported a trace of lipstick and the new short-sleeved Astros button-up her dad had bought her to match her cap. Omar's damp hair preserved the tracks of a wide-forked comb, and he'd replaced one over-sized hand-me-down for a nicer, less worn one. Abby had switched into the low-cut, light blue and yellow summer dress she'd been talking up all week. She'd purchased it at Goodwill with some of her hunting cash and was saving it for fair night. It fit her chest a little better than her T-shirts, but not by much.

After Cel answered everyone's greetings with a smile, Parker hopped onto her bike's back wheel pegs. "All right. Let's go." He pointed over her head toward the setting sun and spoke in his cartoonish deep voice. "To the fair!"

Energetic hoots stabbed the air as they pedaled out of the driveway with Cel and Parker in the lead. The Klepper Fields—a group of eight interconnected soccer fields where the fair had been held for the past eighteen years—were located one block north of Oak Mott High, roughly three miles away. A trip that took closer to twenty minutes on a leisure ride, took just under fifteen due to their enthusiasm. When they rounded First Baptist Church and turned north onto Jasper Street, which passed directly in front of the high school, they breached the edge of the fair's aura.

The school parking lot was full, and the shoulders of Jasper Street and the roads intersecting it were lined bumper to bumper with parked vehicles. Traffic on Jasper had slowed to a standstill as parents holding their kids' hands, laughing friends, and smiling lovers darted across the road, eager to reach the entrance.

Parker hopped off of Cel's bike as they approached the high school gymnasium, and as she wedged it into the bike rack, a realization gave her pause. They would probably never do this again. For five years straight now, they'd ridden their bikes to the fair together and parked them in this same rack, but by this time next year everyone except Natalie, who'd skipped first grade because of her advanced reading level, would have a driver's license. Parker would get his in two months. They'd probably drive to the fair. Probably in the beat up, mustard-colored '88 Dodge Ram that Parker's dad had inherited and promised to give to Parker next summer on his sixteenth birthday.

The thought of arriving at the fair next year in that truck, riding in the cab with Parker while the other hunters rode in the bed, brought a ghost of a smile to Cel's face. She cut her eyes at Parker and held his gaze as she untied her flannel shirt and slipped it on like a jacket. She'd stitched the slits Frito had carved into the shirt with matching color threads, rendering the damage near invisible.

Parker nudged her arm as the other hunters lined their bikes up in the rack alongside Cel's. "What are you smiling at?"

She nudged him back. "Nothing."

He pointed at her infinity necklace. "You need to do that thing you do. You know..." He pinched his fingers together on his chest as though grabbing a necklace of his own and brought them to his lips.

Keeping her eyes locked on his, Cel fingered the necklace until she found the clasp, which was close to the infinity symbol. She raised the clasp to her lips, kissed it, then spun it to the back of her neck as she mouthed the same good fortune spell her own mother, according to Yesenia, had recited when completing the same task. Her mom had left the necklace for Cel when she'd dropped off two-year-old Cel at Yesenia's house. Cel had rarely taken it off since Yesenia had wrapped and given it to her as a gift on her seventh birthday.

Screams of happy fright and victory bells rang out above the dull roar of the crowd as the hunters snaked toward the fair. An excitement, a tangible buzz as addictive as nicotine, as contagious as the flu, filled the air. The energy seemed to conjure laughter and lift everyone's feet a foot off the ground. They walked at a brisk pace, silent, their eyes taking in the machines towering above the red tent tops. The rotating Ferris wheel dotted with bright blue and gold lights. The wild, twisting cages on the Zipper. The spinning, green-glowing Octopus Swing, its tentacles almost fully horizontal, brave riders clinging to bars in carts that were tilted completely sideways.

Parker led them to the shortest of the three entrance lines, and within a couple of minutes, they were inside the roped-off field with red bands around their wrists and nostalgic smells of kettle corn and roasted meats caressing their noses. They headed straight for the Ferris wheel. Based on Omar's suggestion four years earlier, they had always ridden it first so they could get a good view of the area, locate the best rides and booths, and plan a route accordingly. Cel stayed right behind Parker to assure she rode with him like last year. Omar rode with Jeff, Natalie with Abby. As the wheel slowly spun, they looked up and down, left and right, pointing out areas of interest and people they recognized.

The six of them stayed together for the next two hours as the night sky took over, and the crowd thickened. They rode the Scrambler and Tilt-A-Whirl and Gravitron. They slammed into one another with bumper cars, and then slammed into their own reflections as they navigated the Mystical Mirror Maze. They threw darts at balloons, tossed ping pong balls at jars filled with water, and hurled softballs at weighted pins, which netted them a knockoff stuffed Bart Simpson doll (won by Omar and given to Jeff), a rubber Texas-shaped keychain (won by Parker and shoved in his pocket), and a handful of participation stickers.

Then they bought tickets to The Fantastic Journey, one of the few attractions not covered by the wrist band, and spent ten minutes in slow carts, meandering their way through a ramshackle structure, laughing at shoddy mannequins dressed as killer clowns and moaning zombies with twitchy arms. After that, they pitched in and bought two funnel cakes, two cotton candies, and two sodas. All the picnic tables were taken, so they found a patch of grass between two booths and sat in a circle. They shared the treats while jokingly recounting so-

and-so's face on this ride, so-and-so's lame attempt at this game. By the time they tossed their napkins and cups in a nearby trashcan, it was only a little after nine. They'd convinced their parents to tack an extra thirty minutes onto their regular ten-thirty Friday night curfews, so they still had nearly two hours.

"So, what do we hit up next?" Parker asked.

"The Octopus Swing is the closest cool ride, but I bet the line is long," Omar said.

"I love that one," Abby said, shuffling from one foot to the other in obvious discomfort. "But I really need to go pee first."

Natalie tucked a loose curl back under her cap and hooked her arm around Abby's. "Me too." Her eyes scanned the others. "Anyone else?"

Cel and the three guys shook her heads.

"Okay. We'll meet you guys back here in fifteen minutes."

As Natalie and Abby navigated the crowd, heading for the row of porta potties near the entrance, Cel turned to the others. "It's going to take them way more than fifteen minutes. Why don't we go ride the Zipper then come back here? Its line is never that long."

Parker wagged a finger in front of her face. "No way, no how. I can tolerate loops and shit, but last year I almost puked my guts out when you made me ride that thing. You're nuts if you think I'm doing that again."

Cel punched Parker's upper arm. "Wuss." She met eyes with Omar, and his quick head shake answered her unspoken question. A short, incredulous laugh rocketed up her throat and burst out of her mouth. "Both of you guys suck. I'll just go ride it alone then."

"I'll ride it," Jeff said.

Cel spun on her heels to her left. She'd almost forgotten he was there. He'd hardly said a word all evening. His eyes betrayed the uncertainty lurking behind his brave smile. "Have you ever ridden it before?"

He shook his head. "This is my first fair."

"Really?" Cel bit on her bottom lip. She knew Jeff had never come to the fair with the hunters, but she didn't know he was a fair virgin. The memory of riding the Alligator Coaster and the Merry-Go-Round with *Tia* Dillo at her first fair at the age of five tugged at her heartstrings. Dillo had held her hand when she was scared that night, and they had laughed so much, so hard it hurt her cheeks Cel hesitated for a few seconds, then extended her hand to Jeff. "Come on. You'll love it."

Jeff's brave smile widened, exposing a gap where he'd recently lost a bottom tooth, and he grabbed Cel's hand.

"He's too short." Parker cocked his head and held his hand above Jeff's head as though Jeff were standing next to a measuring stick. "That ride has a height limit, you know."

Cel watched disappointment collapse Jeff's smile. "No, he's not," she insisted and pulled him toward her. "Let's go." She took the Bart Simpson doll from him and tossed it to Omar. When she and Jeff were almost out of earshot, Parker hollered her name. She paused and looked back over her shoulder. "What?"

Parker pointed to his right. "We're going to go..." He raised his arms as if holding a rifle. "We'll meet you back here."

Cel gave Parker a thumbs-up and guided Jeff to the Zipper. They reached the front of the line after one ride cycle, and an acne-plagued teenager wearing a massive cowboy hat and an equally massive belt buckle eyed Jeff and pointed at the height scale. The requirement was four and a half feet. Fifty-four inches. Cel glanced down at Jeff's sneakers as he backed up against the sign. They had a pretty thick sole, but Jeff, small for eleven years old, was still about a quarter of an inch short. The teenager looked at the sign, at Cel, the sign, back at Cel. She rolled her eyes at the guy, reached out, and fluffed up Jeff's thick hair. "There. Happy?" Then she took Jeff's hand and pulled him into the open cage in front of them. The teenager closed the door without responding or making eye contact with Cel, then lowered and locked the padded safety bar.

They each grabbed the bar, and when the ride lurched upward, Cel heard Jeff gasp. She slid her right hand over his left hand. "It's okay to be nervous. That's what makes it fun. The problem is that most people freak out and fight the cage. If you just let it lead you and move with it, you'll love it. I promise."

Jeff looked at Cel and nodded. Uncertainty was still evident in his big dark eyes, but a willingness to trust was there as well. He didn't make a noise for the first few seconds after the ride started, but when the cage began to spin upside down and Cel's stomach started flip-flopping like a fish out of water, causing her to laugh uncontrollably, he began to laugh, too. Louder and louder. So hard tears eventually streamed from his eyes. When the ride slowed to a stop, and once they had finally stopped laughing, Cel squeezed his hand. "It was fun, right?"

Jeff wiped the wet from his cheeks and eyes with the bottom of his shirt, and then looked at Cel and nodded rapidly. He was beaming, and the look of uncertainty in his eyes had died. Only joy remained. Pure, all-encompassing joy. The same joy *Tia* Dillo must've seen in Cel's eyes at this same fair years earlier. Cel smiled back, took him by the hand, and hopped out of the cage. She held his hand until they were approaching Parker and Omar, and Omar tossed the Bart Simpson doll back to him.

"Well?" Parker asked.

Cel glanced at Jeff who was grinning ear-to-ear like a birthday boy and winked. "We had a blast."

"Oh yeah." Parker started poking Jeff in the side and stomach, reaching between and around Jeff's hands when he blocked and squirmed. "I bet you feel like you're about to puke your guts out now though, huh? Don't lie."

Cel knocked Parker's hands away. "Please. He's ten times the man you are."

"Yeah," Jeff agreed, his bold tone and outthrust chin screaming confidence. "I could ride it a hundred more times without puking."

As Omar laughed and gave Jeff a high-five, Cel scanned the area. "Have you guys seen Abby and Nat?"

Parker copied her, searching faces in the crowd. "Nope."

"Knowing those two, they probably got lost," Omar said.

Cel chuckled. "Right. I should probably go find them. I need to pee, anyway." Her eyes slid from Jeff, to Omar, to Parker. When none of them hinted at wanting to accompany her, she added, "Why don't you guys go play a game or something, and we can all meet up at the Octopus Swing in about fifteen minutes?"

"Sounds good," Parker said, and then threw his arms over Omar's and Jeff's necks and energetically ushered them away.

Cel moved slowly, checking every booth and ride for Natalie and Abby as she worked her way back toward the entrance. She saw some classmates and Gateway neighbors, but not her friends. She also noticed how the crowd had changed since they'd first arrived. More teenagers and young adult couples were milling about, less middle-aged parents pushing toddlers in strollers and grandparents holding onto little kids' hands. When she finally reached the porta potties, she spotted Abby on the opposite side of the lines, which were each ten people deep, talking to a guy in front of a face painting booth. She had a golden, sparkly star painted on her cheek, a flirtatious smile on her face. Natalie was sitting on a stool behind Abby, the bill of her Astros hat tilted up. A large woman was running a paint brush up and down her cheek.

Cel began to loop around the back of the lines, moving their direction, but stopped mid-step when the guy talking to Abby glanced her way. Her heart jumped up into her throat. Although a Dallas Cowboys hat partially shaded his face, she immediately recognized him. She didn't remember his name but knew she'd seen him at Maria's house when she'd gone over there with *Tia* Dillo. The pointy nose and chin scar gave him away. He was one of Jose's best friends, one of the guys who'd laughed when Jose had teased her about her flat chest. Which probably meant Jose was nearby. And if Jose recognized Abby, then...

Cel's eyes flitted from face to face as she hustled toward Abby, hoping not to land on Jose. She angled her head down as she approached the guy in the Cowboys hat from behind. In one swift motion, she swooped around him, grabbed Abby's arm, and jerked her away like a teacher forcing a disobedient kid out of the classroom.

Cel led Abby about ten or fifteen yards, making sure to keep their backs to the guy, before Abby pulled loose and glowered at her.

"What the hell is wrong with you?"

"Motion for Natalie to come on." Cel spoke through gritted teeth. Her eyes were wide with urgency. "He's one of Jose's best friends. We need to get out of here."

Abby held Cel's gaze for a long moment before glancing over Cel's shoulder in the guy's and Natalie's direction. Cel watched Abby's eyes slowly change from surprised anger to fear as the realization of the possible consequences settled in.

"Hurr—"

Cel broke off when Natalie yelled out her and Abby's name in succession. "What are you guys doing?"

"*Chingao*," Cel whispered. She cocked her head in Natalie's direction. The guy was staring at her. Natalie was staring at her. The lady painter was staring at her. Many of the people in line were staring, too. She gestured with her hand for Natalie to come to them.

Confused, Natalie hesitated, but when Abby frantically gestured as well, she nodded, hopped off the stool, and headed their way. As she hurried past the guy in the Cowboys hat, movement to her right caught Cel's attention. Cel looked that way and saw Jose emerging from the nearest porta potty, sauntering toward his friend. He was in jean shorts and a tight, solid white tank top, the kind Yesenia called a wife-beater. Following his friend's eyes, Jose looked at Cel, and one corner of his mouth briefly crept up in a cocky smirk. But when his eyes shifted to Abby, the smirk vanished, and his eyes swelled with recognition. He didn't say, "Tits," loud enough for Cel to hear, but his lip movements were unmistakable.

Cel nudged Abby. "Get out of here."

As Abby fled, Cel darted over to Natalie who was about five yards away and grabbed her by the arm. "Come on! We have to get out of here!"

Cel pulled Natalie through the crowd, slamming into unsuspecting fair-goers as she tried to catch up with Abby. She didn't bother to look back and verify that Jose and his friend were chasing them. She didn't need to. Like his mom, he had a vengeful spirit. On more than one occasion she'd heard him brag about beating up guys, and even slapping a few girls around because they'd disrespected him in one way or another. No, she didn't need to look. He was a predator, and now he knew his prey.

They ran for what seemed like hours, jutting around booths, cutting between lines, anything in hopes of losing Jose and his friend. When they rounded the Test Your Strength hammer game, where a young man wielding a sledge hammer told them to "watch the fuck out," they finally caught sight of Abby. She was standing next to Parker, Omar, and Jeff at the back of the line for the Octopus Swing. She had her hands clamped on Parker's forearm. Her mouth frantically moving, her feet pumping up and down as though she were standing on hot coals. She pointed in Cel's and Natalie's direction and Parker glanced that way, locking eyes with Cel as she and Natalie approached.

"We have to get out of here," Cel said, struggling to catch her breath. She let go of Natalie's hand, pulled off her flannel shirt, and tied it around her waist. A good forty pounds heavier, Natalie was struggling even harder to breathe. She stooped and placed her hands on her knees as though about to collapse.

"Jose is here," Cel said. "He's com—"

"I already told him," Abby cut in. Then she glanced over Cel's shoulder and sucked in a sharp breath. "There they are."

Everyone looked.

Jose and his friend were fighting through the crowd about twenty yards away, searching the area like two determined bloodhounds.

"There are only two of them, and they don't know me and Omar are with you guys," Parker said, forgetting to mention Jeff. "If we split up, it'll be easier to avoid them."

Before anyone had time to fully contemplate the idea much less refute it, or suggest a meeting point, Abby grabbed Parker's hand. "Let's go." As she tugged him toward her and they started skirting the metal railing that surrounded the Octopus Swing, Omar pulled the hat off of Natalie's head, took her by the arm, and pushed her into the bulk of the crowd, moving toward the Zipper on the far edge of the fair.

Meanwhile, Jeff sidled up next to Cel and forced his sweaty hand into hers. She glanced down at him and was disheartened to see that the unbridled joy she'd last seen in his big brown eyes had been replaced by fear. She leaned over far enough for her breath to tickle his ear, whispered the protection spell that Yesenia had tattooed onto her psyche, hoping it would soothe him and her alike, and then they cut across the crowd Omar and Natalie had joined, traveling in the opposite direction of Parker and Abby. They slipped between a concession stand and game booth, headed for the perimeter rope in order to follow it and loop back toward the entrance, when Jeff's hand jerked out of Cel's.

Cel spun around. Jose had grabbed Jeff from behind and lifted him off the ground. He had one arm wrapped around Jeff's torso, pressing Jeff's back to his chest. His opposite hand covered the lower half of Jeff's face to muffle his screams. Jeff's feet flailed about six inches off the ground, slapping into Jose's shins. Cel surveyed her surroundings, looking for a stick, or a rock. Anything she could swing or throw. But she couldn't make out much. It was too dark. The booths in front of them blocked out most of the fair's glow, and the soccer fields on the opposite side of the rope serving as parking lots weren't lit.

"If you scream, I swear I'll snap his neck," Jose said.

Cel stepped toward him, where she could see his face well enough to make eye contact. "Leave him alone. He's just a kid."

"Looks old enough to take a beating to me." He squeezed tighter on Jeff's chest, the muscles in his bare arm constricting like a python, forcing the air out of Jeff's lungs. "Especially if he helped you guys break into my house and steal my mom's familiar for your *abuela*."

A chill as deep as February slithered up Cel's back, and the pee she'd been holding in threatened to flood out. She bit her bottom lip and squeezed her thighs together until the urge passed. "My *abuela* didn't send us to your house." She took another step forward. "And nobody touched your mom's stupid fucking cat."

Jose's friend, the guy in the Cowboys hat, emerged from in between the booths and walked up behind Jose. "I don't see the other two anywhere."

"They're out there somewhere, so go fucking find them," Jose ordered.

Cel waited for the guy to nod and walk away before saying, "I asked a couple of my friends go to your house with me. And I," she tapped her chest, "crawled in through the window to look for a book that could help me reverse the curse your mom put on *Tia* Dillo." She pointed at Jeff whose eyes were swollen with terror. "He's eleven years old. He didn't know anything about it. He was at home asleep for God's sake."

"Don't fucking lie, Cel. We know you took Frito, and I don't care if this shithead was there or not. He's with you now, and someone's got to pay."

"Then I'll pay." Cel held her hands out in front of her, palms up like she'd seen in movies, as though willing to be handcuffed.

Jose's eyes fell to her hands, moved back to her face. When he cackled, she lunged at him, reaching for his face, thrusting her thumbs into his eyes. He let go of Jeff and grabbed her hair as he lost his balance, and they all fell to the ground together like a mutated blob of flesh and bone.

Jeff worked himself free of the pile, crawled a few feet away, and jumped up. Cel grunted and struggled with Jose, biting his wrist and scratching his cheek deep enough to draw blood, but at nearly twice her weight, he gained the upper hand in no time at all. After stunning her with a head-butt to the temple, he rolled her onto her back, pinned her arms down with his knees, and rested his backside on her sternum.

"You always have been a scrappy little bitch," Jose said, fingering the scrape on his cheek. He reached in his pocket, pulled out a pocket knife, and flipped out the blade.

Cel tried to scream but Jose's weight on her chest made it impossible to pull in a deep enough breath. She could barely breathe. She closed her eyes and was in the middle of mentally reciting a strengthening spell when Jeff howled and jumped onto Jose's back. She opened her eyes as the jolt of both of their weight crushed down on her and watched Jose lift Jeff off and toss him aside like a sack of trash. Jeff landed flat on his back with a sickening thud and writhed and groaned from the pain.

"He's a feisty little shit, too, isn't he?" Jose ran his hand over his shaved head and pointed the knife at Cel's face. "Now, where were we?" He stroked his lucky stache. "What did you do with Frito?"

Cel raised her eyebrows and shook her head as if she didn't know what he meant.

He inched the knife closer. "Where is he?"

"I don't know," she managed.

"If you don't tell me, I swear, my mom will do stuff—"

He cut off when Parker slammed into him, driving his shoulder into Jose's chest and knocking him off of Cel. The impact jarred the knife from Jose's hand, and as he fumbled to pick it back up, Parker began punching him in the side of the head. After six or seven solid blows, Jose covered his face and head with his arms. As Parker jumped up and gave him a series of hard kicks to the stomach, Cel helped Jeff to his feet.

"Parker," Abby hollered. "Let's go." She was standing outside the perimeter rope, in between Natalie and Omar, who were holding up the rope for Cel and Jeff to duck under. Once Parker joined them, they fled the fairgrounds, zigzagging through the rows of cars back to the bike rack. Cel looked back over her shoulder only once, when Jose's final threat caught up with them in the middle of the parking lot.

"You will pay! You hear me? You! Will! Pay!"

Chapter 18 - Cel

At the bike rack, Parker removed Cel's bike, and without asking her permission, straddled the frame and placed a foot on the highest pedal. She hopped onto the pegs and held onto his shoulders as he aimed the bike away from the fairgrounds, homeward. They looked back over their shoulders and watched everyone else arrive, mount their bikes, and line up behind them. Everyone was breathing hard, faces slathered with sweat, eyes wild with adrenaline, but no one said a word. Natalie was the last to arrive and frantically struggled to remove her bike. When she finally jerked the front tire free, the handle bar jabbed her ribs, and she dropped her hat and yelled, "Damn it."

"You all right?" Cel asked.

Abby shot daggers at Cel with her eyes. "Like you care."

"What is that supposed to mean?"

"It's *your* fault if she's hurt. That's what it means." Abby jabbed an accusatory finger at Cel. "All of this is *your* fault. It's *your* fault Jeff's hurt. It's *your* fault Parker had to beat the crap out of Jose. It's *your* fault they recognized me and ruined our night. It's *your* fault they're even after us to begin with." She shrugged her shoulders. "And for what? Do you really think that stupid cat you stole was worth it? Your aunt isn't getting any better."

If anyone else agreed or disagreed with Abby, they didn't voice it. A silence as thick as a blanket, as cold as snow, shrouded the Cricket Hunters. Cel knew Abby was technically right, and part of her felt intense guilt for causing her friends pain and distress, putting them in harm's way. But another part of her, the lifetime Cricket Hunter card holder, the one-for-all, all-for-one member, the one who knew she didn't force anyone to do anything, felt needlessly attacked.

Eventually, Cel gathered enough moisture in her mouth to speak. "I didn't mean for anyone to get hurt." Her voice cracked with the last word. She cleared her throat, stepped off of the pegs, and faced Abby. "I had to try something to help my *tia*." A deep, shaky breath. "And I told you two or three times that night you didn't have to come with me, anyway."

Abby shook her head and continued spitting accusations as though she hadn't heard a word Cel had said. "And it's going to be *your* fault when they come after us again, too. Because now that they know who we are —"

"Hey, hey," Parker interjected. "Will you two knock it off? You can settle this *after* we're a safe distance away from them? Get on, Cel. We need to get out of here."

"Yeah, come on," Omar chimed in as he nervously glanced back toward the fair. "We should get a move on. Pronto."

"I don't have anything else to say, anyway," Abby said. And with that, she pedaled away, and the others followed suit.

As they made their way back to the Gateway neighborhood, their bikes tearing holes in the still night air, Omar was the only one to speak, and he only said one sentence as everyone slowed when they reached his and Natalie's turn off. "I think I'll start the round robin in a little bit so we know everyone made it home okay."

Parker nodded in agreement, but no one else responded.

Round robin was the circle of communication the hunters had started using in the first grade. Nobody could remember who'd had the initial idea, or why they'd first used it, but it was undoubtedly a spinoff of the whisper game they'd played on the magic carpet in kindergarten. It worked like this: if one person had an idea, or plan, or gossip, or whatever, rather than that person calling everyone, they called the next person in the circle, who called the next, and so on until the person who started the thread received a final call signifying that everyone had been contacted. The circle was alphabetical—Abby, Cel, Natalie, Omar, Parker—because, as first graders, that was the first idea that came to mind, and the calls weren't to last longer than five minutes. As they'd aged, they'd used the method less and less, and when they did, it was usually for silly reasons, a form of nostalgia on whimsical nights mostly. This was the first time any one of them had suggested using it for safety.

Parker, Cel, Abby, and Jeff continued on as Natalie and Omar cut down Garrett Street and rode out of sight. When they reached Abby's driveway a few minutes later, Abby and Jeff rode up into the yard and hopped off their bikes. After retrieving the house key she'd hidden in the mailbox and unlocking the door, Abby briefly locked eyes with Parker before marching inside and flicking on the porch light. When Cel glanced back a few seconds later as Parker continued down the street, Jeff was standing in the doorway with his Bart Simpson doll under his arm, his face lit by the light's warm glow. She threw her hand up in the air, and he did the same.

Rather than standing and holding on to Parker's shoulders like she did when the other hunters were around, Cel looped her arms around his chest, closed her eyes, and laid her head on his back. They rode in silence, inhaling and exhaling in unison. As Parker slowed to a stop behind his dad's truck in the driveway, a sharp, urgent pain suddenly blared through Cel's lower abdomen. Now that she'd calmed down and her adrenaline rush had subsided, her need to pee returned with a vengeance.

She jumped off the bike, dashed over to the dark walkway between the garage and the Dodge Ram on the side of the house, pulled down her shorts, squatted, and relieved herself.

Parker approached her as she pulled up her shorts and thumbed at the house. "You know we have toilets inside, right?"

"Ha, ha," she replied while buttoning her shorts.

"They flush and everything."

"Smartass." She stepped forward and tried to punch his shoulder, but he grabbed her wrist and pulled her to him. They studied each other's eyes for a moment, lips inches apart, breaths colliding, then Parker wrapped his arms around her waist, forcing their hips together, and kissed her. She could feel how much he liked her, and, as one of his hands slid down her backside beneath her jeans and underwear, she reached down and rubbed his crotch. The kissing intensified, and he spun her around and backed her up against the house. He ran his other hand up her shirt, under the bra, and she moaned and forced her hand down his pants.

They had gone this far before. She had even finished him off a couple of times, let him touch her down there with his hand, too, but she'd always been able to resist the urge, and his persistence, to go all the way. Tonight, though, the combination of the excitement of the fair, and the danger of the Jose chase, and the fact Parker had come back for her, rescued her, made the urge harder than ever to subdue. Tonight, her cautious inner voice, the voice that had always usually overridden her urges (*No. Stop. You're too young. You could get pregnant.*), sounded farther away than ever before. Tonight, maybe—

Cel's eyes snapped opened, and she pulled away from Parker when the roar of an engine startled her. She reflexively crouched as headlight beams crept down the road and stopped at the foot of Parker's driveway. Parker copied her and turned his head so his better cricket ear pointed toward the road. They watched the lit road for a moment, listening to the car idling just out of sight to their right. It had a monster engine, a muscle car engine. Like Jose's Mustang. But it wasn't loud enough to disguise the sound of a car door opening and closing. Cel grabbed Parker's hand as images of Jose marching across the lawn with an anger-forged face and a baseball bat in his hand like he had outside his own house that night she'd stolen Frito flooded her mind. Parker looked at her, gave her hand a firm squeeze and nod of assurance, and then led her to the corner of the garage where they peeked at the street.

A blue Firebird with the glass T-tops removed was parked in front of Parker's neighbor's house. Not a red Mustang. Not Jose's car. Not Jose. Cel released a shaky sigh of relief. The white guy driving the car had a mullet, a wide grin on his face, and one hand cockily angled atop the wheel. Parker's seventeen-year-old neighbor Cindy Lowden was skip-walking to her front porch with a stuffed animal in one hand and a balloon in the other. When she reached the front porch and glanced back at the car, the guy waved, then cranked up the radio and eased away from the curb.

Once the car was out of sight, Cel faced Parker and let go of his hand. "That freaked me out. I was worried it was Jose."

Parker smiled a nonchalant smile, as if the notion of worrying were both foreign and absurd. "He'll never come here." He grabbed the front of her shorts and pulled her closer to him. "Now, where were we?"

She turned her head down and sideways when he tried to kiss her. "He will find out where you live, you know? And he will try to get revenge." She looked up. "He said so himself. Especially on you. Maybe even on your family." She shook her head. "And what if he brings friends with him? And a bat? Or that knife? Or a gun? I know Maria has a couple." Cel's heart rate escalated with each spoken fear. Sweat began collecting on her palms. The possibilities kept coming. "And what is Maria going to do? Will she try something on us or my *abuela*? If she could do that to *Tia* Dillo then—"

Parker put a finger on her lips as if she were a child. "Calm down."

Cel knocked his finger away. "Don't tell me to calm down. This is not a joke. This is real. We need a plan." She bit her lip and looked moonward. For the first time that evening, she noticed chirping crickets in the distance.

Parker watched her until he found the right words. "I'm sorry," he said. "I know it's real."

A few seconds ticked by before she met eyes with him. "We need to call the cops and tell them that he attacked me with a knife at the fair."

"But then he'll tell the cops about you breaking into his house and stealing Frito."

"I'll deny it. It'll be his word against mine. There's no proof I was ever there."

"He'll just do the same thing about the fair. There's no proof of that, either. The charges won't stick."

"So what? At least it'll let him know other people are watching. I think if the cops question him, he'll be way less likely to come after any of us. At least for a while. I guarantee you he doesn't want to go to jail. When he was busted with pot last year, *Tia* Dillo said he bawled like a baby at the thought of spending any real time behind bars."

Parker glanced up and down the street, at the front door, and then his eyes landed on Cel's. "What about Maria? You really think she'll try cursing us or something?"

Cel inhaled, held it, nodded, then exhaled. "I'll have to talk to my *abuela* about it. Which means I'll have to tell her about Frito, too."

"What do you think she'll say?"

"She'll be mad." Regret gushed over Cel as the realization of the coming dark stint settled in, causing her chest to tighten and her eyes to tear up. She shook her head in self-disappointment. "I'm so sorry, Parker. Abby was right. This is all my fault." Tears streamed down her cheeks. "I shouldn't have dragged you guys into this."

Parker pulled her in for a hug, and she rested her head on his chest. "You didn't drag us into anything."

He sounded honest and sincere to Cel, and though she felt an inkling of an urge to look at his eyes to verify her belief, she held back.

They stood there for a full minute before Parker's porch light popped on. Cel snapped her head up and hurried to her bike at the end of the driveway, wiping her eyes with her flannel sleeve as she went.

Parker called out her name twice, once when she hopped onto her bike, and again when she was rolling out of the driveway, but she didn't look back. She stared straight ahead and pedaled as fast as she could.

At home, she used the spare key hidden on the back porch to enter the empty house. Yesenia wasn't home yet, and Cel guessed she'd probably fallen asleep at the hospital again. After walking through the house with a steak knife in her hand, whispering the protection spell over and over, turning on every light, checking every closet, under every bed, the small attic and single car garage filled with furniture and boxes, she took a quick, hot shower, crawled into bed, and pulled the covers all the way over her head.

She was exhausted. She had just dozed off when the retro, clear phone on her bedside table rang, streaking fluorescent blue light across her room. She shot upright and stared at the phone for a moment before answering.

It was Abby, playing her part in the round robin. When she greeted Cel, she didn't sound angry, which surprised Cel almost as much as her willingness to even call, but she didn't sound happy, either. She was floating somewhere in between, in the bored, obligatory zone. She probably wouldn't have called if Parker hadn't been her round robin caller. Cel figured he'd talked her into it somehow, maybe even asked her to "please do it, for [him]," knowing that would work. She didn't say much, only a few arbitrary comments about the *Singled Out* rerun she was watching on MTV, Jeff's obsession with his stupid Bart Simpson doll, and how tired she was. Anyone listening in on their two or three minute conversation would've never guessed at the magnitude of their night.

Chapter 19 - Cel

Two days after the fair, Cel, Natalie, and Omar stopped by Oak Mott Memorial Hospital after school for their daily visit and learned that *Tia* Dillo had suffered two massive strokes and had been moved to the Intensive Care Unit (ICU). The doctors had used the defibrillator paddles on her heart three times after the second one in order to bring her back. Now she breathed via machine. Her prognosis was grim. Twenty-four hours to live. Maybe.

After Natalie and Omar left, Cel was allowed to sit at Dillo's bedside with Yesenia. She slid her hands inside her flannel shirt sleeves, pulled her legs up onto the chair underneath her, and placed her backpack on her lap to help combat her intermittent shivers. For the next two hours, she barely moved. She just sat there listening to Yesenia continuously whisper healing and strengthening spells as the heart monitor and breathing machine beeped and chugged in the background. Cel purposefully stared at the floor a majority of the time, only stealing brief glances at her *abuela* and *tia* when a young, lithe, blonde-haired nurse in pink scrubs came and went twice at the top of each hour to check the machines and IV bags. She knew that if she looked at *Tia* Dillo or Yesenia for too long or too hard, she'd burst into tears.

Tia Dillo looked nothing like *Tia* Dillo. Her skin hung off her meatless skull like wet paper, and her chest twitched awkwardly when the breathing machine forced air into her lungs. That, along with the mainline jutting out of her chest, IVs in her hands, blood pressure cuff around her bicep, catheter tube trailing out from under the sheets, and the fat snake of a tube shoved down her throat, she appeared more like a cog in a machine than an organic human.

And Yesenia looked nothing like Yesenia, either. Sure, she had her hair neatly braided down her back, her blue dress starched and pressed, and sat with perfect posture, hinting at her typical composure and strength, but when Cel looked into her eyes, she didn't see the eyes of a strong, confident, vibrant, wise, woman. She saw the eyes of a scared little girl. She saw helplessness, desperation. A crushed soul hiding behind the veneer of a stable structure. And seeing her *abuela* in such a state made her bowels churn with guilt. What if Maria had performed a new curse, a new ritual, to finish off *Tia* Dillo, after hearing that Cel had been the one to break into her house? What if, by killing Frito, Cel had caused this escalation? Yesenia had been angry when Cel had told her about the cat and the following fair incident. She'd scolded Cel for a good hour, but she'd also forgiven her almost immediately afterward. The day after the fair, she'd even helped Cel create protective talismans for the hunters to hang above their beds, and she had gathered them in a circle in the backyard and performed a shielding ritual to help protect them from curses. But what if, Cel thought as she sat in the cold ICU room staring at the white tile floor, her *abuela* blamed her for *Tia* Dillo's rapid downfall? What if that's why she would barely look at Cel?

Thirty minutes after the Cricket Hunters had planned to meet in Cel's backyard to hunt, Natalie appeared outside the glass wall looking into Dillo's room and gave a tentative wave when Cel finally looked up. Cel raised an acknowledging hand, patted Yesenia's shoulder, gestured at Natalie, and said, "I'm going to go talk to Natalie. I'll be right back. Do you need anything?"

Continuing to whisper spells, Yesenia shook her head without looking at Cel.

Cel knew it was selfish to leave Yesenia alone, but she needed a break from the cold room, from the steady beeps and chugs counting down the last hours of *Tia* Dillo's life, from her *abuela's* incessant desperate whispers. She needed a brief respite from the crushing pressure of lingering on Death's porch. So she left the room as gingerly as possible, like a guilty sinner exiting a rapt congregation during the heart of a sermon.

Natalie greeted her with a one-armed hug in the hallway. She had switched to sweatpants since leaving the hospital and had put on her Astros cap. She raised the paper bag in her right hand. "Me and Mom made you guys some bread. It's not much, but…" She shrugged.

Cel took the bag and smiled weakly. "Thanks."

Natalie's eyes moved to *Tia* Dillo, but then quickly moved back to Cel, as if she didn't want to look at a dying person too long or too hard, either. Other than the loss of family pets like dogs and cats, hamsters and gold fish, none of the hunters had experienced much death, and never firsthand. Never face-to-face. Parker had lost both of his grandparents on his father's side, but they'd died before he was born. Natalie's aunt, Bonnie McIntyre, had drowned in Lake Travis when Natalie was a toddler, so she barely remembered her. And one of Omar's grandfathers had passed from a heart attack recently, maybe a year or year and half ago if Cel remembered correctly, but he lived in Mexico, and Omar had met him only a handful of times and hadn't attended the funeral.

"Any changes?" Natalie asked.

Cel shook her head.

Natalie nodded sadly and looked down, shielding her eyes with the bill of her cap as she fidgeted with her hands. "Everyone else is in the waiting room." She looked up. "Me and Omar met Parker and Abby at your house and told them what happened. Will your grandma care if you...or do you want to..." She drifted off and thumbed behind her.

Cel simply nodded, and then followed Natalie to the ICU waiting room.

The hunters were the only people in the waiting room save for one elderly man dressed in dingy overalls sitting alone in the corner. Between his legs, a cane rested against his thigh, and he stared at the nothing in front of him with a faraway look in his eyes. On the opposite corner of the room, Parker, Abby, and Omar had arranged five of the chairs to form a closed-off circle. Parker closed his copy of *The Illustrated Man*, and Abby's and Omar's hushed discussion stopped as Cel and Natalie approached and sat in the two empty chairs.

"How is she?" Parker asked in a hushed tone, as though Dillo's condition were a secret.

Clenching the top of the sack of hot bread on her lap with both hands, Cel met eyes with him. "Bad. Very bad."

He touched her knee. "Sorry." After Abby, Omar, and Natalie echoed his condolences, he added, "Are you okay?"

Cel bit down on her bottom lip and nodded, lied, her eyes brimming with tears. She was far from okay. Such an overload of emotion. On top of the sadness and guilt she felt about *Tia* Dillo's situation, she was also terrified she'd been cursed.

Since the day after the fair, the day Yesenia had taken her to the Oak Mott police station to file a report about Jose assaulting her, she'd had trouble sleeping. And not because she was overly worried about Jose anymore. She was a *little* worried, had even purchased small cans of mace at Kmart for each hunter to carry in their pocket just in case, but none of them had seen him since the night at the fair, and she assumed he'd lay low for a while. The reason she'd had trouble sleeping was because of the crickets lurking around Yesenia's house. They seemed louder than before, closer, their relentless chirps triggering surges of paranoid thoughts in her. Lying in bed alone while Yesenia was at the hospital, she had been covering her head with her pillow, and repeating out loud what Parker had assured her. That they only seemed louder because the hunters hadn't been hunting. That their numbers had grown simply because the hunters had been going inside before sunset the past two nights as an added safety precaution. But no matter how many times she repeated the rationale, she couldn't quiet the crickets. She couldn't dispel the fear that Maria had sent them—*espiritus venganza*—to torment her just like she had with *Tia* Dillo, and that her *abuela's* protection attempts would do no good.

Natalie leaned over and put her arm around Cel's shoulders, and Cel closed her eyes. No one spoke. Seconds stretched into minutes.

When Cel opened her eyes, she scanned her friends' solemn faces, and Omar asked, "Have you been sleeping any better?"

"Not really."

"The crickets still bothering you?" Parker asked.

She hesitated when Abby leaned back and pushed out a loud breath, but eventually nodded.

"You want me to steal some of my mom's sleeping pills?" Parker asked. "They might help."

Cel instinctively shook her head. Through teachings and by example, Yesenia and *Tia* Dillo had ingrained in her the idea that medications wouldn't trump magic. "If Maria's cursed me, they won't help much."

"But what if she hasn't?" Abby fired back. "What if you're just freaking out about *Tia* Dillo and the Jose thing, and those pills will help you rest and feel better?" Her eyes moved up to the ceiling for a moment, then moved back to Cel. "I mean, if she cursed you, why hasn't she cursed me or Parker? She knows we were involved, too."

Cel stared at Abby. Her expression remained neutral, her lips zipped. She didn't have the energy to debate Abby about her family's beliefs tonight, or defend herself against the notion that she was freaking out, or purposefully strange, or too superstitious, or just flat-out crazy.

"What if we go hunt the crickets around your house when we leave here?" Parker asked. "I'm up for it if everyone else is."

Cel wanted to jump up and hug him for the offer, kiss him for understanding her, show the others how he was her favorite, but she simply held eye contact with him instead, hoping her eyes relayed the same message. "Thanks, but you don't have to. I'll probably be staying here all night tonight, anyway."

"What if," Omar said, and all eyes snapped his way. He was looking at the ground, through the ground. His face was pinched with the deep thought of someone who'd been crunching numbers and percentages, running through a litany of possibilities, searching for the best solution to a problem. "Her curse is hurting you more than us because you believe in the power of her curses more. Kind of like in that movie, *Nightmare on Elm Street*, or that book, *It*."

"That's what *I* said," Abby professed. "It's all in her head."

Omar jerked his head toward Abby. "That's not what I meant." He met eyes with Cel and curved his eyebrows in an apologetic gesture. "I didn't mean it that way. I was just saying that maybe since you're more saturated in magic than we are, since you've been raised on it, live it all day, every day, are surrounded by it, and you're a lot more connected to Maria than we are, that's why it's affecting you more." He dipped his head and lightly shook it. "I don't know. It was just a thought."

Abby bumped his shoulder with her fist. "I think you think too much."

Omar looked up, a faint smile on his lips. "So does my mom."

Everyone, including Cel, lightly chuckled.

Natalie took her arm off of Cel's shoulder and pressed it against her own chest. "Well, I personally do believe there are powers out there that we can't all control or understand. Unexplainable things happen every day. Miracles happen all the time."

Cel flashed Natalie a shadow of a gracious smile, then looked at Omar. She knew he meant well. His analytics never carried malice. "I know what you're saying, but I think if it was that easy to block her curses, my *abuela* wouldn't be so worried, and *Tia* Dillo wouldn't be dying."

Whether they agreed with her or not, everyone gave slight nods, and then looked everywhere but at Cel. While the uncomfortable silence dragged on, Cel glanced at the sack in her lap and lay her hand flat across the bread. It was no longer hot, barely warm. That's what this place does, she thought. Death's doorstep. It drains the warmth and love and life from everyone and everything. She lifted the bag. "I better take this to my *abuela* before it gets too cold."

The other hunters' eyes found her, and they all nodded again. But rather than the awkward, uneasy nods she'd received minutes ago, these came quick, with a sense of relief that the unsettling pow-wow was ending. They didn't like being in the hospital any more than she did, and that was okay.

"You guys better leave so you can get home before dark, anyway."

"Are you sure you don't want us to stay a little longer?" Natalie asked.

"I'm sure. I need to get back in there with my *abuela*."

They all stood and hugged Cel, and she told them thanks for coming. Natalie told her to call if she needed anything and that they'd come by tomorrow after school if they hadn't heard from her. Parker asked if he could please borrow her bike for the ride home, promising to bring it back in tact whenever she wanted. Tonight, even. He could have his dad drive it back up in the back of his truck. She said of course he could use it, and not to worry about bringing it back; her *abuela's* car was there. Natalie waved as they filed away, and just before he was out of sight, Parker glanced back over his shoulder and winked, striking a warm flame in the center of Cel's chest as she spun and headed for Dillo's room.

But the flame quickly extinguished and the warmth vanished the second she turned onto Dillo's hall. She momentarily froze when a loud continuous beep pierced her ears and she saw an elderly nurse in blue scrubs rush from the nurse's station into Dillo's room. A few seconds later, the young blonde nurse who'd been checking the monitors all evening appeared in Dillo's doorway. She had one arm hooked around Yesenia's shoulders, the other locked onto her forearm. Yesenia was looking back over her shoulder. Indiscernible Spanish words streamed out of her mouth as she fought the nurse's attempt to guide her into the hall.

Cel dropped the sack of bread and ran toward Dillo's room, the blaring beep growing louder and louder as she went. When she reached her *abuela's* side, the young nurse passed Yesenia's arm to her as though it were a baton. "You need to keep her out here."

Yesenia continued spewing Spanish heartache as they stood there shoulder-to-shoulder and stared through the glass wall into *Tia* Dillo's room. A prim doctor with a puddle of white hair atop his head was inside with two nurses who were frantically removing blankets and clothing, exposing Dillo's bare chest. He had defibrillator paddles in his hands, urgency in his eyes. As Cel and Yesenia looked on, their eyes locked on Dillo's protruding ribcage, he yelled, "Clear," and *Tia* Dillo's body was violently jolted for the fourth time in twelve hours in an attempt to restart her heart.

Looking back, Cel wasn't certain if she saw the doctor paddle *Tia* Dillo five, or six, or even seven or eight or nine times. What she was certain of, however, was that after each paddle, as she held her breath in anticipation, the heart monitor continued wailing, its unyielding cry as knife-like to her mind as fingernails down a chalkboard.

Chapter 20 - Parker

Sans Cel, the hunters walked out of the hospital to a colorful sunset. Various shades of red and pink and gold and blue colored the cotton ball clouds hovering above the day's last edge of sun. The onslaught of hues and their otherworldly smearing brought to mind a description Parker had read in *The Illustrated Man* earlier in the waiting room. Something about a sky of diamonds and sapphires and emeralds and streaking comets. That summer, his sister Jennifer had given him her worn copy with a bald tattooed man on the cover, and he'd quickly discovered that Bradbury was a painter with words, his descriptions often conveying more in one sentence than most authors did in an entire chapter. As Parker followed the others around the north end of the two-story brick building, he felt as though he were looking at a Bradbury crafted sky. As though God Bradbury had whispered a sentence into existence.

When they reached their bikes, which were propped against a hurricane fence behind a row of dumpsters on the side of the hospital, Omar, Natalie, and Abby mounted theirs, and Parker mounted Cel's. All four aimed their bikes in the direction of home, at the dying sun. Pockets of chirping crickets provided the only noise.

"How long you think until it's all the way down?" Abby asked.

"Fifteen minutes or so," Omar said.

"Just enough time to get home before dark if we hurry," Natalie said.

Abby glanced at Parker. "You don't *really* want to go cricket hunting at Cel's do you?"

Parker listened to the nearby crickets for a moment, then shook his head. "It doesn't matter."

"Good," Abby said, and pedaled away. "Let's go."

The clouds morphed and the sky lost color as the hunters crossed streets and cut across lots. By the time they merged onto Sylvia Street on the outer rim of the Gateway neighborhood, only a sliver of burnt orange lined the horizon. They stopped on the sidewalk beneath a street light where Sylvia merged with Yankee Road—the road Omar and Natalie needed to take north, Abby and Parker, south.

"Well," Parker said. "This is where we part ways."

Natalie took off her hat, wiped the sweat from her forehead with her forearm, and slid the hat back on. "Do you guys think we should—" She cut off and turned her attention to the road behind them when the sound of an approaching engine challenged her words.

All heads swiveled to follow the red Mustang with tinted windows as it sped by at well above the posted thirty-mile-per-hour limit.

"Oh, shit," Parker said as the car's brake lights lit up, and it abruptly pulled to the side of the road about half a block away. "Is that Jose's car?"

"I don't know," Omar answered. "It's the same color and model, but I didn't look at the plate. His starts with BLP."

As they squinted at the backend of the Mustang trying to make out the plate, waiting for any sign of movement, an unsettling quiver danced up Parker's legs and spine, urging him to move. No matter how miniscule, he at least had a chance of surviving a face-to-face encounter with Jose. But he and the other hunters had no chance at all surviving a car-to-bike encounter. His eyes bounced from Natalie to Omar to Abby, back to the taillights and rumbling exhaust pipe. The engine revved, relaxed, revved. "I think we should get out of here." He met eyes with Omar. "You guys stay off the roads as much as you can. I'll start the round robin in thirty minutes."

Omar nodded, and with Natalie on his tail, rounded his bike north and pedaled into the dark alley that separated the houses facing Yankee Road and a seemingly endless line of storage units.

When Parker turned to tell Abby to follow him, she was already veering into the same alley but on the opposite side of Sylvia Street, heading south. Parker called out her name as he wheeled Cel's bike around. At the foot of the alley, he paused and glanced back at the Mustang again. A few seconds passed before it peeled away from the curb, U-turning his direction. When the headlights popped on, he chased after Abby with everything he had. The cat and mouse game was on.

He passed three backyards before he heard the Mustang turn into the alley. Abby was two houses ahead of him. "Cut through the Collins' yard," he yelled, and she curved into a fenceless backyard on her left.

At the edge of the Collins's yard, Parker looked back over his shoulder. The Mustang had stopped twenty yards behind him, where a dumpster had been irregularly set and partially jutted out into the alley, shrinking the space for vehicles to pass. That along with the uneven terrain fraught with craters and loose, large rocks had apparently given the driver pause. The Mustang engine gave a defiant throaty roar, and then it began reversing out of the alley.

Parker hurried through the Collins yard and turned south onto a fifty-yard uphill section of Yankee Road. Abby was on the sidewalk two houses away, struggling to maintain her speed, repeatedly checking the road behind her. Parker caught up with her and encouraged her onward, repeatedly glancing back as well. When they reached the top of the hill, the Mustang swerved onto Yankee Road, headed straight at them.

"Come on!" Parker hopped the curb into a vacant lot, and Abby followed.

Near the back of the lot, Parker's front tire clipped a hunk of discarded metal hidden in the overgrown weeds. The impact jolted his hands off of the handlebars. As he slammed onto the ground and the bike crashed down on his back, the Mustang screeched to a stop in front of the lot.

Abby slowed as she approached Parker, panic etched on her face. "Parker? Are you okay?"

He squirmed his way out from under the bike and jumped to his feet. "Keep going," he ordered as he righted the bike. She obeyed, and as she slipped down the alley at the back of the lot, the Mustang driver gunned the engine. Parker threw his leg over the frame, found the pedal, and then chanced a glance at the Mustang. The driver's side window was lowered about six inches, smoke curling from the opening. When Parker forced his weight down on the pedal and began rolling toward the alley, waves of amused laughter drifted from the car. As he picked up speed and disappeared behind the neighboring house, a number of Spanish words caught up with him before the Mustang sped away, leaving the rustle of flung loose gravel in its wake.

Though massive surges of adrenaline were tracking through Parker's veins as he raced to catch up with Abby, his fears of confrontation subsided. The chase was over. If Jose had really wanted to fight, to hurt, to maim, he wouldn't have stayed in the car. He'd had plenty of time to get out and rush Parker in that lot. But he hadn't. He'd simply laughed like someone watching a dog dosed with beer stumble around the backyard bumping into things. Maybe he was too high to give chase, or maybe he was waiting for a more isolated scenario where no one would be able to hear the commotion and call the police. Either way, or any other way, Parker didn't care. For tonight, he believed Jose had just been fucking with them, teasing them, trying to torment them. Nevertheless, Parker proceeded with caution as he crisscrossed through the alleys and streets of Gateway searching for Abby.

The starry, moon-bright night sky had taken over by the time he emerged from an alley onto Chaparral Street, Abby's street, ten minutes later. The trip had taken twice as long as it should've because he'd looped back a few times, checking different routes he thought Abby might've taken to make sure she hadn't crashed or been injured or something. Two houses from hers, he saw that her porch light was off, but her bike was lying in the center of the driveway on its side. He pedaled to the side of the house, and as he hopped off of Cel's bike in front of the gate that led into Abby's backyard, the scent of fresh cigarette smoke tickled his nose. He tried the gate but found it locked.

"Abby," he whispered forcefully.

No response, so he tried again, a little louder.

Seconds later, the gate flew open, and Abby hurled herself into him and wrapped her arms around his neck. She turned her head sideways and pressed her damp cheek on his neck and whimpered. She was trembling.

"Are you okay?" he asked.

Eventually, she pulled away and nodded. "Are you?"

"Yeah."

She crossed her arms over her chest, careful to keep the glowing cherry away from her skin, and then nervously looked over his shoulder at the road. "We should go inside. What if he comes here?"

Parker rubbed her upper arms as if trying to warm them. "Don't worry. If he wanted to hurt us, he would've. He won't come here. He was just trying to scare us."

Holding eye contact with him, she took a shaky puff off the cigarette and offered it to Parker. He partook and handed it back. She glanced over his shoulder again, her eyes darting left to right, scanning the road.

"I'm going to put our bikes in the backyard just in case he drives by," Parker said, hoping to somewhat mollify her.

She puffed, blowing the smoke out of the side of her mouth to avoid assaulting Parker's face with it. Pockets of crickets were singing somewhere in the alley behind the house. "I don't really think that'll matter. This is Oak Mott. *Six degrees of everyone*. I'm sure he already knows where we all live, anyway."

"Probably. But I don't want to give him the chance to damage or steal them." He took the cigarette from her, used it, passed it back, and then retrieved both bikes and rested them up against the back of the house under her bedroom window. "Besides." He threw his hands out to his side as if he were a magician's assistant displaying the bikes to an awestruck audience. "If you ever need to make a quick escape, just hop out the window and off you go on your fully fueled escape pod."

A flicker of a smile moved over Abby's mouth. "You're ridiculous." She shook her head, then glanced back at the road again. "You want to come in for a minute? It's probably been close to thirty minutes. We should call Nat and Omar."

He nodded, and after quickly going back and locking the gate, he met Abby on the back porch and followed her into the house through the sliding glass doors.

In the kitchen, Abby grabbed the cordless phone off the receiver and dialed Natalie's number while Parker made his way into the adjacent dining room. He sat across the table from Jeff who was spooning chocolate ice cream from the carton into his mouth. Jeff's mouth was a sticky brown mess. Bart Simpson was perched on his lap, his spiky hair and button black eyes barely visible over the table top. Parker flashed Jeff a tight-lipped smile as Abby walked into the room and stopped behind his chair. The analog clock hanging on the faux-wood panel wall behind Jeff read ten after eight.

"Hey, Nat. You guys make it home okay? Good. Yeah. Yeah. It followed us…No. No, we're okay. Yeah. Yeah. No. He's here with me and Jeff right now. Okay. I will. Okay. Bye."

Abby returned the phone to the receiver in the kitchen and then came back to the dining room. "They're fine."

"Who?" Jeff asked with the spoon between his lips.

"Don't talk with your mouth full," Abby shot back. "Besides, it's none of your business, twerp." She pulled out the chair next to Parker and sat down. "She wants me to call her back after you let me know that you made it home okay, too." Staring blankly at her brother, she sucked in a deep breath. Her shoulders rose and pinched inward as she inhaled, loosening her shirt to expose a long line of cleavage.

Parker noticed but pretended not to when she pushed out the breath and her shoulders dropped. "What's wrong?" he asked.

"I just wish Cel hadn't dragged us into all of this." She shook her head. "We wouldn't be running around scared all the time if it wasn't for her stupid ass. She's so fucking immature with all that magic shit." She turned her attention to Parker and measured him, her dark eyes sliding back and forth across his. He knew she wanted validation, backing, and he gave it to her with a nod.

"She's not stupid," Jeff said. "She saved me from that guy at the fair."

"She's the reason *that guy* was after you in the first place. She stole his mom's cat because she thought it had magic powers for God's sake." Abby put her palms on the table, squinted, and shook her head as though baffled at herself. "Why am I explaining myself to an eleven-year-old? You need to go to your room."

Jeff plucked the spoon out of his mouth. "I don't want to."

"I don't care." Abby stood and pointed down the hall. "Go."

Focused on scraping ice cream from the carton wall, Jeff calmly replied, "No."

She marched over to him and grabbed him by the ear and pulled him to his feet like Ms. Bogan, the Oak Mott Grade School music teacher for five decades running, often did to disobedient students. He dropped the spoon on the table, and Bart toppled to the floor. "If you don't stop, I'm telling mom."

"Go ahead."

He grabbed her wrist with both hands, and as she twisted his ear, three hard pounds sounded on the front door, and she froze.

Parker jumped up.

Jeff took advantage of his sister's paralysis and knocked her hand away. "Get away from me," he said, shoving her.

"Shut up," Parker ordered him in an angry whisper, glaring at him with narrowed eyes.

Jeff and Abby eyed Parker. A look of terror haunted Abby's eyes. Jeff appeared both shocked and confused by the ferocity behind Parker's expression. "Why are you—"

Abby pressed her hand over Jeff's mouth, and Parker put his finger to his lips. "Shhhh."

Three more knocks.

"No one ever knocks this late," Abby whispered. "Do you think it's Jose?"

Parker shook his head. "No way he'd knock on your door. Could it be your mom? Maybe she forgot her key?"

"She doesn't get off until ten-thirty."

Two more knocks. "Abby! Jeff!"

Abby's eyes enlarged. "It's my dad."

Jeff's eyes suddenly filled with terror, mimicking his sister's.

"I know you're in there!" The door knob jiggled. "It's not right for your mom to leave you alone like this! Let me in!"

"What are we going to do?" Abby whispered. She took her hand off of Jeff's mouth. He scooped up Bart Simpson and pressed him tight against his chest.

Parker held Abby's gaze, his mind reeling, adrenaline coursing through his body like a raging river for the second time in an hour. Long seconds passed, the clock on the wall ticking like a doomsday countdown. When a series of slaps came from the sliding glass door followed a deep voice calling out Abby's and Jeff's names again, he flicked off the dining room light, and crouched low to avoid detection through the kitchen window. Then he snuck into the kitchen, snagged the cordless phone, and hurried back. "Is there anywhere we can hide while we call someone for help?"

"The basement in the garage," Jeff whispered. "The light down there doesn't work, but there's tons of stuff to hide behind. Mom can never find me when I hide down there."

"Perfect," Parker whispered. "Let's go. And be quiet."

He shoved the phone in his pocket and followed the Powell siblings down the hall and out the door leading into the garage, locking the door behind him from the inside, hoping that might dissuade Tom from suspecting they were out there if he broke in.

In the corner of the garage, they raised the rectangular door, which opened and closed via a fifty pound counter-weight attached to a pulley system on the wall, and slipped down the dark staircase. Jeff went down first, and quick. Parker went last pulling the door closed behind him, careful to keep it from slamming shut. Halfway down the narrow staircase, he bumped into Abby's back, and she grabbed his arm to keep from falling when gravity forced her forward. Once she steadied, he grabbed her by the hand, and they proceeded to the foot of the stairs.

"Jeff," Abby whispered into the lightless void.

"Over here." His whisper came from behind them, somewhere under the staircase, seemingly somewhere far away. "There's another hiding spot behind the boxes over there."

"*Over where?*" Abby whispered in frustration. "We can't see shit, and I never come down here."

"Follow the wall, and you'll feel them."

Parker eased in front of Abby and followed Jeff's instructions, running his free hand along the wall until he came across a stack of cardboard boxes. He slithered around a few uneven stacks, shimmied behind them, and sat down with his back against the cool cement. Abby sat next to him and pulled her knees up to her chest. "You got the phone?" she whispered.

Parker fished the cordless from his pocket. "I can't see the buttons."

"Here." Abby touched his arm and traced it to the phone. "I can do it. Should I call my mom or 9-1-1?"

"9-1-1. They'll get here quicker."

"Okay."

Parker listened as Abby fidgeted with the phone, punched rubber buttons, and then a loud dull beep echoed through the room. More button mashing, and the beep stopped. Abby repeated the motions with the same result. "I think we're too far away from the receiver," she whispered.

She tried one more time to no avail, dropped the phone onto the cold cement floor with a clatter, and pressed her forehead onto her knees.

When Parker heard soft sobs, he put his arm over her shoulders but didn't immediately speak. He breathed in the scent of moist cardboard for a moment, long enough to push back the fear creeping to the forefront of his own mind. Well aware he was the oldest hunter, the strongest, the biggest, and that the others often looked to him for leadership, he knew the words he needed to say, and that he needed to say them with confidence to assure Abby, to keep her calm. "It's going to be all right. We're safe down here. There's no way he'll find us."

Abby twisted sideways and rested her head on his shoulder, wrapped her arm around the front of his midsection. Stroking her hair, Parker angled his cricket ear toward the door and listened to the pressing silence. Seconds turned into minutes. Eventually, Jeff started whispering, most of the sentences a string of indecipherable hush, but Parker occasionally thought he heard the name Bart. In the darkness, usually unnoticed sounds suddenly became audible, tiny discomforts intense. Parker could hear a slight, annoying nose-whistle every time Abby exhaled, and the spine of the paperback in his back pocket seemed to be digging into his butt cheek harder and harder with each passing second. When Abby momentarily lifted her head off his shoulder to reposition herself, he tilted and pulled *The Illustrated Man* out of his back pocket to remedy the discomfort.

"You know, after tonight we should have smooth sailing for a while."

"*What?*" Abby laid her head back on his shoulder.

"My mom always says bad things always come in threes, and today has given us all three." He counted on his fingers. "Dillo, Jose, and now your dad. So it can only get better from here, right?"

Abby inhaled and exhaled, her whole body inflating and deflating. She looped her arm around Parker's midsection again, tighter this time. "Do you think he's gone?"

Parker looked upward as if he could see through the darkness and the ceiling and know the truth. "Probably." He started running his hand through her hair. "Do you remember much about him?"

"Who?"

"Your dad."

"Good or bad stuff?"

"Either."

"I know my mom told everyone he was molesting me, and I don't think she'd make something like that up, but I don't remember any of it. I do remember watching him beat on my mom, though, and I remember not liking being alone with him, especially after he'd been smoking his pipe out back in the shed. But..." Abby shook her head without lifting it off of Parker's shoulder. "I don't know. I don't like to think about that stuff."

"What about good stuff?"

Parker felt a change in Abby's face, a smile. "He liked to dance. Sometimes when he got out of the shower, he'd strut into the living room in his white underwear with his hair slicked back and pick me up and dance around the room. Mom hated how he'd turn the radio up real loud and toss me into the air, but I loved it. He smelled so good."

A gap of time passed with nothing but breathing sounds and Jeff's faint whispers.

When Abby adjusted her position again and moved her hand to Parker's inner thigh, he placed his hand on her back. She started rubbing back and forth, inching toward his crotch, and he mimicked her, his hand sliding up her back beneath her shirt, into the waist of her shorts. She sat upright and kissed him, her warm tongue swirling rapidly inside his mouth. She threw her leg over his, straddling him, facing him. He ran his hand up her shirt, over her huge breasts. They moved and touched and kissed as Jeff whispered in the background. Parker lifted her shirt and put his mouth on her. When she moaned loud enough to quiet Jeff, he pulled away. She cupped her hands under his chin and kissed him hard.

"What is Cel going to think about this?" she asked.

"What do you mean?"

"Please. You know she has a major crush on you." A beat. A change in tone. "Do you like her?"

Unseen to Abby, Parker shook his head.

"Do you?"

"No," Parker lied. He did *like* Cel, a lot. He found her attractive, mysterious, witty, and challenging, but that didn't mean he couldn't like Abby, too. Or a handful of other girls in Oak Mott. He was young, enjoyed having options, liked flirting in general, and it wasn't as if he'd ever asked anyone to stay true to him. On his fifteenth birthday the previous year, his thrice divorced Uncle Marty, while sharing a secret beer with him in the backyard as his parents argued inside, had advised him to "take advantage of variety while he was still young and able," "play the field before he got old and fat and bald and tied down." Heeding that advice, Parker had made out with Somer Young at Huber Park a week earlier, and had been regularly talking on the phone deep into the night with Amy Lister—a sophomore lifeguard he'd met at the community pool in August. They had plans to go to the Buena Vista Drive-In sometime soon for a double matinee.

"But I don't think she needs to know about this," Parker added. He swallowed down the salty taste of Abby's saliva. "She might get pissed, and I sure as heck don't want to get cursed or hexed or anything." He poked her in the belly. "Do you?"

When Abby chuckled, he did too, and she smashed her lips onto his.

Chapter 21 - Yesenia

Yesenia stood bedside and held her dead sister's hand, waiting for Cel to return with the bag of supplies she'd stored in the back of her '82 Starlet. The IVs and tubes had been removed from Dolores's body, a white sheet pulled up to her chin. Her salt and pepper hair splayed out on the sides of her head like open pigeon wings. The fluorescent lights stole what little color remained from her face. Yesenia alternated between whispering an awareness spell and calming spell. The awareness one to prepare Dolores's spirit, the calming one for herself. Her chest and head ached, but she needed to stay vigilant, on point, and perform the death ceremony in a timely manner to ensure Dolores's safe delivery into the afterlife. Her mom had schooled her and Dolores on the ceremony shortly before her own death many moons ago.

When Cel returned, Yesenia instructed her to pay close attention, and then set the stage. She placed plumeria petals on the pillow around Dolores's head, a yellow plate with dried mango slices and *pan de leche* on her belly, a cup of *yerba buena* in the center of the plate—Dolores's favorites.

On top of Dolores's heart, she laid the doll their mom had made for Dolores when Dolores was a baby. Dolores had named the doll, made from used blankets and horse hair, Fatima. Yesenia had named hers Gabriela.

After placing four white stones on the corners of the bed, Yesenia lit a white pillar candle and began swirling it in a circle over Dolores's body. The doctor had granted her permission to perform any rites or rituals she wanted, so long as she didn't damage the body or light any candles. Yesenia didn't care what the white doctor had said. He didn't understand. With Cel sitting in a chair behind her softly crying and sniffling, she whispered the death acceptance spell and the transition spell, each four times in Spanish, then she raised the candle up high and whispered a guidance request to *Santa Muerte, La Huesuda*, The Bony Lady, The Hand-Holder.

She lowered the candle and moved it in a circle over Dolores four times clockwise, four times counter clockwise, and took her sister's hand. She spoke each sentence in Spanish once, then English once, so Cel would fully understand.

"Dolores Josefina Garcia-Ayala, *Tia* Dillo, Daughter, Sister, Friend, Witch, Healer.

"By the firmness of the earth, you were grounded in the physical world.

"By the swiftness of the air, you were open to knowledge and communication.

"By the light of fire, you were inspired with passion and love.

"By the flow of water, you were allowed to dream your dreams.

"By the greatness of the Source, you were given access to life.

"So now, by earth, air, fire, water, and the blessing of the Source, shall you pass into the next stage of your existence with strength, peace, and purpose."

Yesenia kissed her sister's forehead, whispered, "*Te amo, dulce hermana,*" and blew out the candle. She clenched her teeth and swallowed to keep from bursting into tears before facing Cel. "Do you want to say anything to her?"

Cel stood, and as she made her way to Dolores's bedside, wrapped her arms over her chest as though hugging herself. Following Yesenia's lead, she kissed Dolores on the forehead, and then whispered something into her ear, a short statement that Yesenia couldn't make out. When she met eyes with Yesenia and was unable to stifle her sobs, Yesenia pulled her in and hugged her as desperately as she had Dolores after their mother's death ceremony. Though separated by time and circumstance, the wakes of both instances were the same; two Garcia-Ayala females were left to share the pain of the worst losses of their lives.

"Is everything okay?" the young nurse in pink scrubs asked as she stepped into the room, startling them despite her cautious tone.

Yesenia rounded on the young nurse who was eyeing the candle, her expression suggesting she caught the hint of smoke clinging to the air. Yesenia glanced at the candle, dropped it into the bag on the ground beside the bed. "Yes. We're finished here. Will you please see to it that the items we left stay with her?"

The nurse's sympathetic eyes met Yesenia's. "Yes, ma'am. I'll make sure everything accompanies her to the funeral home."

"*Gracias.*"

Yesenia led Cel out of the room, past the nurses' station where the elderly nurse in blue scrubs looked up from her computer and offered condolences, and down to the main lobby. To mollify her growing anxiety that she hadn't specified the proper funeral home, she stopped at the check-in station and asked a large woman wearing a thick film of make-up and nametag reading SHONDA, to please call Dr. Bernard on the second floor to verify that Dolores would be transported to the Fernandez Funeral Home. Satisfied with Shonda's quiet confirmation, Yesenia and Cel made their way to the car, serenaded by chirping crickets as their feet smacked on the tarmac beneath a starless night sky.

They traveled the empty roads without speaking until Cel broke the silence two blocks from home. "I'm so sorry, *Buela*. If I hadn't killed Frito maybe *Tia* Dillo wouldn't have…" She dropped her face into her cupped hands, shaking her head. "I know you hate me right now."

"I don't hate you, *mija*." A deep breath. "And what Maria did to her was not your fault."

"But I made everything worse for her. I was trying to help, but I made it worse."

Yesenia agreed with the outcome of Cel's actions. She had made things worse. But not for Dolores. Sure, Frito's death, which she believed Maria had felt the second it happened due to their indelible connection, had hurt and infuriated Maria, but it hadn't caused an escalation of Dolores's death. Maria had already damaged Dolores beyond repair at that point. No, the impact of Frito's death had fallen on Cel and Yesenia, the duo she blamed for stripping away her familiar. And now, with Dolores out of the picture, Maria could focus her vengeance squarely on them.

Reciting a calming spell, Yesenia rubbed Cel's back. She needed Cel to remain mentally and spiritually strong. "*Esta bien*. Everything you did for her, you did to help, and she knows that."

Cel looked at Yesenia. She had the same scared expression on her face that she'd worn as a toddler when thunder rattled the windows. "Do *you*?"

Yesenia pulled the Starlet into her driveway and shut off the engine. She didn't agree with Cel's actions, but she knew her granddaughter's intent was good. She made eye contact with Cel, hoping the unconditional love she felt for her was evident in her gaze, and touched the center of Cel's chest with two fingers. "*Conozco tu corizon, mija.*"

Cel let out a relieved sigh, and Yesenia hugged her.

Inside, while Cel grabbed a fresh pair of pajamas and headed to the bathroom to shower, Yesenia placed the teakettle on the burner, turned the heat to low, and then made her way to her bedroom. She retrieved a mottled key from the tin Band-Aid box in her nightstand, and holding it between her lips, tugged the wooden chest filled with grimoires out of her closet. She slid the chest to the foot of her bed, sat down, and shoved the key into the lock that had protected the chest's secrets for more than two centuries. The key was hard to turn, the mechanism inside worn and clunky, but with some jostling, the lock finally released. Yesenia raised the lid and gazed down at the mess of books and scraps of paper, the handwritten recipes and spells and instructions.

To assure herself she had done all she could to help her sister, over the past week Yesenia had spent many of the quiet hours in the hospital recounting the exact dates and ingredients of every healing potion she'd concocted for Dolores, the step-by-step details of every ritual she'd performed over her, and the full list of protection spells and counter curses they'd cast. In the end, there was only one potentially potent ritual she knew of that she hadn't performed. She and Dolores had discussed the ritual, one of the strongest they'd come across, one evening shortly after Dolores had moved in and they were flipping through the grimoires. But the recipient of the ritual had to have a familiar, which Dolores did not have. Her latest familiar, an albino ferret named Aurelia, had inexplicably died about a month before the crickets' songs began tormenting her.

Yesenia's familiar, however, was alive and well. Yesenia had walked out onto the back porch to water her plants one morning and found the grey, skeletal kitten hiding behind a pot. When she met eyes with the kitten, she felt a surge of recognition. She immediately knew its name, knew they were spiritually bound, knew that Mina had come to protect and serve her. Their bond wasn't as seasoned as Yesenia would prefer for this particular ritual, Mina being barely a year old, but, at this point, she had to try. She wanted no regrets.

She rifled through the chest and found the tattered purple grimoire with the word FAMILIARS stitched in gold thread on the cloth cover. The book was thin, maybe around sixty pages, and filled mostly with information on how to recognize and spiritually bond with familiars. There were only a handful of minor spells written in the margins here and there, and only instructions for one ritual—the taking (*tomar*) ritual on the second to last page. Yesenia ran her finger under each Spanish word as she read the instructions, making a mental note on what she would need to gather and prepare.

When Cel emerged from the bathroom and walked into the kitchen an hour later, Yesenia had already placed a tourniquet on Mina's front right leg just below the shoulder. She was sitting with her back to the stove. Mina was wrapped tightly in a small blanket on her lap, only her gray head visible. A mug of steaming tea, a candle, a knife with a bone handle, a length of twine, and a lock of her hair were on the table in front of her. A pot of water seasoned with the proper herbs was slowly heating on one of the stove's back burners, a searing comal on a front one.

Cel stopped toweling her hair when she noticed Mina. "What are you doing?"

"Sit down."

Cel glanced at the stove and items on the table before obeying.

"I know it's late and you're tired, but I need your help with a ritual."

"Okay." Cel set her towel on the table. "What's it for?"

"It's a taking ritual." Locking eyes with her familiar, Yesenia stroked the gap between Mina's eyes with her index finger.

As Cel appraised Mina, Yesenia could see the gears turning in Cel's head, grinding through the information, trying to make sense of it. "A *taking* ritual?" Cel asked, more to herself than Yesenia. Her eyes lit with recognition. "You're going to take power from Mina."

Smart girl. Yesenia nodded. "It'll help strengthen my healing spells, counter curses, and protection abilities."

"How can you do that?" Cel's eyes swiveled to Mina, the knife, back to Yesenia. "Do we have to kill her?"

"No. She has to stay alive for it to work. But I do have to cut off one of her legs, which is why I need your help. I gave her some calming drops and tied her back legs together, but you'll still have to help hold her down for me." Yesenia scratched behind Mina's ears. "She knows what needs to be done and understands, but it's natural for any living thing to fight pain, so she'll struggle."

Yesenia glanced at the clock. It was a little after one in the morning. The tourniquet needed to be on for at least two hours before they began. "We'll start around two."

Over the next hour, Yesenia and Cel sat at the table in the center of the kitchen sipping tea and chatting. They talked about Maria and Frito, Jose and the fair, Parker and the hunters. They recalled *Tia* Dillo stories, some eliciting laughs, some tears, some both. Five minutes before two, the conversation turned back to the ritual.

"It's time," Yesenia said. She stood, pushed in her chair, lit the candle, and laid Mina on her side on the table. Cel stood, too. "You need to put one hand on her hip and the other on her back, and then push down hard enough to keep her from moving. I'll slide the blanket down just enough to expose the leg and hold her head."

Cel nodded and did as she was told.

Yesenia readied the sanctified, bone-handled knife she'd purchased from a *curandero* in Mexico many years earlier, partially removed the blanket, and pinned Mina's neck and head down. After giving Cel a single nod, she whispered the ritual's opening line and placed the blade just below the tourniquet. Mina fought and caterwauled as Yesenia sliced through her flesh and snapped through bone. Only a small amount of blood spilled onto the table when the lifeless leg fell free. Yesenia set the knife down and ordered Cel, "Pick her up, and hold her tight."

As Cel pinned Mina to her chest, Yesenia slipped a pot holder on her hand, picked up the screaming hot comal, and pressed the edge to Mina's wounded nub. She rolled it back and forth multiple times. The fur crackled, the skin hissed and sizzled like frying bacon. Mina yowled and jerked and bit down on Cel's hand, causing Cel to yowl, too.

Yesenia set down the comal and helped Cel retighten the blanket around Mina's entire body. "Sit and don't let go of her."

Yesenia continued, whispering the words she'd memorized from the grimoire. Using the sanctified blade, she cut the removed leg in two at the middle joint, knotted twine around the lower half, looped it around her neck, and tied it off. Then she wrapped her lock of hair around the upper half and moved it back and forth over the candle flame, purposefully inhaling the scorched-hair scent. Once the flesh was exposed, she tossed the leg into the pot of boiling water and started chanting. She chanted the curing verse one time for each year of her life, and once for each year of Mina's as well, before retrieving the leg with tongs.

Cel's chin dropped in awe when Yesenia took Mina from her and then began chewing on the boiled leg. Eyes locked on her familiar, whispering as her mouth worked, she ate what little leg flesh there was and then gnawed the bone until it broke in two, completing the ritual.

After slathering Mina's wound with a homemade salve and giving her two more Aspirin, Yesenia spent the next hour recasting every protection spell and counter curse she knew while Cel looked on in silence.

SEPTEMBER 2013

Chapter 22 - Cel

Detective Hart called Cel at a quarter past nine and told her they'd finished searching the house and she could return home. When prodded, he wouldn't elaborate on what, if anything, they'd found, saying they needed more time to process the items they'd gathered and fully examine the electronic devices. She told Yesenia what Hart had said before heading out to the back porch where a moonlit sky and a choir of distant crickets greeted her.

Two hours earlier, the sun had been burning bright when she'd walked to the edge of Hunter's Haven. She'd followed the tree line south until the only dirt road leading into the woods came into view. Peeking around the trunk of a giant elm, she watched officers in yellow vests come and go from unmarked cruisers parked on the road for twenty minutes before a Mickey's Towing Services truck emerged from the forest with Parker's Camry in tow. The sight twisted her insides and brought tears to her eyes. She gripped the rough trunk and clenched her jaw to keep from sprinting over to the car. She wanted to rip open the door and catch a whiff of Parker's Stetson cologne that always clung to the seat. She wanted to see what radio station he'd last listened to. She wanted to see what he'd left behind. She wanted answers. But she knew they'd deny her request. The car was not her property. Or Parker's, for that matter. Like their house on Matador Lane, the Camry technically belonged to Beverly Lundy. She'd bought the car for Parker three years earlier, after his Buick's engine crapped out, and she'd never transferred the title into his name.

Cel inhaled a deep breath and pushed it out in the form of a calming spell as she slipped on her *chanclas* and stepped down into the backyard. She hoped the cops had finished their search, or had at least left Hunter's Haven for the evening. They would find it suspicious if they caught her, the spouse, a suspect, sneaking around a potential crime scene. They would never believe she needed to stand where Parker stood, walk where he walked, to see if she could sense any residual aura he'd left behind, any hint if he was in distress when he was out here or not. They would think that was ridiculous and stupid, a lie or a ruse. Cops were fact people. Physical world people. They didn't believe in spiritual detective methods.

She followed the tree line south like earlier, but this time found the dirt road vacant, as white as chalk under the moon's glow. No cruisers. No tow trucks. No cops or canines, flashlights or voices. Thankfully, they'd left. For now, anyway. They'd probably come back at the first sign of daybreak. She quickly skirted the tree line back north until she reached the field separating Hunter's Haven from her *abuela's* backyard and then cut into the forest.

Fewer and fewer shafts of moonlight penetrated the canopy the deeper she progressed, so she pulled her cellphone out of her pocket for a ready light source. Although she hadn't ventured into the heart of Hunter's Haven in almost fifteen years, since the searches for Abby seemingly a lifetime ago, it only took a couple minutes and a few quick bursts of light to locate the game trail she'd used hundreds of times as a kid, a trail which led her to the dirt road.

As she walked down the center of the road, intermittently moving her phone's flashlight left and right, ahead and behind, a lump of anxiety filled her stomach, bulky and cumbersome, the size of a soccer ball-sized tumor. She had recited the finding spell three times like Yesenia had insisted, and she was trying so hard to reach out with her feelings, to focus on connecting with Parker, but the uncomfortable sensation in her gut coupled with the incessant cricket choir dampened her concentration.

"Parker?" Desperation spilled out of her. "Where are you?"

She stopped dead in her tracks when her phone's light hit on a length of yellow police tape wrapped around a tree in front of her. The visual brought her mental dialogue to a halt. Sadness clogged her throat. She swam the light around, revealing large sections of pounded down flora on either side of the road. She was there. Where Parker's car had been found. Where the cops and canine had trampled and scoured the earth, searching for clues.

Her eyes and light flitted from the flattened greenery to the tire tracks on the dirt road to the strands of yellow tape screaming for attention for what felt like hours before her mental engine kicked back into gear and picked up steam.

"Why did you come here?" she whispered as she cautiously moved forward. "Were you meeting someone?" She stopped next to the yellow-taped tree and aimed her light deeper into the thicket. The question that came next, she didn't ask aloud because it was absurd. She'd already rejected the idea when Detective Hart had posed it. There was no way he'd ever kill himself. Not Parker. He wasn't the type. Besides, if he had, or if he'd fallen and or been injured in some other way, the police hounds would've found him. Hunter's Haven was large, but nowhere close to Yosemite large.

She closed her eyes, took slow, measured breaths like when she meditated in the afternoons, recited the finding spell three more times, focused her energy and tried to reach out with her feelings again. Slow seconds ticked by. Her gut danced. Crickets chirped. Just when she was about to give up and open her eyes, a hopeful thought sprouted her mind. A simple thought.

Parker had driven out to Hunter's Haven because he didn't want to go home.

Tension had been building at 216 Matador Lane for months. Cel had confronted him about Lauren this morning. Fought with him. Accused him. He had probably come to Hunter's Haven to think. To contemplate. Formulate a plan on how to deal with Cel when he went home. Decide whether to lie or tell the truth. Fight to save their marriage or propose divorce. But if he'd left the comfort of his car on his own, where had he gone? For a walk? To where?

Cel opened her eyes and looked northeast, toward Mesquite Creek. If Parker wanted a meaningful, secluded place to collect his thoughts and weigh his feelings and future with Cel, there was no better place than Table Rock. The place where *they* started. The place they first kissed. A stone's throw away from where they first made love. It was also the place where they had spent countless summer afternoons with the other Cricket Hunters, debating songs and movies, aggrandizing and reminiscing about their experiences, predicting and dreaming about their futures.

Confident she had connected with Parker's lingering aura and now had a grasp on his true intentions for coming out here, Cel made a beeline for Table Rock. She powered through low limbs and tangles of thorny vines that clawed at the tops of her feet and lower legs, and, within a few minutes, reached the game trail she wanted to find, the one that wound its way to the sweet-scented water source slicing through the center of Hunter's Haven.

On top of Table Rock with Mesquite Creek moseying along in front of her, she closed her eyes and reached out with her feelings again. She stood motionless, face angled upward, arms out at her sides shoulder-high, breathing slow and deep, focusing, but this time no hopeful thought came. No matter how many times she repeated the spell and pled with Parker to find her, no connection was made. Eventually, she pushed out an exasperated sigh. "Where are you?" she whispered. Why hadn't he gone back to his car? Where else could he have—

She snapped her eyes open when a startling rustle drifted across the creek. Her heart rate jumped up five notches. She flicked on her phone's light and brushed the glow back and forth over the dense foliage. The longer she scanned, the faster her heart raced.

She understood that the last twenty-four hours of her life had turned her into a frazzled, sleep-deprived, mess of tender nerves, and she also knew that Hunter's Haven was named and known for its abundant wildlife, most of which was active at night, but she still couldn't shake the eerie feeling that she was being watched by something other than an animal. She sensed a human presence. An aura. Keeping her light and eyes aimed over the water, she stepped off Table Rock, picked up a stick, and hurled it, hoping against hope to see a deer or rabbit bound away when it slapped the ground, but nothing fled.

"Hello," she called out.

When a soft giggle answered, she was the one who fled.

She backpedaled a couple of steps, then turned and hurried down the same game trail she'd followed to the creek. Her light swooped up and down with the swing of her arm as she navigated the narrow path as quickly as she could in *chanclas*. Sections of the cricket choir hushed in her wake, allowing her to hear rustling in the brush on the right side of the trail. Every instinct she had warned her she was not only being followed but chased. Hunted.

She moved faster, not slowing when one of her *chanclas* flew off. When she chanced a glance back over her right shoulder, the tip of the other *chancla* caught on an exposed tree root, causing her to tip forward and fall to her hands and knees. She sprung to her feet and pointed her phone's light to the right, toward the rustle, holding it with both hands as though it were a loaded pistol.

"Who's there?' she asked.

Her breath caught in her chest when the farthest reaches of the light's glow hit on what looked like a pale face peeking out from behind a tree.

"What do you want?"

The face didn't budge.

Cel remained still, kept vigil. The longer she stared, the more she doubted. Was it really a face, or were her eyes playing tricks on her? Night time and forests and fear did that. The moment stretched. But then the face turned, and the blur of a body ran from behind the tree to behind another directly to the left. Cel chased the blur with her light. The face emerged again, and she quickly switched her phone to camera mode and held down the picture button.

In the darkness after the first flash, she heard rustling again. Maybe a giggle, too. She wasn't certain. Her heightened senses made the smallest sensations grand. She could feel her pulse pounding in her ears. Each inhale and exhale sounded like a gust of stiff wind. Each flash seemed pure white. After the sixth picture click, she let go of the button and held her breath, listening. Only the songs of distant crickets remained. She flicked her flashlight app back on, but rather than aim it where the person had been, she aimed it at the game trail and ran.

By the time she reached her *abuela's* back porch, she was slick with sweat. She'd traveled more than five miles roundtrip. Her mouth was as dry as sandpaper. The soles of her feet tender and scraped from pounding uneven ground. Her legs and arms and cheeks stung where whip-thin branches had caught her. She needed to catch her breath. She needed water. She needed to rinse off. But she needed to look at the pictures more. She sat down on the top step and opened her phone's photo gallery.

The first picture revealed a pale face peeking around the trunk, just like she'd seen. The flash hadn't reached any farther into the thicket than the flashlight, making details of the face, anything that might help determine age or gender or ethnicity, undiscernible.

Cel's finger had blocked the lower two-thirds of the second picture, but above that there appeared to be a thick mane of blurry hair flowing behind the profile of a blurry face.

In the third image, the smear of a person had their back fully to the camera. The hair fell below the shoulders. The dark ground foliage covered their legs up to knees. Above the knees was a dress that extended all the way up the back. A dress with the slightest hues of blue and yellow swirled in the blur.

The fourth, fifth, and sixth images were too dark and unfocused to make out much more than a general body shape as it dissolved into the forest background.

Cel flipped through the photos again and again, searching for answers that wouldn't come. Not until she went inside and was showing them to Yesenia did she make the connection. The location. The hair. The dress color. The giggle.

Abby.

Chapter 23 - Yesenia

Yesenia brewed a kettle of *yerba buena* while Cel washed her wounds in a hot shower. Yesenia had felt a stirring in her chest before Cel had left for Hunter's Haven and tried to convince Cel to wait until morning to venture into the woods. She had lectured Cel about being in peak emotional and spiritual health to attempt the finding spell, told her how darkness can be unforgiving for the weak, but *terca como una mula* like her mother sometimes, Cel had insisted she go. Now look.

After leaving a glob of homemade salve on the bathroom counter for Cel, Yesenia returned to the kitchen, filled two mugs with tea, and waited at the table. She briefly watched the steam dance out of the two mugs before picking up Cel's phone and examining the pictures again.

Yesenia had no doubts that under the right circumstances; spirits could be seen, felt, communicated with, and even occasionally captured on audio devices or photographed. She'd experienced the phenomenon in all forms. In fact, tucked away inside one of her grimoires, she had two convincing Polaroids of a ghost boy named Gabino that Dolores had taken in Matamoros in the mid-seventies. So the question circling her mind wasn't whether or not the girl in the images was a spiritual or physical being, but why the spirit, in particular Abby Powell's spirit, had reached out to Cel.

She set down the phone when she heard the hall floorboards creak under Cel's approaching feet. Cel entered the room, sat across from Yesenia, and picked up her mug. The dim oven hood light stretched just far enough across the room to illuminate Cel's face. Her wet hair was tucked behind her ears. The salve on the two short parallel scratches on her left cheek glistened like pond water in the glow.

"I see you found your old robe," Yesenia said.

"I can't believe you kept this thing." A faint smile tickled Cel's lips as she glanced down and ran her hand through the shaggy purple fabric, but when she looked up, her eyes landed on her cell phone, and the trace of happiness vanished. "I feel cursed." She lightly shook her head, chewed on her bottom lip. "First all the stuff with Parker and Lauren...then Parker disappears...then the picture thing with Abby and the crickets…and now…" She gestured at her phone. "That." She shook her head again.

"*Que* picture? Crickets?"

Cel met eyes with Yesenia, and Yesenia raised her eyebrows, imploring Cel to elaborate.

Yesenia listened and nodded as Cel explained how on the night Parker didn't come home, she'd heard noises in her house, like someone else were there, but when she investigated, all she found was Parker's books knocked off a shelf in the computer room closet and a picture of Abby on Table Rock sticking out of his copy of *The Illustrated Man*. A picture she'd never seen before. Then she explained how a day later, she'd found crickets in all three sinks and both bathtubs in the house in the morning after Natalie left. In all the years she'd lived in the house, that had never happened. Maybe a roach or water bug every now and then after a big rain, but never a cricket apocalypse.

Concern gripped Yesenia's chest as memories of Dolores's final months scraped her thoughts. "Did the cricket's songs sound—"

Cel waved her hand, cutting Yesenia off. "No. Nothing like that."

Yesenia nodded, the pressure on her chest subsiding. "Maybe Abby's reaching out to you," she suggested. "Trying to tell you something. *Darte un mensaje.*"

Cel immediately shook her head, as though she'd contemplated and rejected that idea years ago.

"Maybe her disappearance has something to do with Parker's."

Cel shook her head again, with more certainty this time. "No. That was so long ago. There's no way."

Yesenia surveyed Cel over the top of her mug as she took a sip of tea. Cel looked upset, on the verge of tears. Yesenia knew dredging up particulars about Abby's disappearance would upset her even more, but she had to pose the question. The question Cel had refused to contemplate or discuss since the first day Abby went missing, and even more so after she was officially declared dead years later. The question that Yesenia had debated in her own mind time and again. "What if Parker had something to do with Abby's disappearance?"

The corners of Cel's eyes tightened. "Don't even."

"*La policia* said he was the last person to be seen with her that night."

"Yeah, they did," Cel said with an edge to her tone. "But *he* said when he last saw her, she was fine and headed back inside her house. He would never have hurt her."

Yesenia paused, set down her cup, took a deep breath. "It would be an answer as to why you found that picture in *his* favorite book. And the crickets. And why she appeared while you were looking for *him*. Presenting herself in the same colors she was last seen in. *Con el.*"

Cel swallowed hard, began nervously gnawing on her bottom lip, dropped her gaze to the table top.

"Maybe Abby appeared to Parker the afternoon he went out there, too," Yesenia added.

"What are you saying?" A disbelieving, airy chuckle popped out of Cel's mouth, and she looked up. "That Abby's ghost kidnapped Parker?"

Yesenia gave her granddaughter a look that screamed sincerity. "I don't know what happened to him. But maybe Abby does."

"Maybe Lauren does," Cel shot back like a rebellious teen.

Yesenia shrugged. "Maybe. You've already discovered more than a few secrets he carried when it comes to her. But I still think that if Abby's spirit is reaching out to you right now, it's for a reason. Whether Lauren has anything to do with it or not."

"How am I supposed to...I can't...I can't..." Tears fell down Cel's cheeks. "There was so much going on back then. And now..." She lowered her head onto her arms on the table and softly cried. Yesenia hated seeing Cel hurt, but knew accepting the pain of the situation was necessary if Cel wanted to grow strong enough to face whatever answers were coming her way. Yesenia moved to other side of the table, sat in the chair next to Cel, and whispered a soothing spell as she rubbed her back.

A couple of minutes passed before Cel sat upright and wiped her eyes with her fuzzy purple sleeve.

"I'm just trying to help," Yesenia said.

Cel nodded, and her mouth opened but no words tumbled out. The weary expression on her face and her despondent eyes told Yesenia that she had emotionally and mentally checked out. The mounting stress had finally tripped a breaker inside her, temporarily shutting down the communication line. Yesenia took Cel by the hand and stood. "Come on, *mija*. You need sleep."

Cel allowed Yesenia to guide her down the hall to her childhood bedroom. Like Dolores's room at the end of the hall, and the kitchen, and the living room, and Yesenia's own bedroom for that matter, Cel's hadn't changed much in fifteen years. Yesenia trailed Cel to the wire-framed daybed nestled in the far corner of the room—the same daybed she'd bought at garage sale on Cel's seventh birthday—and waited for Cel to lay down. Then she tucked Cel in, kissed her on the head, and told her she loved her, like she had every night for the first ten years Cel had lived with her, until Cel hit her teenage years and refused the efforts.

On her way out, she whispered a soothing spell, and then closed the door only halfway so the nightlight in the hall would touch the carpet, the way Cel had liked it when she first moved in and was scared of the dark. The old nighttime routine felt natural, seamless, as though she'd just done it the night before, and the previous thousand nights before that.

In her bedroom, she turned on the overhead light, lit an incense stick, and after retrieving the key from the Band-Aid tin in her nightstand drawer, slid the wooden chest out of her closet and unlocked it. She leaned forward when she lifted the lid and inhaled slow and steady. The scent of aged paper and ancient herbs the chest concealed possessed its own magic. The magic of time travel.

Every tattered grimoire and yellowed scrap of paper and hand-drawn image carried a piece of Yesenia's past. Her story. Her most cherished memories. And every time the scent hit her nose, her memory floodgates opened.

Her mother reading to her and Dolores while they sat side-by-side under a single blanket on cold nights as toddlers. Her and Dolores sitting opposite one another on their shared mattress on the floor as kids, practicing reciting basic spells, quizzing one another, laughing. Her mom having her and Dolores copy down bits of information from the books to aid neighbors in need. Her and Dolores poring over the books as teens, experimenting with the ability to manipulate matters of hurt and revenge, desire and joy, as they traveled through the haze of adolescent curiosity. All the times she gained help and comfort from the books as she entered adulthood and had to navigate jobs and ownership, hatred and racism, passions and men. The times she and Dolores communicated with their mom's spirit. The times she summoned Dolores's. Her excitement when passing along the knowledge to her own daughter, Rebecca, keeping the family traditions alive. Then again with Cel. It was all there, every moment of her past, every emotion, her heart, in the chest, in the smell.

As she picked through the stacks, Yesenia looked at each grimoire longer than needed, read small snippets, handwritten notes, allowing the memories to filter though her slow and easy. She found the spirit board and two books she needed about halfway in but continued rifling and reminiscing until she reached the splintered bottom of the chest. The older she got, the more she tended to do this each time she lifted the lid.

It was after four in the morning by the time she shoved the chest back in the closet and headed to the kitchen with the board and two books under her arm. She prepared another batch of tea, gathered a pencil and notepad from the junk drawer, sat down, and began copying. She wanted to be ready to help whether Cel decided to contact Abby or not. The choice would have to be hers.

First, she copied the spirit talk ritual, including the pre-spells and conditions the primary summoner should adhere to in order to have the best chance at getting a response, from the grimoire that had the word ESPIRITU written on it in her mother's handwriting. Then she copied a rejection spell, cleansing spell, and steps to perform a spirit cast off ritual, all from a grimoire with a large X stitched on the cloth cover.

After rechecking her work and returning the books to the chest, she peeked in on Cel before heading out to the back porch. Tired but wise enough to know sleep wouldn't come, she gently swayed in a rocking chair with a warm mug of tea between her thighs, watching the horizon, drifting in and out of the past, waiting for the sun to rise and Hunter's Haven to awaken.

Chapter 24 - Cel

Cel woke to the smell of *migas,* bright sunlight, and Mila's weight and warmth on her ankles. She shot up right, realizing, remembering, she was at her *abuela's,* not home. She looked at the clock. It was almost ten, four hours past her typical wake up time. Before she took three breaths, the previous day's and night's events—Lauren, her kid, Parker's car, the search warrant, the ghost girl—burst into the forefront of her mind, bringing with them a sense of urgency and anxiety.

She hopped up, threw on her robe, and headed for the kitchen. She froze mid-step in the hallway when a deep voice, a man's voice, touched her ears. She couldn't make out what he was saying, or who he was, but she knew it couldn't be too serious by her *abuela's* throaty laughter that followed. She cinched her robe's belt, tucked her disheveled hair behind her ears, and continued.

Her anxiety receded when she entered the kitchen. A genuine smile born from the relief threading through her spread across her face. Yesenia was manning the stove, spooning diced potatoes and onions into a sizzling pan of eggs. She wore the same white dress she'd had on the night before, the same single braid down her back as always. Her greenish-gray eyes were bloodshot-tired but happy. Natalie and Omar sat on either side of the table in the center of the room, remnants of *migas* on plates in front of them. They both looked radiant, put together. The opposite of how Cel felt.

Since graduating from the University of Texas, Omar had traded in his over-sized hand-me-downs for standard accountant attire. He wore a white long sleeve button-up, black slacks, and shiny black shoes. He had shaved his beard since Cel had last seen him six months earlier, but his hair was still stubble-length with hints of gray brushed into the temples. Natalie wore a red skirt, black sleeveless top, and black heels. Her hair was damp and scalloped into tight curls, her face highlighted in all the right areas with makeup. All three returned Cel's smile, and Natalie and Omar rose to greet and hug her.

"I remember that robe," Natalie said, running her hand over the fuzzy purple fabric. "I was so jealous of it. It still fits you the exact same."

Cel sat next to Natalie, and Yesenia placed a *migas*-rich plate and mug of tea in front of her. She thanked her *abuela*, and then looked at Natalie, at Omar. "What are you guys doing here?"

Natalie briefly eyed the scratches on Cel's cheek before replying. "I tried to call and text late last night after Craig's cousin—Dennis, you remember him? He's been on the Oak Mott PD for about six months now." Cel nodded. "Called and told us the cops were searching your house, but you didn't answer or text back. So when I went by your place this morning and you didn't answer the door, I came here." Natalie patted Cel's thigh. "Are you okay?"

Cel pinched her lips together and nodded, a lie she didn't expect them to believe and could tell neither one of them did.

When she didn't elaborate, Omar said, "I'm sorry I didn't get in touch sooner. I wanted to come yesterday after Natalie called and told me about Parker, but I had to finalize some reports at work before I left town." Omar lived in Halo, a suburb east of Austin. He and his partner of eight years, Kris Ashton, lived in a two bedroom apartment, and both worked at the Dell corporate offices where they'd met. He and Natalie had remained close over the years, texting and chatting regularly, but Cel only communicated with him once every couple of months or so.

Cel met eyes with Omar, reached across the table and squeezed his hand. "It's fine. I'm glad you're here."

"Have you heard from the cops since the search?" Natalie asked. Then she shook her head in apparent disgust. "I can't believe they did that. Dennis said Parker's mom demanded Chief Sterling do it."

"She's always been a bitch," Omar said. With a cheek full of *migas*, he cut his eyes mischievously back and forth from Natalie to Cel, and smiled a closed lip smile, eliciting chuckles from both of them. For a flash, Cel glimpsed the boy he used to be. The boy who rode an electric motor-assisted bike and always carried a calculator in his pocket.

"All Detective Hart said when he called last night was that I could go home if I wanted, and that they needed time to examine Parker's laptop and stuff." Cel looked down at her plate, jostled the food around. "I think they think I have something to do with it."

"That's stupid," Natalie said. "They know he'd been at work all day, and they found his cell phone and briefcase in the car, so they know he never went home afterward, too."

Cel's heart leapt into her throat. So much for relief. One of her last remaining hopes was that the cops would be able to track him via his cell phone. If he didn't have his cell phone, that sliver of hope was lost. "I didn't know they'd found his phone."

Natalie's eyebrows rose in an apologetic expression. As if she'd done something wrong. "Yeah, Dennis said it was in the passenger seat of the car with a book and his briefcase. I don't know why they wouldn't tell you that."

Cel felt her eyes heating up, filling with moisture.

Yesenia pulled out the chair next to Omar and sat down. "Because they want to see if she'll admit to knowing something about the scene that she couldn't know unless she was there."

Natalie's eyes tightened. "They're such assholes," she said.

Cel bit at her lip in an attempt to steel her emotions. "They're just doing what they need to do. The spouse is always the first suspect when anyone goes missing or…you know."

"I understand the percentages," Omar said, his voice suddenly tight with indignation. "But they need to fucking hurry up and eliminate you so they can find out what really happened."

"Right," Natalie agreed.

When Cel looked down and picked at her food without responding, Natalie and Omar followed suit, fiddling with what little food remained on their plates in silence. Cel scooped *migas* into her mouth but struggled to find the desire to chew. Usually salty and spicy, the food was tasteless, like a glob of moist Styrofoam. She wanted to spit it out. She wanted to cry. She wanted to grab her phone and earbuds and go outrun the pain. But she could feel her *abuela's* eyes on her and didn't want to worry her any more than she already had. She also wanted to avoid another lecture about how she needed to rest and eat and stay strong like she'd received after refusing dinner the previous night. She forced the glob down and managed six more forkfuls before downing half of her tea in large gulps. "What are you guys' plans for the rest of the day?" She looked at Natalie. "Do you have to show any houses?"

"I showed one this morning, hence..." She waved her hand sarcastically over her shirt and skirt. "But I have the rest of the day off."

"Do you think you can take me to my house so we can see what it looks like? I don't have my car, and I don't want to go in alone."

Natalie smiled and touched Cel's forearm, and Omar nodded. "Of course," they answered in unison.

"Thank you." Cel stood and pushed in her chair. "I'm going to brush my teeth and change real quick then."

Yesenia stood, too, and began clearing the table, waving off Omar's and Natalie's offers to help. "Your clothes are on top of the dryer with your phone, *mija*."

My *chanclas* are out in Hunter's Haven though, aren't they? Cel's inner voice responded, bringing the hairs on her arms to attention as she nodded and left the room.

Chapter 25 - Cel

Cel sat in the backseat of Natalie's Scion with Mila on her lap, a pair of Yesenia's *chanclas* on her feet. She met eyes with Natalie in the rearview when the car stopped at a red light at the Sylvia and Yankee Road intersection, tipped her head toward Omar in the passenger seat, and mouthed *He knows, right? The baby.*

She could only see Natalie from the nose up, but she could tell Natalie smiled when she nodded. She guessed Omar was the first one Natalie had told about her pregnancy, but she wanted to be sure before speaking up. "How have you been feeling? Still nauseated?"

"It comes and goes," Natalie said. "Hopefully I can hold those *migas* down. They were pretty spicy."

"You better," Omar joked. "I've cleaned up enough of your stinky ass puke for two lifetimes already."

Natalie elbowed Omar's arm and laughed. "Shut up. If I do puke, you *will* clean it up, and you'll do it with a smile."

Somewhat jealous (she and Parker used to banter like that) but at the same time grateful (she loved that they hadn't lost their connection), Cel chuckled at their back and forth, a welcome calm before the storm she expected to find inside her house. She stroked Mila as the light turned green, and Natalie's attention returned to the road. She stared out the window and tried to fight off any thoughts about their destination as they zoomed past familiar fast-food franchises and car dealerships, churches and houses. She wanted to hold onto this moment of normalcy, a moment with her friends where friendly banter was okay, laughter was okay, feeling safe was okay, for as long as she could.

When they reached 216 Matador Lane, Natalie parked in the driveway behind Cel's Envoy. She twisted sideways, facing Omar, and cocked her right leg up in the seat. She glanced at Omar before meeting eyes with Cel, and Cel saw something pass between her two friends. An invisible nod of encouragement. Omar knew what Natalie was about to say. "I know this is bad timing, and it may seem stupid because of everything that's going on with you, Cel, and I'm sorry, but we are rarely all three together, and I wanted to talk about this with just you guys, in person." Her eyes moved nervously back and forth from Omar to Cel. "As you guys know, Craig and I aren't church people, but we still wanted to know if you guys would be our baby's godparents? In a symbolic way. Like if something happens to us..." She flapped her fingers in front of her teary eyes. "Sorry." She chuckled. "Hormones, I guess."

Cel leaned into the gap between the front seats and hugged her. "It's not stupid. Of course. Of course."

Omar took Natalie's hand in his and smiled a proud smile. Another unspoken message passed between them before he let go and looked at Cel. "Ready?"

On the front porch, Cel paused after twisting the knob. She feared the house would no longer feel like a home if the cops had ransacked it like in crime shows. Mila meowed at her feet, eager to enter and restore her ownership of the place. When Omar placed a friendly hand on Cel's shoulder and Natalie touched her lower back, she mentally recited her go-to calming spell and opened the door.

They made their way down the hall, searching the living room, spare bedroom that served as an office, hall bathroom, kitchen, and every closet they crossed. The place was far from ransacked. For the most part, they found the same mess Cel had left in her wake after searching for evidence that Parker had been communicating with Lauren.

The pillows and cushions on the couches and chairs appeared to have been lifted and checked under, unzipped too, maybe, but they weren't sliced open, their billowy guts torn out. Clothes and coats hanging in closets were abnormally slid all the way to one side or the other but not tossed onto the floor. Some drawers and kitchen cupboards were still open or only partially closed, hinting at an intrusion, some of the contents stacked on the floor or furniture nearby, but nothing was unorganized. Some of the furniture and pictures on the walls also sat askew, but not drastically.

Not until they searched Cel's bedroom and bathroom did they perceive the sincerity of the search. The bedspread, sheets, and pillowcases had been removed and piled on the floor at the foot of the mattress, which had been flipped (Cel rotated it regularly to prevent sagging, and last week the tag had been facedown, not visible.), and a watermelon-sized section was crudely cut out. Similarly, two swatches of carpet in front of bathroom door had been excised. The cops had obviously detected the blood stains on both the mattress and carpet, stains that would match Cel, not Parker, when tested. Reminders of dark stints they went through after her third and fourth miscarriages.

Natalie put her hands on her hips and cursed the cops when she saw the missing carpet, and Omar backed up the sentiment as he ran his hand over the damaged mattress. But what stung Cel the sharpest wasn't the carpet or mattress, or anything else that had been taken or moved or rifled through. It was what Natalie found wedged in the heap of linens moments later. When Cel walked out of the bathroom after checking the cupboards under the sink, she found Omar and Natalie standing at the foot of the bed, staring at a book in Natalie's hand.

"What's that?"

Natalie cocked her head in a gesture of pity, like a teacher about to show a failing grade to a hardworking yet mentally-challenged kid, and passed the book to Cel.

It was Parker's abused copy of *The Illustrated Man*—the same copy she'd found on the floor of the computer room closet two days earlier and placed back on the shelf with his other books. The same photo of Abby on Table Rock was poking out of the top—the photo she'd wedged inside the center of the book before re-shelving it.

"Why would they bring it in here?" Cel whispered to herself. She kept her eyes glued on the book as she backpedaled to the mattress and shrunk down. Her mind was knotting up with questions and possibilities like it had too many times in the last forty-eight hours. Would this fucked up roller coaster ride ever end? "Did Hart want me to see it? Was it an accident? A coincidence? Or…is…"

"Cel," Natalie said. "Are you okay?"

To Cel, Natalie sounded as if she were speaking from the bottom of a deep hole, far away. "Was *Buela*…" Cel whispered. She looked up, her eyes aimed at Natalie but not seeing her. "Abby…" Cel's eyes fell on the book again. "But she couldn't have…"

Natalie sat next to Cel. "Cel. You're scaring me."

Omar squatted in front of them and put his hand on Cel's knee. "What's wrong? What's going on?"

As her stress-laden eyes seesawed from Natalie to Omar, Cel pulled her cell phone out of her pocket, handed it to Natalie, and told her to open the gallery. She described her trek into Hunter's Haven in long, run-on sentences as Natalie flipped through the photos. She told them everything. The yellow police tape. The finding spell. The connection with Parker's aura. Table Rock. The maybe-Abby's–ghost in maybe-Abby's-dress. The giggles. The running home barefoot, scared out of her mind.

Natalie handed the phone to Omar, who began scrolling through the pictures as she gestured at Cel's cheek. "Is this how you got those scratches?"

Cel nodded.

"I wish you would've called me. I would've gone out there with you."

Cel's non-reply reply was to hold up *The Illustrated Man* and unleash another string of run-ons. She told them about hearing the strange noises in the house the night Parker vanished. Finding the book and picture on the floor. She pulled out the picture and gave it to Natalie and asked if she'd ever seen it, and she said no. When Omar passed Cel her phone back, he looked at the picture and said he'd never seen it either. Then she told them about finding all the crickets in the sinks and tubs the morning after finding the book and picture, and how Yesenia thinks Abby's spirit wants something from her, or is trying to contact her for a specific reason. Maybe something to do with Parker.

"And now this book, out of all of his books stacked in the computer room closet, his favorite book back then, is in here when I come home. With Abby in it."

Cel inhaled deeply. It felt good to uncork. "What do you guys think?" But not so good to see the expressions on her friends' faces when they looked at one another in response to her question and shared a silent conversation with their eyes. A conversation she read as: *Do you believe this could be Abby's ghost? I really don't either. Everything that happened can be rationally explained. She's just stressed and upset, probably relating the two disappearances out of desperation. She's been through a lot. Poor her.*

Before they could respond, Cel answered her own assumptions. "I know you guys think I'm stressed out, and that to still believe in all this aura and spirit and spell stuff is childish and stupid, but—"

"Wait," Natalie interjected. "You're right. We *do* think you're stressed. And for good reason." Omar nodded in agreement. "But it's not fair to say we think your beliefs are childish or stupid. We've never said or thought that." Natalie searched Cel's face with heartfelt eyes.

"You've known me since third grade. You know I believe in powers beyond our full understanding just as much as you."

Cel bit at her bottom lip for a moment before nodding. "I'm sorry. That wasn't fair." She gulped. "I just get the feeling you guys think I'm crazy, that I'm grasping for answers and connections that can't exist."

"We don't think that," Omar assured.

"We're just trying to process everything," Natalie added. "I mean, Abby disappeared fifteen years ago. Now thinking about her ghost being in Hunter's Haven…and those pictures you took…and the crickets…and Parker vanishing… It's a lot to filter through and try to connect."

Cel cracked a weak, knowing smile. It was a lot. Too much. She hung her head, letting her hair shield the sides of her face, and opened her phone's photo gallery. As she scanned through the pictures, worried she might be over analyzing, she sensed Natalie and Omar meeting eyes again, talking without talking. When Natalie brushed Cel's hair away from her face, Cel closed the photo gallery and looked up. "I'm sorry," she said again, this time softer and slower. "This whole thing is just so fucked up."

"It's going to be okay," Natalie said, smiling a motherly smile that touched her eyes.

Cel squeezed Natalie's hand. "You're going to be such a great—"

A series of loud thuds cut her off. Four jarring knocks on the front door. The same as when the cops had arrived yesterday. Cel, Omar, and Natalie looked back and forth from each other, waiting. Four more knocks echoed through the house. "It's the cops," Cel said.

Omar and Natalie followed her to the front door. Omar stepped into the living room and peeked through the blinds. "There's one guy in a suit. He's tall and skinny and has a goatee."

"It's Detective Hart," Cel said. *If they'd found Parker's body, there'd be more of them*, she thought. *But if they found him alive, or a clue that he was…*She flung the door open. "Did you find something? Is he okay?"

Detective Hart studied the scratches on Cel's face before making eye contact. He looked exhausted and dehydrated. His lips were flaky, eyelids heavy. "We didn't find him. Yet." He glanced over her shoulder at Natalie and Omar, locked eyes with her again. "We'd like you to come down to the station to answer a few questions that might help, though."

"How can I help? I told you everything I know. He went to work and never came home. You found his car. Now *you* need to find him."

"These questions aren't about Parker's disappearance per say."

Cel's brow furrowed. "*What?*"

"I need to talk to you about Lauren Page."

Chapter 26 - Cel

Detective Hart escorted Cel to a small cold room that was as colorless as the hospital room *Tia* Dillo had taken her last breath in. There were no windows, no pictures on the white walls. Only a black camera perched in the corner opposite the door, aimed toward the center of the room. The uncomfortable chairs resembled giant plastic ice-cream scoops, the table between them a chunk of wood covered in the cheap faux-wood paneling that covered walls in the eighties. To combat the vent shooting cold air directly at her, Cel sat across from Hart with her knees pinched together, her arms folded across her chest.

"Can you turn down the A/C? It's freezing in here."

"Sorry, I can't. Out of my control. One thermostat controls the entire building."

Hart made eye contact and spoke sympathetically, but Cel thought the excuse sounded rehearsed—Oak Mott PD protocol for suspects undergoing questioning. When he offered her his suit jacket a moment later, she knew. She'd seen more than one *Dateline* episode where interrogators explained how they would create an uncomfortable environment for suspects on a basic, primal level (thirst, hunger, cold, etc.) and then offer relief in order to build trust. She accepted the jacket, laid it across her legs, and thanked him.

Hart opened the manila folder on the table in front of him and proceeded to flip through the sheets of paper as if he'd never seen them before, as if he'd been ordered to bring Cel in and the folder held the reason why. When he finished scanning the pages, he pulled out his cell phone and examined it for a moment. "Sorry," he eventually offered. "Just looking over my notes from our talk the other day." He gave her a crooked smile. "Still not a fan of using the cell phone. I know it may be faster for some people, but it just seems like twice the work to me since I still have to fill out paperwork later." He sat the phone down. "Okay. So, you said the other day that you and Parker argued about him spending a lot of extra time with Lauren Page, correct?"

"Yeah, that was part of it. Why?"

"How well do you know her?"

"What do you mean?"

"Would you say you're friends, acquaintances, enemies?"

"Acquaintances, I guess. She's Parker's mentee. I talked to her a few times when I went to the school to have lunch with him, and maybe once or twice more, but that's about it." Cel straightened her back when Hart shuffled through the papers again. When he plucked a pen out of his pant pocket and jotted something down, she shoved her hands under his jacket, wedging them between her thighs.

"When was the last time you saw her?"

Nervous about where Hart was headed, Cel crinkled her nose and shook her head. "What's this about?"

He laid the pen down and met eyes with her. "You've been cooperative with us, so I'm going to be straight forward with you." He propped his elbows on the table and locked his hands together. "Lauren Page is missing, and we have good reason to believe foul play is involved."

Cel's eyes bulged with shock. "What? That's crazy. Do you think it has something to do with Parker?"

"We're looking into that, which is why I wanted to talk to you. And I'm just going to be blunt. Where were you last night at around eleven?"

"You think *I* had something to do with it?" A hard swallow. "I didn't."

"I don't know what to think, yet, Cel. I just know that this morning when she didn't show up for work, a co-worker went to check on and found her front door unlocked and wide open, and there appeared to have been a struggle just inside the doorway. Her keys, cell phone, purse, and Jeep were all still there, but not her."

"Oh my God," Cel said. "I swear, I didn't...I was at my *abuela's* all night. Officer Wilson drove me over there, remember? I didn't even have my car?"

He wrote something down. "Have you ever been to her apartment?"

The question caught Cel off guard. How much did he know? As she held Hart's gaze, struggling to find the right words, a way to make her reasoning sound rational, she nodded.

"Thank you for being honest." Hart flashed a closed-lip smile. "Because when I was talking to some of Lauren's neighbors this morning about an argument they heard around eleven last night, they said they saw you there yesterday around noon, and that you two got into an argument that turned physical on the sidewalk. Is that true?"

Cel nodded again. "We argued, but we didn't physically fight."

"You didn't shove her, or slap her, or anything aggressive like that?"

"It was a heated argument, but I didn't hurt her."

"Did you threaten her?" He raised his brow in a submissive way, as if to imply Cel could've been a victim. "Or vice versa?"

"No. We argued about Parker. That's all."

"Why did you go there in the first place?"

Cel pushed out a shaky breath. "I was freaked out about Parker's disappearance, and I wanted to see if he was there. I thought maybe he was hiding out over there. I never expected her to show up, and when she did, I asked her if she knew where he was, and she said no." Cel rolled her eyes in self-disgust at the memory. "Then I called her a liar and she called me crazy, and then I accused her of sleeping with him, and she told me she'd call the cops if I didn't leave, so I left."

"Had you ever been to her apartment before yesterday?"

Cel lied, shook her head.

"So you're saying you've never been inside her apartment, and our crime scene detectives gathering evidence over there right now won't find your fingerprints or anything inside where it appears an altercation took place, right?"

Cel's bowels constricted. She'd been inside, all right. To place the doll under the bed and perform the blocking ritual. Then again to remove it. Thank God she'd worn gloves. Thank God she hadn't touched anything in the living room by the front door. But she also had a key to the front door. She'd instinctively taken it out of her back pocket when she got home from Lauren's and tossed it and her Envoy keys in the brass bowl on the runner table in the entry room, the bowl she and Parker kept all their spare change and keys in. Shit. How could she explain that without looking guilty? "Right," she answered as confidently as her conscience allowed.

"And how did you know exactly where she lived?"

"Parker told me. He had a key to her apartment," she said, in case Hart had found the key and was trying to paint her into a corner. "He fed her fish when she went out of town once."

"And you were okay with that? Him having a key to her apartment?"

"Honestly, no. That was one of the reasons for our argument the day he…" She glanced up at the camera, fighting back the swell of emotion collecting in her eyes.

"You believe they were having an affair?"

She did. Maybe not a full on fuck-fest physical one yet, but an emotional one, no doubt. The calls and texts and lunches. The key. The note Parker had written about meeting her son Sammy. "I can't be sure exactly how close they were. They both denied it, but…" She shrugged in surrender to the full truth.

Hart pinched his lips and nodded, his deep-set eyes doing a convincing job relaying the message that he understood the pain and heartache of uncertainty. He wrote on the paper in front of him, then pointed at Cel's cheek with his eyes and the pen. "Out of curiosity, how'd you get those scratches?" He glanced at her arms and swiped the pen back and forth. "And those? You didn't have them when we talked the other day."

Cel fingered the two scrapes on her cheek. She knew what it looked like, but she had nothing to hide. None of her DNA would be found under anyone's fingernails. "I went for a walk in Hunter's Haven yesterday evening to collect my thoughts and stumbled across an angry wasp nest." *Not a ghost.* "And some branches got the better of me when I took off running."

"I see." As Hart wrote down her response, the door opened and Chief Sterling lumbered into the room. He wore boots and jeans and his tan-tinted glasses. His chief badge hung from the left pocket of his long sleeve button-up shirt as always. He greeted Cel, shaking her hand over the table, and sat across from her.

"Sorry I'm late," he said to Hart, which sounded even more contrived than when Hart claimed the inability to lower the thermostat. Cel assumed Sterling, Beverly Lundy's lifelong friend and rumored lover, had probably been watching the interview in a separate room, and Hart probably knew exactly when he'd walk in the room, exactly what he'd say. "What did I miss?"

"We're just wrapping everything up," Hart said. "She admits to arguing with Lauren yesterday afternoon but says she was at her grandma's all night and has no idea where Lauren is."

"Okay." Sterling turned his attention to Cel and smoothed his mustache. "Are you willing to turn over your cell phone, take a polygraph test, and give us fingerprint and DNA samples?"

He spoke the request so soft and gentle, like a grandpa telling a folktale to a grandkid perched on his lap, that it took a second for the severity of it to sink in and ignite a flame of indignation in Cel's chest. She narrowed her eyes. "That sounds a little bit overboard."

"Don't take it personally," Hart said, holding up a hand like a small shield. "It's just a formality."

"How can I not take it personally when it seems like you think *I* might've done something to her?"

"Then let us prove you didn't," Sterling answered. He shifted in his chair, crossed one leg over the other, his comfortable demeanor matching his dulcet tone. "You need to help us if you're innocent because right now your husband, who was probably having an affair with Lauren Page, a situation which caused problems between you and him, went missing two days ago, and now she, a woman you admit to having an altercation with outside her apartment yesterday, goes missing, too. You're a smart girl, Cel. You have to know how bad this looks not only to us but everyone else involved."

Unable to see more than a vague outline of his eyes through his tinted lenses, Cel focused her attention on the center of the glass. "Involved? You mean Beverly Lundy?" She shook her head. "She's always had it out for me, and you know it."

"We're just doing our job," Hart said. "Not the bidding of anyone else, I assure you." He twirled his pen, looked at Sterling, back at Cel. "But like both of us, you grew up in Oak Mott. You know how fast suspicions can spread and damage people's lives. If you continue cooperating with us on all levels, it'll help you just as much as it does us."

"We'll be able to eliminate you as a suspect in everyone's eyes," Sterling added.

"Fine." Cel jerked Hart's jacket off her legs and tossed it at him. Then she pulled her cell phone out of her pocket and slid it across the table so hard it flew into Sterling's lap. "But not because I give a shit about what anyone else thinks. I just want to clear my name so you can get back to looking for what really happened to my husband and Lauren."

In the booking area, freckle-faced Officer Wilson fingerprinted Cel, photographed the scratches on her face, arms, and legs, swabbed the inside of her cheek, then led her to a white room that was a twin of the first one save for the polygraph machine and laptop sitting on the faux-wood table. Wilson had Cel sit in the bucket chair closest to the door, facing the camera in the corner, away from the table, and said Detective Langmore would be there shortly.

Sitting with her legs folded crisscross like when she meditated in the afternoons, Cel closed her eyes, recited a calming spell, and focused on her breathing while she waited. When Langmore arrived five minutes later, she felt centered, calm, warmer. He was wiry, had a twangy accent, and made little eye contact as he introduced himself, described how the machine worked, what it measured, laid out the parameters of how he would ask questions and how she should answer. After she confirmed she understood the process, he placed a cuff on her arm, monitors on her fingertip and chest, and sat in front of the laptop, out of her direct line of sight.

Cel stared upward in the direction of the camera without focusing on any particular point as she answered. She fought off waves of nervousness by focusing on her breathing in the five to ten second breaks between questions. Questions, some simple and mundane (*Is your name Celia Rebecca Lundy? Are you sitting in a chair?*), others complex and specific (*Were you involved in a car accident on November 4th 2009 that resulted in your 2004 maroon Envoy's front right fender being damaged?*), that she was to answer with only a yes or no. Questions that delved deeper into what Hart had already asked her about both Lauren and Parker. Questions she believed sometimes had no black and white answer.

Have you ever been inside Lauren Page's apartment? Harmed Lauren? Wanted to harm her? Do you know where she is today? Believe she was having an affair with Parker? Did you know she had a son? Have you met her son's father? Followed her? Did you know Parker had taken Lauren's son Sammy to his parent's house? That he'd visited Sammy at Lauren's parent's house in Austin? Bought him birthday presents? Have you ever harmed Parker? Do you know why he went to Hunter's Haven two days ago? Do you know where he is today? Did you hurt or kill Parker in your bedroom? Do you own a gun? Have you left Oak Mott city limits in the past forty-eight hours? Destroyed any household items? Replaced any?

And on and on.

The longer time dragged on and the questions mounted, the harder Cel found it to keep calm. In the silent gaps between questions her thoughts continued to circle back to the knowledge that Parker had introduced Lauren and her fucking kid to his family. And that he'd visited her family in Austin. And that he'd done it all behind her back.

When done, Langmore thanked Cel for her cooperation, unhooked her monitors, removed the sensors and finger clip, untethered his laptop from a larger machine sitting in the center of the table, and left without a goodbye or any hint of what she should do. She stood and paced back and forth, occasionally glancing up at the camera, wondering who was watching, what the results would be, what Parker saw in Lauren Page, the look on his face when he played with her son, how guilty she would look if she marched out of there with her chin held high and arms swinging confidently, leaving without offering a goodbye of her own.

She stopped moving when Detective Hart entered the room and refused his request for her to sit down. "I've been sitting down long enough. I'm ready to get out of here."

"I understand, but I have a few more things I'd like to discuss real quick."

Cel crossed her arms over her chest. Her mouth set in a hard line. "No. I've cooperated. Done everything you wanted me to do. I want to go now."

"You're free to leave, if you want," Hart said, gesturing at the door. "But then you won't be able to explain to me why the results of the polygraph test showed signs of deception on certain questions."

Cel was well aware she'd lied. A little. White lies. About being inside Lauren's apartment, following her, knowing that she had a son or why Parker had gone to Hunter's Haven. But she'd only fibbed about small things. Nothing that had anything to do with Lauren or Parker's disappearance. "This is bullshit." She stepped close enough to Hart to smell his sweat stench. "I. Don't. Know. Where. Lauren. Or. Parker. Are." She cut her eyes at the camera in case she had an audience.

Hart threw up a hand-shield again, at chest level. "It doesn't mean you're guilty. I'll be the first to admit these tests aren't one hundred percent. There are variables we're willing to take into consideration. Maybe you were too nervous or stressed. Or misunderstood the question. If you'll agree to come back and retake—"

"No. I'm done here."

Cel held eye contact with Hart. He didn't blink. She didn't blink. The air surrounding her felt solidified and warm despite the whooshing air conditioner. The thought of whether or not she looked guilty didn't re-enter her mind as she marched passed Hart with her chin held high and arms swinging confidently.

Chapter 27 - Parker

Parker awoke covered in sweat, his red boxers clinging to his legs and crotch, the balled-up shirt beneath his head damp. The stench of his own waste stewing in the bucket-toilet assaulted his nose seconds after he opened his eyes and found the room lit. The overhead bulb had fluctuated between lit and unlit for random chunks of time, but not in long enough intervals to coincide with night and day. He had no idea how long he'd slept. Or how long he'd been chained to the floor. Without clocks or sunrises or communication of any kind, the steady passage of time had abandoned him.

After his eyes adjusted to the light, he sat up and immediately noticed a change in the room. The small rectangle in the center of the far wall. A wallet-sized picture. He sprung up and almost fell when his foot tangled with his slacks. He'd taken them off God knows how long ago and slid them down his right leg over the chain. He regained his balance and moved forward until the chain snapped taut.

The photo was a headshot of Cel from not that long ago. Her face obviously cut out of a larger picture. A small piece of Scotch tape held it to the pocked wall. Her hair was pulled back in a ponytail, and she wasn't facing the camera. She had on her blue jogging tank top and was smiling wide enough to reveal her signature Garcia Family crooked incisor. The photo appeared creased and worn. As though it had been taken in and out of a wallet hundreds of times.

Parker pitched forward, lifting his chained ankle up off the ground, and reached for the picture, but his fingertips stopped six inches away.

"Damn it!" He yelled out of frustration as he reached down and jerked on the chain hard enough to send barbs of pain shooting up his leg, a reaction he'd found himself giving in to more and more as time passed. Or didn't.

He stared at the picture of Cel for a moment, then turned toward the coffin-sized cellar door at the top of the slender staircase. He hadn't seen his captor since the first time he'd awoken chained to the floor. Whoever it was must've slipped in while he slept and taped the photo to the wall.

"What do you want?!"

He could feel his skin reddening, his heart jackhammering, his veins bulging in his hands and temples. His tongue felt like sandpaper against the roof of his mouth. He glanced at the water jug on the floor to his left and realized it had been refilled sometime while he slept, too.

He shot a middle finger at the cellar door. "Fuck you!"

He wanted more than anything to chug the water, the entire gallon. His muscles and organs ached for moisture. But he knew better than to indulge. He'd concluded early on that he was either being drugged or poisoned. He initially attributed the waves of drowsiness and disorientation he was experiencing to a concussion from the blow to the back of his head, but soon realized the waves hit him hardest after he drank water from the jug. Water that when swished and held on the tongue carried an unnatural bitterness. The more he drank, the harder the punch. So he started drinking as little as possible, as infrequently as possible, in order to stay as alert as possible. Ready to seize an opportunity to escape if it arose.

He knew he should lie down and try to relax in order to lower his blood pressure, but he was too keyed up. His mind was racing and his feet begged to follow. He paced back and forth in front of the mattress as far as the chain allowed, balling and opening his fists. The slacks insulating the chain muffled the irritating scrape of metal on cement as he moved, allowing his stressed mind to run uninterrupted from one tangent to another, his emotions to stretch from tears to laughter.

First, he questioned the picture. *Who could've taken it, placed it there? Why Cel? What was the message? Was she being held captive, too? Or...there was no way she was involved in this, right? Had she hired someone to kidnap him like she'd hired Josh Teague to kick his ass?*

Which led to him weighing his entire relationship with Cel. The highs and lows, good times and bad. Moments they were the only two people on the planet. Ones filled with cursing and punches and pain. The sex and miscarriages. Regrets and missteps. Could'ves, would'ves, should'ves, and ifs. *Did he still love her as much as he once did? As much as a husband should?*

Which led him to Lauren. *Was he falling in love with her, or just infatuated with someone new, someone perkier?*

Which led him to the last argument he'd had with Cel. *How much did she know about Lauren? Or the other girls over the years, during what she called their 'dark stints?' Did she know Lauren had a kid, or that he'd met Sammy?*

Which led to him revisiting Sammy's birthday party at Peter Piper Pizza in Austin, smiling at the thought of the boy's joy when he opened his presents and ate cake with his friends.

Which led him to speculations about the four sons or daughters he had almost had. What they would've looked like, acted like, laughed like. As toddlers, teens, adults. Their hobbies, habits, idiosyncrasies. Hairstyles, height and weight, sexuality. *Would they be a momma's boy? A daddy's girl?*

Which led to him revisiting his own childhood: Christmas mornings and board game nights with his mom and dad and sisters. Egging and teepeeing houses on Halloween with his neighbor Billy before the Hamiltons moved away. Beers and poker with Uncle Marty when his parents went out of town. Fairs and movie nights and Hunter's Haven with the Cricket Hunters. Enemies like Jose. Girls. Like Abby. The real one who disappeared and the ghost one he chased through Hunter's Haven. *Had that really happened?*

The span of time between when Parker started pacing to when his legs and throbbing head started singing for relief could've been ten minutes, or it could've been ten hours. He couldn't be sure. Time no longer existed as far as he was concerned. He sat on the foot of the mattress, picked up the water jug, and took a long hard pull. The water tasted bitter, like the first batch, but that didn't diminish the relief his body expressed as wetness coated his mouth and throat and pooled in his empty stomach. He took two more decent sized gulps before lying down.

After positioning his shirt under his head, he closed his eyes, focused on breathing slow and steady, in the mouth out the nose like Dr. Gordon had taught him, and dove into one of his favorite childhood books.

He'd already swum through countless titles to stave off the hunger and isolation and fear. Sometimes he'd recited the stories aloud, sometimes silently. Sometimes he imagined turning actual pages filled with words as he read. Other times, he would visualize the action like a movie. He'd already traveled to Mars and The Shire and Derry, Maine. Anywhere to escape. This time, he decided to go to a "great town," as Roald Dahl called it, and follow Charlie Bucket on his quest for a golden ticket.

SEPTEMBER 1998

Chapter 28 - Cel

On the outer reaches of Twin Tree Cemetery, Cel, Parker, Abby, Omar, and Natalie stood shoulder-to-shoulder in front of a heap of dirt, looking into a hole at *Tia* Dillo's homemade, hand-painted coffin. At Yesenia's request, they were dressed in colorful, casual clothes, and not the typical dark, formal funeral attire. This wasn't a regular religious funeral, after all. There had been no obituary in the Oak Mott Daily, no viewing or church service. There would be no graveside sermons or prayers or speeches. There would be no line of mourners. It was simply a burial, a returning of *Tia* Dillo's vessel to the Source.

A few days earlier, Yesenia's and Cel's next door neighbor, Mike Stabel, had built the coffin in his garage, using leftover locally harvested oak he'd purchased for a patio project the previous summer. Mike was Cobalt Street's retired, jack-of-all-trades handyman, and one of the few people on the street who treated Yesenia like a human rather than a plague. He'd helped her with many plumbing and electrical issues over the years, replaced many hoses and gadgets on her '82 Starlet, and when she'd knocked on his door and offered him cash to build a simple wooden box to bury her sister in, he'd accepted without batting an eye. But as always, he'd refused payment. When finished, he and his son Mike Jr. propped it on sawhorses in Yesenia's driveway, where she and Cel had spent the afternoon painting it.

The glossy colors they'd chosen shone bright in the Saturday afternoon sunshine that spilled into the hole.

"It looks good," Parker said, shoving his hands into his deep cargo short pockets. "The swirly star things are cool."

Natalie adjusted her Astros hat to better block the sun from her eyes, then pointed at the foot of the coffin. "My favorites are the red and yellow flowers down there."

"I like the crescent moon," Omar said. "And the white cat in the tree."

"It's supposed to be a ferret," Cel said in a monotonous tone. "Dillo's favorite familiar." Her eyes were aimed at the coffin, but she wasn't seeing colors and images like the other hunters. She was seeing what lay beneath the coffin lid: Too-skinny *Tia* Dillo in her now too-big favorite dress on top of the quilt her mother had sewn for her when she was a child, surrounded by the personal items Cel and Yesenia had placed around the too-pale body at the funeral home before the final ritual was performed and the lid nailed shut.

"Oh, right," Omar said, fidgeting, sliding his hands in and out of his oversized sleeves. "I see it now. My bad."

After a short hesitation, Cel blinked away the image of her dead aunt and gave Omar a slight smile. "Don't worry. I painted it, and I can't even tell what it is."

"I thought it was a squirrel," Abby admitted demurely, keeping her hands clasped behind her back and not looking up.

"I thought it was a rat," Natalie said.

"Chihuahua for me," Parker said. "I thought *Tia* Dillo said they were her favorites once."

Cel chuckled, and everyone joined in. She fingered her necklace and found the clasp wedged up against the infinity symbol. She kissed the clasp, whispered the good fortune spell as she repositioned it, and then looked over her shoulder at Yesenia.

Twenty yards away, on a blanket in the only shaded spot in the cemetery, Yesenia sat cross-legged like a little girl. The two long-limbed oak trees that had given the cemetery a name lorded over her. She sat in between the two, below where their branches tangled. Supposedly, the trees sprouted the day after two young lovers, a white woman and black man who'd been secretly meeting in the field, died in the late 1800s. Yesenia had told Cel she would've preferred to bury Dolores in a more secluded place, Hunter's Haven maybe, naked and wrapped in a shroud, like they had their mom on their homestead. But since *Tia* Dillo died in a state hospital, and Texas has strict rules about known burials, she had no choice. Twin Tree was the cheapest cemetery in Oak Mott, so Twin Tree it was.

"Should we go back over there?" Parker asked. He and the others had briefly greeted Yesenia when they'd arrived on their bikes thirty minutes earlier.

Cel bit the corner of her bottom lip and looked at him. The concern she detected in his voice comforted her. She nodded, and he nodded back, took her hand in his, and led her and the others toward the trees.

She felt lighter with each step, as if his hand, his touch, somehow had the power to lift her off the ground and whisk her through the air, causing the blue and black flannel shirt tied around her waist to flow behind her like a cape. He'd called her every night since Dillo's death, talking her through the sleepless hours, promising her an exciting future with him by her side. Now, here he was, choosing to hold her hand out in the open, in front of the other hunters. She hoped they noticed. Especially Abby.

They sat in a semi-circle facing Yesenia. Two tight braids hung down either side of Yesenia's head and rested on her chest. In between them, Mina's severed leg bulged beneath her heavily embroidered *quechquémitl*. A Saran-Wrap-covered paper plate of *pan de leche* sat in the center of the blanket in front of her. She and Cel had baked the batch of *Tia* Dillo's favorite snack at sunrise and placed the largest one inside the casket. Yesenia peeled off the wrap. "You kids eat before the flies do."

They each took a piece of the sweet Mexican milk bread and started eating. The muggy air made the gummy dough stick to their fingers and lips. Parker finished first. "Delicious as always, Mrs. G," he said, wiping his hands on his shorts.

Yesenia gave a slight nod and smile of gratitude.

"I'd like to learn how to bake them," Natalie said. "My dad would love them."

"*Bien*," Yesenia said, her eyes moving from her sister's gravesite to briefly meet Natalie's before returning.

Robins chatted in the oak trees overhead as everyone silently finished their treats.

After dumping the crumbs into the grass and folding the paper plate into a small triangle, Yesenia's eyes moved across the kids' faces. "I told Cel last night I'd like for you all to keep hunting the crickets around the house until the cold weather comes. They're getting louder. I'll keep paying if you do, like I promised."

Natalie shot Cel a quick glance before looking at Yesenia. Her eyes were fraught with worry. "Are they starting to bother you now, too?"

Yesenia shook her head. "They're just a bad reminder, and we all had a deal." Then she locked eyes with Cel, her expression asking her questions.

Why did Natalie give you that look? What haven't you told me?

Cel felt the weight of her *abuela's* expectant eyes pressing on her. She hadn't told Yesenia about her fear that Maria might've sent the crickets after her, too. She'd only told the other hunters. With all Yesenia had gone through, she didn't want to stack any more worry on her plate. "When *Tia* Dillo was in the hospital, I had trouble sleeping because of the crickets, but they haven't bothered me ever since the night you did the…" Cel's eyes dipped to the bulge on Yesenia's chest, then swung back to her face. "Rituals." The inside of her mouth felt dry. She force-swallowed. "I'm sorry I didn't tell you, but I think they just bothered me because we hadn't been hunting as much, and I was home alone, and I felt guilty about *Tia* Dillo, and they reminded me of her, and I regretted that I'd…" Cel's eyes welled up.

"*Esta bien, mija,*" Yesenia said, and stood. "*Esta bien.*"

Cel stood, too. "I swear they haven't bothered me since then."

As Cel hugged Yesenia, the other hunters stood and brushed the crumbs off their clothes.

"We'll do it for free," Parker said.

Abby met eyes with him and nodded in agreement. "Of course, we will."

"Yeah, we don't want any money," Omar added.

"We'll do it to honor Dillo," Natalie said.

Yesenia released Cel and smiled big enough to expose her crooked Garcia incisor. Her eyes were bleary, matching Cel's. "*Gracias, mis pequenos.*"

All their attention turned south when an engine roared in the distance. Parked in front of the cemetery gate about fifty yards away was a red Mustang. Jose's Mustang. The passenger side faced the cemetery. The window was down, revealing Maria's chubby face and thick head of wavy hair. Jose leaned forward to see past his mom, one hand on the wheel. He gunned the engine, and Maria smiled and waved. "How is it, Yesenia?"

"Bitch," Parker said.

When he bolted toward the car, Abby grabbed his arm with both hands. "Don't, Parker."

He raised his middle finger high in the air and yelled, "Fuck you!"

Jose jumped out of the car, his bare chest and arms visible above the Mustang roof. He threw his hands in the air. "Bring it, *ese*! I'll put you in the ground, too."

Parker jerked free from Abby, but Yesenia grabbed his shoulder and spun him around. "No, Parker. *Detener.* This is what they want. They want us upset so they can laugh. Don't give that to them."

"But—"

"You better get back in the car with your mommy, asshole!" Cel bellowed from behind Yesenia. She pointed at Jose. "Before we put *you* in the ground."

Yesenia spun around. "Celia! *Basta!*"

Jose picked up a loose rock and hurled it at the hunters. When it landed a good twenty yards shy and no one responded, he threw his hands forward as though shooing a swarm of flies away. As though the hunters and Yesenia weren't worth the time or effort. When he ducked back into the Mustang, Cel noticed a cat's head peek out of Maria's window. A cat the same color as Frito. Her breath caught in her throat—*it couldn't be*—as Jose gunned the engine two hard times, and then shot gravel and dirt into the air as he peeled away from the cemetery gates.

Cel met eyes with Yesenia once the car was out of sight. "Sorry, *Buela.*"

"Me, too." Parker said. "He's just…They're so…ugh."

"Right," Abby added, crossing her arms over her chest.

Natalie shook her head. "I can't believe they would come out here and do that."

"I can," Cel countered.

"Some nerve," Omar said.

Yesenia took in a deep, audible breath. "You kids need to go home now." She spoke with an authoritative tone.

"But Cel said you needed to fill in the hole yourself," Parker said. "And we wanted to help."

"You can't," Yesenia said. "We only have two shovels."

"We could take turns," Natalie suggested.

"No." Yesenia motioned the kids off the blanket, scooped it up, and shook off the crumbs. "It's to be done by family only. Now go," she ordered. "I don't want you here if they come back."

Parker and the others looked back and forth at one another for a moment before heading toward their bikes. The southernmost road in the Gateway neighborhood nestled up against the back end of Twin Tree Cemetery. Cel had ridden with Yesenia and entered through the front gate, but the other hunters had taken the back way and propped their bikes on the outer side of the hurricane fence bordering the cemetery.

Cel snuck glances their way as she helped Yesenia fold the blanket and saw Abby hook her arm around Parker's and Natalie throw one of hers over his shoulders. They were out of earshot, but she could tell he was angry. His arms flailed wildly as he spoke. She hoped he wouldn't go looking for Jose without her.

Yesenia recited a protection spell for the hunters as they hopped the fence, which inspired Cel to cast a calming spell of her own for Parker. A simper formed on her face when he mounted *her* bike and smiled at her over his shoulder before pedaling away.

Graveside, Cel and Yesenia picked up the two shovels lying on the mound of dirt and began scooping soil onto *Tia* Dillo's casket. Thirty minutes in, covered in sweat, her arms and shoulders aching, Cel was glad they were not allowed to both dig and fill the hole like Yesenia had wanted. The cemetery owner, Tom Schneider, a hefty man who trimmed his beard in a way to remind people he had both a face and neck, had told them Texas required a certain depth and size for a burial hole, and he could be fined if those specifications weren't met. He demanded his team dig the hole, but that Cel and Yesenia could refill it as long as they didn't damage any nearby graves.

The soil was dry and airy, but each scoop and toss seemed heavier, harder to maneuver. They spoke little, and other than occasional glances at the cemetery gates, focused solely on shoveling. They stopped for water only once during the two hours it took to finish the job, when Mr. Schneider arrived in his small truck and approached them with two cold bottles, praising their efforts. Shortly after they'd finished, he returned with a second bottle for each of them, offered his condolences once again, and reminded them the flat grass headstone would take about four weeks to arrive. Having already spent countless hours over the past few days talking about Maria and Jose, curses and safety, Cel and Yesenia sat at Dolores's graveside without speaking about the incident. They rested with their own thoughts, drinking water, watching the sun slip toward the horizon in a wash of blues and purples and oranges.

At home, Yesenia insisted Cel shower first. Cel set the water as hot as she could tolerate and stood under the showerhead with her eyes closed, allowing the heat to soothe her sore muscles. She could've stood there all night but only stayed around twenty minutes to make sure her *abuela* would have plenty of hot water, too. When she walked into the living room in her purple robe, she found Yesenia asleep. She was in her chair, feet propped up on the coffee table, head tilted sharply back, mouth open. She snored at a steady pace, the cat-leg-bulge on her chest swelling and falling with each deep breath. Cel considered waking her but decided against it. Her *abuela* hadn't slept more than a couple of hours since *Tia* Dillo had passed. She needed rest. So Cel untied and slipped off Yesenia's shoes, laid the couch quilt over her legs, turned off the lamp, and headed to her bedroom.

The alarm clock on her window sill read eight-fifteen. She knocked the folder stuffed with school make-up work off her pillow onto the floor and lay down. She placed her phone onto her lap, intending to call Parker, but the relief of being horizontal forced her to close her eyes. She felt like they'd only been closed a few seconds, a long blink maybe, when a tap on her window jolted her upright, the bright green numbers on her alarm clock read nine-thirty.

She waited motionless, thinking she might've dreamed the noise.

Another couple of taps. This time followed by a loud whisper. "Cel? It's me. You in there?"

She peeked out the blinds and Parker waved at her. Her bike was on the grass behind him. The excitement in his eyes made her heart jackhammer. Warmth filled her chest as she raised the blinds and slid the window open. "What are you doing?" She tried to sound serious, tried to fight back her smile, but was unable to dampen her happiness.

"I felt bad that I've had your bike so long and wanted to bring it back."

Cel cocked her head and arched a doubtful brow. "If you were that worried about it, why didn't you give it to me at the cemetery?"

He stepped back and threw his hands in the air as if given orders by a police officer. "Okay. Okay. You've got me." He dropped his arms. "I didn't come to give your bike back. But you can have it, though. I really came because I wanted to see you. I wanted to make sure you were okay. Jose and Maria didn't show back up out there, did they?"

Cel sucked her bottom lip between her teeth and shook her head. "Did you guys run into them?"

"Nope. We just hung out at Abby's until her mom got home."

Cel kept her eyes glued to Parker's as he stepped up to the window and leaned his face to within inches of hers. His breath smelled sweet.

Like a combination of chocolate and vanilla. "I would invite you in, but I don't want to wake up my *abuela*. She passed out in her chair in the living room when we got home."

"Is she still mad at me?"

"She wasn't mad. She just didn't want you to get hurt."

Parker rose up on his tiptoes and dropped a quick kiss on her. "If I can't come in there, why don't you come out here?"

She raked her hand through his wavy hair. "I don't know if my *abuela* is awake or not. If she comes in here and I'm gone, she'll freak out."

"Come on," Parker plead. "We haven't spent any time alone together in days."

Cel bit at her lip to keep from beaming. "If I do, will you help me do something?"

"Anything. What?"

Cel held his gaze for a long second. "Did you see that cat on Maria's lap earlier?"

Parker shook his head. "No. Why?"

"It looked just like Frito."

As the statement sunk in, Parker's eyes widened. "It couldn't have been though…right?"

Cel shrugged.

"What did your grandma say about it?"

"I didn't ask her. She was so mad about what I did to Frito before. I was hoping she didn't see it, so she wouldn't worry."

Parker looked skyward, dropped his eyes back to Cel. "You want to go check the grave real quick? Make sure?"

A swell of warmth filled Cel's chest. It was like he could read her mind sometimes. She looked back over her shoulder at her closed door. She knew she shouldn't leave. She was tired and sore and emotionally wrung. Jose could be hiding around any corner. Yesenia would kill her if she found out. But she needed to check the grave, not only for her safety but also for her *abuela's*. On top of that, the idea of having Parker's undivided attention for a while was too inviting. "One sec."

She snuck down the hallway, avoiding the creaky spots, and peeked into the living room. Other than her head being turned to the side, Yesenia hadn't budged. She was still snoring, too, only quieter. Cel carefully made her way back to her bedroom, eased the door shut, and met Parker at the window. "All right. She's still asleep. But not for too long. Wait there. I need to change."

Without closing the window or lowering the blinds, Cel plucked a T-shirt and jean shorts out of her dresser. Turning her back to Parker in the center of the room, feeling his eyes on her, wanting them on her, she shrugged off her purple robe and stood still for a moment in her underwear and bra before stepping into her shorts and sliding on her shirt. After slipping on shoes, she climbed out the window.

Parker grabbed the garden shovel off of the back porch and took Cel's hand in his as they headed for Hunter's Haven. He met eyes with her in the field behind the backyard. "Are the crickets bothering you? Should we take our sticks? I have my little flashlight."

Cel shook her head. With Parker holding her hand, by her side, nothing would bother her.

They reached Frito's burial site within minutes, and Parker slid aside the giant rock they'd placed on top, knelt, and patted the dirt. "Feels solid. Doesn't look like it's been disturbed or anything."

Cel knelt and touched the ground, too. She agreed, but she had to be certain. The best forms of magic were often the hardest to detect. "Give me that." She took the garden shovel and started digging.

The scent of decay wafted from the earth almost instantly. Aiming his flashlight at the growing hole with one hand, Parker buried his nose in the crook of his other arm. "Whew. I think he's definitely still dead."

Cel gagged a couple of times but continued digging. About twelve inches down, the garden shovel finally met resistance. She and Parker leaned over the small hole. The flashlight highlighted globs of fur and the sliver of a bone. Cel looked at Parker. "I guess it was a new familiar."

Parker nodded. "Probably." He handed the flashlight to Cel, shoved the loose dirt back into the hole, and then slid the large rock back into place. When they stood, Cel threw her arms around Parker's neck and kissed him. She felt his desire growing when she ground her pelvis into his. Her heart was beating so fast she couldn't detect individual beats. She had a million thoughts running through her mind, but they weren't the type of thoughts you said. They were the type you turned into action. By the way Parker was eyeing her, she assumed—*hoped*—the same thoughts were running through his head.

"You want to go back?" Parker asked. "So you don't get in trouble."

"If my *abuela* woke up, I'm already in trouble, so I might as well make the most of the night."

Parker looked left, right, thumbed behind him. "Since we're already about a third of the way to Table Rock, I guess we could…"

"Go all the way," Cel finished, her eyes betraying her intended use of the innuendo.

Parker's mouth curled into a smile as he registered the offer in her eyes. Without responding, he took her by the hand and led her deeper into the woods. They exchanged nervous glances as they moved. Their pace quickened with each step, as though they were trying to keep up with their out-of-control hormonal desires. As though the prize of a lifetime waited for them at Table Rock.

When Table Rock came into view and the trickle of Mesquite Creek hit their ears, Parker jerked to a stop and spun her toward him. He pushed into her, kissing her, wrapping his hands around her waist, running them up the back of her shirt, down the back of her shorts. She reciprocated.

They lowered to the ground on a bed of leaves and twigs under a gnarled elm tree, undressing from the waist down.

"Are you sure?" Parker asked. "Out here? Like this?"

Cel pulled him onto her. Fear of being too young, or not waiting until marriage, or not using a condom or diaphragm, or getting a disease, or getting pregnant after only one time like Rita Owen said happened to her sister—everything her *abuela* and health teacher had lectured her about, everything the cautious voice inside her head usually screamed—couldn't best her lust and love for Parker. Not tonight.

She squealed when she lay back and a twig poked her shoulder blade. Parker rose to his knees. "Here." He took off his shirt and put it underneath her. "Better?"

She nodded although she could still feel the twig digging into her shoulder blade, the weight of him on her sore muscles.

What followed didn't take long and was nothing like the Skin-A-Max movies she'd seen. It didn't feel good or pleasurable or make her moan, but it felt right. Having Parker inside her felt right. Like a lock only has one right key. Parker was right for her. Lying underneath him, listening to him whisper her name as he enjoyed her, she felt as far away as possible from the grief and guilt she'd been buried under for days. She felt free. Like she'd proven to Parker how much she loved him.

They dressed with their backs to one another and walked out of Hunter's Haven hand-in-hand. They didn't speak, only exchanged furtive glances and hesitant smiles. Cel didn't know what to say. Questions were erupting inside her head, but she couldn't find the confidence to voice them. *What's he thinking about? Is he thinking what I'm thinking? Was this really his first time, too? Is this something we talk about? Did he like it? Was I good at it? Should we have done it? Does he see me different now? Better or worse? Are we going to keep it a secret?*

When Cel's window came into view, she breathed a sigh of relief. The inside was dark, which meant Yesenia hadn't awoken. She turned her back to the house, wrapped her arms around Parker's neck, and kissed him. When their lips parted, they held eye contact. As Cel searched his eyes and he hers, she sensed that similar questions were erupting inside his head, too. They were on the same plane. They had been all night. Before and after. During. Together. Connected in more than just a physical way. She'd made the right choice.

"Will you give me a boost?" Cel asked.

"Of course." Parker squatted and laced his fingers together.

She stepped into his hands, climbed into her room, and turned back toward the window.

"You good?" Parker asked.

"Yeah. You?"

"Yeah."

He smiled. She smiled bigger. They shared a moment.

"I'll call you tomorrow," he said.

"You can help me with all the make-up work I have from the four days I missed last week."

"On second thought, I'll have Omar call you tomorrow."

"You're stupid."

"Exactly. That's why I'll have Omar call you tomorrow." Parker up-righted Cel's bike and gave her an imploring, charming look as he threw his leg over the seat. "Can I? For just one more night?"

She rolled her eyes playfully. "Fine."

Right then, she would've given him the bike forever had he asked.

Chapter 29 - Parker

Riding Cel's bike, Parker escorted Abby and Jeff home after school on Monday. After the incident with their dad a week earlier, where he'd pounded on the house and scared them into the basement, Abby had been terrified to enter the home alone, fearing Tom Powell might've broken in and be waiting inside. Four out of five weekdays, her mom left for work at three-thirty, leaving the house empty for nearly an hour before she and Jeff arrived home. Her mom had filed a restraining order against Tom that night, but the cops hadn't been able to locate him yet. Abby asked Parker to please follow her and Jeff home and check the house with them, promising him "anything" he wanted if he agreed. He was more than willing.

Parker led Abby and Jeff through the house, checking closets, under beds, the garage, and the basement. Just like the checks the previous week, they found nothing amiss, no sign of an intruder. After sharing a menthol and school gossip on the back porch, Parker turned on the TV in the living room while Abby forced Jeff to get a snack, go to his room, and shut the door.

Abby sat on the couch next to Parker, close enough for her leg to rest against his. "Thanks for doing this again for me," she said. "You're a life saver."

Parker smiled. "No problem." He put his hand on her thigh, and the moment they met eyes, she threw her arms around his neck and kissed him. Ever since they'd begun this routine last week, their make-out sessions had started more quickly each day, lasted longer, progressed farther. She shoved her tongue into his mouth. He loved the way she always madly swirled it around like a tornado. Like a possessed corkscrew. As he pawed at her chest, she pawed his crotch. They kissed and touched and moaned. She guided his hand under her shirt. She unbuttoned his shorts and was snaking her hand beneath his boxers when she heard footfalls behind the couch.

She jerked her hand free. "What the fuck?"

Fumbling to button his shorts, Parker looked over his shoulder. Jeff stood a few feet away, clutching the Bart Simpson doll from the fair. Determination was etched across his face, rebellion pouring out of his eyes.

"I'm sick of being in there. I want to watch TV."

Abby grabbed a pillow and hurled it at him. "No! Get the hell out of here!"

He scooped up the pillow and threw it back, hitting Parker in the head.

"Not cool, man," Parker said.

Abby looped around the couch, stomping toward Jeff.

"It's not fair," he yelled as he fought off his sister's attempt to grab his arms. "I'm not your fucking prisoner!"

"If you don't go back to your room." Abby jerked Bart Simpson out of Jeff's hand and held it over her head where he couldn't reach it. Then she positioned her hands as though she were about to twist off its head like a bottle cap. "Your precious little Bart gets it."

"If you do," Jeff countered. "I'll tell mom what you and Parker have been doing on the couch after school every day."

Abby's mouth thinned into a tight rope, and when she twisted Bart's head backwards, Jeff roared and lunged at her. "Give him back!" He fought, got a handle on Bart's leg, then kicked Abby's shin hard enough to knock her leg fully out from under her. She dropped Bart and threw her hands out for balance as she pitched sideways. Her shoulder slammed into the wall, cracking sheetrock before she fell to the floor.

"Jeff!" Parker screamed. "What the hell!"

Cradling Bart like a football, Jeff bolted into his room, and slammed the door.

As Parker helped Abby to her feet, a solid thunk, a wood-on-wood crunch, sounded behind Jeff's door. "What's he doing?" Parker asked.

"Pushing his dresser up against the door. The lock doesn't work."

Parker eyed Abby's leg. The sole of Jeff's shoe had fileted off a patch of skin exposing pink flesh. Blood oozed to the surface. "You okay?"

"I'll be fine," she said as she rolled her arm, testing her shoulder joint for pain.

Parker guided her back to the couch. "Wait here." He made his way to the bathroom in the hall, wet a washcloth, and grabbed a Band-

Aid out of the medicine cabinet. Across the hall, Jeff had turned up his radio, loud. The bass rattled the walls.

After cleaning and bandaging Abby's wound, Parker tossed the washcloth in the bathroom hamper and returned to the living room to find Abby lacing up her shoes. "I want to leave," she said.

"I thought your mom said not to leave Jeff alone."

"I know, but..." She stood, puffed her cheeks, and exhaled. "I really want to get out of this house for a little while."

One corner of Parker's mouth lifted as an idea sprouted in his mind. "Okay." He shoved his hands into his pockets, fished around, and pulled out a five dollar bill. Brandishing it as though it were a worth a fortune, he flicked his eyebrows up and down. "How about we go to Rita's and get a *raspa*?"

Abby smiled, nodded. "What about Jeff?"

Parker held up a finger. "One sec." He walked to Jeff's door, knocked hard, and tried to yell louder than the music. "Jeff! Come out! We're going to go get snow cones!" He knocked again. "Jeff! Come on, man! Let's go!" He turned the knob and pushed against the door with all his weight, but it only opened a crack before the dresser stopped it. "Jeff!" Parker hollered through the crack. He figured if he slammed into the door hard enough, the dresser would fall, but he didn't want to go that far. He looked down the hall. Abby was standing behind the couch, watching him. "He won't come out."

"He's probably in his closet. He hides in there sometimes when he gets pissed. Mom says it's best to leave him alone when he does. Let's just go. We already checked the house. He'll be fine." She held up the house key and flashed an exaggerated smile. "I'll lock the door behind us like a good big sister."

On the side of the house, Parker mounted Cel's bike. "You want to ride with me, or are you going to ride yours?"

Abby paused, appraising the back wheel pegs on Cel's bike as though they were speaking to her, reminding her of the past, before looking at Parker. "Why did you hold her hand at the funeral the other day?"

Parker gave her a quizzical, *are-you-serious* look. "What made you think of that?"

She shrugged. "I don't know." She looked down, up. "I thought you said you didn't like her like that."

It wasn't easy for Parker to lie to Cel and Abby. They were two of his best friends. They were Cricket Hunters. Part of him, the part that had been their friend through thick and thin for years, knew that it was a mistake, that they would eventually figure everything out and his actions would come back to bite him. But another part of him, the young man who felt he knew all and deserved to explore all, liked "the thrill of having the best of both worlds" as his Uncle Marty put it. Cel was a clever, inspiring, beautifully mysterious girl, a challenge. Abby was perkier, sillier, more eager and willing. Easier to cajole. He liked hanging around with both of them. He might even love both of them. He didn't want to have to make a permanent choice between them. At least not yet. He'd fallen asleep twice this past week daydreaming about what would happen if one of Yesenia's magic books had a spell or ritual in it that could somehow meld them together. Now that would be perfect.

"I held her hand because it was *Tia* Dillo's funeral, and she was sad," he lied. "I would've done the same for you. Or Natalie. Or Omar."

"The look on her face when you grabbed her hand was not a friendly look. It was head-over-heels in love look."

Parker let out a nervous, airy chortle. "That's not the way I meant for her to take it." He touched his chest. "And I didn't see it that way."

"Are you going to tell her about us?"

Parker hesitated, his mind spinning, looking for an out. "I really don't think that would be smart because…you know…" He crinkled his nose and wiggled his fingers at her, hoping to turn the conversation down a humorous road. That had always seemed productive with Abby in the past. "She might turn us into toads or some shit like that."

The corners of Abby's mouth hinted at joy, but only for a moment. "I don't want to hide what we're doing. If what we feel between us is real, we shouldn't have to hide it just because she has a crush on you."

His stomach turning sour, his legs antsy, Parker nodded. "But can we not worry about this right now? I just want to enjoy our time together." He gestured at the pegs with his eyes. "Now hop on so we can get there before Rita closes shop."

Abby obeyed, pressing her chest against Parker's back and wrapping her arms tightly around his chest as he pedaled away.

About ten or fifteen people were in line when Parker and Abby arrived. *Rita's Raspas* was a food/snow cone trailer owned and run by Rita Morales and her daughter Isabell. It had been a staple in Oak Mott for as long as Parker could remember. They not only sold the biggest, sweetest snow cones in town, Rita also made fresh tamales and burritos daily. During spring and early fall, the trailer rested in a vacant lot a block away from Oak Mott High School, and during the summer months, in the Woodway Community Pool parking lot. The day after Halloween, when temperatures started dropping and all the cotton crops were harvested, leaving Rita's husband Rene out of work, the Morales's hitched the trailer to their beat-up Chevy and headed south for warmer weather and jobs on citrus farms. But they returned to the vacant lot like clockwork each March, open from eleven to six every day but Sunday.

Parker laid Cel's bike in the grass near the trailer hitch and followed Abby to the end of line. Most of the kids in line were sweaty football players in padded pants, but a few were younger, around Jeff's age. Two Hispanic men were at the front of the line, standing under the awning that was propped open with a broom handle, speaking Spanish to Rita. Music from the Oak Mott High marching band, which Natalie and Omar were members of, drifted up the street from Klepper Fields where they practiced.

After fist bumping a couple of the players, Parker and Abby chatted as they inched closer to the trailer. They made small talk about movies and music, snow cone flavors and costumes for next month's Halloween dance. Parker was mindful about not mentioning Cel, or anything remotely related to her, and was thankful Abby didn't either. When they reached the opening under the awning, Rita greeted them with a tired smile and asked what she could get for them in broken English. Parker ordered a large cherry *raspa* in a cup, Abby a lemon one, both topped with a sprinkle of Lucas chili powder.

"You want to eat them here or take them back to your house?" Parker asked as they approached Cel's bike. "We've been gone about twenty minutes."

Abby slid the plastic spoon out of her mouth and pointed it toward the ground as she swallowed. "Here. It won't take long. Jeff's probably still in the closet, anyway." She shoveled more yellow ice into her mouth and spoke as she sloshed it around. "Sometimes he stays in there for more than an hour."

They sat in the grass in front of Cel's bike with the setting sun at their backs, silently watching customers come and go, and cars pass by on Jasper Street as they ate. Parker had emptied half of his cup when Abby jumped up without warning, as if a steel rod had been thrust up her spine, and looked toward the road.

Alarmed, Parker stood and followed her gaze. She was staring at a small white car that had pulled to the side of the road across the street. The driver opened the door. "What's wrong?" Parker asked. "Who's that?"

The broad-shouldered man in a tight T-shirt and baggy jeans marched across the street with a purpose. His head was shaven to stubble, in tandem with his whiskered face.

"My dad," Abby said. She dropped her snow cone and looked at Parker with panic-stricken eyes. "We have to go."

"Abby!" Tom Powell hollered as Parker tossed his snow cone aside.

Parker's fight or flight instincts kicked in. He righted and mounted Cel's bike. He'd only seen Abby's dad in old pictures, when he was young and lanky and smiling. This man wasn't smiling, and he wasn't lanky. The prison weight yard had done his body well. "Come on."

By the time Abby was secure and Parker's foot hit the pedal, Tom was directly in front of them. He straddled the front tire and grabbed the handle bars with both hands.

Parker tried to jiggle the handlebars. "Let go, man."

Tom kept his eyes on Abby. "I just want to talk for a minute."

"Get away from us," Abby yelled, squeezing Parker's chest so tight he gasped.

"I'm not going to hurt you," Tom demanded, causing the kids and Hispanic woman in line to turn their way. "But you fucking owe me the right to explain myself."

"I don't owe you anything."

Tom's eyes searched the line of customers, then swiveled back to Abby. "Is my boy here?" He glanced toward his car, up and down Jasper Street. "Where is he?"

"He's not here," Abby said. "And he doesn't want to talk to you, either. We both hate you!"

Tom pointed at Abby. "Don't you fucking talk to me that way. You need to show some respect. I'm your dad for Christ's sake." He pointed to the ground. "Now get off that fucking bike."

Realizing Tom only had one hand on the handlebars now, Parker twisted the wheel back and forth as hard as he could. The tire slapped into Tom's calves, knocking him off balance, forcing his other hand to slip off the handlebars. Parker jerked the bike backward, but as he turned the wheel and tried to get a foothold on a pedal, Tom shoved him. The bike toppled over. Abby screamed when she and Parker crashed onto the ground. Parker looked back as he scrambled out from under the bike and jumped up with his hands fisted.

Tom glowered at him. "Who the fuck do you think you are, *boy*?"

Parker kept his eyes on Tom as Abby pulled her leg free from the bike's weight and crab-walked toward him. His attention snapped toward the trailer when the door flung open with a bang, and Rita emerged, leveling a shotgun at Tom.

"You leave those kids alone and go," Rita said. She was tiny and short, ninety pounds and five-feet tall at best, but her steely eyes and unbreakable tone projected the size and strength of a giant.

Tom threw his hands up. "Calm down, lady."

"I am calm." Rita gestured at the road with the gun barrel. "Now go, or I call cops."

Tom nodded. "Okay. I'm going. I'm going." His eyes flicked from Rita to Abby as he backed toward the road. He paused when he reached the curb, holding Abby's gaze. "We'll talk later."

Abby sidled up next to Parker as Tom turned around and sauntered across the street. Along with Rita and all the other customers, they watched Tom pull away from the curb, U-turn, and squeal his tires as he sped south.

Parker looked at Rita, and she lowered the gun. "Thank you."

"Welcome. You okay?"

Together, Parker and Abby said, "Yeah."

She glanced at their spilled cups on the ground. "You want another *raspa*?"

Together, they shook their heads. "No thanks," Parker said.

As Rita headed back into her trailer, Parker turned to Abby, looked her up and down, saw the bandage had ripped off her shin. Blood was flowing from the wound again. "Are your leg and shoulder okay?" he asked. She'd landed on the same shoulder she'd slammed into the wall at her house. Rubbing it, she nodded, her eyes trained in the direction Tom had driven.

"I don't think he'll come back." Parker assured. "Rita scared the shit out of him."

"That's not what I'm worried about." She made eye contact with Parker, and he felt a heavy force coming his way. "He's headed toward my house."

Parker cut his eyes southward down Jasper Street. *Jeff.* They mounted Cel's bike and took off without another word.

They covered the two and half miles to Abby's house quicker than normal, using alleys as a pathway in case Tom had circled back to cut them off. When they reached the back of Abby's house, she jumped off the pegs before Parker fully stopped. She sprinted across the backyard, through the side gate, and was halfway around the house before Parker had steered Cel's bike into the backyard and jumped off.

When he rounded the house, Tom's car was nowhere in sight, but the front door was wide open. He could hear Abby inside, yelling, "Jeff," over and over. He followed her voice.

In the living room, an end table was knocked over, a lamp lying on the floor with its shade askew. Abby's calls for Jeff echoed from the hallway. Parker almost slammed into her as he entered Jeff's room.

"He's not here," she said, shoving past him, continuing to yell her brother's name.

The room was a mess, plastic toys everywhere, a trash can tipped over, food wrappers and paper falling out, the bed sheets torn off and on the floor. The dresser was face-down beside the mattress. Like Parker imagined it would've been if he'd thrown his shoulder into the door earlier. He spun around as Abby emerged from her mom's room and ran toward the dining room.

He chased after her, trailing her into every room, checking every closet, every cupboard small enough to fit Jeff. They searched every nook and cranny, the garage and basement and attic, just like they had when they'd first arrived after school. Then they checked again, continually calling out for Jeff. But Jeff was gone.

Chapter 30 - Cel

Cel waited until Yesenia had been snoring a good thirty minutes before staging her bed and sneaking out of the house. She stuffed her robe under the blankets to simulate a body, threw on jeans and her trusty flannel, and climbed out of her window five minutes shy of eleven. Natalie had called her four hours earlier, telling her about Abby's and Parker's encounter with Tom, and about Jeff's disappearance. Abby's mom had called the cops, and they were scouring the town, searching for Tom and Jeff. Natalie invited Cel to go over to Abby's with her and Omar, for support, but Cel declined. She'd been sick since Sunday afternoon. She and Yesenia both. They spent the day after Dillo's funeral fighting stomach cramps, taking turns retching into the toilet. The nausea had abated some for Cel come Monday morning, but not for Yesenia. They'd rested in front of the TV in the living room all day, sipping *yerba buena,* periodically casting healing and soothing spells between trips to the toilet. They were convinced they'd been sickened not by the chicken they'd eaten before the burial the previous day, but by Maria.

Along with the electric bill and Saturday's coupon booklet, Cel had collected a small envelope addressed to Yesenia when she checked the mailbox Sunday morning. The envelope held two small scraps of paper that reeked of rotten beans and were speckled with black droplets. Cel's name was scribbled on one scrap, Yesenia's the other. Yesenia said she knew the sickening curse well. It was a juvenile curse. Perfect to fly under the radar of most protection spells. She and Dolores had used it on schoolmates who teased them when they were young. Maria was toying with them. Cel had helped Yesenia perform a cleansing ritual, burning the paper, envelope, a smattering of herbs, and chunk of Palo Santo, but by that afternoon, they were sick nonetheless.

So while her *abuela* had napped this afternoon, Cel had pulled the old chest out of the closet and dug through the grimoires until she found the one labeled *MALDICION*. Inside, she'd found what she wanted: the process to cast the name-on-paper sick curse, a simple curse even an inexperienced *bruja* or warlock should be able to adequately concoct. Completing the ritual had only taken her about five minutes. She shoved the envelope holding the smelly, hexed piece of paper with Maria's name and dried drops of blood on it in her back pocket as she hurried across her front yard.

She let down her hair to blanket her cheeks and neck and shoved her hands in her pockets as she headed down Cobalt Street. A cool breeze had pushed out the day's heat, chilling her depleted body. A small cup of tortilla soup was all she'd managed to hold down today.

She needed her bike. It would not only make life easier on her weak legs but would also make escape easier if she ran into trouble at Maria's house. But she hadn't seen Parker since late Saturday night after Dillo's funeral, hadn't talked to him since Sunday afternoon. He'd been at school all day, at Abby's ever since. When she rounded onto his street, she saw his dad's truck in the driveway but not Beverly's car. The porch light was on, but all the windows including his were dark. She lightly tapped on Parker's window and whispered his name a few times, anyway. After trying a second time with no response, she crept around the perimeter of the entire house, hoping, but didn't find her bike.

It might be at Abby's house, Cel thought, and quickly headed that direction. If Parker had ridden it over there after school but then was taken to the police station to answer questions about Tom and Jeff, which would explain why Beverly's car was gone this late, too, it would still be there. Either way, she needed a bike. If she didn't find hers here, she'd take Abby's or Jeff's.

She found Abby's house nearly identical to Parker's. Porch light on, the windows dark. Abby's mom's car wasn't in the driveway, making Cel believe her assumption had been right. Parker and Abby and their mothers were probably at the Oak Mott Police Station. Or the hospital, if something terrible had happened. The thought triggered her to kiss the clasp of her infinity necklace, whisper the good fortune charm, and spin it back into place.

She walked around the right side of the house, opened the wooden gate, and although the back porch light was off, the security light on the electrical pole in the alley provided enough glow for her to see her bike laying in the yard next to Abby's Schwinn. Perfect.

She had crossed half the distance to her bike before a dim, flickering light teased the corner of her eye. She froze and looked toward the house. The light was coming from behind the sliding glass doors. A TV light. The blinds were twisted closed and covered three-fourths of the two glass panes. Curious, she crouched low, made her way onto the porch, and ducked behind the lawn chair to peek inside.

The TV's glow highlighted the coffee table and couch, the brightness growing and dimming when the images on the screen changed. For a brief moment, Cel started to rise and knock on the glass. Parker was sitting on the center couch cushion, facing the TV. But she quickly squatted back down when Abby looped around the couch in a knee-length, nightgown-large T-shirt, sat next to him, and laid her head on his shoulder. When the TV light hit Abby's face, her eyes looked puffy, like she'd been asleep or crying, or both. When Parker put his arm around her shoulder, Cel's barren stomach clinched. He's just consoling her, she thought. He's caring like that. Probably feels guilty for taking her to the snow cone stand. A good friend. Abby on the other hand…

She watched them sit there silent and unmoving for five long minutes before Abby's hand started rubbing on Parker's thigh and slipping her fingertips under his cargo shorts. He didn't respond. But he didn't stop her either. His face stayed fixed on the TV. Cel's breathing grew deep and thick, allowing the smell from the ashtray crammed with menthol butts under the lawn chair to saturate her nose, fill her lungs, absorb into her taste buds. Nervous sweat collected in her armpits, adding to the stench. She wanted to jump up and hurl the fucking nasty ashtray through the glass. Instead, she gritted her teeth and watched, hoping Parker would set Abby straight.

When Abby's hand touched Parker's crotch he put his hand on her and said something short. One or two words. *No, Abby? Don't? Stop?*

Abby stood and stepped in front of Parker, shading his face from the TV's glow and Cel's eyes. Cel pursed her lips as Abby hiked her shirt up to her armpits and held it there. She had on pink underwear and a white bra. *Do you like what you see? Isn't it better than Cel?* Cel didn't know if he was smiling or not, ogling Abby or not, but she did know he wasn't reaching for her, or rising and kissing her, or pulling her onto him like he had Cel.

Long seconds passed. Then Abby dropped her shirt and straddled Parker, her breasts inches from his face. Cel watched Parker's arms, waiting for any sign of movement, willing him to reject her, but before he reacted, Abby scooped the remote up off the couch cushion and flicked off the TV, shrouding the room in darkness.

Cel balled her fists and squeezed hard enough to drive her nails into her palms. Fucking Abby. Tits. She was throwing herself at Parker, trying to manipulate him, seduce him, sway him, tease him, win him, all while her little brother was missing, possibly kidnapped, or being tortured, or even dead, and it was all her fault for leaving the kid alone. Disgusting. Weak. Pathetic. Slut.

Cel stared at her reflection in the dark glass for what felt like an eternity, mentally begging Parker to flick on a light, before finally slinking off the porch, retrieving her bike, and wheeling it through the gate on the side of the house.

She was no longer cold. In fact, her cheeks and hands felt as if they were on fire, the chords in her neck tight. Her heart pounded. Chest ached. Whether more from hurt or anger, she didn't know. She wanted to cry. To scream. She wanted answers. Wanted a fight.

She pedaled toward Clover Lane harder than she'd ever pedaled in her life. The more distance she put between her and Abby's house, the worse she felt. After she dismounted her bike and propped it against the back of the rusty camper three houses down from Maria's house, a wave of light-headedness lapped over her. Her vision blurred, equilibrium tilted. She put her hand on the back of the camper to brace herself, but the sensation traveled down her body. Her knees turned to rubber, unable to support her weight, forcing her to the pavement. She'd pushed herself too hard, stretched herself too thin in too many ways. She lowered her face into her hands and sobbed.

She jerked her head up and scooted her back up to the camper's license plate when she heard a car engine approaching from the opposite direction. When the headlights veered into a driveway across the street from Maria's house, Cel levered herself to her feet and leaned back against the camper. She listened to the engine cut off, a car door open and close, a house front door open and close. The light-headedness had passed, but now she felt queasy. She fished the envelope out of her back pocket. She needed to slip the envelope into the mailbox and hurry home.

She peeked around the camper. Maria's car was in the driveway, Jose's red Mustang behind it, partially blocking the sidewalk, a few feet from the curbside mailbox. The garage door was down, the gate to the backyard closed and padlocked—a new edition since the night she'd stolen Frito. She bet Maria's bedroom window stayed closed now, too. The porchlight was off, the only visible window on the side of the house darkened by curtains.

She followed the neighbors' fence-lines up the street, moving in shadows whenever possible, her eyes locked on Maria's front door. She crouched as she approached Jose's Mustang and paused next to the back driver's side fender. Looking over the trunk, she ran her eyes over the house again, checked the windows and front door, but saw no signs of life. Staying low, she slid around the Mustang bumper and placed the letter in the mailbox, wedging in the middle of the Monday mail the Lopez's hadn't retrieved.

As she crept back around the back of the Mustang, she stopped when she noticed a smattering of green shards on the curb on the neighbor's side of the driveway. A shattered beer bottle. *Dos Equis.* Jose's favorite beer. When at his house with her *abuela*, Cel had heard him claim it was the only brand real Mexicans should drink. He'd probably tossed the bottle there. Such a fucking pig. Inconsiderate and rude. Always insisting he was right. Always demanding he get anything he wanted, when he wanted it. Disgusting. Just like Abby.

Her eyes stolid, wrought with justified vindication, Cel picked up the largest shard, made her way over to the Mustang with purpose and dug the glass into the paint.

"This is for my *abuela*. For *Tia* Dillo. Because you're an arrogant asshole. Because your mom is a bitch. Because I can."

Spittle fumed from her lips as she whispered and scored the door and both adjoining fenders. As a final fuck you, she stabbed the shard at the back tire, but it punctured her palm instead of the rubber, drawing fresh blood. She cursed in Spanish, and without realizing exactly what she'd done until finished, she scratched TITS across the bottom of the door.

She tossed the shard aside, sprinted to her bike, and pedaled back to the Gateway neighborhood as quickly as her legs and lungs allowed. When she turned onto Abby's street, Abby's mom's Escort and Beverly Lundy's Suburban were in the driveway, a police cruiser curbside in front of the house. The front door was closed, all the inside windows now lit.

Keeping her eyes on the front door, she cautiously wheeled her bike up to the gate on the side of the house, and after peeking into the backyard to make sure the coast was clear, she eased open the gate, pushed the bike through, and lowered it to the ground. This wasn't exactly where she'd found it, but considering all that had happened in the home, her bike's exact placement wouldn't be memorable, anyway. Besides, she couldn't risk someone seeing her.

She slipped across the street and headed home without chancing a glance back at the house.

SEPTEMBER 2013

Chapter 31 - Cel

The sun had set by the time Cel marched out of the Oak Mott Police Station after the polygraph test. When she arrived home, Mila emerged from the darkness and greeted her just inside the door, weaving around her ankles, meowing for food. Cel whispered a soothing spell as she flicked on every light she passed on her way to the kitchen. She filled Mila's food and water bowls and was on her way to the bathroom to pee when the landline phone rang. She knew the caller without checking the caller ID. Parker had insisted they have a landline in case of power outages or other emergencies, and Yesenia was the only person other than Parker's mom and telemarketers who knew the number.

Cel had debated stopping by her *abuela's* house on the way home but decided against it. She knew Yesenia would insist on brewing tea, probably cooking something, too, and then want to sit at the kitchen table and talk for hours, discussing what Detective Hart had wanted, what he'd asked, what, if anything new, the cops had learned. Cel wasn't hungry, and she wasn't eager for a long, face-to-face rehashing session, either. She needed time to process everything first. But if she didn't answer, Yesenia might drive over. Over the phone she'd at least be able to keep the conversation short.

She picked up after the second ring. Natalie and Omar had driven back to Yesenia's house after Cel left for the police station to let her know what had happened. They were still there, worried because Cel hadn't answered their texts or calls. Cel gave Yesenia the short version of the interrogation, not mentioning the polygraph or that her phone had been confiscated, and politely rejected Natalie's and Omar's offer to come over, saying she was tired and just wanted to take a hot shower and get some sleep. She promised to call them and swing by her *abuela's* house sometime tomorrow. After she hung up, she filled the tea kettle and placed it on the burner before heading to the bathroom.

She changed into sweatpants and a tank top, and as the hours passed, moved from room to room with Mila on her heels and a mug of tea in her hand, erasing what the cops had done. She flipped her mattress to hide the missing chunk and remade the bed with fresh sheets. She reorganized the closets, emptied the dressers, refolded and replaced the clothes. She removed every dish from every cupboard, washed them and put them back. She re-stacked Parker's paperback books in the computer room closet in alphabetical order by author's last names with one exception; she put *The Illustrated Man* with Abby's picture sticking out on Parker's nightstand. She scrubbed the toilets and sinks and tubs. She vacuumed. The longer she worked, the more isolated and scared she felt. The house seemed larger and larger. The silence heavier and heavier. She left every light on, all closet doors open. Checked and rechecked every locked window and door. Tears occasionally fell from her eyes as her mind reeled, struggling to absorb and process her situation.

When she'd completed every task she could think of, she went to the living room, sat on the couch, and turned on the TV. It was a little after four in the morning. She was exhausted but for some reason couldn't keep her eyes closed. She found an *I Love Lucy* re-run, lay on her side, and stared blankly at the screen. Only after Mila hopped onto the couch and curled up against her belly did sleep finally find her.

She awoke three hours later, not rested but alert. Leaving the TV on for noise, she made her way through the house, turning off the lights and opening the curtains and blinds, allowing the rising sun to light the place. After showering and performing a strengthening ritual, she toasted a piece of bread, refilled her mug with warm tea, and went back to the couch where Mila napped. The local news was on. She watched the weekly forecast and was about to change the channel when a short-haired woman anchor named Jesse Dalton said, "Coming up, Oak Mott Police are asking for help following the disappearance of two local teachers."

Cel gasped when Parker's and Lauren's pictures popped up in the upper right corner. Parker had on a white dress shirt and blue tie—his school picture from last year. Lauren's picture was a headshot, too, but not a school photo. Cel stared at the screen, struggling to finish chewing the bite of toast in her mouth, as three excruciatingly slow minutes of commercials passed. When Jesse Dalton returned to the screen, the pictures returned, too.

Cel scooted to the edge of the cushion and watched wide-eyed as Dalton talked about Parker's Camry being found in Hunter's Haven, how Lauren had disappeared from her apartment days later, and how they both taught English at Oak Mott Middle School. Stock pictures of Hunter's Haven and the Grandview Apartment complex replaced Parker's and Lauren's photos while Dalton talked. She didn't mention Lauren's son Sammy, or that Lauren was Parker's mentee and possible mistress. She ended the short segment by asking anyone with any information to call the Oak Mott police.

Cel turned off the TV, cinched her robe tighter around her waist, and walked to the window that looked out at the front yard. She wondered how long it would be before reporters came knocking on her door. Or her neighbor's. Or *Abuela's*. The Oak Mott Gossip Train had probably already jumped into action, spreading the news far and wide that Lauren Page—a young, beautiful, single mom—had disappeared, too. Cel sighed and shook her head as she scanned the houses across the street. She had no doubt that by lunchtime, Oak Mott would be saturated with hushed speculations about the witch's missing husband and his mistress.

Cel reclosed all the curtains and blinds before heading to the back porch for some fresh air. She would've preferred to go for a walk in Woodway Park instead. She was too tired to jog but still craved the routine and scenery her morning jogs provided. But that would likely draw unwelcome attention. So she watered her plants, rotated them to different spots for optimal sun, and sat in a lawn chair for a while watching the sky brighten, knowing a social storm was headed her way. Soon enough, every eye in town would be casting suspicion and accusations her way. Every head in every car rubbernecking her direction.

She went back inside around nine o'clock to prepare to go to her *abuela's* house. In her bedroom, she changed into jeans and a T-shirt, and then applied enough eyeliner, blush, and lipstick to hide her skin's pallor and the bags under her eyes. She'd just pulled her hair back in a ponytail and was sliding on shoes when a woman called out her name. She gasped and cut her eyes toward the doorway. The voice hollered her name again. It was close. In the house. She hurried to the doorway and looked down the hall as the front door slammed shut. Hadn't it been locked?

"Where are you, Cel?"

When Parker's sisters Jennifer and Jill stepped from the foyer into the hallway, heat flushed Cel's face. She wanted to point over their shoulder and scream, "Get the fuck out of my house," but as the cops had made blatantly clear, it wasn't her house. It was Beverly Lundy's house. Cel fought back her desire to rage but refused to hide her disapproval of their intrusion. She strode down the hall to prevent the sisters from coming deeper into the home. "What are you doing in here? You can't just barge in."

Jennifer, the elder Lundy sister, the spitting image of round-faced, thick-banged Beverly, held up a house key. A key Parker swore he hadn't given a copy of to his mother. Fucking liar. "Yes, we can."

"Just because you have a key doesn't mean you—"

"Yes, it does," Jennifer interjected, her beady eyes swelling with anger. "We're going to do whatever it takes to find out what happened to our brother."

Cel crossed her arms over her chest. "Is that a threat?"

Jennifer didn't respond. She eyed Cel like a charging bull. Chin down, eyes angled up. Her chest rose and fell with each breath beneath her pink shirt. She was twice as wide as Cel. Her midsection blocked a good portion of the hallway. Behind her, Jill glowered, too. Though taller, thinner, and sporting longer hair and glasses, she had the same round face and beady eyes as her mother and sister. She lived in Houston with her dentist husband, Dylan Feck, and their two kids, William and Maci, ages four and five. Cel hadn't seen her since last Christmas at the yearly Lundy gathering, where she maybe said two sentences to Cel. They might've shared two paragraphs of conversation over the last two years.

"What do you want from me?" Cel asked.

"Answers," Jennifer said.

"The truth," Jill added.

"I've told the cops everything I know."

"That's bullshit." Jennifer pointed at Cel. "You know what happened to him."

Cel tilted slightly forward at the waist. "No. I. Don't."

"Then why did the cops find huge blood stains on your mattress and floor?" A smug expression found Jennifer's face. "And why did they make you take a polygraph test, huh?"

Cel scoffed in disbelief. Beverly had obviously talked to her good buddy Chief Sterling and passed the information onto her daughters. "First off, they didn't make me do anything. I volunteered. Second, the stains weren't huge." Cel threw her hands out to the sides as she said the word huge, as if testing how far she could reach, then re-crossed them in a defensive position over her chest. "And it wasn't even Parker's blood. It was mine. Both of them." Cel took one step forward, moving to within a couple of feet of Jennifer. "The blood on the mattress is from when I started hemorrhaging during my third miscarriage, and the blood stain on the carpet is from when Parker hit me in the face and bloodied my nose when we were drunk and arguing one night."

"I don't believe you," Jennifer said. "You know where he is, and I think you know where Lauren is, too." She licked her lips. "I think you and your voodoo grandma did something to them because you were jealous and knew he was going to leave you for her."

Cel hesitated, stung by the statement. Not the voodoo grandma part. She'd been teased about her "witch" grandma and their "satanic" family her entire life. Countless times by the Lundy women, in fact. What stung was the possibility that Parker had told Jennifer he was leaving Cel. A possibility she'd dwelled on internally many times but had never heard voiced out loud. "He wouldn't leave me," Cel proclaimed, though her tone betrayed her lack of confidence.

Cel's rejection seemed to please both Jennifer and Jill. They were smart, she was dumb. "Uh, yes. He would," Jill insisted. "He told me so himself. He said he was sick of your crazy ass mood swings. He said living with you is miserable."

Cel's eyes bounced from Jennifer to Jill, Jennifer to Jill.

"I think you knew he brought Lauren *and* Sammy to our house last week to meet Mom," Jennifer added. "I think you knew he was falling in love with Lauren because she had a good heart and a good womb and would do anything to make him happy, and that's what set you off, made you kill them, isn't it?"

Cel gritted her teeth and shook her head as her eyes shrunk to angry slits and brimmed with tears.

"Is it your fucking goal to destroy our whole family?" Jennifer thumbed at her own chest and then over her shoulder at Jill. "Do you know where we just came from? Huh?" Her eyes misted, as well. "The hospital. That's right. Our mom had a stroke last night when she learned that Lauren had gone missing, too. A stroke caused by you and your lies. You need to tell us the truth, Cel. Or I swear to God, I don't care what kind of hoodoo voodoo shit you can do, I'll—"

"Get out!" Cel screamed

"Or what?" Jennifer taunted.

"Or I'm calling the cops!" Cel licked her lips, eager to sting Jennifer as hard as she'd been stung. "And then I'll curse you so bad it'll make your mom's stroke seem like a joke."

When Jennifer made an aggressive move toward Cel, Cel jumped back and threw her hands up like a boxer. Jill grabbed her sister's shoulders. "No, Jenn. She's not worth going to jail over. Mom doesn't need that to deal with, too. The truth will come out, and she'll get what's coming to her."

Jennifer glowered at Cel for a moment before allowing Jill to escort her to the front door. As Jill pushed the door open and stepped out onto the front porch, Jennifer glanced back at Cel. "You really think you're a fucking witch?" That same smug smirk on her face. "Then you better be ready to be burned alive."

As Jennifer turned to follow Jill outside, Cel rushed her, shoving her from behind. Jennifer stumbled forward into Jill, knocking Jill off the porch and onto the grass. Cel tried to slam the door shut, but Jennifer spun around and jammed her tree-trunk-sized leg into the gap. Cel threw the door open, dropped her chin, and rammed Jennifer's chest with the top of her head. Then Cel wrapped her arms around Jennifer as Jennifer backpedaled onto the porch and tackled her into the yard.

"Get off of her," Jill yelled, tugging on the back of Cel's shirt.

Jennifer easily shoved Cel off, then rolled over and dug her knee into Cel's back, pinning Cel to the ground. "How do you like that, you fucking bitch?"

Cel struggled to inhale much less speak. A strained moan was all she could manage.

Jennifer grabbed Cel's ponytail, jerked her face off of the grass, and twisted her head sideways. She raised her other fisted hand, ready to strike. "You're going to wish—"

A blaring horn cut her off. Jennifer and Jill both froze, looked away from Cel. Cel cut her eyes toward the road and saw the tail end of a big gray truck stopped in front of her neighbor's house. She looked the other way, saw the mailman on a porch three houses down, watching.

Jill grabbed Jennifer's raised arm and forced her off of Cel. "Let's go."

Cel pushed up onto all fours, and after catching her breath, rose to her feet in time to flip off Jennifer's Audi as it pulled away from the curb.

Chapter 32 - Cel

Cel and Yesenia had been sitting at the kitchen table sipping tea for half an hour, discussing Jennifer and Jill, Detective Hart and the polygraph test, when Natalie knocked on the front door and let herself in, calling out, "Cel? Mrs. G? It's me, Natalie," as she made her way through the living room. She set her purse on the floor and sat next to Cel.

Yesenia held up her mug. "You want a cup?"

Natalie flashed a grateful smile. "Sure." She turned toward Cel as Yesenia retrieved a mug from the cupboard. "Do you not have your phone? I've been trying to text and call you all morning."

Cel shook her head. "I gave it to Sterling and Hart yesterday." She threw up finger quotes. "To help eliminate me as a suspect."

Natalie thanked Yesenia, who set a mug of steaming tea in front of her before returning to a chair on the opposite side of the table, then met eyes with Cel again. "Detective Hart came by my house early this morning and told me something similar. He said he wanted to ask me some questions in order to..." She mimicked Cel's finger quotes. "Help clear your name."

"*Pendejo*," Yesenia whispered as she stared at the steam wafting out of her mug.

"What did he want to know?" Cel asked.

"He asked about you and Parker's relationship, the last time I'd seen Parker, if you'd ever mentioned Lauren to me, if I could vouch for your whereabouts the past few days. Stuff like that. He even asked Omar—oh yeah, that reminds me. Omar said to tell you he's sorry he had to leave without saying goodbye. Kris called him this morning and said something was wrong with one of their monthly reports, and he needed Omar to help him fix it before Monday's meeting." Natalie shrugged. "I don't know. Anyway, I answered all of Detective Hart's questions, and then I told him that you didn't have anything to do with Parker's or Lauren's disappearance, and that they needed to start looking at other people, like maybe Lauren's kid's dad or something, and he said they were."

"*Lo que sea*," Yesenia said. "You really think they've polygraphed anyone else?"

Natalie's eyes widened and her jaw slightly dropped as she looked at Cel. "They polygraphed you?"

Cel took a sip of tea and nodded. As she told Natalie about the polygraph test and her morning encounter with Jennifer and Jill, Natalie's wide eyes and dropped jaw gave way to narrow eyes and pursed lips. "They can't blame what happened to their mom on you." She slowly shook her head. "I think they were lying about Parker. I've known you guys my whole life, and I'm around you all the time. He loves you. There's no way he was about to leave you. No way. They've always had it out for you and are just using this as an excuse to bully you. Don't let it get to you. They're not worth it."

Cel put her hand on top of Natalie's and flashed a closed-lip, thank-you-for-your-support smile. Natalie had always been the most naive and optimistic of all the Cricket Hunters. To a fault sometimes, but that was okay. Welcome even. Cel loved her like a sister and was grateful to have someone like her, someone whose bright aura remained unfazed day-in and day-out despite circumstance, in her life. Especially during dark stints.

Natalie turned her hand around, touching palms with Cel, and squeezed. "You'll get through this. Everything's going to be all right."

Cel squeezed back and followed Natalie's gaze when Natalie looked at the papers covered in Yesenia's handwriting that were on the edge of the table. They sat partially atop a hand-painted board. One side of the board appeared water-damaged, and the black paint used to create the partially-visible geometric symbol in the center, the Spanish letters circling the symbol, numbers on the bottom, and the words *Si* and *No* in the upper two corners, were lined with tiny web-like cracks. A crudely cut, black wooden triangle sitting on the papers with a hole in the center was webbed with cracks as well.

Natalie met eyes with Yesenia. "Is that the spirit board you told me and Omar about last night?"

Yesenia nodded.

Natalie looked at Cel. "Were you about to use it?"

Yesenia lifted her mug with both hands and crooked a brow at Cel.

Cel eyed the papers and board. Before she could respond, Natalie added, "I'd like to help if you were. Your grandma said you had to be the leader, but that the more people around who were connected to Abby the better." She glanced at Yesenia. "Right?"

Yesenia nodded.

"It might not even be Abby," Cel said. "It might not be a spirit at all."

"What if it is?" Yesenia asked.

"Yeah," Natalie agreed. "We won't know unless we try. I say we do it."

Cel watched Natalie's committal bring a slight smile to Yesenia's mouth, a spark of achievement to her eyes. Her *abuela* had no doubt told Natalie and Omar about the spirit board the night before in hopes of them convincing Cel to participate.

Cel chewed on her bottom lip, her thoughts filing through her recent failures—the reconnecting ritual for Parker, the blocking doll under Lauren's bed. "What if nothing happens? What if we don't learn anything about what happened to Parker?"

"If nothing happens, nothing happens," Natalie replied. "No harm done. But don't you want to at least try? For Parker." She touched Cel's arm. "I think it'll help you feel better, too."

Cel could tell by the look in Natalie's eyes that Natalie believed the last statement, but she also guessed her *abuela* had fed something similar to Natalie and Omar the previous night. Cel met eyes with Yesenia. "You know not all spirits are good. What if it's bad one? Or a lost one? A desperate? A trickster having fun with me?"

Yesenia tapped the papers on top of the board. "I put all the safe guarding spells to protect you if that's the case. And if it is *muy mal*, we need to know so we can cast the proper rejection spell and perform a separation ritual."

Cel's eyes slid back and forth from Yesenia to Natalie. The two people who'd always had her back through thick and thin, dark and light. Two people she never wanted to disappoint. "Won't we need something personal of Abby's?"

Yesenia shook her head. "The summoning spell I chose is for general contact, which is easier to perform and requires no personal objects. You and Natalie being her friend is enough."

"But aren't general contacts more dangerous?"

"It can be, *mija*," Yesenia said. "But you three are strong enough to handle it if you follow my instructions."

Cel turned to Natalie who was watching her expectantly. Her eyes dropped to Natalie's stomach, rose to her face. "Are you sure you want to do this? I mean…you're pregnant and—"

"I'm sure."

Cel closed and rubbed her eyes. If there was any chance at all that this could help her find Parker…

"Okay," she eventually said. "Let's try it."

Natalie flashed her newly acquired proud-mother smile and looked at Yesenia. "Where is the best place to do it? Here in the house?"

"No," Cel answered for her *abuela*. "We need to do it out in Hunter's Haven, where I took the pictures."

Yesenia nodded in agreement and then eagerly walked Cel and Natalie through her notes. She explained the proper way to summon, ask questions, and handle the planchette, and then she told them about certain signs to watch for that would indicate whether they'd contacted a hurtful or helpful spirit. After answering their questions and forcing them to regurgitate the information back to her, she retrieved glass jars filled with herbs from the pantry and helped them create protection sachets.

Cel struggled to keep the bundle of nerves squirming in her gut from affecting her hands as she filled her sachet with rosemary, angelica, sage, three cloves, and a pinch of salt and tied it around her neck. She had listened to her *abuela* and *Tia* Dillo discuss séances many times, had secretly watched them communicate with the dead on three occasions when they had friends over, but she'd never participated in one. Inciting interactions with the dead, opening a gateway to their influences, was something only the most seasoned *brujas* and *curanderas* should attempt, and even though Yesenia had said she was strong enough, Cel didn't consider herself seasoned by any stretch.

On the back porch, Yesenia performed a shielding ritual over Cel and Natalie, rubbing fresh aloe juice on their foreheads, hugging them, and sending them on their way.

As Cel crossed the backyard and overgrown field beyond the fence, walking shoulder-to-shoulder with a fellow Cricket Hunter, carrying a spirit board under her arm, a candle, planchette, and bag of dried wormwood in her pocket, wearing a protection sachet around her neck and smear of aloe on her forehead, on her way to summon a ghost in hopes of solving a mystery, she felt closer to fifteen than thirty. When they pierced Hunter's Haven and escaped the glare of the afternoon sunshine, Cel said, "This feels surreal. Like we've stepped back in time or something."

Natalie gave Cel a wistful smile. "Right. I feel it, too." She jiggled the sachet hanging around her neck and arched her brow. "Like we're Cricket Hunters again. On another magical mission to right a wrong."

Cel returned a smile, and they continued on in silence, keeping their eyes peeled for Cel's lost *chanclas* as they navigated the game trails. Cel didn't know with one hundred percent certainty where she'd taken the pictures but had a good idea. She knew that when they came across the *chanclas*, they would be close. Natalie spotted the first one in a clump of weeds when they rounded a sharp bend, and Cel found the other about twenty yards up the trail.

Cel scooped up the *chancla*, surveyed the area, and quickly located the two trees she thought the spirit had hidden behind. "This is it," she said, meeting eyes with Natalie. "Let's set everything up."

Cel found a stick, and, while whispering a request for protection and guidance from the Source, drew a large circle in the soil. They sat cross-legged in the center, the spirit board on the ground in between them. Cel lit the candle, set it next to the board on top of Yesenia's notes, and then whispered another incantation as she sprinkled dry, crushed wormwood over the flame. When she placed two fingers from each hand on the planchette, Natalie dutifully copied.

Cel looked at Natalie. "Ready?"

Natalie held eye contact for a moment before nodding and fixing her gaze to the board like a soldier set to task.

Cel inhaled a slow, deep breath of wet-earth-scented air. Anxiety hummed off of her like radio waves. She closed her eyes and mentally recited her go-to calming spell three times. When she opened her eyes, she read the summoning spell word for word off of Yesenia's notes, focused on the board, and asked the first question.

"Is anyone here with us?"

The leaves in the treetops rustled overhead, but the planchette didn't move.

Cel waited, calmly repeated the question, and this time the planchette sprung to life, drifting up to the word *Sí* in the corner of the board.

Cel's pulse quickened. She glanced at Natalie, who looked up. The surprise in Natalie's eyes assured Cel that Natalie hadn't purposefully manipulated the planchette, either. They appraised one another for a few seconds before looking back at the board.

If Cel had cast a specific summoning spell, the next step would've been to verify the spirit's identity by asking for a full name, age, birthdate. But with a generic summoning, getting too personal would make a connection with a bad spirit harder to sever. So Cel cut to the chase. She needed to keep the interaction short.

"Do you want to talk to us?"

Si.

"Do you have a message for me?"

As a gust of wind rustled the treetops and stirred up fallen leaves, the planchette jerked their fingers to the center of the board and moved in a circle, then in the shape of a cross, circle, cross. Yesenia had warned of this type of nonverbal response. It was either a sign of a weak spirit, or a sign of an agitated one. A sign to hurry, either way.

"Did you see Parker Lundy out here three days ago?"

The planchette slid to *Si.* Slid off. Back on. Off. On. The wind escalated. Ripping some of the weaker leaves off their branches and sending them sailing through the air.

"Was he alone?" Urgency highlighted Cel's voice.

The planchette moved to *No* and stopped cold.

"Who was with him?"

The planchette traced the circle of Spanish letters. Once. Twice. Three times. As if unsure how to spell. Then it cut back and forth in jagged, connected lines, creating a continuous star pattern over the geometric symbol in the center of the board.

*Is it messing with us? Or...*Cel let the thought die as the significance of the symbols hit her like a bag of bricks. A chill iced her spine.

"Did someone we know hurt Parker?" Her tone urgent *and* hemorrhaging fear now.

The planchette swirled in an endless figure eight pattern. Clouds moved over the canopy, blocking out all traces of sunshine. The wind strengthened. The candle flame flickered, vanished. The papers beneath it fluttered. Static crackled in the humid air. Cel's arm and neck hairs stood on end. Her legs begged to run. She made eye contact with Natalie whose eyes were scared-big. They should've never come out here. She needed to end this. But she couldn't help blurting out her biggest fear: "Is Parker Lundy dead? Is he there with you? Did you hurt him?"

The planchette ricocheted from *Si* to *No*.

A giggle (*Abby*) echoed in the woods somewhere behind Cel, followed by a deep-throated howl. A bolt of fear shot through her. Her heart fluttered, breath caught. When she took her right hand off of the planchette and reached for the page with the separation spell on it, her two fingers still touching the planchette suddenly felt pinned down. Glued to the wooden triangle by an invisible hand.

As she read Yesenia's words, the planchette pulled her and Natalie's hands around the board. Making a circle then a cross (*Sniper's cross-hairs*). A star. Over and over. Cross-hairs. Star. Cross-hairs. Star. The candle toppled over from a gust and rolled into the brush. Time slowed. A large elm branch cracked, snapped, crashed to the ground behind Natalie, just outside the protective circle in the dirt.

"...thank you and goodbye."

The planchette finally stopped moving after Cel's final word.

Separation.

Natalie jumped to her feet. "Let's get the hell out of here."

Cel nodded, picked up Yesenia's notes, the spirit board and planchette, and ran down the game trail with Natalie on her heels.

They burst out of Hunter's Haven in a dead sprint. Sweat adhered their shirts to their upper chests and backs, strands of hair to their cheeks. The sun shone bright. Not a cloud in the sky. Only a slight breeze. A different world from where they sat minutes earlier. They slowed to a brisk walk as they approached the backyard gate but didn't stop to catch their breath until they reached the safety of the kitchen.

Natalie immediately burst into an explanation for Yesenia when they'd returned. Cel nodded in agreement with Natalie's account and with Yesenia's subsequent assurances based on that account, assurances that their experience was not abnormal, not horrific, that they'd probably contacted a random spirit anchored to Hunter's Haven, the spirit of a long dead hunter maybe, a bored trickster who preferred to manipulate nature rather than communicate, but Cel didn't agree with either. In Natalie's explosive, run-on telling of the short-lived séance, she never mentioned hearing the giggle—Abby's signature giggle—or the deep-throated howl. And she'd said the planchette had "gone crazy" in the center of the board, not drawn the symbols Cel had recognized.

Cricket Hunter symbols.

The cross-hair Parker had carved on his cricket stick.

Cel's infinity.

Abby's star.

Though Cel's version and conclusions differed from Natalie's and Yesenia's respectively, she could tell her *abuela's* assurances were soothing to Natalie and didn't want to disrupt that. Disputing either of them would just reinject fear and anxiety into her friend and her friend's baby. Natalie was still in the high-risk-for-miscarriage stage of pregnancy. Fear and anxiety were two of her worst enemies. Assassins Cel had met face-to-face and had no intentions of introducing to Natalie.

An hour later, Craig texted Natalie, letting her know he was on his way home with Chinese take-out, so Cel walked Natalie to her car, hugged and thanked her, and told her she'd call in an hour or so to check on her. When she went back inside and found the bathroom door closed, she knocked.

"You okay, *Buela*?"

"*Si*. I'll be out in a bit."

Despite having drunk two cups of *yerba buena* since arriving back at Yesenia's, repeatedly reciting her go-to calming spell, and performing a cleansing ritual with Natalie, Cel still felt far from calm. On the contrary, she felt vulnerable. Scared. Targeted. So, with a small window of opportunity, she hustled to Yesenia's bedroom, opened the old chest in the closet, and swiped a page from the grimoire labeled FAMILIARS—the page containing the same ritual she'd helped Yesenia perform with Mina the night of *Tia* Dillo's death.

She'd contemplated asking for a copy on her way inside after seeing Natalie off, but she imagined her *abuela* would say that chopping off, cooking, and gnawing on Mila's leg was unneeded, an overreaction, that the protection measures they'd taken had worked and she'd be fine. Or that her bond with Mila wasn't strong enough for the ritual to work. And maybe she would be fine. Maybe she *was* crazy to think her bond with Mila was strong enough for the ritual to work. Maybe she *was* grasping at straws. But she didn't want to hear, debate, or argue about it. She was teetering on the edge of Meltdown Cliff, and for her own peace of mind, she wanted—*needed*—to perform the ritual as quick as possible. She needed something to grasp on to.

So she took it without asking and hurried home without a goodbye.

Chapter 33 - Cel

Cel parked askew in the driveway and hurried inside her house. She locked the front door behind her, pulled the folded piece of paper out of her back pocket, and called out for Mila.

She made it halfway down the hallway before Mila emerged from the computer room. She knelt and held out a welcoming hand as Mila sauntered her way, meowing. She wiggled her fingers. "Come here, girl. Come here."

She didn't notice the infinity necklace dangling from Mila's neck until Mila was a few feet away and the silver symbol caught a ray of light. She gasped and brought her hand to the hollow of her throat. She couldn't move, couldn't think, couldn't anything.

Spellbound, she didn't notice the figure creep up behind her, either. Not until she eventually mustered the courage to reach out for the necklace and it tackled her, driving its weight into her back, pancaking her into the carpet face-first. She struggled beneath its weight to no avail and screamed in surprised pain when she felt a sharp sting in her shoulder. A burning sensation trickled down her arm and into her upper chest seconds later. Within half a minute, she was too weak to struggle and her extremities went limp.

Half a minute more and her eyelids were too heavy to hold open.

SEPTEMBER 1998

Chapter 34 - Cel

When Cel returned home after delivering the sickening curse and carving TITS on Jose's Mustang, her *abuela* was thankfully still asleep. She stripped down to her underwear, crawled into bed, and pulled the sheets up to her chin. She lay there in the dark, eyes wide open, struggling to stay afloat in a stew of emotion. She sighed. Cried. Ached. Regretted. Tossed and turned. Recited calming spells and soothing spells. Whispered angry words and curses at Abby. Questioned Parker's heart, desire, sincerity. Part of her wanted to call him and demand to know exactly what had happened at Abby's after she'd left. Part of her never wanted to know.

Sleep eluded her. Hours passed.

She didn't have the energy to get up, but she couldn't find a comfortable position in the bed or inside herself. Her brain refused to shut down. She ran through scenarios, possibilities, relived the night's events, the last month's events, every aspect of her and Parker's relationship since their first clandestine kiss four months earlier.

Around six in the morning, she finally passed out. Yesenia woke her an hour later and asked if her stomach felt any better, if she felt well enough to attend school. Cel asked if she could stay home one more day, rolled over, and fell back to sleep as Yesenia rubbed her back.

She slept the morning and half the afternoon away. When she woke a little after three, her *abuela* had tea and tacos ready for her to heat and eat. She ate in the kitchen and then moved to the couch where she curled up under a blanket and watched *Titanic* on VHS. The credits were rolling when someone knocked on the front door.

Startled, Cel sat up and watched Yesenia crack open the door. She couldn't hear what was said, but when Yesenia stepped aside and opened the door, she had an idea. A man wearing an Oak Mott PD uniform and carrying a small notepad stepped into the living room. He had a thin mustache and elephant ears. He appeared young and unsure of himself, new to the job. He gave Cel a closed-lipped smile and acknowledging nod.

"I'm Officer Gary Sanchez," he said. "You can call me Officer Gary. Are you Cel?"

"Yes." Cel shifted under her blanket when something inside her stomach torqued.

"Have a seat," Yesenia said, gesturing at the couch as she sat in her chair.

Gary gave Yesenia the same closed-lipped smile he'd given Cel. "No thanks. This should only take a minute or two." His attention turned back to Cel. "I need to know where you were last night. Specifically…" He glanced at his notepad. "From about eleven to six this morning."

"She was here," Yesenia answered for Cel, her voice sharp and defensive. "Asleep. We've both been sick, throwing up, and we haven't left the house in days."

"Is that right, Cel?"

Cel nodded, fighting as hard as she could to slow her thumping heart.

"What's this about?" Yesenia demanded. "Did someone accuse her of something?"

"Not exactly."

"Then what?"

Gary fumbled to flip to the previous page in his notepad and reread his notes before asking, "Do you know Jose Lopez?"

Cel and Yesenia both nodded.

"Well, he called us this morning and said his Mustang had been vandalized last night, and he wanted to file an official police report so his insurance company would cover the damage. Someone had scratched it up and written the word," he nervously cleared his throat, "*tits* on the door. When Officer Jackson—that's who talked to him, not me—asked who he thought could've done it, Jose said, and I quote." Gary ran his finger under the words on his notepad as he read: "It was fucking Cel Garcia and her friends. I know, because one of them is called Tits." He looked up. "Do you have anything to do with the vandalism or know who does?"

As Cel shook her head, Yesenia said, "*Chingao*." She scooted to the edge of her seat, her eyes shrinking to slits, her brow scrunched. She pointed a teacher-finger at Gary. "Listen, I've known Jose since he was a toddler. I used to be good friends with his mother, and we used to spend a lot of time at their house. He always picked on Cel, and they never got along well, but she didn't have anything to do with this. She was here with me all night." She lowered her hand. "This is all for revenge. That's how the Lopez's work. He's doing this because we filed a report on him a week ago after he attacked Cel and her friends at the fair. Hell, he probably did that to his car himself."

Gary nodded like an obedient grandson. "I didn't know about that incident. I'll look into it when I get back to the station." He jotted down a reminder, met eyes with Cel. "Do you have any friends called...you know, that word?"

"*Chingao*," Yesenia whispered. "Who calls their friend that?"

Biting her lip, Cel shook her head.

"Didn't think so," Gary wrote again. "Do you think *any* of your friends could have anything to do with this?"

Cel shook her head.

"They didn't mention anything about it to you?"

"No. I haven't seen or talked to them since I've been sick."

Gary nodded. "Will you go ahead and give me their names, anyway? That way I can touch base with them, too, since you haven't talked to them in a while."

Cel did.

Officer Gary thanked her and Yesenia for their time and cooperation, and as Yesenia walked him to his cruiser, Cel hurried to her bedroom and dialed Parker's number to warn him, but he didn't answer.

Chapter 35 - Parker

"You know it was her," Abby said. "Who else would've written that?"

Parker passed through the gate on the side of her house, stopped next to Cel's bike which rested against the siding, and spun around. Light sliced through the blinds in Jeff's bedroom window to his left, striping his face and chest. An Oak Mott police officer named Gary had left Abby's house ten minutes earlier, after questioning her about her whereabouts the previous night, and about the altercation with Jose at the fair.

"I don't think she would do that," Parker said. "Besides, she's sick, remember? She hasn't left her house in days. And I have her bike. You remember how far away Jose's house is?"

Abby cocked her hip to the side, planted a hand on her waist. "Why do you keep defending her? Is there more to you guys than you've told me?"

"No. And I'm not defending her, I'm—"

"Yes, you are," Abby interjected. "You're taking her side over mine."

"I'm not taking sides. There are no sides. Jose pisses a lot of people off. He's in fights like every other day. There's no telling who fucked up his car."

Abby shook her head, her arrogant smirk reaching her eyes. "No. She did it. She's in love with you, and she's jealous of us."

Parker waved a dismissive hand and blinked longer than natural. "Listen, I understand. After everything with your dad and Jeff, and then the cops coming tonight to question you about Jose. You're upset. I get it. They came to my house and questioned me, too. But until we talk to Cel and—"

"Let's go. I'm ready. Right now."

Abby moved as though she would march past Parker and led the way, but Parker threw up his hands and blocked her. "No."

"What are you afraid of?" She knocked his hands down and stared into his eyes. "Do you love her?"

A nervous chuckle escaped Parker's mouth. "Love? Really?"

Abby knocked his hands down and tried to inch forward. Their chests collided. Emotions were high. "Move."

"No. Your dad is still out there somewhere. And what about Jose? He's crazy. If he really thinks you did—"

"Move!"

"No!"

Abby grimaced and shoved Parker with all her weight behind it. He absorbed the blow, grabbed her shoulders, and slammed her back against the house just to the right of the Jeff's window.

"Let go!" Abby reached around his arms and slapped his cheek hard enough for the smack to echo.

Parker's temper flared. He pushed his forearm across her neck, pinning her head to the house. A stripe of light lined his angry eyes. "Stop fighting me! I'm not going to hurt you!"

They held eye contact, both breathing heavily. Tense moments slipped past.

A small round shadow appeared behind the blinds.

A head.

Jeff.

The cops had found him hiding in an abandoned house two blocks away earlier that morning. His dad had rushed to his house after the incident with Parker and Abby and entered the house through the unlocked sliding glass doors. When Jeff heard his dad yell out his name, he'd escaped out of his window and ran as his dad busted through his bedroom door, knocking down his dresser. He'd spent the night in the abandoned house, curled up in a ball inside the sleeping bag he'd taken there months earlier when he'd run away for a few hours after a fight with Abby.

Parker pulled his forearm away from Abby's neck, and she slapped the window, rattling the glass. "Go away," she ordered. "Leave us alone!"

The blinds twisted closed, and shadow Jeff vanished.

Watching the window, Parker stepped back.

Abby slowly peeled away from the house.

"Sorry," Parker offered. "Sorry...I..."

Abby straightened her shirt, checked the sides of her hair with her hands.

"I feel like we have something good going here." Parker flicked a finger back and forth between Abby and himself. "I don't want to fight about Cel. I don't even want to think about her when I'm with you."

"Then you need to decide. You either tell her about us and to leave me the hell alone, or I will."

Parker's insides—lungs, intestines, every part of him—felt as if they were inflating beyond control. On a mission to burst. "She's fragile right now. After Dillo and all."

"I don't care. That's no fucking excuse to mess up my life."

"Fine," he said calmly, trying to hide his inner turmoil, his desire to refuse. "I'll tell her."

"Tonight?"

"You know I can't tonight. I have to get home before my parents get back from the church, and I don't want to do it over the phone." Fearing for his safety after the incident at Rita's, Parker's parents had told him he wasn't allowed to leave the house after dark until Tom Powell was found. Abby and Jeff were given similar instructions. "I'll talk to her tomorrow."

Abby searched his eyes. "Promise?"

Parker took her hand in his. "Yes."

She nodded as though she believed him, but her eyes didn't align with the action.

Parker cocked his head slightly sideways, jiggled her hand playfully. "Come on. I promise I'll take care of this."

She half-heartedly nodded again.

Parker stepped forward, their faces close enough for him to smell the remnants of a menthol on her breath. Anger radiated off her in pulses of heat. He took her other hand in his. "Everything's going to be okay. You have to believe me." When he leaned in to kiss her, she didn't throw her arms around his neck and close her eyes like she always had before. And when their lips met, she barely responded. Her lips felt tougher than normal, almost plastic, nowhere close to soft and eager. And there was no tornado tongue action.

"I have to go," Parker said, letting go of her hands. He pulled Cel's bike away from the house, threw a leg over the frame, and glanced at Abby. She crossed her arms over her chest, eyeing the bike with disdain. "See you in the morning."

Her gaze shifted to Parker, but she didn't speak.

They stared at each other for a few awkward seconds before he pedaled away.

Chapter 36 - Cel

After Officer Gary left, Cel and Yesenia exchanged a few cross words about Jose and Maria. Yesenia reiterated her belief they had damaged the Mustang themselves—"*It's a double whammy. An insurance scam to get a new paint job and make us look bad.*"—and Cel let her believe it. She wished she could spill her guts about Abby and Parker, the sickening curse she'd delivered to the Lopez's, and what she'd done to Jose's car. Telling someone, especially her *abuela*, the smartest woman she knew, would be such a relief, a weight off her shoulders. But Yesenia had been so angry after she'd kidnapped and killed Frito, and when she and Parker had lashed out at Jose at the cemetery, that she had to lie. She didn't want to disappoint her *abuela* again. Or get into legal trouble. Last night's truth would have to be hers and hers alone.

They ate a light dinner, tortillas and *queso fresco*, and when Yesenia went to take a hot bath afterward to help ease her arthritic hips, Cel made her way to her bedroom and closed the door.

She turned on her alarm clock's radio, heard Nirvana's *Teen Spirit* playing, and turned up the volume. She shrugged off her pajamas and changed into jean shorts, a black T-shirt, and her blue and black flannel, and then paced back and forth from the window to the door as the night sky swallowed the sun. She thought about Parker and Abby and Jose, reliving, re-evaluating. Repeating what-ifs. Re-feeling. Obsessing. Trapped inside her own head, just like the previous night.

The song ended, and after a commercial another came on. Then another.

She kept pacing. She had a stack of make-up work on the foot of her bed that she needed to complete, but there was no way she could slip into a school mind-frame right now. Her legs were as restless as her thoughts. Eventually, she decided to head outside for some fresh air, more room to walk, hoping a change of scenery and stimuli might help her break her circle of thought, stop the emotional rollercoaster.

She poked her head into the bathroom. The shower curtain was partially closed, exposing her *abuela's* upper half. The water-damaged book Yesenia was reading, Anne Rice's *The Tale of the Body Thief*, blocked her face.

"*Buela?*"

Yesenia lowered the book.

"I'm feeling cooped up after being inside all day. Is it all right if go out back and cricket hunt for a little bit?"

"Okay. But don't go far. And don't stay out long."

Cel slipped on shoes, grabbed a flashlight from the kitchen junk drawer, went to the backyard, found her cricket stick among the others leaning against the side of the house, and started hunting. The night air was warm and dry, the crescent moon bright, the crickets plenty.

She circled the house first. Angling her head sideways, her cricket ear down, she tried not to think. Just hunt. Allow her senses to guide her. She focused on the sound of the chirps, the feel of the stick in her hand, the smell of fresh pine riding the wind, the slight, shadowy movements in the grass and shrubbery. She paused as long as needed when the crickets quieted, held the flashlight steady as she lowered her stick over their bodies, and drove the tip through them in a swift stealthy motion. She killed five crickets hiding in the gap between the foundation and the soil, and then made her way along the backyard fence line.

The more she hunted, the better she felt. Her legs no longer felt uncomfortably restless. Her skull no longer rattled from her mind's relentless pursuit of answers. She didn't feel anger or heartache, guilt or fear. She didn't talk to imaginary Parker or Abby. She didn't miss *Tia* Dillo. She didn't worry about Jose or Maria or Yesenia's well-being.

She hunted.

In a little less than an hour, as she crept through the backyard, the field beyond that, and the outer rim of Hunter's Haven, she killed sixteen more crickets. As she emerged from the woods, headed for home, tired and eager for a shower, the hurricane fence gate opened and a dark silhouette walked into the field.

At first, she thought it was her *abuela*, but as the person approached, she knew it wasn't. The person walked too fast, was too thin.

She waited. "Parker? Is that you?" she eventually called out.

No reply.

She flicked on her flashlight and aimed it at the person who was now ten yards away.

A yellow and blue summer dress.

Not Parker.

Arms crossed over her chest. Angry eyes and a taut, set mouth.

"Abby? What are you doing here?"

Abby slapped the flashlight out of Cel's hand, and when it hit the ground, the light blinked out. "Why did you do it?"

Shocked, Cel stepped back. "What the hell?"

"I know it was you. Parker says it wasn't, but I know it was."

"What are you talking about?" Cel's voice quaked, the question coming off feeble and insincere. Because it was. She knew exactly what Abby was talking about.

"The cops just left my house." Abby dropped her chin and angled her eyes up. "Thanks to you, they think I carved the word TITS on Jose's car last night."

"I didn't tell them you did it." These words came out stronger. "I told them I didn't know who did."

"Just admit it. I want you to admit it. You want me to get in trouble. You want to hurt me."

Cel didn't respond. An anger bubble was forming in her chest. How dare Abby tell her what to do. The cords in her neck tightened along with her grip on her cricket stick.

"Only a few people even know Jose called me that." Abby thrust a finger in Cel's face. "And you're the only one stupid enough to write it on his car."

Cel slapped Abby's hand away. "Don't call me stupid."

That brought a smirk to Abby's face. "Why not?" She jutted out her chin. "You are. It was your stupid ass that got us all in this mess with Jose. You and your *stupid* magic and *stupid* aunt and *stupid* cursed crickets and *stupid* cat stealing."

"I told you that you didn't have to help that night. And I know you really didn't want to. You just didn't want Parker to be alone with me. You can't stand that he likes me more than you."

Abby guffawed. "What a joke. He doesn't like you. He feels sorry for you. He thinks it's sad you've had a little school girl crush on him for so long. He pities you. He thinks you're a flat-chested, crazy-ass tomboy."

"You don't know how he feels about me. We're closer than you could ever imagine."

"In your dreams, maybe. He's in love with me. And I love him."

Cel clenched her jaw, shook her head. "You don't know what love is. Raising your shirt and throwing your tits in his face on your couch when he's just there to be nice because your little brother is missing doesn't even come close to being love. It's desperation."

Abby's mouth fell open. "You were you spying on us last night, weren't you?" When Cel didn't immediately answer, Abby flashed a nasty smirk and added, "Do you want me to tell you what happened when I turned off the TV? Do you want to know if we went all the way?"

"Nothing happened."

"Are you sure?"

"Yes." Cel tapped her chest and spoke with conviction. "I know Parker. He would never stoop that low."

Abby giggled in disbelief. In mockery. In holier-than-thou giddiness. Her I'm-so-cute-giggle. "You're a fucking obsessed psycho, you know that, right?"

"You're a fucking slut!"

Abby lunged, swinging her hands at Cel's face. Cel dropped her cricket stick and threw her hands up to block the blows. She grabbed a handful of Abby's hair and jerked Abby's head down and sideways, controlling her like a dog on a leash.

"Don't ever touch me again," Cel hissed.

Abby twisted and punched Cel in the stomach. Cel gasped and buckled forward. Her hand ripped away from Abby's head, strands of hair sticking between her fingers.

Abby touched her scalp. "Bitch!" Then she rushed Cel, shoved her, and Cel tripped over her own feet and fell onto her haunches. Abby kicked at her head, but Cel ducked under the attempt and tried to crab-walk away.

Abby dove on top of Cel, driving her knee into Cel's pelvis, sending hot barbs of pain down her lower back and inner thighs. Cel collapsed onto her back, and Abby straddled her chest, lorded over her. She knocked Cel in the side of the head two hard times before Cel managed to get her hands up to shield herself.

"Where are all your protection spells now, huh? *Witch*."

Abby grabbed the infinity necklace on Cel's chest and jerked it, snapping the chain. "You and your stupid infinity bullshit." She clenched the necklace in Cel's face. "You probably thought you and Parker would get married and have babies and love each other for *infinity*, didn't you?"

Abby snapped her attention to the right when a series of light crunches echoed out from Hunter's Haven's tree line a few feet away.

Cel seized the opportunity. She balled her hand and punched Abby in the jaw. When Abby canted left, Cel thrust up her hips and used Abby's momentum to force her to the ground on all fours. Cel jumped to her feet and kicked Abby in the stomach, then kicked again, this time her foot hitting Abby's squishy chest. Abby fell onto her side, rolled onto her back.

Cel moved to straddle Abby, repay the favor, smack her upside the head, but when she stepped forward, she kicked her cricket stick and reached for it instead. She lowered it over Abby's face.

"What are you going to do with that stupid stick?" Abby asked, a cocky smile playing at her lips. "Do you think I'm a fucking *demented cricket*, now?" Abby giggled for a moment, and then the giggle morphed into an outright laugh.

Cel held her stance as the laughter faded.

"You're pathetic," Abby said.

Cel didn't make a sound or close her eyes as she drove the stick into Abby's left eye with one swift motion. Abby's right eye flared with shock as Cel pushed the stick until it hit the back of her skull.

When Cel slowly slid the stick out, blood erupted from the eye socket like lava from a volcano. Abby covered the hole with her hands as though that would stop the bleeding. She opened her mouth into a horrified O and as an airy squeal escaped, Cel methodically stabbed the stick into Abby's open mouth, driving it through the back of her throat, piercing the moist soil below her neck.

Cel watched the pupil in Abby's bulging, good eye swell and swell until it blocked out all traces of color. Then her eyes fell to Abby's chest, watching it move up and down, slower and slower. When it stopped, she slid the stick out of Abby's mouth and a death gasp followed it out. Then her jaw twitched.

Cel dropped the cricket stick and stood over Abby. She felt numb, paralyzed. Deaf. Mute. Like someone or something else had taken over her body. Like she was in a dream. She looked toward Hunter's Haven, at her *abuela's* backyard fence, down at Abby's lifeless body.

What had she done? *Oh, shit.* She'd killed…She'd murdered…

Her stomach lurched, and she suddenly was thrust back into her body. Her hands trembled. She could hear her heart pounding, a drumbeat to her whooshing breath. She ratcheted her head left and right. What should she do? Should she call the cops? Explain it was self-defense? Abby had approached her, attacked her, right? But was it really self-defense? Was it? She *had* wanted to hurt Abby. She'd stabbed her through the eye and added another hole to her throat. And it had felt good when she did it. Justified. The right thing to do. But now…

Her cover-up instincts kicked in. She needed to hide the body. She grabbed Abby's feet and started dragging her toward Hunter's Haven, but every imperfection in the soil, every blade of grass, rock, weed, seemed to fight against her efforts, grabbing onto Abby's body, holding it. Abby was so heavy, so cumbersome. So…dead-weight. Tears fell from Cel's cheeks as she tugged. Fearful tears and guilt tears alike. What was she doing? She fell onto her backside, stood, pulled. Was this real or a nightmare?

She'd dragged Abby about a yard into the trees when her *abuela* called out, "*Mija?* Where are you?"

She dropped Abby's legs and hastily wiped the tears off her cheeks as if Yesenia could see them from that distance. Oh my God, she thought. Had Abby knocked on the door and talked to her *abuela* before coming out here? "I'll be right there, *Buela.*"

"Okay."

She picked up one of Abby's legs and tried to tug on the body again, but Abby's arm or head or something was caught on a root or bush. Grunting in frustration and bursting into tears, she pulled harder, but her sweaty hands slipped off Abby's smooth shin, and she fell down again.

She jumped up when she heard dry twigs snap behind her. "Hello? Is someone there?"

Distant crickets were all that answered. She was so hyper sensitive. So Paranoid.

She repeatedly whispered the calming spell. She needed to go inside before her *abuela* came out here. She needed to hurry. She needed to move the body deeper into the woods. But how deep? To where? She couldn't bury it. She couldn't…

Her legs started moving without thought. She marched for the backyard fence. She needed time to think. She would sneak back out here later, after Yesenia fell asleep. By then she would know what to do.

As she approached the backdoor, she could see Yesenia's silhouette in the kitchen window, working over the stovetop, probably brewing tea. She froze when her eyes fell on Abby's bike in the grass to the right of the window, in front of the other cricket sticks. Knowing her *abuela* sometimes sat on the porch to drink a cup of tea before bed, she sprinted to the bike, wheeled it out to where the field met the woods and dumped it on the ground near Abby's body.

When she finally reached the back door, she took in a deep breath, and released a measured exhale. She walked past the kitchen with her head down, and when her *abuela* asked, "How'd it go? You feeling any better?" she replied, "Good, I just need to take a shower and clean off." To her own ear, she sounded so unnatural, so wrong. She expected Yesenia to bust into the bathroom and demand to know what had gone on out there. Why she'd sounded so odd. But she never did. And her *abuela* must not have talked to or seen Abby, or she would've said something about it.

Cel showered until the hot water ran out. Then she showered ten minutes more. She didn't wash her hair, she didn't wash her body. She stood there with her eyes closed, picturing Abby's face. Abby's eye. The twitch of her jaw. Anyone watching would've found it impossible to see the tears mixing with the water raining out of the shower head.

When she finally came out of the bathroom in her purple robe, Yesenia was in her bedroom, lying in her bed with her eyes closed. The TV was on but turned low. Cel tiptoed back to her room, shut the door, and lay in the darkness worrying.

No matter how far into Hunter's Haven she hauled the body, it would be found. There would be searches.

And Abby's blood was all over her cricket stick.

And her infinity necklace was probably still clenched in Abby's hand.

And someone probably saw Abby riding her bike over to Cel's.

And who all knew she was coming over, anyway? Her mom? Parker? Jeff? Natalie? Omar?

And her fingerprints would be all over Abby's body and clothes.

There was no reason to try to hide the body or the bike.

She was doomed. She'd fucked up. Major. There was no point in going back out there.

She pretended to sleep when her *abuela* opened her door at eleven-thirty, came in, gave her a soft kiss on the forehead, whispered a soothing spell, and then closed the door behind her as she left. But she didn't actually sleep until many days later.

Chapter 37 - Cel

Yesenia forced Cel to go back to school the following morning, saying if she was well enough to cricket hunt, she was well enough for math and science. Cel walked to school with her eyes on the sidewalk, books clutched to her chest. She didn't risk a look toward Hunter's Haven as she left the house much less check on Abby.

As the morning crept by, she didn't take notes, participate in class conversations, or complete a single assignment. In the halls, she responded to her teachers' and friends' *welcome backs* with a simple closed-mouth smile rather than words. In the classrooms, she sat in her desk and stared at the door rather than the teacher, her stomach knotted, waiting for a gang of cops to arrive, weapons drawn, stern commands for her to put her hands in the air. In the bathroom, she cried in the stalls, took deep breaths in front of the mirror, splashed cold water on her face.

At lunchtime, she sat on the front lawn with Parker, Natalie, and Omar as usual. But as they talked about school gossip and speculated about why Abby might not have come to school, Cel watched the parking lot and streets beyond, expecting a slew of Oak Mott PD cruisers to speed up at any minute, sirens blaring and lights flashing. When Parker asked why she was so quiet, she said she was tired, still didn't feel a hundred percent.

The afternoon passed more slowly than the morning.

After school, Parker offered to give her bike back, to ride home with her and help her with makeup work, but she refused both taking her bike and his company, telling him she felt queasy and wanted to take a nap right when she got home. She walked home the same way she walked to school: eyes glued to the pavement, arms hugging books to her chest. She paused when she reached Cobalt Street and glanced up at her house. Seeing no cop cars in the drive way or yellow tape surrounding the yard, she lowered her head and continued.

Inside, she greeted her *abuela*, who said she looked exhausted and suggested she take a nap. Cel agreed, went to her room, closed the door, dropped her books on the floor, curled up on her bed, and stared at the wall. She lay there for an hour, fighting off the urge to flop her head into Yesenia's lap and cry and spill her guts, explain how and why Abby's one-eyed, lifeless body was out in Hunter's Haven. Her *abuela* had forgiven her for many things over the years, the most heinous action being stealing and killing Frito, but killing a cat and killing a person were two different beasts. Cel feared—*knew*—the latter was unforgivable. Cel wanted to delay seeing that look of disappointment and heart ache in her *abuela's* eyes, the only family she had, for as long as possible.

She rose from bed an hour later when Parker called and told her Abby was missing.

The investigation and city-wide searches started immediately.

The cops, led by newly elected Chief Robert S. Sterling, questioned the Cricket Hunters, seemingly everyone in Abby's grade level, and everyone close to Abby's family, and what they gleaned from the interviews led them to focus their efforts on three people: Tom Powell, Jose Lopez, and Parker Lundy.

Tom was initially considered the prime suspect because of his relation to Abby, his lengthy arrest record, the threats he'd made since his release from prison, the fact he'd broken into the Powell household just a few days earlier, and the allegations Sheila Powell had made about him molesting Abby. Sterling put out a statewide APB on Tom, who hadn't been seen since the afternoon at Rita's.

Due to the Tits-on-the-Mustang incident and the fair fight, Jose was brought in for questioning, but within thirty minutes he lawyered up and refused to cooperate.

Parker became a key suspect because Jeff told the cops he'd last seen Abby outside arguing with Parker the night she went missing. Jeff told the cops she'd never come back inside that night. Parker denied having anything to do with Abby's disappearance, and his parents and the other hunters, including Cel, professed the same. Four days after Abby vanished, the same afternoon her bike was found in an alley a block away from Parker's house, forcing Sterling to zoom in on Parker even harder, his parents retained a lawyer for him as well.

When Natalie called and told Cel about Abby's bike being found, Cel thought the information had been wrong. Maybe they'd found a similar bike but not Abby's bike. Abby's bike was out in Hunter's Haven, inches away from her decaying corpse. *Right?* She hurried off the phone and sprinted out to Hunter's Haven for the first time in days. Abby's bike wasn't there. Neither was Abby. Or Cel's cricket stick. Everything was gone. Cel nearly fell to her knees with shock. She couldn't find words to complete a thought.

Weeks passed. Time moved in irregular, disjointed stops and starts for Cel. Some days seemed to linger on forever, every minute detail wedging deep into her mind, while others passed in a blur, leaving no lasting memories.

Local newspapers ran front page stories, and TV channels ran short bits with Abby's previous year's school picture in the top corner of the screen. People all over town eyed Parker and Jose and their families with crooked eyes. Rumors whispered in supermarket corners and church pews and in schoolyards spread like wildfire. Abby had run away because she was pregnant, or because she was a closet lesbian. Parker had killed her because she wouldn't sleep with him. She'd overdosed and her body was hidden by her mom to conceal the truth. She had been gang-raped by Jose and his friends and her body had been burned in the dunes behind the town dump. Her dad had owed people money, and they'd kidnapped her for revenge.

The police held four official searches that focused on the Gateway area, but some of Sheila Powell's co-workers formed a group that fanned out and scoured the entire town from top to bottom, searching for any signs of Abby.

The Cricket Hunters joined in on many of the searches, passing out flyers and knocking on doors, and also spent many hours huddled around the table in Cel's kitchen, speculating about what could've happened to Abby, what they could've done different to prevent whatever happened from happening, crying on one another's shoulders.

When with the other hunters, Cel made little eye contact, rarely spoke, kept her hair down to shield her face and her hands drawn into her sleeves. In general, she walked around in a perpetual state of paralyzed confusion. Zombie-like. She spent every night either sitting on the back porch or standing in front of the kitchen window, staring out at Hunter's Haven, wondering what had happened to Abby's body, the bike, her stick. Was she losing her mind? Had she hidden everything and blocked it all out? Had Abby lived? *Could* she have lived? No way. Had someone else taken her? Kidnapped her? The questions were relentless, pressurizing. Day after day, night after night, no answers came. She never felt relief. Out of frustration one night, unable to sleep, needing to feel, wanting to know she was still alive, she went to the bathroom, removed a razor blade from her leg razor, and sliced her upper thigh. As the blood ran down her leg, a wave of relaxation ran through her mind, quieting the relentless questions. This became her nightly routine before bed. First a goodnight kiss from her *abuela*, then a soothing spell, then spilled blood, then sleep.

A month passed.

A vigil was held in the Oak Mott High gymnasium. The Texas Rangers were brought in to re-canvas the town, re-interview suspects and friends, but they found no new suspects, no new evidence, no sign a crime was ever committed.

More months passed.

The Oak Mott Gossip Train slowed. The town's hysteria faded. Wind and rain eroded missing person flyers off of telephone poles and storefront windows. Abby Powell's name was mentioned less and less. Cel learned how to compartmentalize to survive. Her anxiety morphed into depression, which morphed into denial. She stopped cutting. She and Parker began holding hands in school hallways, kissing in public, calling each other boyfriend and girlfriend. It had been difficult and burdensome, the road to get there unplanned, but he was hers. When asked, she told Yesenia she'd lost her infinity necklace somewhere out in Hunter's Haven, but that she knew about where and planned on finding it.

In early January, Tom Powell was caught stealing from a Kmart outside of Houston, and when he was arrested and questioned about Abby, provided an alibi—later proven by fast food transaction receipts and security camera footage in Austin—he'd left town the same night he'd broken into the Powell's house.

In mid-March, Jose and Maria Lopez sold their house and moved to Mexico. According to one of Yesenia's friends who also knew Maria, the police had been following Jose all over town and had also been responsible for Maria losing her job at M&R Liquor. They felt singled out, picked on, harassed, by both the police and media, and decided *suficiente es suficiente*. They wouldn't take the fall for some *chica blanca tonta*. They left and never looked back.

By the beginning of summer, the fate of Abby Powell had been relegated to a footnote in Oak Mott gossip. And after Oak Mott's Prom King/All-State Quarterback Jack Henning died in a car accident two days after graduation, and a Texas Highway Patrol Officer, Oak

Mott High graduate Betsy Fellows, was shot and nearly killed just south of town during a traffic stop a month later, Abby was erased from conversations altogether.

The passage of time resumed a more normal, steady course for Cel the less she heard Abby's name. The Cricket Hunters still hung out but stopped hunting and venturing out to Hunter's Haven. After a while, even they rarely mentioned Abby by name. There were looks sometimes, feelings of sadness or awkwardness that passed between them when something came up that reminded them of Abby, but no more long conversations, no more speculation about her fate, no more tears.

With each passing day, each new experience, each new smile and laugh and change, the memory of Abby's death and questions as to what had happened to her were buried deeper and deeper inside Cel. Eventually, she went weeks at a time without thinking about the mystery surrounding Abby. Then months. Then years. She'd made a mistake murdering her friend, sure, she hadn't needed to go that far, but she'd been attacked and she was sorry and she wanted to move on. Everyone else was.

The last time she heard Abby's name mentioned in Oak Mott by anyone other than a Cricket Hunter was almost a year to the day after Abby disappeared. At her locker at school one morning, she overheard two kids talking about how Sheila, Abby's mom, had died from an apparent heroin overdose three nights earlier, and that her son, Abby's little brother, Jeff, had been sent to live with relatives in Idaho or Iowa, somewhere starting with an I.

SEPTEMBER 2013

Chapter 38 - Cel

Cel woke slowly, groggily. Her eyes fluttered, closed for a couple of seconds, fluttered, closed for a minute or more, then finally fully opened. As her vision cleared and her sluggish thoughts centered, a bolt of realization zapped her heart. She'd been drugged, kidnapped. Her infinity necklace.

She was lying on her side, her cheek mashed into rough carpet, hands tied behind her back. The air was heavy with a damp, stale scent that rose from unseen water leaks and festering mold. She lifted her head and scanned the room. White walls, nicked and scarred from years of neglect. A hole-ridden ceiling with a fan in the center, missing three of four blades, one of its two bulbs burning bright. Brown shag carpet from wall to wall, 70's style. A single window covered with aluminum foil. A new door hung on new, shiny brass hinges with a new, shiny brass knob.

She maneuvered her legs where she could leverage herself into a sitting position. When she craned her neck to see behind her, her breath caught in her throat. A woman with brunette hair parted down the middle and dark eyes big enough to eclipse the sun was sitting in the shallow closet to her left, watching her. The woman had a gag in her mouth, hands behind her back, knees drawn up to her chest, ankles tied together. A bruised cheek, crusted blood on her temple. She wore an oversized T-shirt and underwear. No socks or shoes. Oil greased her hair. Cel's eyes swelled with realization as the woman began scooting forward, squealing into her gag, pleading with her eyes. The woman was not just any woman. She was Lauren Page. Missing Lauren Page. Miss Mentee. Sammy's mom. The Abby look-alike.

Cel rose to her knees and was trying to stand when the door swung open. She froze and watched a man saunter a few feet into the room. His brunette, shoulder-length hair was parted down the middle, his dark eyes hard on Cel, seemingly happy to find her awake. He had slim, toned arms and legs, knobby shoulders and smooth, pale skin. He was barefoot and wore a dress—a blue and yellow summer dress—

that fit him tightly everywhere except the stretched-out chest. He had a black handgun in his right hand.

Except for a bulging chest and the shadow of whiskers above his upper lip, Jeff Powell could've passed for Abby's twin had Abby been alive. They had the same round eyes, same full lips, same bushy eyebrows, same cowlick on the left side of their parted hair. They even stood the same, with their left hip cocked out, right shoulder slightly dipped.

"*Jeff?*" Cel managed weakly.

His mouth bloomed into a smile—the smile Cel saw when they'd stepped off the Zipper all those years ago—that brightened his dark eyes even more. "I knew you'd remember me." He pointed the gun at her. "I've waited for this day for a long time." He extended his hand as if to help her stand. "Come on. I want to show you something."

Cel stared at the hand for a moment, then glanced at Lauren who'd pushed herself into the corner of the closet and had quit squealing.

"Don't worry about her," Jeff said, walking toward the closet. He shut and locked the door, which Cel now noticed also had a new, shiny brass knob. "We can deal with that later. Now come on. First things first." When Cel remained as stiff as a statue, he took her by the back of the arm, helped her to her feet, and ushered her forward.

As she moved through the threshold into the hallway, she glanced left, then right, and immediately recognized the place. The empty living room to her left, the layout of doors dotting the hall to her right. This was Abby's and Jeff's childhood home. Yes, she'd awoken on the floor of Jeff's room. She'd avoided driving by the house for fifteen years. Hell, she hadn't driven down the street in ten or more. The small three-bedroom home had sat empty for four or five years after the Powells left town until a local lawyer bought it and added it to his long list of rental properties. In a casual conversation about a year earlier, Natalie had told her the lawyer had retired and moved to Austin and all of his Oak Mott properties were back on the market.

"Brings back memories, doesn't it?" Jeff asked.

Cel looked back at him. Their faces were inches apart. She could smell menthol smoke on his breath, see pride in his smile.

"Renters fucked it up pretty good over the years, but I got a great deal on it."

The moment spooled. She held his gaze. Eventually, his proud smile faded, and he gestured at the door at the end of the hall that led into the garage. "Let's head that way."

"Why?" Cel asked. The word came out weak and strained, sickly, as if she was suffering from laryngitis.

"Just go." Jeff nudged her in the back with the barrel of the gun before closing and locking the bedroom door behind him.

Cel stopped in front of the weathered door at the end of the hall. It not only had a new, shiny brass knob that matched the others, but also a shiny brass chain and deadbolt. Jeff stopped behind her, his slim gut up against her tied hands. She could feel his breath on her neck, heard him sniff the scent of her deep into his lungs, taking a part of her for himself.

"I know what you did to my sister," he whispered into her ear.

Her blood froze. She slowly turned around and locked eyes with him.

He studied her face, seemingly relishing her reaction, absorbing the moment like a sponge. Like he'd been fantasizing about this moment for a lifetime. "I was there. I followed her to your house that night, on this exact date, September 29th, and I watched you kill her with your cricket stick."

An image of Abby's one-eyed, mouth-open-in-a-scream, dead-face expression materialized in Cel's mind. She hadn't seen the face in years, never wanted to see it again. She closed her eyes and shook her head, as though her head were an Etch-A-Sketch and she could erase the image if she shook hard enough. When she opened her eyes, they were filled with tears. She looked Jeff's blue and yellow dress up and down. Abby's dress, the one she'd died in. Been murdered in. Holy-fucking-shit. Cel met eyes with Jeff.

"Jeff, I didn't mean to—"

"Stop!" Jeff said, shaking his head in apparent disappointment. "I don't want to hear lies. Enough lies. You're better than that."

Cel gulped. Long seconds ticked.

Jeff reached over her shoulder, unbolted, unchained, and unlocked the door. "Go. To the basement."

A corset of fear cinched around Cel's chest. "Jeff, you don't—"

He grabbed her shoulder and spun her around. "Go!"

A bright glow shot out of an opening in the floor in the corner of the garage, lighting a path between dressers and tables and chairs in front of Cel. She shuffled toward the opening, the barrel of the gun a knife in the center of her back, Jeff's bare feet occasionally bumping into her own. She stopped at the opening, glanced at the coffin-shaped door propped against the wall, looked down the narrow wooden staircase. She thought about Parker, Lauren. "What's down there?"

Jeff beamed a joyous grin, and an odd recognition hit Cel. Jeff had grown into his man teeth. They were no longer too large for his mouth like when she'd last seen him all those years ago.

"Did you kidnap Parker?"

His grin grew impossibly wide. Like the Joker's exaggerated, painted maw.

"Is he down there? Is he alive, or did you…" She looked down the stairs, leaned forward at the waist, and hollered Parker's name. "Are you down there?"

She turned her head sideways, angling her ear to catch even the faintest response. When a muffled moan seeped up the stairway, a desperate hope jolted her and she hurried down the stairs, her bare feet slapping the cold wood as she went, calling Parker's name again. The room reeked of old piss. The lightbulb overhead buzzed with effort.

Parker was lying on a bare mattress, gagged, hands and legs hogtied behind him. His red boxers were twisted askew, his hair a mess. Dark stubble carpeted his usually clean-shaven face. Though it had only been four days since Cel had seen him, he appeared to have aged four years. His skin was sallow, loose on his frame, and his eyes had sunk deeper into the sockets. Pounds of gut flab had vanished. Cel scurried to the edge of the mattress and dropped to her knees, straddling a chain anchored to the floor. She lowered her face close to Parker's, could hear the air whistling in and out of his nose.

He briefly met eyes with her, then looked up over her head as footfalls approached.

Jeff stopped behind Cel, lording over her, legs spread wide, and pointed the gun at her. "Move back." When she didn't obey, he pressed the gun to Parker's forehead. "I said, get up. And step back."

Cel hesitated but followed the instructions.

Jeff removed the gag from Parker's mouth and tossed it aside.

Eyeing Jeff, Parker coughed, then swallowed huge gulps of air.

"You don't have to do this, Jeff," Cel pled. "Just let us go. We won't say anything."

"Jeff?" Parker said, scrutinizing Jeff from head to toe. "Jeff Powell?" His eyes flitted back and forth from Cel to Jeff.

Jeff looked at Cel, a sparkle in his eyes, an upturn to the corners of his mouth. "He doesn't know, does he?"

Parker coughed. "Know what?" He met eyes with Cel. "Know what?"

Cel took a step toward Jeff. "Listen, I understand you hate me for what I did. And I understand what it's like to want revenge. But you don't..." She trailed off when Jeff shook his head in disappointment, as if her words had stung him, and then his gaze fell to the floor for a moment.

When he looked up, his eyes had changed. They were thick with sincerity. "I don't hate you for what you did. I could never hate you. Don't you get it? Don't you feel it? I love you for what you did. I admire you."

Flabbergasted, Cel backed up until her bound hands touched the cement wall.

"That's why I've done everything I've done."

The statement washed over Cel, bringing the last few days' oddities to the surface of her mind. "You...put the picture in the closet? And the crickets in the sink? But how..."

Jeff watched her, delighted at her amazement.

"And in Hunter's Haven that night..." she continued. "But how did you..." She brought her hand to her throat to touch the memory of her infinity necklace, a necklace lost to time, and her eyes flared when her fingers actually touched cold metal. He must've put it on her while she was unconscious. She lifted the infinity symbol and stared at the only tangible evidence her mother ever existed as if it were about to swallow her.

Jeff reached for the necklace clasp nestled up against the symbol, touched it to Cel's lips, then spun it to the back of her neck. "But...I do know about you. All about you. I've been watching you for a long time, on and off for years, and we're more alike than you could ever imagine." He winked. "I have ways of getting keys to other people's houses, too." Jeff glanced at Parker, who hadn't budged, and looked back at Cel. "Just like you, I spent a lot of years lying to myself about my past. Lying to myself about who I was, what I'd done, what had happened to my sister. I made myself forget. But at some point, I had to face the truth, embrace it, and I needed you to do the same before we reconnected. I've talked to enough psychiatrists over the years to know some people need help breaking free from the lies they tell themselves, and I wanted to be that help for you. I wanted you to stop lying to yourself. I want you to be as proud of your truth as I am."

Cel held Jeff's gaze, the humming lightbulb seemingly growing louder and louder.

"So, it was you I chased through the woods?" Parker asked.

Jeff shot him a quick grin and ran his hand down the side of his dress as if presenting a one-of-a-kind anomaly. "Pretty convincing, huh? I didn't know how far into Hunter's Haven you'd driven that day, and when you saw my truck and I had to back out of there, I thought I'd screwed up and you'd leave." He looked at Cel. "But I guess fate was on our side."

"Truck," Cel whispered, the previous days' events blasting through her head like a tornado. "You were at Lauren's apartment, watching me."

"I was also the one who honked outside your house when Jennifer was about to beat the shit out of you." Jeff spoke with an air of confidence, cockiness. Heroism.

Cel pointed at the stairs. "But Lauren doesn't have anything to do with Abby. Why did you take—"

Jeff threw up his free hand, shushing her. "After I saw you guys fight that day, I was scared you might go back and hurt her, and I couldn't risk you getting into trouble and possibly going to jail before I had proven myself to you." He shot Parker with a sharp look. "Helped you embrace the truth."

"What the hell are you two talking about?" Parker asked. "What truth?"

Jeff looked at Cel expectantly. "You want to tell him, or should I?"

"Tell me what?"

Cel's stomach lurched. She swallowed slowly to block the bitter bile creeping up her throat from reaching her tongue. She watched Parker watching her. Her knees turned weak, wobbly, as if the weight of the memory of Abby was too much to hold afloat. She looked at Jeff, pleading with him with her eyes. *Don't make me tell him.* A fat tear trickled from her left eye, made a path across the skin blemish below it on its way to falling off her cheek. She began mentally reciting her go-to calming spell. Over and over and over.

"Fine." Jeff sucked in the corners of his mouth, lifted his eyebrows, and gave awe-shucks, okay, whatever shrug. "I'll do it." He spun toward Parker eagerly, like a dancer who'd had his back to the audience when the curtain rose and was excited to face the crowd for the first time. "Cel—"

"I killed Abby," Cel blurted out, bringing a satisfied expression to Jeff's face as he eyed Parker expectantly.

The moment stretched. No one moved. No one spoke. The buzzing light grew impossibly loud. Cel didn't breathe. Couldn't. Parker stared at her. She studied him. She could see the gears in his mind grinding, processing her confession, shooting him back in time to the fall of 1998.

"*You* killed her?"

Cel hustled to the mattress, fell to her knees, and apologized. With a string of words that ran together in an endless chain of sentences, she tried to explain herself, rationalize her actions. She told him how it had happened, when, where, then apologized again. She told him how she'd seen him and Abby together in Abby's living room the night before, how she'd carved TITS on Jose's car in a fit of anger, she'd planned on confessing, accepting the blame and consequences, but…then she apologized again, told him she loved him, was so very sorry. "I should've told you. I should've trusted—"

"Stop the lies!" Jeff yelled, the words ricocheting off the cement walls, stinging Cel's ears. "I watched you. You enjoyed ramming that stick into her eye. You enjoyed shutting her up by shoving it down her throat."

Cel cut her eyes at Jeff. "I did not." She met eyes with Parker. Her heart rattled inside her chest as his eyes filled with horror, the mental image, the same one Cel had blocked out all these years, surely forming inside his head. His disappointment and disgust were as readable on his face as the giant words on Yesenia's grimoires. "Parker…please…"

He dismissed her with a headshake, as if she were an unknown, unwanted solicitor begging for something she didn't deserve.

Jeff touched her shoulder, and she jerked away. "You need to stop lying to yourself. You weren't sorry then, and you don't have to be now. Abby fucking deserved what she got. I was there. She attacked *you*. She'd been jealous of you and fucking with you for years. She made fun of you all the time when you weren't around. She called your *abuela* and Dillo backwood spics. She mocked your magic spells. She called you an idiot and a dyke and a lowlife." He pointed the gun at Parker. "And *he* knew. And he kept it from you. Hell, he partook in the ridicule. And then…" Jeff licked his lips. "And then he fucked her the night before you killed her. She never liked you, much less respected you. And she was a bitch to both of us. She never *got* you like I did. Or wanted to. And neither does *he*." Tension and anger vibrated off of Jeff like bass from a giant amplifier. "He cheated on you and lied to you just as much as Abby did." A glance at Parker accompanied by a fuck-you smirk. "And he's been doing it ever since. Right?"

Jeff walked to the staircase and slid a laptop out from under the bottom step. As he made his way back to Parker and Cel, strutting with a slick air of arrogance, he unfolded it and the screen lit up. He sat on the edge of the bed next to Parker's feet and held the laptop where Cel and Parker could both see the screen. "I'm sure you'll recognize all these women, Parker," he said, and then moved his eyes to Cel. "But *you'll* probably only recognize one or two." He cued up a video. A young woman with dark hair and dark eyes looked into a camera. He pushed play.

Cel watched as the woman gave a statement about how she'd slept with Parker many times in 2008. Then came another woman with brunette hair and dark eyes who made a similar claim for 2009. Another, similar appearance, 2009. Another, 2012. Cel recognized only one, the last one. Janette Willow. The pretty, athletic, pink-scrub-wearing brunette who'd cleaned her and Parker's teeth at Denton Dental for years.

Jeff closed the laptop and set it on the mattress when Janette finished. "And then there's the little lady upstairs, too, of course." He looked at Cel, his expression saying he was concerned for her. "And these are just the women I was able to track down. Only God knows how many others are out there with brown hair and dark eyes and toned legs he's stuck it in behind your back."

Cel slowly blinked. "How…"

"I've been following Parker, too. I knew who he really was. It wasn't hard to find these women. Or to get them to talk. I just put on a nice suit, carried a fancy black brief case and little business cards, and then knocked on their door when their husbands or boyfriends weren't home and told them I was a lawyer representing Parker in a pending, unlawful restraint and rape case." A chuckle. "Then I told them he'd given me their names in order to prove he'd cheated on his wife with many women, but never once forced anyone to have sex with him. I told them if they agreed to give a statement, they'd remain anonymous if the case ever went to trial." Another proud grin found Jeff's face as he made an invisible, paper-sized rectangle in the air in front of him. "I even made up fake anonymity agreements that were notarized and everything for them to sign."

Cel had suspected Parker of cheating many times, kissing or touching other women, maybe even letting one or two give him a blowjob, but not outright fucking them in cars and alleys and dentist offices. She met eyes with Parker. "Is it true?"

Expressionless, he gazed at her and nodded but offered no apology, no explanation.

"There you go," Jeff said, standing. He walked to the shadowed corner under the staircase as Cel's and Parker's eyes stayed glued together.

When he returned, he broke their eye contact by tapping two sticks on the floor between them. First, Parker's eyes moved to the sticks, then Cel's followed. They were cricket sticks. The last two. One with a lightning bolt carved in it, the other, an infinity symbol. Jeff's and Cel's cricket sticks. Shortly after Abby's death, Cel had gathered the other ones leaning against the back of her house, snapped them into pieces, and tossed them into a dumpster. Her eyes tracked her stick down to the sharpened tip, which was stained black with Abby's blood.

"Now that you know the truth," Jeff said. "It's time for me to prove myself to you. To show you just how much alike we are."

Jeff hiked up his dress, slid the handgun into the waistband of his tighty-whiteys. Cel noticed the thin scars on his upper thighs. Cutting scars that mimicked her own. "Stand up," he ordered Cel.

Cel shook her head.

"It's time to stop lying about who you are, Cel. Who we are. Now, get up."

She shook her head again, chewing on her bottom lip, trying to wriggle her hands free from her restraints.

"Get up!" Jeff grabbed her arm and jerked her to her feet. "Why are you fighting this? After all I've done for you, shown you. I dragged Abby's body deep into the woods and hid it for you that night. Do you know how hard that was? I was fucking tiny back then." He pinched the chest of his dress. "I took off her dress and used it to wipe away any fingerprints in case she was found. I made sure to take her bike far away, where it would never be linked to you." He jiggled Cel's cricket stick. "I took your stick. Made sure it didn't get damaged." He flicked the infinity symbol on Cel's necklace. "I pried that out of Abby's hand and wore it around my neck as I was shipped from house to house, family to family, and then left to my own devices in a fucked up world at eighteen. I never betrayed you or lied to you. I thought about you every day." His eyes misted. "Your smile that day at the fair on the Zipper. The warmth of your hand as we spun. The way you protected me from Jose. Defended me when Abby went off on me." He cocked his head slightly sideways. "The times we hunted together in the woods. Laughed. Joked. You let me be me." He pointed his cricket stick at Parker who was struggling to break free from his restraints. "I don't get why you want to defend *him*. Save *him*. He doesn't understand or love you like I do. And he never will. He'll always be looking for another Abby. Hell, his girlfriend upstairs is another Abby. Don't you get it? You and him don't work because there'll always be another Abby." He tapped his chest, gestured at Cel. "You and me. We work. Open your eyes. We're the same. Now watch me remove this cancer from our lives like I once watched you."

Jeff raised both his and Cel's cricket sticks in the air as one, angling them at Parker's chest like a spear fisherman. Fear swallowed Parker's weary eyes. He opened his mouth but no words came out.

Jeff gritted his teeth, rose to his tiptoes—

"Wait," Cel said. "You're right. You're right. I did enjoy killing Abby. I loved the way it felt driving my stick into her eye." She looked at Parker, hoping to connect, silently communicate the way they used to, the way Natalie and Omar did, convey a secret message, her plan. But Parker looked at her like she was an alien, an abomination. Any connection between them had been severed. She looked into Jeff's eyes. "If this is going to happen, it has to happen right. I want to do it together." She watched skepticism pass over his face. "Just like when we rode the Zipper. Me and you."

He lowered the sticks.

"No, Cel," Parker said. "Don't. I'm sorry about the women. Cel? Please."

Cel ignored Parker as Jeff untied her hands and handed her cricket stick to her, beaming like a little kid. Little Jeff after the Zipper. Jeff with a bloody palm after crafting his cricket stick.

Jeff raised his stick and Cel copied him. "Ready?" he asked.

Cel nodded, then looked at Parker. His eyes were on her. "For God's sake Cel, don't do this. I know I've fucked up, but I do love you. I've tried so hard to be a good husband, a good friend."

When Cel heard an angry growl rumble in Jeff's throat and saw his eyes tighten, she turned and thrust her stick at his chest. She thought she'd been quick enough, surprising enough, but he reacted like a whiplash and slammed his stick down onto hers, pinning the tip to the cement floor.

"Don't do this," Jeff said.

Cel glanced at her stick, and when she tried to pull it loose, Jeff lifted his leg and planted his bare foot in the center of her chest. The blow knocked her back a few steps. Her stick fell from her hands as she stumbled.

"Cel, please!" Jeff said. "Calm down."

She glanced down at her stick. Jeff followed her eyes and put his foot on it. They held eye contact. Long, slow seconds ticked off.

Cel eventually slid her eyes from him to his stick, which was aimed at her. Then she met eyes with him again, hoping he read the faux regret in her eyes as real. "Jeff," she whispered pleadingly as she arched her brow and tilted her head sideways in a submissive gesture. She shook her head. "Jeff…I'm sorry…I—"

The moment she saw his stick start to lower, she rushed into him, driving her shoulder into his chest. He gasped and dropped his stick as they crashed onto the cement floor.

"Stop!" he ordered as he fought off Cel's flailing hands.

She clawed and slapped at his face, and when she grabbed a handful of his hair, intending to slam his head into the floor, he backhanded her across the cheek, breaking her grip, knocking her onto her side. A white flashbang of pain detonated inside her head. She writhed and moaned.

Parker squirmed in vain on the mattress as Jeff stood and straightened his dress, looming over Cel like a storm cloud about to release a hailstorm. He kicked her in the gut. "Why are you making me do this?" He dropped a knee on her chest and slapped her. Then he took a handful of her hair and aimed her face at Parker. "You've let him destroy who you are…who you were." He slammed her head down onto the cement, picked up both his and her cricket sticks, and faced Parker. "I hope you rot in hell with Abby. You two fucked up everything around you."

As he raised the sticks, Cel swept her leg across the cement, landing a solid blow to his shin. Jeff squealed in pain from the bone-on-bone connection as he pitched forward, smacking the cement face-first with a sickening thud, the sticks wedged between his body and the floor

Cel crawled on top of him as he tried to roll onto his back and reached up under his dress, feeling for the handgun. Just as she gripped the handle and started jerking, he slammed his hand down on her forearm, knocking her hand free. The gun slid out of his waistband onto the floor, trapped inside the folds of the dress. She rose onto her knees, roared like a lioness, and punched him in the side of the head as hard as she could. With his eyes closed, he threw up his hands and scooted back to avoid more blows. The gun fell onto the floor as he moved, and Cel scooped it up and jumped to her feet.

When Jeff's eyes landed on the gun, he stood and screamed and lunged at her. She pulled the trigger. The blast was deafening, ear-splitting. The bullet hit the right side of his chest but didn't stop him. He grabbed the barrel, twisted it, and, as they fought for control, the gun went off again, the bullet ripping through Cel's abdomen. She released her grip on the gun, doubled over with her hands on the hole, and fell to her knees.

Seconds later, the gun clattered onto the hard cement, and Jeff toppled sideways onto the mattress, moaning, gasping. He had his hands pressed to his chest, trying to stem the blood that spurted from the wound with each heartbeat.

Using the mattress for leverage, Cel struggled upright, looked at Parker and said his name. His name sounded flat and foreign to her ears, felt cold on her tongue. There was no concern in his eyes. He wasn't Parker anymore. Not her Parker, anyway. He appeared horrified at the sight of her, recoiling. She said his name again, wondering if it sounded as off to him as it did her. Was it the effect of the cement walls and floor and ceiling? Or was it something inside her, a sea of change, a new understanding expressing itself in this new voice? She shook her head, realizing it wasn't the walls. It was inside. A feeling of disconnect, of loss. The knowledge that Parker would never love her again. Not like he once had. Not the way she wanted. She deserved. Her secret had destroyed the love he had in her, and it would never regrow. He would never forgive her. She'd killed Abby, and Jeff was right, he'd been searching for her replacement ever since. And he always would. Stick his dick in anyone that resembled her. She searched his eyes, shook her head. Her heart fell through her chest and took all feeling with it. She didn't know him. He didn't know her. She could never trust him again. He would never trust her. Not as a lover. Not as a friend. Not as a neighbor. The second he was free, he'd run and tell the world about his psycho witch of a wife and how she'd killed his teenage soulmate. He'd run to the cops and demand justice, and she'd rot in jail for loving him, fighting for him, saving him. Within a year, he'd marry Lauren, and they'd give Sammy a new brother or sister. What would her *abuela* think of her? Natalie and Omar? Her soon-to-be godchild?

Trying to ignore the searing pain from the bullet, a pain that was constricting every muscle and organ in her abdomen, she picked up her cricket stick. She knew what needed to be done. She knew the ramifications. She'd lived through it all once before and was prepared to do it again. "This is best for both of us," she whispered as she rammed the stick into the right side of Parker's chest between two ribs. She maneuvered it under the sternum, puncturing his heart as he wiggled and caterwauled in agony, pushing until she hit spine.

She held Parker's gaze, searching a pair of eyes she no longer recognized, eyes that wanted to escape her, until a final pocket of air escaped his mouth and his pupils dilated.

Woozy and weak, she jerked the stick free and stumbled back. Warm blood ran down her stomach, sluiced behind her shorts, trickled down the inside of her leg. She centered herself, dropped her stick on Jeff's dress, wrapped the fabric around the handle and wiped it clean of fingerprints. Then, using his dress as a glove, moved the handle up under his hand.

Her vision waivered as she bear-crawled up the stairs, moaning, crying, then scrabbled through the garage and back into the house, leaving a trail of metallic-scented crimson in her wake. She dropped to her belly in the hallway outside Jeff's bedroom door and lay there for what felt like an eternity, slipping in and out of consciousness, growing colder and colder.

She eventually managed to pull herself upright, and leaning against the wall, unlock the door. She stumbled into the room, unlocked the closet door, pushed it open, and fell onto the floor. Lauren slid over to her, squealing, and Cel reached around to Lauren's back and untied the rope holding her wrists together.

"Go," she mustered, closing her eyes and fully collapsing onto the floor. "Get help." She couldn't breathe. "I shot him." Gasp. "But he stabbed Parker...and..."

OCTOBER 2013

Chapter 39 - Cel

Panic was all Cel knew when she first woke. She had no idea where she was, when it was, why she was. A steady beep beckoned her, scared her. She caught a whiff of sage and rosemary. She tried to sit up with a purpose, but the movement knifed intense pain into her stomach and brought a light-headed dizziness to her head, forcing her to lie back down and close her eyes.

She took deep breaths, reciting the calming spell over and over, until she felt centered, balanced, and then opened her eyes and surveyed her surroundings.

The square room had one bed, white walls, and a white floor. A small TV perched in the upper corner adjacent to a window that revealed a starry, night sky. A handmade talisman hung next to a white dry-erase board at the foot of the bed. The name Nurse Patty Holmes was scrawled in fat purple letters above some numbers and times on the board. Two vacant chairs were on her left, one of Yesenia's seashell bags on the floor between them. So many machines surrounded her. Machines with hoses and tubes that connected to her arm, chest, stomach, and bladder. A table on wheels beside the bed held a cup of water, a pile of *pan de polvo* on a paper plate, one of her *abuela's* healing sachets, and a worn Deborah Harkness paperback. Flowers, six or seven vases of flowers, stood on the window sill, two more on the counter with a sink to her right. A white blanket covered her from the waist down, a thin white gown her chest.

Hospital. She was in the hospital. But…

Then the memory struck her as fast and powerful as a bolt of lightning.

Her infinity necklace.

Jeff…in Abby's dress.

The gun.

Lauren.

The fight.

Gunshots.

Her cricket stick.

Parker.

A feeling of dread accompanied the image of Parker's dilated pupils that formed in her mind. She reflexively moved to sit up again, as though she could jump up and outrun the image. But pain and dizziness denied her once more. She closed her eyes, whispered her go-to calming spell again, a soothing spell, a strengthening spell. She drifted back into a dreamless sleep.

She woke hours later to find her *abuela* sitting in one of the two chairs at her side. Yesenia's chin was on her chest, eyes closed, single braid draped over her left shoulder, hands clasped together on her lap. She was lightly snoring, Mina's mummified leg moving up and down on her chest beneath her bright yellow shirt.

Cel tried to say "*Buela*," but the word clawed to a stop in her dry throat. She gathered spit in her mouth, forced it down, and tried again. "*Buela*."

Yesenia's head shot up, and she immediately leaned forward and ran her hand over Cel's head. "Celia." She looked upward. "*Gracias. Gracias.*" She brushed her rough hand over Cel's cheek. "Are you okay?"

"I'm thirsty."

Yesenia made her way to the sink, filled a tiny paper cup with water, and brought it to Cel. Cel swished the water around inside her mouth before swallowing.

Yesenia sat back down, leaned toward the bed, and rested her hands on the metal bedrail. "Do you remember what happened?"

Cel met eyes with her *abuela* and nodded. "Parker...he's..."

Yesenia's eyes reduced to solemn slits, and she dipped her head and nodded as she placed her hand on top of Cel's. "He didn't make it, *mija*."

Cel bit on her bottom lip, her eyes brimming with tears. She looked away from her Yesenia and out the window at the night sky. The tears were genuine. She was not the type who could cry on command. No, her hurt came from a mixture of guilt and loss, an unavoidable consequence, two dreadful emotions she knew from experience would dominate her life for the foreseeable future.

Yesenia squeezed Cel's hand. "I'm sorry, *mija*."

Cel looked at Yesenia with a desperate gaze, eyebrows up. "What about Jeff? I know I shot him, I had to, *Buela*, I had to. But when I left to get help, he'd fallen, but I wasn't sure if he had..." She shook her head.

"*Se murio*," Yesenia said. "And rightfully so. You didn't do anything wrong." She took in a deep breath. "How did he get you?"

"He was waiting for me when I got home after using the spirit board with Natalie. He'd put..." She felt her chest, felt the infinity symbol below the thin gown, pulled it out, and stared at it.

"The cops said he probably stole it a long time ago and has had it all this time," Yesenia said. "The doctor wanted to take it off, but I made him leave it. I told him *yo los maldigo* if he didn't." Cel glanced gratefully at her *abuela*, then kissed the clasp, spun it behind her neck, and tucked the symbol under her gown as she mentally recited the good fortune spell.

"Did he tell you why he took you?" Yesenia asked.

Cel shook her head.

Yesenia looked away and also shook her head, disgusted. "That boy was never right in the head. *Loco follador.*"

The moment passed.

"What about Lauren?" Cel asked. "Is she okay?"

"She's fine." Yesenia gestured at a red vase of wilting daisies on the window sill. "Those are from her family. For saving her."

"How long have I been here?"

"Two weeks." Yesenia glanced at Cel's stomach. "You lost a lot of blood. The bullet went through your stomach and pancreas."

Cel dropped her chin and looked at her abdomen, bit her lip again, chewed for long seconds. Yesenia squeezed Cel's hand, and Cel locked eyes with her *abuela*. "Did Parker's family already have a funeral for him?"

Yesenia nodded. "It was nice. I went with Natalie, Craig, Omar, and Kris. He's at Gallagher Cemetery, close to where his father is buried. Beverly, Jennifer, and Jill have come by here with flowers to check on you a few times, too, *por extrano que parezca.*"

Cel's eyes widened, her expression saying, *Really?*

Yesenia's brow rose. "I know. I don't think they want to be friends or anything, but they said they're sorry for blaming you about what happened to Parker."

As Cel's eyes moved around the room, Yesenia said, "Lots of people have been coming by. Natalie comes every day and Omar on the weekends." She gestured at the *pan de polvo* on the table with her eyes. "Natalie and Omar brought those yesterday. Last week I taught Natalie how to make them, and those are from her third try by herself. She said the first two didn't turn out so well."

Cel eyed the cookies and a slight simper touched her dry lips.

"Sterling and Hart have stopped in, too."

Panic seized Cel's chest and must've also touched her eyes because Yesenia squeezed her hand again. "Don't worry, *mija*. You're not in trouble. They know it was self-defense. They just want to talk to you about what happened, get your side of the story. They assume you were kidnapped like Lauren and Parker, and Lauren already told them how you crawled upstairs after Jeff shot you and told her you'd killed him but that he stabbed Parker."

Cel pushed out a long breath, the work of her diaphragm sending barbs of pain through her abdomen, and closed her eyes.

"Everything will be okay, *mija*," Yesenia assured, stroking Cel's head. "I promise. This dark stint will pass."

Cel knew her *abuela* was right. It would be hard, but it would pass. It would just take time. Time for the heartache and guilt and paranoia to subside. Time for the reassurances of justification to take root and sprout and cover everything else. Yes, eventually, she'd be able to forget what she'd done, to erase the image of Parker's dead eyes from her mind, to feel happy again, find purpose. She just had to keep breathing, keep drinking, keep eating, keep moving, keep living. Bury her wayward emotions so deep they couldn't survive. Break apart and compartmentalize her past actions so well they couldn't form a cohesive narrative in her mind. Remind herself daily that she wasn't a bad person, that she'd made the right choice, the only choice. That she was strong and patient and resilient. Of course she was going to miss Parker something fierce, always, but she could get through this dark stint. Just like after Abby.

When Yesenia began whispering the same soothing spell she'd whispered over Cel a thousand times before, Cel joined her.

ABOUT THE AUTHOR

Jeremy Hepler is the Bram Stoker-nominated author of *The Boulevard Monster* as well as numerous short stories and nonfiction articles. He received the Texas Panhandle Professional Writer's Short Story Award in 2014, and his debut novel was a Bram Stoker Award finalist in the Superior Achievement in a First Novel category in 2017. He lives in the heart of Texas with his wife and son where he's working on his next novel. For more information, you can follow him on Twitter, Facebook, Instagram, Goodreads, and Amazon.

Also from Silver Shamrock Publishing:

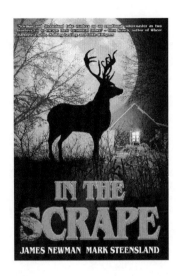

Most kids dream about a new bike, a pair of top-dollar sneakers endorsed by their favorite athlete, or that totally awesome videogame everyone's raving about. But thirteen-year-old Jake and his little brother Matthew want nothing more than to escape from their abusive father. As soon as possible, they plan to run away to California, where they will reunite with their mother and live happily ever after.

It won't be easy, though. After a scuffle with a local bully puts Jake's arch-nemesis in the hospital, Sheriff Theresa McLelland starts poking her nose into their feud. During a trip to the family cabin for the opening weekend of deer-hunting season, Jake and Matthew kick their plan into action, leaving Dad tied to a chair as they flee into the night. Meanwhile, the bully and his father have their own plans for revenge, and the events to follow will forever change the lives of everyone involved . . .

Coming soon from Silver Shamrock Publishing:

October 2019

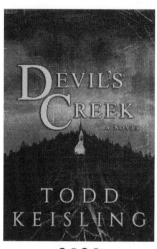

2020

Made in the
USA
Columbia, SC

81566280R00157